FOREVER
TEXAS

Look for these exciting Western series
from bestselling authors
William W. Johnstone and J.A. Johnstone

The Mountain Man

Preacher: The First Mountain Man

Luke Jensen: Bounty Hunter

Those Jensen Boys!

The Jensen Brand

MacCallister

The Red Ryan Westerns

Perley Gates

Have Brides, Will Travel

Will Tanner, Deputy U.S. Marshall

Shotgun Johnny

The Chuckwagon Trail

The Jackals

The Slash and Pecos Westerns

The Texas Moonshiners

Stoneface Finnegan Westerns

Ben Savage: Saloon Ranger

The Buck Trammel Westerns

The Death and Texas Westerns

The Hunter Buchanon Westerns

FOREVER TEXAS

WILLIAM W. JOHNSTONE
AND
J.A. JOHNSTONE

KENSINGTON
PUBLISHING CORP.

www.kensingtonbooks.com

KENSINGTON BOOKS are published by
Kensington Publishing Corp.
119 West 40th Street
New York, NY 10018

All Kensington titles, imprints, and distributed lines are available at special quantity discounts for bulk purchases for sales promotion, premiums, fund-raising, educational, or institutional use.

Special book excerpts or customized printings can also be created to fit specific needs. For details, write or phone the office of the Kensington Sales Manager: Kensington Publishing Corp., 119 West 40th Street, New York, NY 10018. Attn. Sales Department. Phone: 1-800-221-2647.

This book is a work of fiction. Names, characters, businesses, organizations, places, events, and incidents either are the product of the author's imagination or are used fictitiously. Any resemblance to actual persons, living or dead, events, or locales is entirely coincidental.

To the extent that the image or images on the cover of this book depict a person or persons, such person or persons are merely models, and are not intended to portray any character or characters featured in the book.

PUBLISHER'S NOTE: Following the death of William W. Johnstone, the Johnstone family is working with a carefully selected writer to organize and complete Mr. Johnstone's outlines and many unfinished manuscripts to create additional novels in all of his series like the Last Gunfighter, Mountain Man, and Eagles, among others. This novel was inspired by Mr. Johnstone's superb storytelling.

KENSINGTON BOOKS and the WWJ steer head logo are trademarks of Kensington Publishing Corp.

ISBN: 978-1-4967-4776-5 (ebook)

ISBN: 978-1-4967-3534-8

First Kensington hardcover printing: November 2020

First Kensington trade paperback printing: May 2022

10 9 8 7 6 5 4 3 2 1

Printed in the United States of America

FOREVER
TEXAS

Chapter 1

The first shot pinwheeled the tall man's hat off his head. The second sent him diving for cover, and the third spooked his mount and sent it crow-hopping and snorting into the pucker-brush.

He heard a harsh, barking laugh followed with shouts of "Die, gringo!" . . . then shots volleyed at him from all sides.

The tall man managed to crank off a shot of his own. He heard a groan and a curse drift up on the still, hot air as the gunfire echoed and tapered off. Regis Royle had enough time to suck in a sharp breath between his tight-set teeth before a fresh fusillade pinned him tight in a wedge of sun-warmed sandstone.

He counted what he thought might be several guns still blazing, or someone was good at reloading. He trailed his fingers to his gun belt and felt his sheathed knife. He had three shots left in his gun. Fresh ammunition rested snugly in his saddlebags on the ass end of the horse he'd likely never see again.

"What you want here, gringo?"

Regis Royle spun his gaze toward the voice and closed his hand tighter on the walnut grips of his revolver. He saw nothing save for an anaqua tree. In the blue sky far beyond, a lone gray cloud teased apart on a breeze. A meadowlark bobbed on a spiny jag and warbled its morning song.

"Who's asking?"

Ragged laughter echoed off the slabs of sandstone chiseled by wind and time.

Not a man prone to twitching at imagined spooks, Royle nonetheless felt a shiver of ice ripple his backbone. He hunkered lower and eyed around the boulder, looking longingly toward the receding view of his squirrel-headed, bucking mount, and with it his shiny new rifle.

He held the pose as if he were part of the warming stone. The meadowlark rose into the air, trailing dewy notes, and in a series of short swoops landed on a jut of gnarled mesquite some distance to the west—two hundred, three hundred feet.

Could be the bird was a friendly sort. Could be if Regis were a betting man, and at times he was, that bird was looking for a handout, a morsel from a kindly stranger. Could be that bird found the curious laughing man for him. Could be now was the time to place a bet.

Regis almost shrugged, almost smiled at his fanciful notion. Then he didn't smile, for he noted a shifting of light, less than a shadow's worth, in a darkened gap in the stony declivity beyond and below the twitchy, curious little yellow-and-brown bird.

"Thanks, bird friend," he whispered, and licked away a slow drop of sweat from the corner of his mouth, unseen beneath his thick black moustache. Too early by half for this sort of tomfoolery. He had land to check on, friends to catch up with, and an appointment in Brownsville to keep.

Now he was more annoyed than afraid for himself. He'd known, of course, of the danger of brigands out here, and had even been reminded of the cautions he should take when friends at the docks learned he was riding inland alone, on his way to Corpus Christi to visit other friends.

"Why you want to do a thing like that, Cap?" Lockjaw Hames had said. "No sir, if I was you I'd stick to the water. Safer around here. No injuns or Mexicans out to lay a man low, steal his boots and his hair, then pillage what's left out of his middle."

Lockjaw, who earned the odd moniker because his lips rarely seemed to move when he spoke, a task he was unafraid to undertake, had shuddered then as if he'd had a vision of something horrific happening that was fated.

Lockjaw was as solid a seaman as they'd come. Reputedly a former slave and now self-proclaimed free man, he was also the biggest man Regis had ever met, and that was saying something, as Regis himself was north of six feet tall by several inches.

Lockjaw was a steady presence on the steamers and riverboats, turning his hand to whatever task Regis or his partner in the shipping trade, Cormac Delany, asked of him.

Didn't mean Regis was about to take his advice to heart. He'd chuckled and said, "I appreciate your concern on my behalf, Mr. Hames, and I will endeavor to remain on the good side of the soil with breath in my lungs."

The big black man had paused, sacks of quicklime balanced on each shoulder, his bulging arms steadying them, and said, "Ain't no call to get uppity about it, boss. But you don't come crawling back to the safety of the docks saying how come ol' Lockjaw didn't warn you!" He'd stomped off, loading the hold of the *Missy B.*, a recently acquired craft Cormac had christened after a younger sister long dead, or as Cormac had said, "called to her glory."

And now here Regis was, pinned down in the rocks and grasses of this pretty river valley by an outlaw, no doubt. "Looks like you were right, Lockjaw," Regis mumbled.

Another shot, this time slicing in from east of him, scored a fresh groove in the dusty rock above his head. "Okay, at least two outlaws."

As if in response to his thought, a third, then a fourth shot, each from different directions, pinged and whined in ricochet harmlessly above him. For the moment he was safe, but if they—by his best guess that would make at least four scurvy-addled curs out for his blood—decided to close in, he'd be a dozing fawn to their pouncing lion.

His ire with himself almost outweighed any animosity he felt toward the would-be thieves. Almost. He'd save his full steam for dealing with the prairie scum. And he knew he would, in part because Regis Royle was a man who never failed at anything he attempted.

He had fought his way to his position as partner in a shipping business, co-owner of a growing fleet of riverboats plying the waters of the Rio Grande and up and down the coast. He and Cormac had worked like demons during the Mexican War, the wounds of which were slowly healing, though still bleeding aplenty, since 1846.

Here it was 1852 and he was still scrapping his way through life. He sighed and carefully extended a long leg and flexed it, massaging his knee. A bullet pinged a few inches below the heel of his stovepipe boot. He yanked it back and sucked in air through his teeth.

He needed a plan, because sitting here wasn't getting a damn thing done. What sort of plan could he hope for? Stand up and shout, "Hey, gents, how about we talk this over?" He grunted at the folly of his thoughts. No, best wait them out, keep alert, and take advantage of the relative safety of this rocky hidey-hole he'd managed to wedge himself into.

Then another thought came to him: What if he weren't the only critter in this hole? If it got cold at night, which it would surely do, would a pesky rattler slide out of that crevice behind him and try to get cozy with whatever warmth might exude from his cramped body?

The idea didn't do much for his mood. Regis cursed his horse again, a feather-headed thing with a balky streak a mile wide. When he got back to Brownsville, he was going to buy it from the hostler he'd rented it from and either train it right or shoot it in the head and start with a fresh beast.

A smile tugged a corner of his moustache upward. He was thinking of the very reason he'd ventured out on this fine jaunt in the first place. It had been three days since he'd left Brownsville and ridden northward to Corpus Christi. He'd intended to pay a call on friends who'd moved there, attend a fair he'd heard was to take place in that bustling town.

Really, it was little more than a convenient excuse to get away from his beloved steamers. He still enjoyed the work, but he'd been at it for years without letup. He was still a young man, but sometimes he felt like he was ninety and ready for a rocking chair by a fireplace.

He knew the itch, for it had never really left him. He wanted to—no, he needed to venture beyond the waterways. And a trip on horseback, even if only for a few days, would help scratch that pesky, restless feeling.

But a funny thing happened on his way north. He'd cut inland a bit, in a northwesterly fashion, and he'd found a distraction he'd not even known he had been seeking. In fact, it up and smacked him in the head before he knew what was happening.

Actually, it had been more of a slow saturation of his senses. The day had been hot, as were most days in April in southern Texas, and he found himself riding without care or hurry. In light of his current situation, he knew he'd been lucky to make the journey unmolested.

Even the balky buckskin had seemed lulled into peacefulness by the green rolling prairie Regis found himself in. The wind played over an ocean of long floss-tipped grass stems, as if they were the surface of an endless sea. A little farther on and the land sloped gently to his left. Soon he smelled it, the earthy richness of flowing water. And then he saw it at the same time he heard it.

Or rather, he heard a splash. His horse's ears perked, and he reined up and watched something he'd never before witnessed. The scene fascinated him and hooked him in all at once. A herd of wild mustangs, perhaps half a hundred, were wading into the river to his left, dipping their muzzles and sipping long of the cooling flow.

All of them, that is, but a magnificent dappled brute of a stallion with wide flexing nostrils and a near-black mane and tail. His gaze scanned the far bank and raked across the all-but-hidden presence of Regis and his horse. Then the stallion's gaze swung back and locked with Regis's eyes.

The mustang stallion stared for long moments, an unfelt breeze riffling his topknot. He flicked his ears, snorted once, and stomped a foreleg. The splashing alerted the other drinking horses, and the entire mass of them—brown, fawn, black gray—swung their dripping muzzles upward and seemed to stare at him.

Regis felt at once awed, at home, and unnerved, a combination of feelings he'd not experienced since the war's battles. The herd wasted no time in stomping up and out of the river. In moments, there was little more to prove that their presence had been real but dissipating swirls of mud that soon the river carried away.

He guessed the water for what it was—the Santa Calina, a flowage of clear, cool water that fed live oaks and anaquas along its banks. Those trees gave way to the waist-high grasses of the prairie he'd been admiring.

He took the mustang herd's advice and guided his horse through the grasses until they broke through and emerged along the muddy creek's bank. He slid from the saddle but held the reins as the horse sipped long and deep, glancing often at the spot where the mustangs had been across the river but moments before.

When the horse had slaked its thirst, Regis squatted low upstream and lifted his hat free. He squinted—the sun had been given free rein to annoy his sight—and scooped the refreshing liquid onto his face, down the back of his neck, and finally over the top of his head.

It felt so good that he remained squatting at the edge of the water and let his eyes close as he breathed in the lush, verdant smells surrounding him. A kiskadee called out, and another answered, somewhere up in the high, blue sky.

With a sigh, he stood and mounted up and kept riding, spying turkeys, quail, antelope, and deer, all eyeing him with interest and perhaps a twinge of suspicion as the wayward breeze carried his strange scent to them. They would scatter in all directions, coyotes as much to blame as Regis's presence in this otherwise seemingly untouched place.

It wasn't so much a valley as a wide, endless sea or rolling green cut through by the Santa Calina. Rough, wild, vague thoughts formed in his mind, drifted out again, and reformed, telling him little more than one thing. He knew, somehow deep in his guts and bones, that he wanted to be here for longer than just the duration of this pleasant ride.

He surprised himself by realizing he wanted to live here, to possess it somehow. But how? And why? Did he not have a life, a thriving business, friends, several women—prominent young things themselves the daughters of men of society—who wished to impress him? Why here, then? What was it about the place, other than its obvious raw beauty?

In this manner, Regis's thoughts rambled and ricocheted off one another as he rode, much of the time at little more than a leisurely walk, the horse in no hurry, either.

It wasn't until he heard a crashing and a stamping in a thicket to his left, between him and the river, from which he'd strayed, that something happened that would alter forever the course of his life, the lives of countless others, and the very land on which he rode.

For Regis Royle, steamship captain, saw cattle. A vast herd of them—feisty feral beasts little more than ornery goats with wide horns and blood-red eyes and burr-stickled hides. Cattle that fought and stomped one another and rubbed their rank hides raw against mesquite trees. But they were cattle. And in that moment an idea came to Regis Royle almost wholly formed. He would ranch this very land.

He knew instinctively that if it weren't him, someone would, for it teemed with life. And what gave life its very essence? Water, the tincture of life itself, for without it life will not last. But here in the midst of this hot-as-sin place known as South Texas, there was ample water and lush green grasses, and massive herds of wild mustangs, hundreds, perhaps thousands strong, barely outmatching herds of balky, crazy-eyed cattle. And that wasn't to mention the wild game.

Here a man could own land, good and valuable land—though he knew some might debate those descriptions—and never go hungry. And more than that, he could raise beasts, horses, and cattle and sell them to others for profits that one day might far exceed the solid earnings he'd made from plying the waters of the Rio Grande.

And here, here it all was. He might be no landman, but he, by golly, knew opportunity when he saw it. And this was it—prime ranching land, water and all.

That had been three days prior, and thoughts of the place throughout his long, slow trip had leeched into his mind, his heart, the marrow of his very bones, and would not let him be.

He'd been poor company, he knew, to his kind friends in Corpus Christi, but he'd been haunted by the place, and he had cut short his trip by a day in order to repeat the journey from north to south, half expecting the mystical place to have been little more than some fiendish trick of the brain, some devilish whim sent from on high to torment him, for what purpose he knew not.

But it had not been the case. Instead, he had been, if possible, even more impressed with the sights and smells and sounds and feel of the Santa Calina range. All of it had been repeated—the stretches of lush grasses, gamma near water, the ample game and stock roaming the hills, the very creek, the Santa Calina itself.

Only this time his thoughts of it were anything but vague. They were sharp and shrewd and calculating, all the things that had made him a solid businessman now came into play, and he knew he had made a decision. Or maybe some unseen hand had made it for him. No matter, he was a practical man and now was the time for action. He would have the Santa Calina range.

He knew he would be bullish, ruthless if need be, in his pursuit of it. He'd not intentionally cause anyone harm, but neither would he mince in his pursuit of his goal. To the devil with anyone or anything that might get in his way.

Regis knew there would be plenty who would dare to stop him. This region was famous for Apaches and Mexican and Texas outlaws, all eager to lay low newcomers with blind ambition and money to burn.

Regis snorted. They'd not have reckoned on Regis Royle, for once he set his mind to a task, let alone his heart and his wallet, it would take all the Indians, outlaws, and the US Army, too, to peel him from his dream.

He'd just have to convince his pard, Cormac Delany, to back his play in laying claim to the Santa Calina. Regis wasn't exactly sure how much this land was selling for, but he doubted a place like this would come too dear. On the other hand, what did he know? How much land had he bought? Exactly none. So it could well come hard, and his own coin purse, while healthy, wasn't what he'd call fat.

Yet somehow he knew that Cormac would be intrigued, too, and not just because he'd want to humor Regis. He'd been a father figure to young Royle when he had been little more than a skinny starving stowaway on one of Delany's steamers.

Delany could have tossed him overboard and been well within his rights to do so. Instead, the seemingly surly Irishman had scowled at Regis, told him he was too thin to be of use to anyone, and fed him.

He'd plied him with more food than the kid had seen since the Christmas before, when his mother's family back in Maine had hosted dinner for her and her two young boys, a kind but charitable gesture given that Regis's philandering father had gambled away their savings some months earlier.

Cormac had then made Regis a cabin boy, and he'd worked his way up, year after year, with Delany teaching him to read and cipher at night by light of an oil lamp.

Yes, Delany would back his play because he'd trust Regis and his intuition, in part because it was his own teaching that guided Royle. And it had paid off handsomely in the past. It had landed them shipping contracts that had rewarded the pair well, allowing them to expand their holdings.

Regis also knew he had to have Cormac in on such a deal because the older man's cultured ways would more than compensate for Regis's own reputation for a distinct lack of tact when it come to protracted negotiations.

And so, wedged in his rocky nest, Regis had smiled and nodded, caught in his blissful dream of the future despite the grim situation in which he now found himself.

And that's when the bullets, which had trickled to a random but steady flecking on him with rock chips that stung and nicked, poured on him once more. Through the long hours, the bandits never seemed to gain any ground, nor did they seem to lose interest in him.

They'd lobbed insults and sneers and jeers and hoots, and twice he heard glass shatter. So they'd been drinking. That was a two-edged sword. Good because their senses might be dulled, but bad because they would be emboldened for even more of this fool's fight.

"Well, let's get to it," he mumbled. He had decided to shuffle to his knees and prairie-dog up to see if he could size up one of the rats, when a fresh voice shouted from afar, and it kept shouting.

It was a yip—no words, but it sounded an awful lot like a man trying to imitate a drunken coyote. Or maybe the other way around. But curiously, the awful yowling was accompanied with the increasing loud sound of pounding hooves and, most important, fresh shots. Sounded as if it was coming at him fast and from the northeast.

Regis bent low and risked a peek around the base of the rock, hoping he'd not get a third eyehole for his trouble.

It was definitely a crazy rider, barreling pell-mell into their midst. Puffs of blue smoke from three directions told him the rider was not one of his attackers. Whoever he was, he was still yipping and howling and cranking off shots with a revolver and what looked to be a shiny new rifle. And he was tugging along a second horse behind. Hmm.

The man seemed to be pounding at everything in sight, except at Regis. Maybe his luck had turned. He resumed his own firing, measuring his shot and taking his time. Regis heard a scream and saw the back of a man as he emerged from behind the rock pile he'd suspected the first shots came from, thanks to the bird. The man bolted for a ground-tied speckled horse and leapt on, one hand held to the side of his head.

Regis saw spatters of blood on the man's white tunic. He also saw that the man wore an unusually tall blue-banded sombrero and a bright red sash about his waist. Regis aimed for the man's back, raised his barrel to adjust for distance, and . . . he held his shot. He'd not fired at many men in his life, and he'd certainly not shoot one in the back, marauder or no.

That didn't seem to bother the man who'd apparently ridden to his rescue. Friend or foe, he'd yet to find out. But the man wasn't bothered by shooting at the retreating bandits.

Regis risked a wider peek and counted four, five of them. He looked again at the man barreling on in. He was still smoking the blue blazes out of the pan-hot afternoon. And what he saw surprised him almost as much as the events of the previous hour. It was most definitely his own horse lined and trailing behind the newcomer.

Regis stood, visoring his eyes with his left hand and holding his cocked revolver on the slowing howler with his right. The man raised the rifle and butted the stock on his thigh as he trotted up.

The sun was in Regis's eyes, but he swore there was something familiar about this fellow. Then the newcomer spoke and removed doubt.

"That any way to treat kin, Mr. Royle?"

No, couldn't be, thought Regis. He goosed his neck forward and peered up at the mounted man now but three paces from him. "Shepley? That you?"

"The one and only, big brother!" The newcomer slid from the saddle and landed with a plunk, his boots raising dust.

If a full-bore circus troupe had wandered at him out of the shimmering landscape, Regis Royle could not have been more surprised. And yet, the impossible had just happened. Before him stood his very own little brother, his only sibling, one Shepley Royle, who until that moment Regis had assumed was still a student at that Quaker boarding school in Connecticut he'd been paying for.

"What . . . But how . . . What are you doing here?"

The younger man doubled over as if he were choking on a hunk of cheese, laughing and smacking his leg with a palm. "To think . . . Regis Royle at a loss for words! Hoo-boy, I never thought I'd see the day!"

Regis shook his head and strode forward and stuck out his hand. "Shepley, I . . . I don't know what to say!"

"Start with thank you, you big ninny! I come all this way, show up in time to save your sorry hide, and all you can do is shake my hand?"

Before Regis could react, the kid jumped up and locked his free arm around Regis's neck. "Good to see you, big brother!"

They smacked each other's backs for a few dusty pats, then stood back, Regis holding the youth's shoulders. "Let me look you over." He saw little and yet everything of the youngster he'd last seen four, five years prior? "Still the whip-snap, hell-raisin', risk-taking kid brother, I see."

"And a good thing, too, from the looks of it. I'm not sure how you ever got along without me all these years."

"Oddly enough, I managed." Regis smoothed his moustaches. "Question is, What are you doing out here? And at just the right moment, too."

"Oh, I come looking for you, of course. I had your address in Brownsville from that last letter you sent a few months back. Talked with a huge man, funny name . . . Big Jaw? Something like that. Anyway, he said you'd ridden out this way, but he forbade me to go after you."

"That'd be Lockjaw. And how'd you get away from him? He's not an easy man to disobey."

"He made a big mistake when he told me not to do something. Cause then I just had to do it! It's as certain as the moon and stars coming out at night or the sun rising and baking our heads off out here in this cursed wasteland! It's just the way it is with me, Regis. Can't explain it."

"I believe you just did."

Shep shrugged and smiled. "So I hopped my horse and rode on out. And the rest, as they say"—the kid looked around him as he untied Regis's horse and led him over—"is now history."

"Or dumb luck on both our parts. No matter, I see you are as humble as ever," said Regis, still smiling. He didn't think he'd ever smiled so much all at once in all his days. "Funny thing. I promised Ma I'd look out for you."

"Well, looks like you got it backward, big brother."

Regis worked his jaw muscles. Nobody in the world could be as exasperating to him as Shepley, and that included a pile of annoying, ornery old businessmen of his acquaintance. By gaw'd, but he'd forgotten how the kid could set him off. And this, despite the fact he was mighty glad to see him.

"Won't happen again." He stabbed his left boot into the stirrup and paused, looked up, then over at his brother. "Thanks, Shep. Appreciate it."

The younger man nodded. "Of course, brother."

Regis scanned the distance where the banditos had ridden. He fancied he saw puffs of dust growing fainter with each passing second. Whoever they were, they were not interested in a second dose. "I best find my hat. Oh, by the way, I'm pleased to see my rifle worked for you."

The kid raised the long gun and nodded. "Yep, just fine, just fine." He admired the blued barrel and rich walnut stocks. "Course it's tricky to load and ride fast, so I switched to my revolver." He patted the gun on his belt.

Regis nodded and mounted up without asking for the rifle back. "Where'd you learn to shoot like that, anyway?"

"That fancy school you sent me to," said Shep as they rode eastward. "Best part about it was the riding and shooting lessons."

"I thought they were Quakers."

"Oh, they are, but that doesn't mean I didn't pursue the more practical arts on my own time."

"Uh-huh. So you still didn't tell me what you're doing here. South Texas is a long ol' way from Connecticut, unless I'm forgetting something about maps."

Shepley smiled and sighed. "Mighty thirsty work saving your hide."

Regis didn't say anything but slid from the saddle and retrieved his hat. He held it up and poked a finger through a fresh bullet hole angling from left to right across his top knot.

"Yep, mighty good to have me around, huh, big brother?"

Regis felt the twinge, the momentary urge to clout, playfully, the kid on the ear. Instead he nodded. "Doesn't mean I don't want answers from you, boy. But thanks again."

They rode in silence for a few moments, then Shep cleared his throat. "Course, this means you'll stand the first beer."

Regis, slightly ahead, cracked a smile. "Only if you beat me to it." He tucked low and spurred his horse into a hard gallop, knowing Shep's brown eyes were wide and a growl was already crawling up out of the kid's throat.

Regis glanced back and saw his younger brother jam heels into his buckskin. Then the kid's old beaver topper, more hole than hat, whipped off his head. He didn't slow a hair. Time for hats later. Regis grinned and looked forward again. He had a brother to beat—and a beer to drink. A free beer, or he wasn't fit to wear the name of Regis Royle.

Chapter 2

It was close to dark by the time they rode down the dusty main street of Brownsville. All about them, squares of light shone long across their path. Bawdy, bold shouts from men, laced with good-natured shrieks from their fair counterparts, filled the night air, still warm but with an edge of ease only night in the desert can bring.

Piano music, pounding and urgent, leaked from over and under a set of poorly hung, puckered batwing doors.

"How about that beer, brother?"

Regis looked over at the slouched youth riding beside him. "I guess one for celebratory purposes wouldn't hurt."

"One?"

The kid's bald disappointment made Regis smile. "Unless you'd rather have milk?"

"Oh no, anything but that. I ever have enough money I'm never going to drink milk again."

"Thought you liked growing up on the farm back in Maine."

"Ha!" Shepley shook his head. "You're confusing me with you."

"Wasn't me! Why do you think I made for the coast?"

"Yeah, and left me to . . ." The kid's words pinched out, and he looked ahead at nothing. Regis didn't question him.

"How about here?" said Shep.

Regis eyed the cantina. "The Lucky Dog? Nope, too rough for the likes of us."

"After what we've been through?" The kid angled his horse toward the hitch rail out front.

"Nope, Shep. I mean it. There's a decent place down the lane. You go in there, you'll come out poor and dead. Place is filled to brimming with card sharps and worse."

Regis noticed how the kid watched through the open doorway, his gaze lingering on the dimly lit action taking place at the games tables.

Shep pulled on his wide smile and said, "Okay then, lead on, oh fearless brother of mine."

A half-minute later, Regis stopped his horse before a quiet, well-lit establishment.

"Millie's?" said the kid, reading the sign. "This a . . . bordello?"

Regis chuckled. "Not that I'm aware of. And don't let Millie hear you say that. But they do make a sinful apple pie, and I'm about ready to indulge. Figured we could fill our bellies before that beer." He looked at Shep, who eyed him back with the same dark-eyed stare. "I'm sorry to disappoint you, little brother, but if I don't eat something soon, I'm not going to be fit company for man or beast."

Shepley climbed down out of the saddle and sighed, then clapped a hand to his waist and offered a short bow. "To err is human, to forgive divine."

Regis regarded Shepley. "Well, sounds like something from that school stuck."

"Yep," said the young man. "The sap from that pine I climbed down to make my escape from their dastardly clutches." He laughed as he looped his reins around the rail and strode toward the diner's front doors.

It was apparent to Shep that Regis was a regular customer at Millie's. A thick-waisted German woman a good decade beyond Shep's seventeen years batted her eyes at him and fanned her shining face as she took their order. Regis barely had to speak when she let loose with a giggle that seemed never to end.

"Good girl," said Regis after she'd left. "Can't understand a lick of English, but she manages to bring out something tasty every time I wander on in here."

"Mmm, I'll just bet she does," said Shep, looking everywhere but at his scowling big brother.

"Don't let Millie catch you talking like that," said Regis.

"That wasn't Millie?"

"Nope." He leaned over the table. "She's even bigger."

The youth's eyebrows rose, and he looked toward the closed swinging door that led to the kitchen.

The feed was true to Regis's words, and despite Shepley's initial hesitation, Shepley tucked in with a vigor only a Royle could muster. "Only person I have ever seen put away that much food at once," said Regis wiping his ample moustache with his napkin and reaching for a last swallow of coffee, "is Lockjaw. Or maybe me."

"What about Pa?"

Regis's grin slid from his mouth. "I guess." The old man hadn't been the easiest critter to get along with and was much of the reason Regis left home. "I'm sorry I left you back there like I did all those years ago."

Shep shrugged. "I'm tough. I could take it. Besides, Ma kept the worst of it from me. Then the old man left us, and we were better off. Then we heard he up and died, but you knew that."

Regis nodded. *Good riddance*, he almost said, then cleared his throat. "How about that school, then? You on a break? Odd time of year for it."

Shep looked away, his face reddening. Then he looked back at Regis. "I haven't been going."

"What?"

Shep sighed. "I don't go there anymore."

"But . . . I've been sending the money. It's a good school, Shep. You'll get a good education there. More than I had. Ma wouldn't let you up and quit. What's she say about this?"

Shep looked away, then at Regis's eyes. "She doesn't have a thing to say about it."

"What do you mean?"

But even before Shep replied, Regis knew. He could tell by the misting of the kid's eyes, the tuck of the kid's bottom lip. "She's . . . dead. Ma's dead."

They didn't talk for long minutes. Finally Regis said, "How long since?" His voice sounded hollow and old to him.

"Four, five months now."

The air left him. "How?"

"Doctor said pneumonia. I . . . I was there. Got home in time. I was with her." The kid cried, shame reddening his face as he dragged the back of his hand across his eyes. He wadded his napkin and coughed into it, then scrunched his eyes and wiped them.

"I been meaning to write again." Regis clenched his own red-and-white cloth napkin in his big fist. "So busy these days."

Shep didn't say anything.

"I'm so sorry, Shepley. Truly. I'd always meant to get back home before this."

"I know. Didn't help, though, did it?"

"Why didn't you tell me? Someone could have sent for me."

"Tried. I sent a couple of letters but never heard back."

Regis sighed. "I've been busy. Shipping . . . new steamer." He couldn't finish. Anything he said was a pathetic excuse not worth uttering.

After he paid the bill, Regis clapped a hand on his brother's shoulder. "Okay, I'll get us a couple of rooms at the Brownsville Arms. Maybe grab that beer before we turn in. I'll meet you in an hour or two in the lobby, okay? I have business to tend to. You're welcome to come along."

"That's all right," said Shep, yawning.

"Okay, if you're as tuckered as I am, I imagine you'd like to make it an early night. We can catch up more later. Sound good?"

"You bet."

By then they were on the sidewalk. "Good." He handed his reins to the boy. "Then you can take these two nags to Bowdrie's yonder." He nodded at a livery stable diagonally across the street. "Tell Tom I'll catch up with him in the morning. We go way back, helped each other out in the war."

Regis would later question why he didn't take his brother's enthusiasms for taking on a chore in stride. Maybe he thought the boy was growing up. He was, after all, seventeen now. He'd come to regret his lack of scrutiny.

But for the moment, he was headed to the office of his and Cormac's shipping company. He intended to leave Cormac a letter explaining what he'd found and his intentions for the Santa Calina range. He didn't want to waste any time in getting the purchase in the works, but he also didn't want to roust Cormac at his house. The man worked hard, doubly so while Regis had been gone. No need to bother him at home, despite the sense of urgency Regis felt. He was confident Cormac would back his play on this. He'd find out for certain in the morning.

After he did that, Regis turned left from their office and made for Joplin's boarding house, where he suspected his friend, one Jarvis "Bone" McGraw, would be holed up in the kitchen, trying to finagle his way into Mrs. Joplin's good graces and, with any luck, out of her knickers.

He grinned and shook his head as he strode up the street and two lanes over. As it turned out he didn't need to make the full journey to the boarding house. From somewhere inside Barnard's Tonsorial Parlor, all windows alight, he heard a boisterous, deep-throated braying he knew could come from only one man. He stepped up onto the boardwalk and opened the door.

A man looked up at him from over a checkerboard. "Regis Royle, as I live and breathe."

"Bone, Mr. Barnard, how are you both on this fine evening?"

"Fine?" said the proprietor of the barbershop, a squat, bald, fat man with huge ginger muttonchops and a Donegal brogue as thick as the drifts of hair piled up in the corners of the room.

The man did not like to tidy up much, Regis noted—not for the first time—with a suppressed grimace.

The barber mopped his sweating red face with a voluminous handkerchief. "The last time the weather in this hellish hole of hell was fine, the Good Lord himself was in knee pants and all was right with the world."

Bone was a tall, lanky, raw-boned man roughly Regis's age. He stood—still not wobbly, Regis noted—and shook Regis's proffered hand.

Royle prided himself on his solid handgrip when greeting folks, but Bone, without trying to, had a way of commanding a situation with that one grip and looking you square in the eye every time. It was one trait among many that Regis admired about his friend.

"What brings you into town on such a night, Regis?"

"Oh, this and that, that and this."

"Uh-huh," said Bone as if reading his mind. He stretched and yawned. "Well, Barnard. Much as I like your company, you ain't getting any prettier, and I suspect it will be a cold day well south of here before you're a comely woman, so I'm going to take my custom elsewhere. And besides"—he inclined his head toward the portly Irishman—"you told me an hour ago that Myrtle had supper on the stove. I don't want to take the blame for you missing a meal. Lord knows you can't stand that!"

He raised his eyebrows and reached for his hat—a mammoth, wide affair. He pinched the brim and walked out, ignoring the muttering Irishman. "He's just sore because I licked him at checkers. Again. Man will never learn."

"I heard that!"

Bone winked at Regis and said, "I know, you Irish devil. Now get on home!"

"Sure, this lousy Texas Ranger thinks he can throw his weight around my shop, tellin' me what to do. If I were a fightin' man, I'd . . ." Barnard's muttering drifted to silence behind them.

"Man never changes," said Regis. "Hey, how about a quick beer? I have a notion I'd like to float your way."

"Sounds serious," said Bone. He stopped and tapped his chin. "If a conversation's going to take place, then we best do it somewhere we can hear each other. How about Stump's place?"

Regis considered the suggestion, nodded, and led the way across the street. Once the two men found a table and seated themselves with glasses of warm beer before them, he leaned forward. The place wasn't as empty as he'd have liked, but it was better than the alternatives—loud bars with louder people getting louder as their evenings ground on.

He sized up Bone, one of his oldest friends, a swaggering, womanizing Texan through and through, and a Texas Ranger to boot. And, Regis knew, one hell of a cattleman.

"I just got back from a few days up Corpus Christi way."

Bone nodded. "Decent town, growing like a weed in a rainstorm."

"Yep, but it's not what impressed me most."

"Oh?"

"It was the Santa Calina range."

"Ah, should have known. She got to you, too, huh?"

"You know of it?"

"Who doesn't? Oh, there ain't much of this region I haven't

ridden through. It's surprising what you'll find down there flanking the creek."

"That's what I want to tell you about. I aim to buy it."

"You don't say?"

Regis nodded, noticing Bone didn't seem overly surprised. "Yep, and run cattle all over it."

"What do you know about ranching?"

Regis smiled and shook his head. "What I know of it could fill this beer glass." He emptied it, then said, "But you, Bone, know more about such endeavors than any other fellow I know."

"If you're buttering me up for something, you'd have more success with whiskey."

Regis ordered a bottle of their finest and poured them each a shot. "What I have in mind is a partnership, Bone. I aim to buy that range. There's fine water, ample cattle, horses, game, all just waiting for someone to put shape to it."

"And that someone is going to be you?"

Regis shook his head. "Not just me. You too. That's what I meant by a partnership. You have the experience running a ranch. You know cattle and cowboying and the land better than anyone I know."

Regis's voice rose, then he looked around at the few patrons aside from themselves in the dark little hole of a place. "I have my commitments with the fleet, but I'll work with you as I can."

"That's just what we need—a greenhorn rancher with one foot in the water!" This struck Bone as humorous, though Regis could not see why, and the former Ranger guffawed.

Regis looked around. Any more of that and he'd have to tell him to keep it quiet. He didn't want to tip his hand, not when the plan was so fresh.

"What?" said Bone, seeing his chum scanning the room. "You think you're the first to have this harebrained idea, Regis Royle?"

"It's not harebrained, and no. Well, I don't know. Hadn't really thought on it." He leaned forward and poked the table-top with a ramrod finger. "There's a big difference between dreaming and doing, Bone. I haven't failed at much I've turned my hand to. Why do you think Cormac partnered up with me?"

The Ranger lost his smile then and got that windburned crinkly look about his eyes as he studied his friend. "You're serious, ain't you?"

"Serious as a frigate full of gunpowder."

"By gaw'd." Bone nodded and drummed the tabletop with his fingertips. He was silent a few long ominous moments. "It'll take a pile of cash to get started, you know."

"I know it."

"I mean"—Bone drummed his chin with his fingertips—"got to build corrals, hire a passel of men, the works. Then there's a cookie for chuck and such, quarters for them to live in, can't expect them to hang their hats in the thin air!"

"Never thought I would."

"You saying you're serious? All in on this?"

"Yep." Regis nodded solemnly.

"Cormac in on it too?"

"He will be, soon as he reads the note I left him. The idea's solid. Just have to track the deed, find out who owns it, and make it happen."

"Hmm. That'll take some doing, if I know anything of it. I expect you'll be dallying with old Spanish land grants and such. But it's probably nothing that money can't handle."

Regis leaned back and shook his head when Bone offered him a second shot of whiskey. "That's for you. Paid for the bottle. Figured it might help you think this thing through. But I would like to introduce you to someone, if you have a few more minutes to spare."

Bone's bristly brown eyebrows rose, and the shot of whiskey

stuttered in midair halfway to his face. "You get yourself hitched to a woman in Corpus Christi, Regis Royle?"

"God no!" Judging from Bone's reaction, Regis knew his face wore a mask of horror. Maybe one day, but marriage now? No, no, and no.

"Okay, then. I reckon whoever you're about to spring on me can't be all that bad."

Regis shook his head and shoved back from the table. He waited to rise while Bone gathered the bottle and tamped in the cork.

Behind him, at the far end of the bar, a thin man in a colorful serape that barely concealed a blood-spattered tunic slid off a barstool and turned toward the door.

Had Regis been looking, he would have seen that the man's dark hair bore thick wrappings of muslin, with a brown stain along one side of his head.

He also would have seen a red silk sash about the man's waist. And in his hand the man held the brim of a distinctive sombrero with a wide, bright blue band. He also wore a smile that lifted the corners of his wide, bristled mouth as if he had just overheard very interesting news. Because he had.

Had Regis been paying attention, he also might have heard the man chuckling softly as he left the cantina.

As they walked to the hotel where he'd told Shep they'd meet up, Regis wondered just what sort of person his younger brother had become. It wasn't as if Regis really knew the kid. When Regis had left home, Shepley was less than a shaver. Then they'd seen each other, what was it? Three, four times in all those years, not counting today.

Regis groaned to himself. What did the kid want with him now? Best to get him sorted out, then send him back to that school in Connecticut to finish his education. *I guess a little interruption—of a few months of traveling solo—never hurt anybody*, he mused. As valuable as sitting in a classroom, in its own way.

But Regis always regretted not having had more formal schooling. With Cormac's help he'd been able to get a leg up on reading, and within a couple of years of being taken under the man's wing, Regis was tallying accounts books like a professional money man.

As soon as Regis entered the lobby of the Brownsville Arms and didn't see his brother, he frowned. The woman at the desk, a perky young thing he knew to be the daughter of the owners, likewise wasn't helpful. She'd not seen anyone answering to Shepley's name or fitting his description.

"Your brother, huh?" said Bone, not working too hard to tamp down a smile. He cradled the half-filled jug as if it were a child. "Why not let him have the run of the town? Never did me any harm."

Regis said nothing, but his raised eyebrows told his opinion of that idea. "Kid's seventeen—a mighty young seventeen— and fresh off the trail. Or stage. Or boat or train. I don't know which he took to get himself out here. But he's my charge now, and I won't have him come to harm, nor cause it for others." A twinge of guilt stabbed him in the gut as he said it. Thoughts of his old mama dead these five months threatened to upset his apple cart.

"You okay?" said Bone.

"Yeah, yeah. I got an idea where the kid might be. Passed the Lucky Dog on the way in. He seemed keen to test it."

"If he has a half dime in his pocket, it'll go amiss in that rat hole." Bone took a pull on the bottle. "We best make certain he's not in there. That's not a place even I choose to frequent."

But Regis was already legging it back up the street toward the loudest spot ahead. "He's there."

"How do you know?" said Bone.

"That's my horse and his, tied out front. Likely half my gear'll be missing, too. Told him to take them to Bowdrie's, dammit." He ended his sentence with a growling, groaning sound that caused Bone to pop the cork on the bottle once more.

Regis glanced at Bone and suspected his friend was secretly thankful he wasn't Regis's kid brother at that moment. Regis knew enough about himself to know that when his back was up, he was one wild-haired mountain lion.

Chapter 3

Shepley Royle had smiled as he draped the reins over the hitch rail out front of the Lucky Dog saloon.

"What Regis doesn't know won't harm him." He rummaged in his saddlebag and pulled out a drawstring sack and stuffed it in his pocket. Then he thumbed his leather braces, sucked in a lungful of night air, and stretched to his full height, a couple of inches shy of six feet.

"In for a penny, Shep, old boy," he told himself, using one of his sainted mama's pet phrases, though he knew it would not please her were she to know where he was headed. He shrugged and shoved his way through the sagging batwing doors.

If he thought he'd draw attention, he was mistaken. The establishment buzzed and heaved with activity. A scatter of baize-topped tables were barely discernible beneath a cloud of gray smoke that hung like a sagging circus tent over the vast room.

In a far corner, a bald man in a striped shirt and arm garters weaved on a stool, pounding on a piano that even from his own meager experience with such instruments Shep knew was missing keys. No one seemed to care.

Laughter of men and women stabbed through a steady din of clinking glasses and poker chips and enough chatter that it sounded to him like a gaggle of geese way up in the New England sky in late autumn of the year. Honking and honking over one another, making sense only to each other, and in here maybe not even that.

Shep stepped to the bar to his right. The barkeep was a barrel of a man with too much hair oil and with tiny curled moustaches, though one side had some time before it lost its fight with the strictures of the wax that held it stiffly curled in place. He wore a white-and-blue-striped shirt similar to the piano man's. Garters, too, on his arms.

"What you want, sonny?" he said to Shep. "Don't serve no mama's milk in here, boy."

A bleary-eyed man leaning on the bartop, a dented brown derby hat by his elbow, found this humorous, and he raised lazy eyelids. His chuckles turned into a series of hiccups and coughs. "Okay, okay. . . ."

Shep gritted his teeth and laid his hands on the sticky bartop as he met the barkeep's bulldog gaze. "That's good, 'cause I don't want no milk. I want whiskey. Pure and straight, no gargle. You understand?"

"Boy, you best go on home and suckle on the sugar teat. I have to say it once more and I'll lay a mesquite stick upside your bean, you hear me?"

Undaunted, Shepley canted his head, sniggered, and tugged out a fawn-color wax cloth sack with a drawstring top. He plunked it on the bar and looked at the barkeep. The burly man looked from the sack to Shepley, uncertainty on the man's face for the first time. Shep's grin widened, and he nodded slowly as he untied the drawstring.

The barkeep matched the boy's grin. "Was that a whiskey you asked for?"

"Why, yes, yes it was."

The man set the bottle and a freshly toweled glass before the kid, then poured a drink and began to whisk away the bottle.

"Not so fast, my good man. Leave the bottle. I plan on roving the room until I find a suitable game."

"Uh-huh. Well, see that group yonder?" He nodded toward a

full table in the back. "With the one in the red dress dancing like she knows something?"

Shep nodded, one hand clamped on his cash bag.

"You're gonna want to go over there, introduce yourself. Tell them Charles sent you. That's me." He said that as if Shep should be impressed.

"Okay, Charles." He slid out a silver coin and pushed it toward the burly man but didn't let it go. "More where that came from if you put in a good word with the head man at the table."

Charles snatched the coin from Shep. "*That* you got to earn on your own, kid. Go on and prove yourself. I'll be here to powder your backside and send you home to mama."

That burned Shep's ears, but he pasted on what he hoped was a hard scowl and thrust the sack into his front trouser pocket. He did not fail to notice that his interaction—and his cash—had attracted the attention of a few folks. Two of them were women in gaudy dresses and glass beads, more fooferaw than he'd ever seen on any one woman.

He threaded his way through the yammering crowd, getting odd looks and not a few sneers. "Gentlemen," he said once he reached the table, interrupting two conversations and the deal. The man with the cards squinted at him through red-rimmed eyes as copious black smoke chugged upward from a cigar nub as thick around as a fat man's finger.

"What?"

"I'm here to play."

"Get gone, boy."

And so it went, a near repeat of the verbal dance he'd had with Charles until he remembered to use the barkeep's name. "Charles sent me."

"Oh." The dealer glanced toward the bar, weaved his head back and forth until he got a sight line he found acceptable. He nodded and turned a sudden smile on Shep. "Well, any friend of Charles is a friend of mine. And the boys here, too. Ain't that right, boys?"

The other men about the table chorused their agreement and matched the dealer's lippy smile.

"Only one thing, kid. You got to have cash to sit in on this game. We're the . . . ah, top dogs in these parts, you see?"

"I see," said Shep, wanting to wipe off the sweat stippling his upper lip and forehead. "I see. Well, you make room, give me a chair, and I'll meet your bet. And raise it."

Eyebrows rose and cigars wagged. Chairs squawked to the side and another was dragged from a nearby table by the woman in the red dress. She smiled down at Shep and winked and laid her long fingers on his shoulders. Next thing he knew she was whispering in his ear. He couldn't make out the words, but he sure liked the feeling of a woman's breath on his ear and neck. Liked it a lot.

A few of the men laughed and shook their heads, and he knew he was in over his head, but what could he do? He breathed deep of the smoke and sweat and beer and some underlying stink of burned beef that clung to the edges of everything, like grease you can't wash off. And he repeated his mama's mantra in his head: In for a penny, in for a pound.

Shep tugged out his sack of coins and wished he'd thought to separate some of it into his other pocket. Too late now. He set it on the table before him, and the men all stared at it, no mirth on their faces now. The sack's obvious weight had attracted their stares like moths to candle flame.

A couple of them swallowed and nearly lost their cigars. He fancied he heard the woman suck in a sharp breath. Shep brightened at that and had himself another shot of whiskey, not burning his throat or warming his gut nearly as much as the first had. He could get used to the gambling life, yes sir.

"Let's do it up, boys. I'm fixing to get rich tonight." He grinned at them.

And that's what Shep did, at least for the first two hands. He didn't fail to notice the theatrical groans or the accompanying winks among the assembled gamblers at his table. And even a few from other tables. But he chalked it up to a combination of genuine jealousy and annoyance that a kid was doing the winning.

After those first couple of shots, the whiskey slid down his gullet nice and smooth. The room, too, took on a mellow brilliance that warmed him in and out. Or maybe that was the whiskey. Twice he thought this and giggled out loud, but no one seemed to notice. The haze of smoke that had hung in the air somehow didn't bother him as much after a few hands. He noticed, though, that he'd been passed by as dealer maybe once or twice and that somehow didn't seem right.

"Hey," he said, trying to blink all those cards in his hands into focus. Surely someone gave him too many cards. "Hey, now. What's going on here? I'm s'posed to deal, too, you know!" He slammed a hand down on the table, and chips and glasses danced.

"Take it easy, sonny," said the first man he'd talked with. What was his name again?

Shep decided he didn't like the man. He'd make sure he bled his little pile of cash dry first, then move on to the others. Money, yes, that's what he was supposed to focus on. He looked down at his spot at the table and noticed his sack of cash looked thinner than before.

"Hey, now. . . . Who's stealing from me? Huh?" He slammed his hand on the table again.

"All right, that's enough, kid."

Shep looked up to see not the pretty woman he expected, but the thick, fleshy face of the barkeep. What was his name? Oh yeah. . . . "Charles!"

"Yep, kid, that's me. Only now we ain't friends, okay? You're done here. You're broke and you're too loud, and my patrons have had enough of you. Just a kid, anyway."

Shep felt himself rising up out of the chair. How was that happening? Whatever it was, he sensed he didn't want it to happen. He thrashed out with his left hand, and it connected with something, felt like a person's arm.

His cards fluttered free, and he noticed, too, that the piano music and all that loud chatter and laughter that moments before felt comfortable and just right had stopped.

"Hey—" he said, but felt a harsh slap across his face. The blow whipped his head to the side, and for a moment he could see straight and true, and what he saw was the pretty lady sitting on the lap of the man who'd invited him to sit down. The man he didn't like so much anymore.

The lady didn't look happy, and she was whispering into that grinning man's ear and the grinning man was looking straight at him. Then the grinning man nodded toward him. Not at Shep, he knew, but maybe at somebody behind him.

Shep was yanked the rest of the way out of his chair by people from both sides of him, from behind. As he slopped backward, he looked up and saw the leering face of a big, big man. But it was no one he'd ever seen before.

As he looked to his left he saw a big fist, and then he saw nothing more but bright pulses of light, like summer's heat lightning in a purple sky—no sound, just flashes of light. Then he felt himself being dragged, even as other blows fell on his face and head and chest like huge drops of impossible, painful rain.

Chapter 4

The woman's long hair, black as the soul of a demon, swayed ever so slightly with each light touch she made on the ornately carved silver pistol's hair trigger. The blue-gray smoke from the shots boiled up from the gun, hovering about her, wreathing her beauty in cloud before breaking up on the breeze.

The shots, measured yet rapid, driven home by instinct rather than calculation, burst bottle after bottle in the long row of glinting green glass lined atop the stone wall.

She paused only to hand the revolver to a servant, then received a freshly loaded gun in the same proffered hand. As the harsh sound of gunfire echoed down the long stone canyon, a man cleared his throat. "Senorita Valdez?"

The woman did not turn, but the man saw her shoulders lower slightly as if she had sighed, perhaps in disappointment. Oh, he thought, let it not be disappointment, at least not in him. And yet, how could it not be so?

"Speak, Hector."

The man turned his blue-banded sombrero in his hand, worrying the brim with grimy fingers, the nails too long and caked beneath with filth. He squinted and licked his lips. The sun reflected off the bottles still standing. Sweat stung the graze wound above his left temple, and his stubbled face prickled in the heat.

"I have news, senorita."

"And I have less patience with each moment that passes."

"Yes, senorita. I was in Stump's cantina, senorita."

"Not news, Hector. That is your second home, is it not?"

"No, senorita, I live in the bunkhouse . . . oh, *si, si.*"

"I am waiting."

"Yes, the man. His name is Royle."

The woman straightened and fiddled with the revolver. "You mean the man you failed to kill?"

For a moment Hector's breath seized in his throat. She knew. How could she know? But then . . . of course she would know. Tomasina Valdez knew everything. He had worked for her for three years, and in that time he had seen her do things that convinced him she was nothing short of a witch, a thing of the spirit world.

She had received word from an acquaintance in Corpus Christi that a man named Regis Royle had talked with friends there, had told them of the wonderful place he had ridden through on his way to Corpus Christi. He had told them of his intent to buy that land, come what may, for he wanted to ranch that land.

When Senorita Valdez's men had heard this news from the acquaintance, they had all laughed. It was too much! They fell down from the laughter, tears stinging their bloodshot, pulque-strained eyes.

Ranch the Valley of Death? Ranch the domain of the wild horses? There was nothing there but wild beasts too numerous to ever die—horses; terrible scrub cattle; and snakes, snakes, and more snakes. Let the gringo ranch it and he would die a thousand times over. And in the first week!

Yet Senorita Valdez had not laughed at the news. She had grown angry at the news.

So yes, of course she would know Hector had failed her. He also knew she could turn and fire and give him an eternal headache before he would blink once more from the blasted sun. He expected it.

She did not turn and fire, but she did keep playing with that gun. It made Hector nervous.

"Yes, senorita, that is the man. But I know more now. I learned of his plans."

"Yes, yes, he wishes to buy the land. We know this already."

He did not respond, because he knew she was not asking his opinion.

"The question is, when? And how? And does he have the money to do so? It would seem we have to meet with the Don very soon. Even if he has not yet invited us, eh?"

"*Si*, Senorita Valdez."

"Why are you still here?"

Hector looked at the kid cleaning the pistols, but the young man did not return his gaze. He felt very alone, very worried about his life. He could say the wrong thing and senorita would shoot him where he stood. He licked his lips. "The money, senorita."

"Yes?"

"He has it. Or at least he will."

"And how do you know this?"

"Because I heard him speak of it at the cantina. He was there with his friend, the Texas Ranger called Bone."

Valdez snorted, and her head jerked back in a short laugh. "That fool of a Ranger has no money."

"No, senorita. But he has agreed to run the ranch for Senor Royle."

Her laughter stopped. Finally she spoke. "And the money?"

"Senor Royle is going to talk with his partner." He leaned forward, as if they were standing inches apart and he were re-laying confidential information. "That Cormac Delany has much money, huh?"

"It is not only money that will win the day—and get me my

family's land back—I assure you, Hector. It is up to me to convince the Don of that."

"*Si*, Senorita Valdez." He wasn't certain what else to do. He'd told her what he knew, though he was certain that more of what he overheard might be of use. But somehow he thought their conversation might have gone better. It was always so confusing to talk with her.

"Oh, Hector?"

"Yes, senorita?"

"You may leave. Tell the men to saddle up. We leave within the hour to visit the Don."

"*Si*, Senorita Valdez."

"Oh, and Hector? Pray he does not turn me down. For if he does, you will be the first to know. The first to feel my anger."

The last word had barely passed from her lips before she peeled off a shot, then another, each tripping on the next. Green bottles exploded almost in unison, their shards pluming skyward like raindrops bouncing off rock.

Hector gulped hard and scurried from the woman's presence, each second expecting to feel a bullet core his heart from the back to the front and a red bloom bursting from his chest.

As she felt the heft of the freshly loaded revolver in her hand, Tomasina Valdez growled a low, harsh sound, deep in her long tan throat. Her long black eyelashes fluttered, and she ground her teeth. She wondered, not for the first time, how her life had come to this. El Jefe to a band of monkey-brain fools, living in a grimy, cave-riddled canyon at the back end of a dry wash where lizards and snakes crawled off to die. This and little else was left to her by her failure of a father.

The man who'd gambled and lost it all, his own meager family fortune and the more impressive, sizable holdings of his wife's family.

"Oh, Mama," whispered Tomasina Valdez, her thoughts drifting back to not so many years before when she was a little girl, a girl among girls, the only child that mattered to her mama. Her sister, a deformed thing, had been sent away years before to live out her days in a monastery. And so Tomasina spent her days dressed in pretty frocks, pretty ribbons holding her long plaited hair, happiness her only companion.

Her mama braided her hair each morning, singing to her, humming softly. She recalled the touch of her long, soft fingers as she fondled Tomasina's hair, telling her stories of her own childhood, so close to royalty.

Tomasina's own papa had once been daring and bold and brash, but his carefree ways had caught up with him and their lives slowly changed. Less of this, less of that, more chores because there were fewer servants, more arguments between Mama and Papa because he had sold off this slice of land or that piece.

"You had no right!" Mama would say over and over again. "That land was my father's and his father's father's! It should have been for our children!"

"I have all the rights because I am the man, do you hear me?"

Always the arguments went on and on like this, over and over, never ending and never getting better. For once land is sold, Mama had told her, it could never again be yours, not truly yours.

"I will prove you wrong, dear Mama. I swear it. I will have our land once more. The Spanish land grant shall be once more in the Valdez name. Certainly not in the name of some filthy greenhorn gringo. No matter the lives it takes, I shall have it. This I swear."

Gunfire echoed once more, spiraling upward from the little sun-baked stony wash. Bottles burst skyward and Tomasina Valdez growled, and her servant boy never even flinched.

Chapter 5

"Hey, mister. . . ." A soft voice called from the shadows to the left of the building.

Regis stiffened. "Who's there?"

Bone nodded once as Regis glanced toward him and stepped back into the street. He moseyed to the left.

"A friend," said the voice. A woman?

A figure stepped from the shadows, quickly followed by Bone, who braced the stranger. The stranger uttered a sharp cry, a distinctly female cry.

Regis bolted forward and held her shoulders. "Ma'am, we aren't here to bother anyone, but why did you call to me?"

She looked toward the saloon doors, but no one seemed to hear her from inside. If they did, they didn't much care. "I heard you talking about the horses. They belong to that kid, don't they?"

Without thinking, Regis gripped her shoulders harder. "What do you know about him? Where is he?" He gave her a shake, and she made a pained sound and tried to pull away from him.

"Regis, let go of the lady, okay?" Bone laid a hand on his friend's arm. Regis pulled back and shook his head. "Sorry. I'm sorry, ma'am."

He could see by the way she was dressed that the word

ma'am wasn't something most folks would call her. He took in her gaudy red dress, her piled hair, the scent of too-strong perfume wafting off her. She was a dance hall floozy, a dime a dozen in the growing town of Brownsville. But she stood straight and tall and looked him in the eyes.

"Hurry," she said, turning from him. "They beat the kid." She turned back. "In the alley. Follow me."

Regis strode after her, but Bone snatched his sleeve. "Could be a trap."

"Since when were you afraid of the dark?" said Regis, and disappeared into the dim space.

"Ain't afraid of the dark, you polecat, just trying to save your fool hide." His mumbling continued as he edged in beside Regis, each man with a hand on his sidearm as they entered the dark mouth.

A gash of moonlight lit the alley enough for Regis to see the woman bent over somebody laid out on the ground. He rushed over, dropped to his knees. "Shep!" He leaned closer. Yep, it was the boy.

"Shep!" He patted the kid's face. "You okay?" Then he looked at the woman. "What happened?"

"They beat him pretty bad. He came in all swagger and no brains, already liquored. Then he plopped himself down at Mr. Sampson's table. He's a . . ."

"Don't care right now, ma'am. Shep, you okay?" The kid murmured and coughed.

"I don't think they did anything more than beat on him."

Regis bent low, sniffed. The kid stunk, like he'd swum all the way to the bottom of a bottle of crap liquor, then slurped his way to the surface again. "Damn fool boy."

"There's another thing, mister," said the girl, smoothing Shep's hair back from his forehead. "They took his money. He asked for it, practically begged them to, dared them to. Said he was going to take them all for everything they had, but he's just a boy, anybody can see that. They were merciless. Picked him clean and let him play the fool." She looked at Regis and Bone and lowered her voice. "If they find out I've said anything, they'll . . ."

"Don't you worry, ma'am," said Bone. "They'll have to answer to me first." He helped her to her feet and escorted her to the alley's mouth. "Go on down to Millie's, tell her Bone sent you. She'll treat you right. I hope you like pie. And I expect you could use some coffee. You done good. We'll take it from here on, though. And when we talk with this Mister Sampson, your name won't need to come up."

She smiled slightly and straightened. "Why, thank you, Mr. . . ."

"It's Bone, ma'am. Friends call me Bone."

"All right, then, Mr. . . . Bone. I'll be seeing you." She glanced left, then right, then walked briskly down the boardwalk toward the café.

"If you're done courting, I'm going to get Shep over to our rooms at the hotel. Then I'm going to go on inside this den of thieves and introduce myself to this Mr. . . ."

"Sampson," said Bone. "Me too. Imagine making a poor woman like that live in fear? I have a good mind to button up that man's eyes for him."

"Not before I do."

Bone leaned over the boy. "So this is your brother."

"Shepley Royle, yep."

"Looks like a green-as-they-come whippersnapper, all right. Let's get to it."

Between the two of them they got the kid's arms up and over their shoulders. He wasn't their height yet, so his toes dragged. They received sideways looks from the few folks still on the street but made it to the hotel without trouble.

In the lamplight of the lobby, Regis cocked an eyebrow and Bone whistled at the look of the kid's face. It was freshly thumped, still pinked and puffed but with an emerging hue of sunset purple beneath.

"Hooey," said Bone. "He is going to feel that head of his, inside and out, come morning."

"Serves him right. But it doesn't mean he deserved what they gave him."

Bone nodded in agreement, and they lugged the loll-headed kid up the short staircase, the wood treads creaking under their boots.

They flopped him on his bed, and Regis pulled off the kid's boots. "Should have left them on," said Bone, pinching his nose. "He needs a bath, starting with them feet."

"Tomorrow he'll get all that and more. Fool kid." Regis walked back to the door. Even before they closed it, they heard the kid snoring.

Despite the mess Shep's face was in, the two men couldn't help chuckling as they walked back down the hall.

The barkeep was a stout fellow with a broad chest, but Regis suspected the brute wore a jaw of bone china that would crack under a quick blow.

"Where can I find a Mr. Sampson?"

"Who?"

Regis sighed.

The man stared at Regis.

Bone drew back a fist.

Regis drew back a fist.

With two ham hands aimed at his face, the burly barkeep nodded toward the table in the back, where faces were turning their way. In fact, the commotion up at the bar had begun to reach everyone in the room. Several men were squawking back their chairs and standing.

The first fist thrown came from Regis. He'd never had a problem opening a ball, or closing it down. He was big enough and had enough of the Irish in him, as his mama used to say, that he would never want for women or fights. She'd made him promise long before he really knew what he was promising that he'd not indulge in or abuse either one. Well, not too awfully much.

By the time he knew what that was, he'd already sampled the delights of two women. The first one he swore he loved, though he'd found out that three other of his shipmates all claimed the same.

He'd also had his share of brawls, one of which resulted from what he'd heard his shipmate say about that very woman. Alas, he'd aged since then and had come to enjoy a good fight for the fight's sake.

But tonight, well, tonight was different. He'd taken a pull on Bone's bottle before they stepped into the Lucky Dog. Unbidden thoughts of his mother had come to him right at that moment, dying of a sickness no one could stave off, and burned hotter than the whiskey in his throat. He was primed for a fight.

Out of the corner of his eye, Regis had seen the burly barman reach for something beneath the bar. He leaned sideways and snatched the man's shirtfront just under his thick chin. His other fist, the opener, drove hard and fast. He'd been correct. The man's eyes rolled back in their sockets. Regis let go of the wad of cloth, and the plug of a man dropped in a heap behind the bar.

"I know you?" said Bone, ducking a quick but sloppy shot lunged his way by a wobbly fellow at the bar. Bone rose up before the man as if he'd been launched straight off a catapult and peppered the wobbling drunk's face with a combined flurry of tight rabbit punches. They jerked the blinking man's face fore and aft as if his head were being yanked by a string.

Regis caught sight of the move and thanked his stars he was chummy with Bone. He was no slouch in a fracas, but the Ranger was downright quick and brutal.

"You see Mr. Big yet?" said Bone.

"Not yet, but if he's here I will." And Regis strode forward, deeper into the room, his fists held loose but ready, his knuckles itching to snap somebody's teeth.

By then every face in the place had swiveled toward the two big strangers. "Which one of you is Mr. Sampson?" said Regis as he stopped before the table the surly barkeep had indicated. "Answer my question, or you all go down, one at a time."

"Now, friend," said a man who looked as though his gray wool attire would be better suited to a life of ease on a riverboat. The man, from the deep South judging from his thick accent, slowly plucked a reeking fat cigar from his plump face and smiled. The smile didn't make it to his eyes. "I am Mr. Sampson. What seems to be the trouble?"

"Trouble is, Mr. Sampson, you and your boys here took advantage of my little brother. And while I won't argue that he spouted off, knowing him, or that he had too much whiskey and not enough years on him, there was no call for you all to do what you did. Now I have one question for you. Are you going to hand over his money the easy way or the hard way?"

The man at the table stuffed the soggy end of his black cigar back between his lips and puffed. He squinted through the smoke up at the ceiling as if an answer were written there on the timbers. He glanced back at Regis and said, "Horton! Melville! Get your sorry hides over here!"

While this little charade unwound before them, Bone stood catty-corner to Regis so they could both take in the entire room.

Two large men parted the crowd behind Sampson and flanked his chair. They were wide as doorways at the shoulder and as tall as Regis and Bone, but with meat enough on their frames that they'd be taken as oxen if they lay down in a pasture.

They stared with blind malice at Regis and Bone through piggy dot eyes. Regis could almost see the steam curling from

their flexing nostrils. He'd seen their type before at every harbor town—no brains to speak of, just enough to thrive on a
fight. They each flexed their big meaty hands. There was his
answer.

"Hard way, huh?"

Mr. Sampson smiled around his cigar. "What makes you
think I got to where I am by giving away my hard-won money,
Mr. . . . ah, didn't catch your name?"

"Royle. Regis Royle. Remember it, because you'll come to
regret what's about to happen."

"I, on the other hand," Bone spoke in a low, cold tone, "will
enjoy every last second of it. You ready, pard?"

Regis ran his tongue tip over his teeth. "Yep."

"Then let's get to it, son."

And they did. The first thing Regis tackled was the piece of
games furniture that stood between him and the still-seated
Sampson. While his left mitt snatched the edge of the baize
table and jerked it upward, the right drew back into a hard knob
of knuckle and bone. It was set to drive into the throat of the
nearest ox-faced brute—Melville or Horton, he didn't know
which, nor did he care.

The table arced up, spraying Mr. Sampson and the other
men still stupid enough to have remained with chips and drinks
and ashtrays and cards and money. *It's fool's confetti*, thought
Regis as the debris whipped by his head and showered the sag-
jowled Sampson and his wide eyes.

Regis's right fist did exactly what he hoped it would. It felt,
from the collapsing sensation beneath his knuckles, as if the
first big man's windpipe were giving way. From the look on the
wide face—even the piggy eyes bulged round—he was right.
The brute dropped to his knees, causing the puncheons to
tremble. Regis felt the twin thuds right up his legs and sidestepped to let the man gag and try to bellow in peace.

He was set to dole out more of the same to the other ox-man, but found Bone had beaten him to it. The Texas Ranger's muscle-corded arms looked like mesquite branches in a mighty windstorm and flailed with solid, precise blows on the wide shape bearing down on him. Trouble was, those blows didn't appear to be doing all that much.

Regis closed in on the brute from the side and landed a quick jab to the man's fat-cupped ear. It was enough to rattle the beefy head and spin it in his direction. He could almost see the thinking going on behind those little curious, hateful eyes.

He didn't give the man time enough to finish the thought, though, because his left fist drove upward. While he'd intended to send the blow up under the man's chin, he didn't reckon on the fact that he stood too close.

His fist caromed off the man's half-soft chest, doing little more than annoy the brute, who grunted and swung a wide left at Regis's head. As the beast swung, he opened his mouth, revealing a black round hole, home to a mass of pink tongue but no teeth. *So much for knocking his chompers in*, thought Regis as the brute's punch slammed into his right ear.

The blow knocked Regis into Bone and Bone into the up-ended table, which wedged harder into the scrambling shape of Mr. Sampson, who'd pitched backward when the table first landed on his lap mere moments before. Some piece of debris had cut his forehead, and the ample flow from the slight wound gave his face a frightening look his cigar-chewing threats could never achieve.

Bone grunted something about being sick just looking at him and swung his right fist at the jowly face. But the table kept the blow from doing anything more than glancing off the man's pointy nose.

"Only thing hard on you's that nose, anyway," said Bone, shoving up off the table and focusing his efforts once more on the brute currently pummeling Regis.

The wide man had Regis by the shirtfront and was fixing to

pop him on the face. Regis appeared dazed, shaking his head and trying to focus his gaze. Bone knew when a situation was turning, and this one looked to be well on its way.

He had one trick left in his toolbox, especially if they were going to take on the rest of the bar. He needed Regis somewhat coherent. So he pulled back his right boot and kicked hard and fast up into the darkness at the nexus of the big brute's spraddled legs.

The air that wheezed from the puckered face and wide eyes told Regis and Bone why the ham-size fist had jerked to a stop in midair.

Regis, his senses somewhat returned, looked at Bone with his brows drawn. Bone shrugged. "Old Ranger trick. Last gasp sort of thing, if you know what I mean. I forgot I have a pretty lady waiting for me tonight, and I don't need to limp my way over there only to have her tell me she doesn't recognize my handsome face."

Regis smiled. "Whose wife is she?"

"Why, Royle, I am shocked you'd say such a thing. You know back in merry old England, those are fighting words."

"Ha."

That was all the time they had for chatter, because Mr. Sampson had dragged himself out from under the table and scrambled to his feet. He made a squealing sound as he shoved his way through the tight-packed throng behind him. "Out of my way!"

But he didn't get far. Regis walked around the small crowd to the back, Bone legged in from behind the overturned table, and they closed in on him.

Regis leaned over. "Going somewhere, Mr. Sampson?"

The chunky gambler gulped, his face a quivering mass of blood and snot-sodden moustache. "No, no, that is to say I . . . my men, they've never . . ."

"Yeah, well, big doesn't equal smart. But you'd know all

about that, eh, big man?" Bone laid a hand on Mr. Sampson's shoulder. The gambler flinched.

"This your establishment, Sampson?" said Regis.

"No, no. I have an agreement with the owner."

"Oh, you drink for free, they feed you the suckers, and you split the takings. That sound about right?"

The man looked at his soiled gray wool jacket, his blood-spattered shirtfront, and then up at the crowd, a renewed zeal in his eyes. "You all saw this! These two men came in here of their own accord, came in threatening us, threatening me! You all know me, right?"

The looks on the faces of the patrons of the now less-than-packed saloon were less than sympathetic. Several people backed away, as if being too close might somehow acquaint them with the blubbering man.

"Sammy! Gobel? Pritchard?"

No one by those names stepped forward.

"My brother's money, if you please. Just what you took. And don't think you can cheat me, because I know to the penny what he came in here with and I know there wasn't a cent in his pockets when I found him in the alley yonder."

Sampson gulped, his head tremoring from side to side as if he'd had far too much coffee and no sleep for a week. "I . . . I don't know the exact amount. I don't know, I tell you!"

He reached into his jacket, and Bone tensed. "Easy now, Sampson. You pull a hide-out gun and I'll gut you like a snare-caught rabbit. With my bare hands."

"It's just my wallet, I'm reaching for my wallet. . . ."

"Okay, then."

Regis suppressed a smile. He was enjoying himself. Might even thank the boy for the distraction. It'd been a long ol' time since he'd indulged in a brawl. Last time had been down at the docks, more than a year back.

"I tell you I don't know the exact amount." Sampson's hands trembled as he thumbed through the bank notes.

"Round up, then," said Regis. "Hey, what's that?" He pointed at the man's parted coat. Hanging from his inside pocket was the flopped top of a cinched sack, fawn colored. Regis reached for it even as the man flinched. He drew out the empty sack and looked at it.

"The kid," said Sampson. "He had his cash in it."

"Yeah, he did," said Regis, his jaw muscles bunching as he smoothed the old, worn thing beneath his thumb. "Was our mother's. Used to keep her pin money tucked away in it. Belonged to her pappy, from the old country." He looked up from it to Mr. Sampson's eyes. "Give me the boy's money. Now." His voice was low and cold. The words forced themselves out between his gritted teeth like sand ground between steel.

The portly gambler whimpered and thrust the full wad of notes and coins into Regis's waiting hand.

Regis clamped the money in his hand, along with the old cloth sack. "That's for the boy," he said, and drew back his right fist. "And this is for my mama." His knuckles rammed sharp and fast into the center of Sampson's quivering face. The man sagged like a sack of wet cornmeal.

"Okay, boys, fun time's over. Come with me."

Bone and Regis looked up to see Marshal Clem Corbin standing in the doorway, a sawed-off gut-shredder draped over his arm. Flanking him were two deputies with equally foul-looking firearms. These were held less casually, their deadly snouts pointing in Bone and Regis's direction.

The two men nodded, and Bone stepped in front of Regis. Regis took the moment to thrust the cash and old cloth-scrap wallet deep into his left pocket.

"Just getting what's ours, Clem," said Bone.

"Didn't say I cared, Bone. Just got to let the folks know I do the job I'm paid for." He turned to his deputies. "I'll take these two in. You two deal with the fatback brothers laid out yonder." He shook his head. "Never seen them two beasts get bested before. You and Royle ought to take more care of our citizenry. Liable to hurt someone."

"What about Mr. Sampson?" said Regis.

"What about him?" said the lawman. "He's out cold. He comes to, he'll find his reputation hereabouts has been, shall we say, sullied by you two. He was a powerful man, so normally I'd say beware of your backtrail, but in the end he's a two-bit gambler. He'll light out, and with any luck we'll be shed of him for good and forever."

Chapter 6

"Gentlemen, gentlemen!"

The booming voice dropped on the ears of the two sleeping men as if it were thunder from on high. Regis flickered an eye, Bone shook his head slowly.

"Gentlemen! Your attention, please!" This time the booming voice was joined by a rattling, clanging sound that jerked both men awake. Another few moments of the same racket brought their booted feet to the floor, eyes wide and unblinking.

Regis saw he was in a jail cell, seated on a chain-hung cot beside another of the same construction. He faced a web of steel, and beyond that stood a pudgy, well-dressed Irishman, grinning and dragging a tin cup back and forth across the cell's strap steel door.

Regis couldn't help but smile.

"Good to see you're awake, Regis, my boy. Thought you'd expired and I'd have to carry on alone, with double the wealth and half the headaches."

Regis's smile widened. No matter the situation, you could count on his partner, Cormac Delany, to show up, grinning and lobbing pithy comments.

"You're lucky I wasn't in my cups last night, otherwise you'd be rattling that cup of yours with broken fingers and yammering through split lips."

"Ah, lovely to see you, too, Regis. And a fine morning it is."
Cormac flicked his gaze toward the yawning Bone. "I see you
found your foreman."

Regis perked up. "You got my note about the land?"

Cormac nodded. "I did, indeed."

Bone looked up at him through tired eyes. "I didn't have so
much to drink last night I don't know what you're talking
about. And yes, if it's still a consideration under the cold light of
this new day, I'm willing. Seems a tall order, though." He
yawned.

"Tall order?" said Cormac. "How so?"

"Gonna take some doing to get the owner of that land to
mull over an offer. Last I heard he was not inclined to sell."

"You know who owns it and you didn't think to tell me last
night?"

Bone shrugged. "I was busy."

Cormac tut-tutted and shook his head.

Regis stretched. "Cormac, did you come to talk all day and
stare, or are you going to get us out of here?"

"I have been informed," said Cormac, nudging the cell door
to swing open with a long, slow squawk, "that the door's been
unlocked the entire time you've been here." Once more he
turned his attention to Bone. "As to your guess about Don Mallarmoza's inclinations, well, we'll find out soon, won't we?"

"Who?" said Regis. "And how soon?"

"Didn't I tell you?" said Cormac. "The Don is the owner of
the Santa Calina range you told me of in your note, Regis. And
he is spending this very day entertaining . . . shall we say, offers
on the land."

"What?" Regis swung the door wider. "Explain yourself,
Cormac. I don't have the time for this."

Delany sighed. "Okay, okay. But for the record, you're no
fun." He leaned against the doorframe. "I have learned to tease
out good and bad news for the same reason. Seems that one

Don Mallarmoza, at his estate not terribly far from here in Reynosa, will very soon see and hear the pleas of a fetching young woman who has never been told no in her life."

"What's that mean, Delany?" Bone joined Regis at the cell door.

"As luck would have it, there's sudden interest in the land you wrote to me about, Regis. Too sudden to be coincidence. I don't believe in coincidences, I believe in work."

"I know," said Regis, edging past the man. "Tell me more about this Don fellow and his situation that's not a coincidence."

Cormac stopped him. "How many people have you been telling of your plans?" He spoke in a low tone, eyeing his partner.

"Just you and Bone. And a couple of friends in Corpus Christi. And Shep. Why?"

"Your brother's here?"

"Yeah, I forgot to mention it in my note to you. I didn't mean to get tossed in the jailhouse overnight. It was for . . ."

"Fighting, I know. I can tell by the state of your face, bruised as it is, and your scuffed knuckles. Really, you two are a sorry sight."

Regis sighed. "The Don, Cormac?"

"I've already paid your fees here. Let's walk and talk. We don't have much time to spare, I'm afraid. If I know anything of the other interested party, it may be too late already."

"Cormac," said Bone. "You're making as much sense as a man lost three days on the Tanglefoot Trail."

"And he says I'm confusing? Texans!" said the dapper Irishman. "I'll never understand them. Oh, I'll take their money, but I'll never understand them."

The trio conversed as they strode up the street, two of them tall and rumpled and sporting bruised, whiskered faces. The third, a shorter man, prone to softness and dapper in a boiled wool suit and a brown derby hat.

Cormac looked left and right, then said, "The Santa Calina, as I've been able to find out, is eighteen thousand acres of land, much of it not considered worth the time it takes to talk about. But apparently you, Regis, found its hidden gem, the heart of it. But you're not the only person who wants it."

"Who's the other?"

"Near as I've been able to discern, it's an angry heir, or rather one who would have inherited the land had the original Spanish land grant not been lost or sold or appropriated somehow in the war."

"And now this heir wants it back? Was the deal fair and square?"

Cormac nodded and waited for two narrow-eyed women to pass them by. "Yes, I believe so."

"This heir, then," said Bone, looking longingly toward Millie's and sniffing the morning breeze for a whiff of the woman's bold-brewed coffee. "He intends to buy it back? Or maybe he thinks he's got a legal leg to stand on in getting the land back?"

Cormac smiled as he came to a stop before the hotel. "The he in question, gentlemen, as I indicated earlier, is a she. And from what I have heard, she has much in the way of influence, if not in money, and . . . oh bother, let's just say she has things neither of you could offer the aging and widowed Don Mallarmoza that he'd find of particular interest."

"Wait," said Bone, his eyes widening. You don't mean . . ."

Cormac nodded. "I do."

"What?" said Regis, looking from man to man. "Who?"

"Go on inside and clean up, Royle," said Cormac. "And make it snappy. I'll pour some coffee into this poor Texas wretch, and we'll meet you back here in"—he tugged out his pocketwatch and clicked it open—"ten minutes." He clicked it shut and slipped it back into its pocket in his brocade waistcoat. "And then we ride for Mallarmoza's. Now make haste, man!"

Regis trudged up the stairs, the twin, nearly foreign feelings of uncertainty and defeat nibbling at his thinker. "Damn kid," he muttered. "He hadn't come along I might have gotten a shoe in the Don's door." Then he realized he was wrong.

If Shep hadn't come along when he did, he might well have died out there in the Santa Calina, pinned down until those demons sniped him or snakes bit him to death in his hidey-hole in the rocks.

He was going to knock on Shep's door, but then he just snorted and opened it wide. There lay his brother, in much the same position he and Bone had left him long hours before. He looked awful in the dim light. Regis crossed the room and pulled the curtains wide, then raised the window.

The clattering stirred the boy. "Wake up, Shep. Time to rise and shine."

A long, low moan was all Regis heard.

"Oh . . . oh no. Not this again."

"Again? Shep, you've been drunk before?"

The kid cracked an eye and looked up, shut it again as fast. "Light, too much light."

Regis sighed and looked around the room. His eyes settled on the pitcher atop the chest of drawers. He smiled and lifted it and stood over his bruise-faced little brother, shaking his head. "Sorry, kid. Time to rise." He upended the full pitcher of wash water on the kid's face and stood back.

Regis enjoyed seeing the sputtering exasperation on the boy's face as it warred almost immediately with the hot, thudding pain that surely pounded within and without Shepley Royle's egg-thin head. "Gaah! Ohh . . ."

"So, Shep, how you feeling?" Regis set the pitcher on the chest of drawers and crossed his arms, not trying in the least to hide his smile.

Shep dragged a hand down his face, wincing at what he felt. "What happened. . . . Oh yeah." He sat up, swung his feet to the floor. "Oh, oh yeah."

Regis watched the kid whisper to himself several times more as the previous evening's events drifted back to him.

Then Shep clawed at his trouser pocket, then the other pocket, then stood and spun in a circle, looking for the rest of his clothes. "I've been robbed! Oh!" He looked up as if seeing Regis for the first time. "I've been robbed!"

"Nope," said Regis. "That's my line."

"What?"

"That money. Where'd you get it?"

"I . . . I don't understand." Shep's face reddened and he looked away, around the room.

"Yeah, you do. You're hung over, you're not an idiot. Well, might be I'm wrong about that. Where'd you get it?"

Shep took a few hesitant steps across the room, looked out the window, then pulled in a deep breath and looked at Regis. "You know that money you were sending for the school?"

Regis took no pains to hide the dark disappointment on his face, and it made Shep look away.

"Naw," said Regis. "Ma wouldn't let you do that. She wanted you educated." He shook his head, not wanting to believe what Shep was saying. "I promised her I'd see to those expenses. I kept my word on that score."

The kid shook his head. "I rode it out at school awhile, and I kept the money. They tried to contact her, but by then it was too late. She was gone, didn't have anything to say about it."

Neither said anything for a full minute. Then Regis spoke. "That's why I asked where you got the money. I was afraid it might have been something like this."

He stepped close to the boy and looked down at him. Shep looked up at Regis through puffed, red-rimmed eyes. "I'm glad you didn't lie to me, Shep. That means a whole lot. In ways you won't even know for a time, I expect."

He hugged his brother then, not the back-clapping, gusto-filled greeting of the day before, but a genuine hug. The kid felt small and frail to him, and Regis knew as certain as he had ever been of anything in his life that he had to take charge of the kid now. For that's what he was, just a kid. And Regis was the kid's only relative worth spit on this side of the dirt. He stepped back.

"I'll pay you back, I swear it, Regis." Shep looked up at his brother and nodded his bruised, comical face. "I promise."

"They only took you for a few rounds. Me and Bone—that'd be my friend you still haven't met—we persuaded them it would be in their best interests to leave you be."

"I . . . I don't remember that."

"That's because you can't hold your liquor, boy."

"But my money. . . ."

"You mean *my* money."

"Yeah, okay."

"It's safe."

Shep looked up. "What?"

Regis pulled out their mother's bulging money pouch and dangled it in the air between them. "I'm going to invest it for you. Since paying to have your head filled long distance didn't work out so well, I've decided you'll do your learning here. With me."

Shep narrowed his eyes. "What do you mean?"

"It means I'm your new schoolmaster. I'm also your new boss."

"I don't understand."

"I told you. I'm investing the money. You keep your sniffer clean and do what I say, you'll earn back the money I invested in you all these years. In the form of a partnership in the ranch I'm building. Unless you have other plans."

Shep smiled and held a hand to his temple. "No, I guess I'm free. For now." He turned and looked at himself in the mirror.

"Good. Now get cleaned up—you're beyond ripe—and dress yourself properly. I brought your bag up last night. Meet you downstairs. We ride in five minutes. Then we have a lot of work to do. I'll see if I am going to keep you on. For now." He opened the door, then leaned back in. "Oh, one more thing. Stay away from the gaming tables. And the whiskey."

"Don't worry about that," said Shep. "Never again."

He turned back to the mirror and looked at his wrecked face. "Who or what is Bone, anyway?"

Regis laughed long and loud as he walked down the hallway to clean up in his own room.

In the street out front of the Brownsville Arms, Regis, Bone, and Cormac Delany stood beside their mounts, a fourth horse in line with them. Shepley Royle walked down the steps, squinting at the day's light and moving like a ninety-year-old man who's been tromped by a rogue bull.

"Over here, Shep."

The kid looked up and nodded and moved toward Regis.

"Cormac, Bone, I'd like to introduce you to my kid brother, Shepley. Shep, this here's Bone, and this is my business partner, Cormac Delany. Mostly they're my friends, so be nice."

Shep straightened and did his best to paste on a smile. "A pleasure to meet you." He shook Cormac's hand.

Then he turned to Bone, who pumped the kid's hand with vigor and spoke in a rather loud, slow voice. "Good to know you. We met last night, only I expect you don't recall all that much, seeing as how you were laid out in the alleyway, your sniffer full of tonic and whatnot." He winked at Regis but kept holding the kid's hand. "Name's Jarvis McGraw, but my friends call me Bone."

"I . . . I'm pleased to meet you . . . , Bone."

"Oh, I said my friends call me that, kid."

Shep's eyebrows rose. "Oh, I'm sorry. I hope I haven't offended you. . . ."

His shock slid from his face as he saw the three men chuckling. Cormac handed him a flask. "Take a slug or two. Trust me, this and a jug of water and you'll be a whole lot more useful to us than trying to chase away your demons in one go."

Shep looked to Regis, who nodded. "Not the best cure, but it'll do for now. Hair of the dog that bit you. Then get on your horse. We have miles to go yet, and we've wasted enough time candyfooting with you." He said it with a harsh tone but winked at the boy.

"And here." He tossed a new fawn-colored wide-brim hat to Shep. "Can't have my junior partner looking like a squinty back-East schoolchild."

"What did you call me?"

"You heard me, boy. Now let's ride."

Chapter 7

The ride out to Don Mallarmoza's border-hugging Reynosa estate took longer than Regis wanted, even if his compadres and their mounts were lathered and hell-bent, the boy included, knowing their timely arrival could well mean all. The alternative wasn't anything they were interested in thinking about. Yet.

"I've been there once before. Some years back, the Don was interested in broadening his holdings and wanted to buy into a fleet of steamers. At about the same time he discovered that a certain parcel of land could be had for a reasonable purchase price."

"The Santa Calina?"

"The very one. I graciously allowed him to bow out of a deal so he could pursue its purchase."

"So you're telling me he might feel beholden to you," said Regis. They'd stopped to let their mounts blow and drink their fill at a small spring.

Cormac shrugged. "He may be, but don't forget, he's a businessman, and a shrewd one at that. He'd not let such sentiment whitewash a proper dealing."

"Sounds like a hard character," said Bone.

"To some I am, too. It's either that or get yourself eaten for lunch."

"Speaking of," said Bone, "I have a nice greasy hank of pork fat here I'd be willing to share it. Shep? You want a generous dripping slice?"

The kid, who'd been silent for much of the trip, looked at the proffered hunk of oozing meat and couldn't bolt for the nearest snag of mesquite fast enough.

"Hard to believe there's much left in his gut," said Regis, shaking his head and mounting up.

"Exactly my thinking," said Bone. "Best to get a little something in there."

"Maybe don't offer him that rancid fodder you're accustomed to, eh?"

Bone shrugged and bit off a piece of the drippy fat. "Mmm-mm. Near as good as Mama used to make."

Regis and Cormac exchanged raised-eyebrow glances and looked away.

"How much farther?"

"Can't be much longer. Less than an hour, I'd say. I expect his men'll find us before we see them."

"They're expecting us, though?" said Regis.

"That's what my message said. Unless the messenger got waylaid. It happens out here."

"Don't I know it," said Regis, recalling the day before. It seemed like a year before. He glanced back and saw Shep mounted, looking much better, his horse trotting to catch up with them.

It turned out that Cormac's supposition was correct. A contingent of five men on gleaming black horses emerged at a casual yet determined pace toward them from all directions. The mounts were decked out in shined black leather tack studded with silver conchos, and the men wore black, too.

Bone had sensed them before they showed themselves and had palmed his dragoon.

Regis, seeing this, had done the same. Shep wore his sidearm but had instead skinned the rifle and laid it across his pommel. Only Cormac remained unarmed. He held his right hand up, Indian-greeting style, and offered a smile as if he'd gotten a box full of them for free.

"Senor Delany?" The words came from the lead rider of the five, who rode ahead of his fellows and stopped a half-dozen paces before the newcomers.

"Yes, that's me."

The man nodded. "Good. The Don is expecting you. And your men. Follow me." The man to the others. "You will not need your guns. You notice none of my men have theirs drawn. The Don has told me to tell you that you are among friends." Then he sat, not smiling but not scowling, either.

"Cormac? You good with this setup?" Bone asked.

The Irishman nodded. "Yep. Put them away, boys. We'll be okay."

Bone sighed but kept his fingertips on the butt of his holstered dragoon. Just in case.

Turns out they still had another thirty minutes to ride. No one said anything, and Regis didn't feel as though he needed to perfume the air with words. He was thankful the boy was feeling under the weather, as he expected Shep was a chatty sort. Always had been as a young boy.

Didn't mean Regis didn't want to ask the Don's point man if they've had any visitors. And then Cormac beat him to it. "Excuse me, but do you happen to know if the Don has received any other visitors today?"

The man didn't break his horse's stride but looked slightly over his left shoulder. "It is possible, sir. It is also possible she is not a visitor, as you say." The man was smiling for the first time as he looked ahead once more.

"She," muttered Regis. "Hmm." Now his interest was aroused more than ever. Was she that wonderful, this other potential buyer? Maybe he and his men could beat her price. But Cormac hinted she had more charm than money. Or had he? Money was the only thing he could think of that might win the day.

He didn't have to wait long to find out. They topped a rise and looked down upon a vast compound of whitewashed low-lying buildings with red tile roofs. The largest of them sat near the center, a hacienda with ramadas spanning outward like fringe, flanking a courtyard in which burbled a sizable stone fountain carved with angels and serpents. The fountain was easily twice a man's height, perhaps taller.

He saw a clot of people moving about in the stone courtyard amid pots of tall exotic plants. The people appeared to be enjoying themselves. One was a woman in a rippling blue gown that clung to her as if it were painted on. Even at this distance, Regis blinked hard to clear his eyes.

Could that be the woman Cormac had spoken of? His rival for the land? If so, his partner was right—there was no way Regis could compete. And it looked as if she were well on her way to sealing the deal. The person to whom she was speaking was a tall man with a bit of a belly. He sported nearly white hair and a full white suit. The Don. Had to be.

Outside the walls of the inner compound, chickens scratched and three dogs lolled, panting or snoozing in the sun. *Too dumb to seek shade*, thought Regis. If he were a dog, he'd be under whatever threw shade all day long.

From the looks of it, there were plenty of trees about the place. Beyond the walls, crops radiated outward, the rows of plantings looking well tended and precise. Here and there, white shirts indicated workers bent over, hoeing or plucking weeds.

At the far side of the compound, a corral held a small but milling bunch of horses, all black and gleaming in the afternoon sun. A man in white in the midst of them held a whip aloft and watched the churning horses, turning with them and whistling, still a faint sound from far off to Regis.

Their horses followed one another down a switchback-laden road that brought them slowly closer to the Don's hacienda. Soon they found themselves at hitch rails before the home.

"You may leave your horses here. Our stable boys will tend them well and have them ready for your departure, whenever that might be." With that, the point man rode off with his four fellows close behind.

The newcomers dismounted, tied their horses, and stretched, looking about them. The entire place exuded the whiff of money, hard-earned and well spent, in Regis's opinion. He could do worse than to end up with a fine home and grounds like this one day.

Maybe, if the ranch and his holdings in the shipping enterprise with Cormac panned out into anything more than hard work and careful speculation. So far his business dealings had required reinvestment of most of his earnings. That's how a business is built, Cormac had preached from the early days when Regis would inquire about pulling some cash out for spending on themselves.

A tall, dark man with short, black, oiled hair and a smooth-shaven face emerged from the darkness of the house. He wore soft rope sandals and a white tunic over white trousers. With his hands folded before him, he nodded at the waist. He said nothing but looked at the four, each in turn, then turned and slowly walked back the way he'd come, glancing back once at them.

"We follow him," said Cormac, stating the obvious. Shep, despite his lingering discomfort from the previous night's events, couldn't help but be impressed with these surroundings. "You know some fine folks, Regis," he whispered.

"So far, yeah. Stick close, okay? I don't know what to expect in there."

"Okay."

They were led into a cool, darkened space with more exotic plants in pots, a red-tile floor, and a sort of way station for cleaning off the trail dust before entering the house proper.

While the men partially disrobed, shucking out of hats, coats, and shirts, an old woman with a stiff-bristle brush shuffled from one to the other, whisking the hell and the dust out of their clothes.

When she was satisfied she'd tormented the clothing enough, she turned her devil of a brush on them. Her persistence won over any amount of evasion Bone tried to throw her way. The faster he danced from her, the quicker the old thing was. Regis thought she even cracked a grin on that wrinkled face of hers. Bone was no match for her and gave up, standing still while she worked him over with extra gusto.

He yelped a few times for good measure, and soon they were told to tug on their freshened garments. Someone had scented them with rosewater, and now they all reeked as they walked down yet another dark hallway toward a bright portal at the far end.

The closer they drew, the more distinct the voices could be heard. From what Regis could recall of their initial glimpse of the place, they were about to enter that courtyard.

". . . I assure you, senorita, that your offer will be given all due consideration. But as I said before, my dear, I will not have loud words in my home. There is nothing we cannot work out in civilized tones, eh?"

Regis liked what he heard so far. That had to be the Don talking, and the low, feminine growling had to be Regis's ticked-off rival.

They emerged into the brighter but still somewhat shady courtyard. Regis was confused. There was no woman in sight. The man with the white suit and white hair looked over at them. For a long moment he stared at each of them, then his eyes traveled back to Cormac and a smile widened his dark, lined face.

"My friend, Cormac Delany. Welcome, welcome." He walked forward with his arms outstretched and hugged Delany, who responded in kind.

"Don Mallarmoza! It is so good to see you once more. I would very much like to introduce you to my business partner, Regis Royle." They shook hands, and Regis bowed and said, "How do you do, sir? I'm pleased to finally meet you. Cormac's had nothing but good things to say of you."

This seemed to please the old Don, and Regis kept that in mind. The old buck liked to have his feathers stroked. Well, who didn't? Maybe he'd become even more fond of it as he aged, too.

Next came the Texas Ranger. "My friends call me Bone, sir."

"Does that mean I may as well?" said the Don, half smiling and not letting go of the tall Texan's hand.

"You betcha, sir. Good to know you."

Still gripping Bone's hand, the Don said, "Are you not the very Jarvis McGraw who single-handedly held off that band of Comancheros some years ago as a Texas Ranger?"

"Why, yes sir, I . . . I didn't think many folks knew of that."

"Ah, acts of selflessness and bravery are things I do not forget, senor. It is a pleasure and an honor to have you in my home."

Well, thought Regis. Looks like the old Don knows how to stroke the feathers as well as having them stroked.

"And this," said Cormac, tugging Shepley forward, "is our youngest partner, Shepley Royle, younger brother of Regis."

Regis was about to prod the youth to offer his hand, but Shep beat him to it. But first offered a neat, quick bow. "It is my pleasure, sir, to make your acquaintance."

"Such fine manners in your family, Mr. Royle."

Regis noted that the Don was classy enough to not inquire about Shep's bruised, lumpy face.

"And now it is time I made an introduction," said the Don. He looked around and his smile slipped. "Senorita Valdez? Where have you gone?"

Out from behind a nearby cluster of towering flowering plants stepped one of the most handsome women Regis had ever seen.

"Ah!" said the Don, arms wide. "Yes, Senorita Tomasina Valdez, gentlemen." He made the introductions, recalling each man's name flawlessly. She nodded at each, her dark eyes piercing theirs, no smile on her perfect lips, only a nod to acknowledge each man in turn.

"Now we are all here," said the Don. "Let us have refreshment, some wine, perhaps. My people have laid out a meal on the table to your right."

But no one was listening to the Don. They were all looking at the woman who'd emerged in their midst.

The blue dress Regis had seen earlier from on high now seemed to shimmer as she moved, as did her long, flowing black hair. Her lips were full and red-black like the skin of ripe cherries. Her nose was long, thin, and arched slightly, giving her a hawkish beauty. Her black eyebrows rose like raven wings over glittering green eyes that did not smile, but did not need to.

Those eyes, as the rest of the woman, were perfect. But there was something clinging to the woman, something foul and tainted about her—angry, evil perhaps.

Regis had always had an innate skill to sense the worth of a person upon meeting them. It's how he came to trust Delany so readily all those years before. It might also have been because Cormac offered him food when he was a skinny, starving stowaway.

But no, Bone had been the same, true in his core from the start. And the Don, although his kindness as a host was a shield over a cold, business acumen, Regis knew the man was good to his core as well.

But this Tomasina Valdez, she was a coiled serpent inside, and he immediately did not trust her. Admire her beauty, to be sure, but that was a far cry from trust.

He glanced at Bone, Cormac, and Shep, and of the three, Bone and Shep were the ones he'd have to keep an eye on. They stared her up and down without shame, as if she were a horse they were considering purchasing.

The woman seemed to enjoy the attention. She canted a hip and pointed a toe and pivoted to best show off the lines of her long legs. "You like what you see?" she said in a low purring voice. "Too bad for you." Her false smile disappeared, and she strode through the midst of them to stand by the Don, laying an arm atop his. "Shall we dine, Don Mallarmoza?"

She said it as if none of them were there.

"*Si, si,* senorita."

The meal was a tense affair that Don Mallarmoza attempted to loosen through small talk with his guests. Of the four men from Texas, Regis and Cormac were the only ones able to hold a conversation. Shep and Bone let their words drift off to nothing as they stole glances at Tomasina Valdez.

She nibbled a thin slice of cheese and played with chunks of melon on her plate but did little else save stare above their heads as if some cosmic truth were written in the air beyond them, something of which only she was aware.

Finally she sighed and said, "Enough, Don." She turned to face the old man at the head of the table. "I have much to offer you, as I have already told you. For money is not the only thing in life worth having. Even you said that."

"I don't recall saying so. When was this? I must have been dazed or drunk, eh?" He chuckled at his own little joke and nodded at them all.

"The Santa Calina range belonged to my family! This much you know. I am the only person in the world who deserves to own it. I do not know how you could be so blind to this!" She smacked the tabletop with a palm and growled. Even in her rage, with her lips parted and clenched teeth revealed, she was a beautiful thing.

But that beauty did nothing to hurry along Don Mallarmoza. He chewed the bite of melon he'd thrust into his mouth, then wiped his lips with a cloth napkin, sighed, and set his hands on his chair rests. "I will be the judge, Senorita Valdez, of who is the person best to own that parcel of land. A parcel of land, need I remind you, that I currently own."

Something under his smiling demeanor told Regis that the old man was most definitely not to be trifled with where business matters were concerned. He kept the thought in mind.

The woman stood, her chair squawking backward, her ample chest heaving. Fire and sparks seemed to shoot from her eyes, and her gritted teeth seethed. "You mewling, pathetic old man! You are a thief! You are a king of thieves! You, who have stolen from me and my family! That land is mine! It is my birthright! By the time I am through with you, you will beg me to let you pay me for the honor of giving me back my birthright!"

She shouted all this in a barking growl. It was a jarring barrage of sound coming from so fine a visage, or rather what had been a pretty face. Now it was a thing marred by her leering, spittle-flecked diatribe of rage.

"Hey now," said Regis, shoving back from the table himself. "That's no way to talk to our host." He tried a smile on her. "Why don't we all sit here like civilized folks and—"

"Why? So you and these other . . . filthy gringos can rob me of what this old man has already taken?" She turned her head, her long hair fanning outward, and spit on the floor beside her.

Their host stood then, any trace of his former sincere, welcoming smile and kindly countenance gone. He looked at the fiery hellcat with narrowed eyes, and his voice came out as a thin blade of steel. "So this is the way you repay kindness? Hmm? You and your men will now leave my home." He reached for an egg-size brass bell beside his place setting and shook it by its wooden handle.

The sultry woman was already on the move and had stepped from the table with a sneer and a raised eyebrow.

Bone and Shep looked at her as if she were pulling one wonderful trick after another, her offensiveness lost on their infatuations with her. But Cormac had shoved back from the table and was prepared to intervene should the spitfire lunge at their host.

Instead, she pursed her lips and worked up two piercing whistles, quick and shrill. From seemingly all sides, rough-looking men, dark with unshaved leering faces and trail-worn ratty clothes, scaled the walls. Others were already in the garden and had apparently been in hiding behind the ample plantings and secreted in shaded nooks.

That was enough to dislodge Bone from his mesmerized stupor. He shoved backward from the table, snatching Shep's shoulder at the same time and flipping the boy backward in his chair to the floor.

Regis saw this and grunted in approval as he dropped to a knee and skinned his revolver, thumbing back the hammer as he scanned the courtyard. Cormac lunged for Don Mallarmoza and pulled him down behind the table while he tugged free a hideout gun from an inner pocket. His pocket watch dislodged at the same time and swung like a pendulum when he moved.

Regis was on the side of the table closest to the intruders, and the blue-dress-wearing devil slipped behind a mass of plants and barked orders to her men. It appeared as if there were a dozen of them.

How did they get past the Don's own men? Regis wondered. And how many men did the Don employ, anyway?

As if reading his mind, Mallarmoza said, "Do you think you will get away with this, Senorita Valdez? You'll never get out of here unscathed! My men are everywhere!"

Regis wondered if that were true. If so, where in the heck were they? He scooched back until he felt the table's edge catch him in the back. Then he sidestepped, crouched low, and angled to his right. He'd cut wide and trace the wall, see if he could round up a few of the attackers.

He heard strident, hoarse whisperings in Spanish, and boot-steps clunking on the flagged floor. They stopped, then others scattered away in a different direction. How many attackers were there?

"What do you hope to gain by this madness?" shouted the Don. As much as Regis appreciated the man's boldness, he wished the old buck would shut his mouth. It was difficult enough to concentrate without hearing his interruptions.

"Ha!" shouted the girl. "That is exactly right, Don. I will gain and you will lose. Though, can anyone really gain something that is lawfully still theirs?"

Regis pinpointed her voice, ahead to his left, behind the big clot of tall trees. He peered far around them and saw the woman raising her dress high up her left leg. The blue fabric rippled and shone as she dragged it higher and higher to reveal . . . a holster strapped about her inner thigh. As she unbuckled a two-shot derringer, her gaze angled up and caught Regis's gaze. She smiled wide, her eyebrows rising. He gulped, and she whipped the pistol on him and fired.

He felt the slug whistle close enough for it to singe the hair on the side of his head above his right ear. He jerked farther left and rolled, tucking low onto his left shoulder. He came up on one knee and wasted no time in scurrying around the clump of trees. She was gone. But she was one hell of a shot, something he'd have to keep in mind.

He caught a glimpse of Bone beyond, in the far right corner.

Soon he heard a shot that smacked stone and whizzed off into the hot afternoon. A groan followed it.

All was still once more, quiet reigned, save for someone's hard breathing. Regis realized it was his. He'd never had a run of such days as this. The fleetest moment of doubt caught up to him. Was this land really worth nearly being killed twice in two days?

He shook off the foul thought as one dispels an irksome bluebottle. Gritting his teeth, he scanned low, left, then right. On the far side of the courtyard he caught sight of something blue. At first he thought it was the murderous Tomasina Valdez, then realized that was not possible. She was still somewhere, lurking like a viper, on his side of the courtyard.

Where were the Don's men, anyway?

The far blue flash reappeared. It was a tall blue hat atop a blur of white? Was that a bandage? Then he caught sight of something else—a red sash—and he knew what it was. Or rather who it was. The rascal from the day before, one of those who'd shot at him. Must mean the other men were some of those who'd pinned him down. And then it dawned on him that they were in the employ of one Senorita Tomasina Valdez.

So she'd been gunning for him even before she knew who he was. Or maybe she had had an inkling of who he was or who he might be—a rival for possession of the Santa Calina range. Maybe she didn't care and was just protecting her hoped-for investment.

He felt a wash of anger, pierced with a slight skein of admiration for her, ripple through him. She was one feisty woman. But her men deserved to die, if only for trying to lay him low the day before.

He raised the revolver and squinted his eye shut, taking aim at the unusual, tall-crowned, blue-banded sombrero. Anyone who wore such a fixture atop themselves ought to be put out of his misery. The man seemed to sense him and jerked back behind the low wall. In time, Regis eased off the trigger and bit back a curse.

More quiet footsteps, then he saw the Don with Cormac protecting him as they bent low and made for the doorway they'd all used to enter the space. Maybe if he could put up enough distraction, Cormac could get the old man out of there and to safety—and then he could send in reinforcements.

He wondered where Shep and Bone were at—he couldn't see clear beneath the thick dark-wood table. Yips and howls of delight, as if from a bunch of drunken stragglers, rose up here and there. Then Regis heard scuffling behind him and saw Shep crawl over on his hands and knees beneath the table. Regis hissed, "Stay low, keep under there!"

To his surprise, the kid nodded, but he was smiling. "Bone said to tell you he's gone to cut off the head of the snake. Said it was the prettiest snake he'd ever seen."

"Yeah, well . . ." Regis's mind flashed briefly on the sight of the woman slinking her dress up that long, long leg. "I hope he's careful. That's one sly snake. And it bites for keeps."

But Regis had no worries about his Texas Ranger chum. The man was good with guns, good in a fight such as this, and good with the ladies. Seemed like the situation was custom-made for him.

"Where's the Don and Cormac?"

"Gone to get his men," said Shep.

"Good—where in hell are they, anyway?"

"Same thing the Don asked. I think. My Spanish ain't so good."

"Isn't so good."

"That's what I said!"

"Hush now," growled Regis. Fool kid, and fool me for bringing him along. He never expected the situation to turn out as it had.

The woman could gain nothing from what she'd done. Did

she think she could get the Don to sign over the land by force? It was laughable. Maybe she was off her bean. Might explain her actions.

Movement beyond caught his eye once more, but it was Shep from behind him who said, "That's that blue-hatted devil from yesterday!" He had crept closer to Regis and now aimed a finger over his older brother's shoulder.

Regis nodded. "I see him." He raised his revolver once more and squeezed off a shot. The man howled and disappeared from sight.

"You get him?" said Shep.

"Dunno. If I didn't, he's a lippy sort."

Moments later they heard a high-pitched yelp that turned into a low throaty growl and tailed off in a string of Spanish words. Flesh smacked flesh, and they heard Bone shout, "Hey now! Simmer down, little lady!" The voices were closer than they expected, and the brothers exchanged glances of surprise before peering around the nearest raised garden.

There stood Bone struggling with a thrashing, kicking, biting, flailing, spitting, growling woman in a blue dress. Fire shot from her eyes, and vicious Spanish words flew from her tongue. Shep said, "If words could kill, Bone would be a cold corpse by now!"

But he wasn't. He was upright and grinning and doing his best to keep his legs from getting kicked by the now-barefoot woman.

"She sure is something," said Shep as they advanced with caution to help their friend.

"You keep clear of her and her ilk. She's evil to the core, with a dose of venom and a whitewash of pretty, that's all."

"Yeah, but what a paint job."

Regis sighed. No use arguing. He could see everything the boy could and he couldn't disagree. But he had the experience and wisdom age brings. At least he hoped he did. Bone was roughly Regis's age, and age hadn't cured the Texan of his fool-hardy ways where women were concerned.

A volley of shouts and rifle cracks chorused outside the high garden walls, all around the perimeter, it seemed. Shots were traded and shouts echoed with them. Regis hoped that meant the Don's men were finally on the job.

"You boys going to help me, or should I just succumb to this wildcat's wicked charms?" Bone grinned over his shoulder at them—until she wriggled around and landed a knee at the apex of his legs. Air whooshed from him, and a wheezing groan fol-lowed.

The she-devil spun from his grasp and disappeared behind another clot of those infernal trees. Regis darted after her, shouting, "Shep, take care of Bone!" But she was gone.

He had seen her two-shot derringer on the stones by her feet when she'd been struggling with Bone, and he couldn't think of another place on her body where she might conceal other weapons, so tight-fitting had that dress been in the first place. But then again she'd confounded him more than once.

"Lady!" he growled. "Give it up. I'm not one to be trifled with, you hear? You lost the deal, likely to your own foolhardy ways, so be gracious about it. Plenty of land in the world. Don't die needlessly for this."

He was just saying whatever came to his mind. He didn't care one way or another if she lived or died, though he did want to know why she was on the prod even before she knew who he was. Unless she ran a bushwhacking business on the side while she tried to get her pappy's land back.

That would explain the killer with the fancy sombrero and red sash.

Then he saw another blue blur and turned to his right in time to see the woman disappear over the wall. Her black-haired head popped up into view once more, and she looked right at him, some five yards away and up to his right. "You may not be one to be trifled with, senor, but I am. And I will have my land. *My* land! Ha!"

With that, she disappeared. He looked at the wall she'd all but scaled, using only nubs of rock for handholds and footholds. But she'd done it.

By the time he made it to the top of the wall himself, Regis heard the thundering of hoofbeats and saw a mass of more than a dozen horses milling, with some pounding away. The Don's men were dressed in black, and the other half were in ragtag togs. One among them was the tall sombrero man.

His red sash had slumped to one side, as had his hat, and fresh spatters of blood decorated the opposite side of his head and shirt from the day before. He held his head and struggled to maintain his seat on his horse.

Regis fancied he saw the man look over in his direction. He saw a wide set of gritted yellow teeth beneath those drooping black moustaches. The man shouted something in Spanish, likely a threat to do him in one of these fine days. Regis shook his head and watched as the man spurred his mount hard. He was on the heels of another horse topped with a vision of venom in a blue dress that shimmered in the afternoon sunlight as she thundered northwestward.

Puffs of shots rose up on the still afternoon air from the guns of the Don's black-clad riders as they fired at the retreating forms of the bushwhackers. The black guard didn't follow. He wondered what they'd been up to and didn't envy them the tongue-lashing they'd receive soon enough from the Don.

Regis jumped down from his precarious perch on the wall and strode the inside perimeter of the courtyard, searching for stray rascals. He found none, but he did find spatters of blood where he guessed he'd grazed that sash-wearing, blue-hatted fool.

"Gave him a matching pair of scars, I bet," said Shep, appearing beside him. Beyond his brother, Regis saw Bone standing straight, his hands on his lower back, and taking deep breaths.

"She gave him a good shot to the grapes," said Regis, not bothering to hide a grin. "That's what you get when you let down your guard for even a moment where a lady such as that is concerned."

"She ain't no lady," said Shep, looking at the wall as if he could see her in the distance through the stonework.

"Isn't, and you don't know that." Regis eyed the youth. "I'm tempted to judge her, too, but we don't know her full story. Best to leave off the judgment until we do."

Shep shrugged, and they walked back to the table in silence. Cormac and the Don strolled back in, smiling and smoothing their sleeves as if they'd just stepped outside for a cigar. Regis wanted to ask him what in the heck had happened to his men to let those intruders in like that, but he couldn't think of a tactful way to do it.

He needn't have worried. The Don smacked his hands together. "I am forever in your debt, gentlemen." He looked them each up and down, paused on Bone, and said, "Some of you had a rougher time than others, I see." He winked at the suffering Ranger, who offered a weak smile on his still-green face.

"My men are normally most diligent, but it has been a long time since we have had cause for alarm where visitors are concerned. Senorita Valdez is a saucy thing, but I have known her and her family for a very long time. Never did I think she would act this way. Her men surprised my own and caught them while they were enjoying a noon meal, and then tied them up!"

He laughed and shook his head. "Well, that will show them. And it served as a lesson, too. I think things will be different from now on, eh?"

"Why not sell her the land and keep things smooth?"

The Don's mouth drooped in a big frown, and he nodded his

head. "*Si, si,* I could do that, but it would solve nothing. I want money for the land, as is only right. And she has none. Besides, I know what she will do with the land. She will do as she is now doing. Ambush strangers and waste her time when she could build it up! Did you know there are vast herds of horses on the Santa Calina?"

Regis nodded. "More than a man could count in a week, I bet. And cattle, too. And game. It's surely a wonderful place. Perfect for a ranch the likes of which this part of Texas has never seen."

He caught the Don smiling at him. "That is why you should have the land. Not only do you have the money—I assume you do have the price we talked about, Mr. Delany?"

Cormac nodded.

"Good. Then you have the money, grand. But you also have the most important thing, which is the passion, the fire, the spirit, the vision to see what that land could be. It is already a thing of beauty, but it could be so much more. It could sustain a life of structure, a place where families could live one day and cattle could roam."

"That's all I've been able to think about since I saw that land, Don Mallarmoza."

"I know, Mr. Royle. Somehow I know this already, and I don't really know you. Yet. And with family and friends such as these, why, I think . . . I think . . ." He turned from them and wiped at his eyes and blew his nose with a white hanky. "Pardon me, gentlemen, I am overcome with relief. I think this calls for a drink! I insist you all remain my guests here at my hacienda tonight. Your horses are well stabled and tended. For despite what you may think of my men, we are good to our horses." He winked. "And then we can work out the . . . how do you say?"

Cormac said, "Iron out the wrinkles?"

"*Si!* That's it, yes. The wrinkles will be gotten rid of."

For the second time that day they all sat down to a meal at the Don's table. This time without the threat of a blue devil in their midst.

Still, Regis caught Shepley, and Bone, too, gazing toward the far hills where the devil had last been seen.

Chapter 8

Four days following their return to Brownsville from Don Mallarmoza's compound found Regis Royle in much the same place he'd been on the morning they'd ridden out to the old man's residence. There was his kid brother, Shepley Royle, seventeen going on fifty and with a wild hair about him that Regis was finding vexing.

"Get up, damn your hide!" He whipped off the sheets to find the kid stark naked and shining a double-cheeked moon at the cracked plaster ceiling of the hotel room. "Good thing we're lighting out today, else you'll be getting far too comfortable in your life of leisure to ever be of use to me or Bone."

The brief speech did nothing save for elicit a low groan from the kid's pillow-mashed lips.

"What I wouldn't give for a cherry-red branding iron right now," said Regis, doing his best to ignore the kid's backside. "Next best thing," he muttered, and dumped a full water pitcher on the kid.

The effect was a joy to behold, and Shep came up spluttering and howling. He landed on his feet and squared off in a top-form pugilistic stance. "You quit that, Regis! I ain't no kid you can play your silly games with, you hear?"

From across the room, where Regis had collapsed in a lean against the wall, he nodded his head and wiped away a tear. "Calm yourself, Shep. It'll all be over soon, for both of us, anyway."

"What's that supposed to mean?" said the younger man, snatching up the dry end of his bedding and wiping himself down. He cast a hairy eye on his still chuckling brother.

"It means that you won't have an opportunity much after this to ignore my orders. You see, you and Bone and me, we're heading out to the Santa Calina after breakfast to scout the place."

Shep nodded and smiled. "That sounds good. You know, though, I'm going to need a better sidearm, something I can draw quick. Not heavy like that thing I've been using."

"What makes you think you're going to need a revolver, boy?"

"You got to be kidding, Regis! You have a short memory, don't you? Why, it wasn't but less than a week ago that I rescued you from certain death at the hands of Miss Valdez's bloodthirsty riders. Good thing I came upon your horse and happened to stop it, otherwise it might still be crow-hopping all the way to Canada. Why, I snatched those dangling reins as smooth as you please and slowed that beast to a trot. Then I heard gunshots. That's when I knew somebody was in trouble."

Regis listened to his kid brother's animated retelling of the events, which, to his chagrin, wasn't far from the truth. It galled him, but there it was. He'd not be that unprepared again. "Yes, yes, and yes. You can have a better gun, Shep. But I will leave it to Bone as to whether you can wear it. He'll decide the when and where."

"Bone?" The kid stared at his brother, arms wide. "Why?"

"First off, cover yourself up, you shameless little whelp. Second of all, Bone's the foreman of the ranch we'll be building. I'll spend as much of my time as I can out there, but for now and for the foreseeable future, I'll be working with Cormac. Nothing's changed on that score. If anything, we'll have to double down on our workload, try to scare up more customers where the shipping's concerned. Somebody's got to pay for the ranch. I don't expect it will make itself useful for some time yet."

Shep tugged on his clothes and plopped on the bed to tug on his boots. He sat square on the wet mattress. "Oh, for Pete's sake. Now, look," he said, hopping up and pulling on his left boot. "You worry too much, Regis. You take me. I'm cool in a fight. I can deal with ruffians all day long and play a solid hand of poker well into the wee hours."

"Yeah, you proved that, all right, at the Lucky Dog."

"Well, that was different. Those men cheated me. It was only a matter of time before I was ready to jump back in there and give them what for."

"Hmm, let's see. I expect if we hadn't dragged you out of that alley, you would have done just that, huh?"

"Yep, you bet." Shep opened the door and looked back. "You going to dally all day and keep Bone waiting? Lots to do, Regis. Snap, snap!"

As he legged it down the long staircase behind his wild colt of a brother, Regis Royle wondered if he'd made the right decision in keeping the kid close at hand instead of sending him back East. Trouble was, there really wasn't any decision to it. Shep would have gone anywhere but where Regis told him to go. What would make him stick around here in South Texas?

As if in answer to his thoughts, Bone McGraw appeared at the base of the stairs. "Well, look what the dog puked up. I about give up on you two Snoozy Suzies. Was fixing to ride on out and deal with the rangeland myself. Let's get a move on."

"Yes sir," muttered Regis to Shep. "That man's going to make you one fine babysitter."

If Shep heard him, he didn't let on. There was something about Bone that the kid found appealing, something between Bone and Shep that Regis, frankly, envied a little bit. Something he knew he'd never be able to be to Shep, more friend and mentor than brother and father figure.

He was stuck with the latter, but he trusted Bone, for the most part, with his life. So his brother's should be much the same. As long as women and whiskey weren't around, that is. Both of them were cut from the same bolt of cloth where those two dangerous items were concerned. But way out yonder on the Santa Calina range should be a perfect place for them both to get down to the job at hand, with nothing else around in the way of distractions.

The trek back out there was filled with a whole lot of Shep talking about this, that, and everything. And when he wasn't talking, he was whistling or singing low tunes to himself. Every once in a while Regis caught a whiff of bawdy words.

"You learn that at the Quaker school?" he said at the end of one particularly ribald corker of a tune. Shep looked over at him, his face reddening. "Oh, didn't hear you there, Regis. Uh, no, learned a few new tunes . . . here and there."

"Here and there, huh?"

As they neared the tail end of their first slow, steady day on the trail, Bone dropped back out of point position and behind Shep and beside Regis, who'd been riding drag. The kid was chatting up a storm as if he was carrying on a conversation with himself or a hundred unseen folks. "I think I liked him better when he was hungover."

Regis glanced at his old pard. "He'll grow on you."

"You sure you can't find a use for him on one of those boats of yours? He couldn't get up to much trouble on a boat, I expect."

"Him? Ha."

"Yeah, I guess you're right. But what do I know about tending a wet-nose kid, Regis? I'm an old Texas Ranger. I know that and I know cattle. And that's what I know."

"I'll have a talk with him before I light out. Besides, it won't be but for a few days. Early on we'll all be back and forth. It'll all work out just fine, Bone. You wait and see."

"Hey, look at that!" Shep jerked his chin at something ahead to his right and slid from the saddle. Before Regis or Bone could say boo, he was gone, flailing through the mesquite and grass.

"Good way to get yourself snakebit, boy!" said Bone, shaking his head.

Regis snagged the reins of Shep's horse, and they walked over to him. He was bent at the waist, toeing soot-blackened rocks of a fire ring. There was a gnarled trunk of mesquite, too low to serve as a bench, and another stack, now mostly scattered, of shorter, smaller hunks of wood. Close by, a jut of stone sat warmed by an afternoon sun that wormed its way toward the west.

Bone scratched his head. "Good a place as any to call it a day. Got wood and protection, sort of, from the wind."

"But this could be anybody's camp. What if they come back?"

"Kid," said Bone, dismounting and stretching his back. "This is a camp, sure enough, but it ain't been used in a coon's age."

"How can you tell?" said Shep.

"Well . . . no, no, you tell me," said Bone, thumbing his chest. "Come on, put them book smarts of yours to some good use."

"Ah, you want me to employ the art of deduction."

"What? No, no." Bone shook his head. "I want you to figure out why this camp is old."

"Exactly."

Bone looked over at Regis, who shrugged. "I'd just agree with him. It'll all be over soon," said Regis with a grin.

"Okay, then." Shep smacked his hands and rubbed them

briskly together. "First things first." He palmed the blackened coals in the midst of the stone fire ring. "No heat rising from these ashes, so that means there was no fire recently."

He looked up for approval, but Bone sighed.

Undeterred, Shep plowed on. "Other than my bootprints, I don't see any, so nobody's been here for a while." He barely glanced at Bone. "And here, look at this firewood. The pile's been scattered. I assume it was a pile at one point, since the pieces are all roughly the same length. Somebody snapped them for use in the fire. And there's dry dung piles all over the place, so horses have been here—likely cattle, too." He looked at Bone. "How's that?"

"Not bad, not bad," said Bone, shrugging and loosening the cinch on his saddle.

"What do you mean 'not bad'?" Shep scowled.

"Oh, all those things you say are true. But the real reason I know this camp ain't been used in forever is because it's my camp. I forgot all about it. Used it, oh, must have been two, three years back. Shows you how few folks travel through here. Just lucky you spied it. I'm grateful to you. But mostly you should be grateful."

"Why's that?" said Shep, feeling cheated out of his victory.

"Because you won't have to scare up as much firewood tonight. But you should build that stack back up and get a flame going. It's fixing to be nippy. And watch for snakes."

"Okay, Bone," said Shep, not excited but not protesting too loudly, and wandered off to scout up wood, eyes scanning the ground.

During this encounter, Regis said little but went about stripping his horse of the tack and piling it in a tidy heap near where he expected to stretch out in what he hoped wasn't too long from then. He was dog tired.

"If I told him to do anything like gather firewood, he'd do it," said Regis to Bone. "But we'd never hear the end of it."

The thing he'd been most interested in was how the two men got on with each other. Shep seemed to take joshing and even criticism from Bone a whole lot better than he did from Regis. Again, he suspected it was the fact they were brothers, whereas Bone was mostly still an interesting stranger to him.

Chapter 9

Shep felt something prod him in the upper leg. He moaned, tried to say the words "Knock it off," but they came out a mumble. The thing prodded him again. He'd been in the midst of a decent dream, too. Something about a big table heaped with food. And a pretty girl was there. Maybe wearing blue, but as the thing prodded him again the dream faded further away. He cracked an eye. It was dark. What fool trickery was this?

"Get up, boy. Time to eat. The day waits for no man."

It was Bone—a new friend to him, an old one to Regis, and a man he wasn't so sure he wanted to know, especially this early in the day.

"Why?"

"Why what?"

"Why are we getting up so early?"

All he heard in reply was a low chuckle, as if he'd said something humorous. Shep sat up and rubbed his head. He saw his brother's angular face over the bare glow of a freshly reviving fire. It was made sharper by shadow and light fighting for dominance over a long nose, thick black moustache, and a pushed-back hat. The light glinted off his dark, all-seeing eyes.

Bone was over past the horses, urinating, from the sound of it. That made Shep want to get up, but nothing else did. He could hold it awhile longer.

"I thought Bone said it was time to eat."

"He did," said Regis, glancing at him. "Once you cook breakfast."

"What?"

"Best get dressed and get the coffee on. I'm no good without it, and Bone is likely to tear off your head and gnaw the stump if he doesn't get his coffee. And make it hot, thick, and black. Now hop to it."

Shep groaned and grunted and made all the noises he knew wouldn't make a bit of good as he tugged on his duck cloth trousers and tugged the braces up over his shoulders.

"Check your boots before you pull them on, Shep."

"Why?"

Regis sighed and wondered how the kid ever made it out here without harm. "Critters like to crawl in them. Don't stick your hand in there, either. Bang them out."

Shep said nothing and did as Regis suggested. He saw nothing come out, though in truth it was still pretty dark. He held his breath as he pointed his toes and jammed his feet into the boots. Nothing there. Maybe his brother was funning him? Time enough to get back at him.

Making the coffee wasn't something he was used to, so Regis helped him. He'd come to learn that his brother and Bone, too, showed a man a task once. From then on he was expected to be able to tend to the chore forevermore as an expert.

Nearly an hour and two false starts later, filled with burned slab of bacon and mud-thick coffee, the three men watched the sun silently gild the sky to the east. They crunched their way through the charred chunks of pork and supplemented the meal with a couple of hard-as-stone biscuits Bone produced from a cloth sack in his saddlebag.

"Regis tells me you shoot and ride hard pretty well."

Shep sat up a little straighter. "I do okay, I guess."

Bone sipped the coffee, swallowed, and winced. "Better than you cook, I hope."

If he expected to get more from the sullen Ranger, he was mistaken. He'd also learn that it would take Bone much of the morning to warm up to what he called "conversatin'." But then when he did, he was as liable to yammer on about any random topic as he was to maintain his morning silence.

Regis reckoned they'd be good company for each other. He tugged out a folded map from his own traps and spread it between them, once the light was sufficient to see its curving and straight lines. It was a plain map but professionally rendered. Both he and Bone tapped here and there and, as far as Shep could tell, didn't really exchange words, though they each nodded or shook their heads now and again as one of them tapped the paper.

Shep cleaned the cups and wondered about the last of the coffee that no one seemed to want. "Should I dump it on the fire now, or wait awhile?"

"Lord, boy," said Bone, not looking up from the map. "I wouldn't wish that brew on my worst enemy, let alone a harmless fire."

All of a sudden the Ranger jerked his gaze up from the map and swiveled his head to his right, to the northeast.

"Stay down," he hissed, slicking his rifle from its scabbard. "Apache, I think," he said to an unasked question from Regis. "From yonder."

The brothers looked toward a slight hump some hundred yards to the northeast.

"How can you tell?" whispered Shep.

"Shh." Regis hunkered lower and eyed the terrain. He glanced at Shep. "Rifle."

The kid nodded and slid it out. He held it at the ready, not certain what that would be, or what he should do should the moment come. He'd never had much trouble once a fight began, but thinking about it beforehand wasn't something he was good at or keen on.

"Cock it."

"Oh yeah," said Shep, reddening.

The trio waited for what seemed a week to Shep. He was about to ask either one of them, he didn't care which, why they were wasting their time, when they heard a howl that sounded as if it came from the throat of a beast not yet discovered. Then an arrow whistled above their heads and kept going, thudding far off, a scant cloud of dust the only clue that it had been sent their way.

"Well, that's that," said Bone, standing.

"What are you doing?" said Shep, horrified and expecting to see Bone pierced through any second by an army of arrows.

"It was who I guessed it might be, though I wasn't sure at first. That's why I kept us low for so long."

Regis stood and smacked dust off his trousers. "Who?"

"Oh, that's right, you don't know him yet. It was old Two Claw. Half Apache, half Mexican. And all loco." Bone swirled a finger beside his head and jerked his chin toward where they'd been watching. "See? There he goes now."

Sure enough, they saw a squat, bow-legged man ambling at a solid lope away from them.

"Why don't you shoot him?" said Shep.

"Why would I do that?" Bone looked as if the boy had smacked a lady right in front of him.

"Well, he tried to kill us, didn't he?"

"Two Claw? Nah, he was just sending us a warning."

"Warning us about what, Bone?" said Regis.

Shep was glad to hear that his brother was as nearly in the dark about this Two Claw fellow as he was.

"Oh, well, I don't know yet. Either he thinks we're trespassing on his property or there's some sort of danger around, waiting for us. Likely both."

Bone turned from them and set to work tidying his gear and saddling his horse, leaving the two brothers slightly confused, one more so than the other.

As they rode, even though the landscape was growing greener in patches—maybe even kinder to the eye—Shep grumbled to himself. If this was the wonderful land his brother was so excited about, they sure had their work cut out for them. He didn't see how much could be raised out here other than horned toads and snakes and blisters and sunburn.

But the look on Regis's face made him look again at the land, to try to see it through his brother's obviously besotted eyes.

Bone had pointed out huisache trees, with their dainty yellow flowers riffling in a slight breeze, and mesquites, the rough-barked anaqua, and more yuccas than Shep could count.

He saw a green bird, much like a jay, with a purple-blue crown as if it were a kingly bird. Doves in clusters fluttered up about them as they rode, and high above, hawks circled, scanning the land for rabbits, which they also saw darting from the safety of one scraggly shrub or mesquite tree to another.

Then Bone halted them with an extended arm. "You got your spyglass, Regis?"

The tall man was already reaching for the buckle on his bag without looking, while keeping his vision locked on the thing Shep was just now seeing.

Far off, across the river they'd been traveling along to their left, sat a vast sward of land that rippled silver with an unfelt breeze. He realized it was grass, looked to be waist high, and then he saw they were soon to be engulfed in it.

But what had attracted Bone's gaze, and now held Shep's, was a black mass that moved, dust rising from the rear of it. As he looked, it grew larger and larger from the rear, advancing in their direction. It seemed never to end. Whatever it might be was traveling toward them from a great distance.

"What is it?" he asked, not daring to look away for fear it might disappear.

"Mustangs. Wild. Herd of them."

"Really? That many? Now I know you're funning me." Shep grinned, satisfied he'd not fallen for another of Regis's jokes.

But his brother glanced at him. "They're mustangs, Shep. This range is crawling with them. Too many, actually."

"Yeah," said Bone. "Might choke out our cattle. But man alive, ain't they a pretty sight."

All three men watched awhile and began to pick out individual beasts at the fore of the herd.

"They're headed to the river to drink," said Regis. "I saw a small band of them across the way when I was out here alone not long ago. They have to be the prettiest things I've seen in a long time."

"Then you weren't paying attention to Miss Valdez," said Shep, still watching the horse.

Bone chuckled and shook his head. "Boy, you best keep your powder dry. That is one matchstick you don't want to light."

Shep reddened again. He was doing a whole lot of that around these two.

After a while, Regis said, "We'd best keep on." He nudged his horse into a walk. It didn't look to Shep as if he were in any hurry.

"When we going to get there? To your land, I mean."

"Why, Shepley," said his brother, turning in the saddle. "I thought you knew. We've been on it since, oh, midday yesterday."

"What?"

"Yeah, we're just scouting for the best place to site the ranch proper. Isn't that right, Bone?"

"Yep, and I'd say that slight rise yonder is the perfect spot. The very one we marked on the map this morning."

"Oh, so that's it, huh?" Regis halted his horse and looked at the terrain once more. "Mmm, close to water, that stand of trees looks promising, mesquite nearby, and look at this land! I tell you, boys, I have a good feeling about this."

His friend smiled. "If I had a shiny penny for every time a woman told me that." He looked at Shep and winked. "Last one to it's an old maid!"

The trio thundered toward the spot. Bone made it first and wheeled the horse in a circle, dust rising where it stomped. "Look good to you, boss?" he shouted to Regis, who thundered up moments later.

"Sure does. But it's not *boss*, it's *partner*. Partnerships come in all shapes and sizes, of course." He nodded as Shep hammered up beside them. "But we're all in this venture together, okay?"

Regis slipped a hand into his saddlebag and pulled out a corked bottle of amber liquid that glinted like honey in the sunlight. "A drink to the Royle Ranch!" He swigged and handed it to Bone, who did the same. Then he handed it to Shep. The boy looked hopefully at Regis, who smiled and nodded. "Go ahead, junior partner."

The boy swigged, gasped, and handed the bottle to his brother. Instead of corking it, Regis raised it high and said, "To Cormac Delany, who not only couldn't be here but didn't want to be here. He said one adventure with us in a month's time is plenty for him. Besides, as he said, somebody has to run the shipping business while I'm off playing out here."

They toasted to Cormac, the absent partner, then Bone raised the bottle. "To Don Mallarmoza, for coming through in the end."

"Here, here." Again the bottle was passed.

After he sipped, Shep was about to hand the bottle back to Regis but instead held it high. He wanted to toast to Tomasina Valdez. Devil or no, she was something else. Instead, he looked at his big brother, a smile on Regis's sunburnt face and that big moustache perched above a smile. Maybe he'd grow one of those, too. Then Shep knew what he wanted to say.

"To our mother. And to my brother. May I be more like each of them. But not too much!" He smiled and swigged, then passed the bottle to Regis.

"Thank you, Shep. I think."

"Okay, it's late enough. What say we bed down here tonight?" said Bone. "I'll see if I can jump some game down by the river. You two brothers set up camp on the site of the future Royle Ranch house, okay?"

While they worked, Regis and Shep talked.

"We'll be riding back tomorrow. You and Bone will provision up. I expect he'll hire some men while we're in town, then you all will be coming back here. You should be back at this very spot in, oh, four, five days."

"What about you?" Shep paused in arranging rocks for a fire ring.

"I'll be along in a few weeks. I've been gone from the fleet too long as it is. How else do you think we're going to pay for all this?"

Shep knew this was the way it had to be, but he was disappointed. He'd hoped to spend more time with his brother, not less. Not that he wanted to tell Regis that.

Regis sensed this and walked over, draped a hand on Shep's shoulder. "It won't always be this way. But anytime men begin a new venture, it takes some sacrifice and a pile of hard work to make it a go. You see that, otherwise you wouldn't have traveled all the way out here to find me, right?"

Shep nodded and Regis continued. "That journey you made was one whale of a trip with a whole lot of chance involved. But you did it. You have sand, Shepley, and that's something you can't just buy at the mercantile. You're a Royle, don't forget it. But don't let it go to your head, either." He tugged Shep's hat brim hard and wedged it down over the boy's eyes.

"Quit it!" said Shep, but he was grinning when he said it. A little sacrifice—he guessed he could do that all right. "I'll be taking orders from Bone, then?"

"Yep." Regis stripped the saddles from the horses. "He's the foreman, after all. For that matter, I'll defer to his judgment on a good many things, too. But don't tell him I said that." He chuckled. "I'm only funning—Bone's a good man. Hard when he needs to be, but he's fair. And if he doesn't know it about cattle, it hasn't been invented yet. The man's a rancher from way back."

Chapter 10

As Regis had promised, Bone, Shep, their two mounts, and a pack horse had made the trip back out to the Santa Calina range within days of returning to Brownsville. They had tools and provisions enough for a week or more, then Regis would be bringing a wagonload of goods and spending time there himself.

Shep looked forward to that, though he didn't let his brother know. He'd learned it didn't pay to tell Regis too much. The man never forgot a thing and always expected you to prove up on a promise. It could get annoying.

They'd not had luck in rounding up any extra help in town, though Bone did get a tip from a cowboy of his acquaintance who was passing through. He told him of a couple of ranches well north of the Royle Ranch whose hands might be looking to move on to other ranges. The drought was playing devil with every rancher in the land, it seemed.

Bone had told Shep, given the scarcity of help and given their genuine need for it, that it would be well worth their time to "sniff out the possibility."

True to his word, on the day Regis was due, Bone's fidgety feeling got the better of him. They'd worked hard at building a shelter and then a corral, but without more men, it was obvious to them both that the ranch Regis envisioned would not come to be.

Bone decided to finally ride north to round up more hands. He hated to think it, but he couldn't help it: If he hadn't had the kid, who really was nearly a man, to wet nurse he would already have been there and back, maybe with a passel of hired help.

"I'll be gone some days," said Bone. "But your brother'll be here by sundown, I expect. He'll have provisions with him and more equipment. Meantime, we have that rock pick, that steel bar, and that shovel."

He reached in his saddlebag and pulled out a pair of used but solid gloves, the fingertips not yet worn through. "There's another pair."

Shep looked them over. "Thanks, but I already have gloves."

The man chuckled. "You go scrabbling around in this dirt too long and you'll be glad you have a second pair. And a third and a fourth before this place is built. Lots of hard scratching to come in this dirt. That rise where the house is going looks to be decent soil, but this here"—he stamped his boot and dust clouded up—"this'd choke ol' Scratch his own self."

He mounted up. "Pace yourself and drink plenty of water. If he ain't careful, a man can dry out and powder off, never to be seen again in these parts. You hear?"

"Sure," said Shep. "But you don't have to mother-hen me. I'll be eighteen before I'm seventeen again." Shep folded his arms and regarded the older man, trying to look big in every way.

"Yeah, I expect so, but I promised your brother I'd see to it you were here and in one piece when he come back. I hate to leave like this before he gets here, I surely do. But if I don't get a start today, it'll be another day, or longer. You know how Regis is with his lists of things that need doing yesterday." He worked his hat back and forth as if he were wearing a groove in his head.

"Don't worry so much about me, Bone. I made it all the way to Texas from Connecticut alone. Well, there were passengers on the stage, but you know what I mean."

"Okay, then." Bone circled the horse. "Just keep yourself alive and whole for a few hours more. I'll be along in a couple of days with a passel of men. See ya, Shep!"

And he was off, a dust cloud trailing him.

Shep watched for a while, then turned back to the corral in progress. "Don't see why I can't go with him. Stuck here like a child." Shep slammed the nose of the shovel into the hard-packed dirt. It clanged. "'Wait for your brother,' he says. Why? I'm no wet-nose child!"

His voice drifted off across the flat landscape. Nothing responded except the piercing screech of a patrolling hawk.

"Easy for you to say," muttered Shep as he sunk a steel bar into the spot where the next bent, gnarled mesquite corral post would stand.

Over and over he jammed the thing into the earth, dust rising up, sweat beading on his forehead, running down his long nose and dripping off the tip. He dragged a hand across his eyes and set to his task again, ramming the steel bar once more into the unforgiving earth, mumbling the entire time. He had been at it a half hour, maybe more, when he heard a sound, as if a boot dragged on gravel. Then a horse whickered, and as he spun, a voice behind him said, "Hey, mister. . . ."

Chapter 11

A half hour up the trail, northwestward, Bone slowed Buck, his grulla, and glanced back over his shoulder. He couldn't see the ranch from there, but he could picture it—hoped what he was seeing in his mind's eye was indeed what was going on there. Nothing but Shep working his fingers to the bone—no troubles, no worries, nothing but a whistle on his lips and a smile on his face.

"Yeah, that's likely," said Bone. More likely, he knew, was that the kid was complaining and getting half the amount of work done that he was capable of, biding his time until he was certain Bone was well and truly gone, then he would lie low in the shade. Maybe take a dip in the creek. Then Bone smiled. That's exactly what he would do—used to do on his pap's hard-luck farm back when he was a weanling pup.

He turned back around and urged the horse into a trot. "Live it up, Shep. Regis'll be there soon enough and then you'll be kept hopping." Still, he hated to leave the kid alone out there, even for a few hours, but they'd all agreed it would be okay. Well, he and Shep did. Regis, he'd been back in town working the boats. But knowing Regis, he had been mired in thinking about getting back to the ranch, itching to do it, more likely.

Still, Bone hadn't been able to trot the idea by him of leaving the kid alone there. But Regis said he trusted him, and they'd not seen hide nor hair of border-hopping bandits or crazy Comanches or rogue Apaches in all the days they'd been pounding away out here.

No, Bone had to get to the two nearest ranches north of here, and quick. He'd had word that Orliss Pushaw, one of the ranchers, as well as Mack Deemworth, an old friend Bone had worked for in the past, were cutting back on hands and stock, maybe land, too. Neither was connected to the Santa Calina range, but Mack's would make a fine property to buy.

Maybe somehow he could finagle it on his own, talk Regis into partnering up on it with him. He'd not sunk much of his own money into Regis's venture, mainly because he'd not been asked to. Regis had it covered. Or Cormac did.

But ol' Mack Deemworth's place, now that would make an all right ranch for Bone to settle on. Worth a thought. But first, he was taking Regis's money; he was riding for that man's brand. Another thing he had to arrange. They needed a brand of their own. Regis was supposed to have talked with the lawyers about ironing out the last of the wrinkles of ownership so they could put their minds and money and back muscles into more important matters. Like brands and borders and stock.

He was hoping he wasn't too late to catch any of the stock and the few men Mack might be letting go before they drifted away. He knew the cowhands because he was one, or had been for long enough, once the Texas Rangering work slid into a lull.

"Damn," muttered Bone.

He'd enjoyed his time Rangering, and there had been real and sore need of them, still was. But it was hard to stick with something when the money wasn't there. A man had to eat. Funny thing was, there seemed to be more need of Rangers now than ever, what with all this border thieving going on. But he knew this was raw country, still wide open and up for grabs. It'd get tamed, but not for some time. And they'd need the Texas Rangers to help do it. He hoped.

First, it needed to be ridden point on by folks like him and Regis Royle and Mack Deemworth and all the others. Even stove-up, broke-down, no-luck characters such as Coop. He'd known the man for years now, both when they were younger Rangers.

Then Coop went up and married that woman he'd drug back to Texas, and they had a passel of kids and set to dirt farming up north on some of the poorest land you ever could hope to find. But as Coop had said at the time, "I ain't no farmer anyhow, so I reckon good land would just be wasted on me."

"Ol' Coop," said Bone, smiling. And . . . what was his wife's name? Pretty thing, though too flinty by half for Bone. He'd done his best to stay on her good side whenever he visited and then he did his best to not overstay his invite by more than a minute.

Bone rode most of that day in silence, his rifle across his lap, at the ready to whip up to his shoulder and fire. Wouldn't help much, of course, if someone took a notion to open up on him from behind, or even from the front, from a distance. He was as exposed as a naked man riding out here, but what could he do? It was South Texas, and it wasn't going to change. Just have to hope for the best and not dawdle along.

He saw the commotion long before he got to it, up ahead and smack in the direction he was making for. And from that distance he had no idea what it was. Maybe a horse with a busted leg? Or a man? If so, what was he up to? And why was he waving his arms like that?

Nah. He squinted. Too light in color, lighter than buckskin. Had to be a critter of some sort. He raised the rifle and circled wider, coming in on it from the east. It would rise up, flail, then disappear from sight below the rabbit brush.

Bone aimed the rifle, held it aloft with both hands, and with his knees he urged the horse on at a walk. The big grulla, a normally calm gelding, kindly but not the cleverest animal Bone had ever worked with, gained on the commotion, ears perked, step by hesitant step.

When they were five yards from it, the thing reared up again and spooked Buck. The big lummox jerked, rose up on its hind legs.

"Calm yourself!" growled Bone, snatching at the reins and jerking the horse hard and down. He nearly lost his seat but managed to pull the reins hard and taut to keep the beast from bolting and crow-hopping and whatever else he set his mind to.

He wasn't much concerned with the source of the kerfuffle coming after him while he was busy calming the horse, because in the instant before the horse spooked, Bone had seen up close what it was they'd been creeping up on.

It was a deer, full grown, or nearly so—a doe, from the looks—and she'd gotten herself tangled somehow in a thick snag of brittle old gray branches. They were clogged and wound tight together so as to form a yarn ball of sorts. At least that was his quick assessment from the speedy glance he'd been given before the horse kicked up his fuss.

He led the snorting beast over to a nearby mesquite and tied him tight, then cradled the rifle and made his way back to the ensnared beast. Could be she was already damaged and would need a speedy bullet to end her suffering.

When he got there, the deer seemed to have been as alarmed by his presence as Bone was of it. The small beast's brown hair was a lathered, sopping mess. Its rib cage heaved from panting; its tongue, a thick blue-purple thing, hung out of its parted mouth, foam flecking its black-gray nostrils that flexed with each hard-drawn breath.

Bone smelled the musky fear wafting off her and saw more of that fear in her wide brown eyes. They barley blinked and kept him in sight the entire time he slowly stepped closer, still out of striking range of those flailing hooves, though.

"No sense getting a gash for my efforts," he said in a low, soothing tone. Or what he hoped was one, anyway.

The beast's breathing was harsh, ragged, more labored than any he'd heard of from an animal for some time. It was sure sign of extreme distress, and if he didn't free the deer, or at least get her to calm down and drink, she was going to expire of exhaustion, a drawn-out process that surely could not be pleasant.

He'd been in similar situations. Far in the past, he and Coop had been pinned down by Comanches in a dried-out old wallow they'd been lucky to make it to. Once they reached it, they turned, forcing their horses down and shooting them in the heads so they might use them as a bulwark, something on an otherwise barren stretch of the Llano Estacado to take cover behind. It had worked, though they had nearly died.

They'd run out of water. And though they'd had jerky left, they had no desire to eat the salty, hard meat. It would only have made their thirst all the greater. He later was reminded by an old trapper of some renown far in the north country, in the Shining Mountains, that he and Coop should have opened the neck veins of the horses and drank their blood. As foul as it sounded, Bone knew they should have done so, and had they thought of it, they would have.

Those Comanches likely went away long before the two haggard men crawled up out of the bullet-pocked wallow and trudged their way to safety.

They'd had no thoughts of surviving the journey, but somehow they had lived. It had been largely thanks to one thing—a horse belonging to one of the three Comanches they'd managed to kill. It had gotten itself tangled in a great bramble snag. By the time they reached it, it had long since given up thrashing to free itself and was simply standing still, breathing slow and steady, angling itself with the shifting sun so as to keep its head hidden from the brutal orb's glare.

At the time, Coop had been in far worse condition than Bone, so Bone insisted his chum climb aboard the horse and they would walk toward far-off safety in the north. They knew it would take the better part of a week of serious daily travel to get them close to where a passerby might, just might, come upon them and give them water.

And wonder of wonders, it had happened something like that. But the important part of this sudden and dredged memory to Bone was the tangled horse. It reminded him much of the predicament this deer now found itself in.

Bone knew it would be easy and perhaps most kind to shoot the deer in the head and be done with it. But he stayed his hand.

He was too far from the ranch to use the beast for food. He suspected he would have shot the deer and skinned it out were he traveling back to the ranch. But he did not need the meat, at least not where he was headed. He also felt a silly connection somehow to the horse he and Coop had found, a beast that truly saved his backside, and frontside too.

But he made a deal with himself that if the beast did not drink and regain her strength before he attempted to free her from the thick tangle, then he would have to kill her to cease the deer's suffering. But what if it would drink?

He sighed and stared at the deer. It regarded him with those same liquid-clear, wide eyes. He looked to the horse and fancied he saw the beast squinting and sneering back at him.

"I know," he muttered. "Foolishness." He walked back to the horse and thought for a moment before tugging out his chipped gray enamel tin bowl and lifted down the fuller of the two canteens.

He had to get the deer to drink before he could attempt to free her. It was risky because she might feel revived and lash out at him. He knew he would were he the deer and some bony goober of a man with a gun came upon him all fetched up and exhausted.

But if he waited and freed the deer, she would not take water from him and would stumble off into the hot desert, with an addled brain and no hope of surviving. The blame, silly as it sounded, would lay across Bone's shoulders like an unwanted burden.

The irony of that thought was not lost on him. He'd shot and eaten more critters than he could count, plus there were all the others, vermin such as rats and snakes, unwanted around camp or barnyard, that he'd cored the brains out of with a bullet or a quick slash of a shovel. Once, a diamondback tasted his boot heel when he had no time at all to draw his revolver.

He'd camped in an area he should have known better than to bed down in—it was smack in a rocky chasm that fairly buzzed with snake warning. But he'd been dog-tired and weak from rationing water and not in his full mind. And he'd almost paid a brutal price for it.

But luck and one last burst of reflex action had been with him. He'd stomped that snake just behind the head as it was fixing to lunge. He ground down even as the rest of its three-foot body whipped and rattled and coiled, not willing to give up the fight for a long time after. It was still writhing and flopping as Bone hastily saddled and thundered on out of there.

He returned to the deer, and though she didn't thrash about, the beast was still breathing as if she had run without cease from Oregon Territory on down to South Texas. All the while she kept her wide eyes on Bone's every move. He wanted to avoid riling the deer further, so he moved as if he were an old, old man on a scorching day. Not that it wasn't. Already summer and they weren't through with spring yet. At least not in his mind.

Bone poured cool water into the bowl. At the slight tinkling, glugging sound the water made, the deer's gaze shifted quickly to the flow, then back again to Bone's actions. She was calming now because her mouth was not so stretched and gasping as she panted for breath. Slowly, slowly, with the bowl gripped by the rim, he set it on the baked hard pan by the deer's head and let it sit. The beast wasn't able to reach it at that distance, but he wanted to get her used to it.

After a moment, he nudged the bowl forward. It vibrated slightly, and a few drops splashed out. The animal started but didn't thrash. He nudged it closer still, now within reach of the deer. And then Bone slowly backed away until he knelt well out of a threatening proximity.

The deer hesitated, and Bone saw he'd made a mistake, as the deer couldn't see both him and the water at the same time. He slowly moved to his right, angling on his prayer bones, one slow knee-step at a time, until she was accommodated. It did the trick.

He'd expected the animal to dither and fidget and thrash and knock over the water, but she was desperately thirsty; she looked once to the bowl, then sucked down the water, all the while keeping her gaze on Bone.

As she sipped, Bone watched her mouth tremble. He knew the feeling, had often felt it when thirsty. And a few times when working on the first of several glasses of beer after a long day in the sun.

He repeated the act, filling the bowl and backing away three times more before the deer showed sign of at least of slowing her desperate taking in of the life-giving liquid.

"Now comes the hard work," whispered Bone. He hoped the beast somehow might trust him a little, enough at least to sidle closer and pull apart the constricting branches. Her two rear legs were hopelessly tangled, and one foreleg would soon be if the deer didn't stop its occasional thrashing.

Bone looked about him, but he had no logs or stout branches he might use as a lever to jam in there and pry apart the criss-crossed thicket. He'd spent the entire time the deer drank eye-balling the tangle, and he believed he'd identified the cause.

Its lower foot—the right—stood on another branch that,

when jammed downward, compressed several higher-up cross-ing branches. These, in turn, whipped together with force each time the deer tried to stand or bucked and thrashed. All it did was make the deer tired and keep her stranded, and maybe make it a little worse each time, too.

With a twinge of hesitation, he finally stuffed the rifle barrel down in a spot between branches he thought might do the trick. He pried back and forth and wedged it. For a moment he was certain it, too, was stuck. But it wiggled and he jammed it a little deeper, then shoved it to the side.

The entire time he did this, sweat rolling down his face and off his nose, fetching up in his moustache, he wondered why in heck he was putting so much effort in on a beast that would like as not kick him in the face with one of those razor-sharp hooves and scramble on out of there with nary a look back.

"That's not the point, Bone," he muttered. And as he did, something below shifted in a different way. At the same time, the deer kicked and jerked, and her right rear leg lifted free. The black hoof rested inches from Bone's face.

He was in a lousy spot. Not only was he dangerously close to that hoof, which could whip backward any moment, but the deer's backside was right beside his left cheek. It stunk because the critter had continued to expel whatever it had eaten, and some of it had also smeared on the beast's hind hair.

"Gaah," wheezed Bone, hoping he'd free that second leg and quick, then he could scramble on out of there before the leg found purchase and shoved the animal upward.

And then, just as he was about to sit back and consider what a next step should be, with a final grunting thrust upward, the deer raised her back end high. The rear right hoof slid back-ward into Bone's right arm, and she used his limb as leverage to hoist up the last hoof, straining to stay on top of a branch. The deer stood still, her haunches shaking from the strain. She swung her head around and looked down at Bone.

Bone didn't dare move for fear of jostling the branches and

dropping the deer back into its trap, but neither did he like the idea of the thing thrashing once more out of fear and striking him.

She must have read his mind, for with two shoves forward, the feet sliding on the topmost branches as if they were on a skin of ice, the deer bounded off the branch pile and stumbled, went down on her front knees, and stayed that way, tongue once more outthrust as she wheezed and heaved for breath.

Bone slid the rifle out and gave it a quick glance—it didn't look too bad for the wear. A few minor scratches in the forestock, but the steel was fine. He knee-walked backward and pushed up to his feet, his own knees popping and cracking from the strain.

"You and me both, deer," said Bone as he bent over, rubbing his sore knees.

The deer swung her head his way once more but didn't seem overly concerned by his presence.

He retrieved the tin bowl and filled it again, then slowly brought it to the deer, which was still on her front knees and panting. He placed it within reach and backed away.

The deer strained for it, couldn't quite reach it, so she forced herself to her feet and, still shaking as if her muscles were being poked from within by hundreds of tiny needles, she drank the bowl down.

Bone shook the canteen, weighed how far he had to go, then recalled he still had better than half of the other canteen full on the horse. The grulla, from a glance, looked to be half-resting, angled as much as he could beneath the gnarled mesquites, yet watching with perked ears the entire escapade with the deer as if he could not believe what had happened.

Bone gave the deer a last drink, which she once more took gratefully, then she walked, stiff-legged, southward. She progressed ten paces or so, then stopped and regarded Bone, ears perked forward.

Bone looked at the thin animal, her hair darkened with sweat, the brown-black eyes staring at him as he stared at her. "Take care where you step from now on," he said, raising an arm. "I may not be traipsing through next time!"

He chuckled as his words caused the deer's ears to pinch backward and swivel. The entire animal perked and tensed and swung her head back around toward where she was headed. Then she trotted, slowly at first. Soon instinct bubbled once more to the fore and she lurched away, settling within one hundred feet or so into a natural, comfortable-looking stride. She did not look back.

Bone sighed and watched the beast go. He wondered if he'd ever be able to stomach eating venison again. He reckoned so.

Chapter 12

At the sound of the voice behind him, Shep spun. There stood the prettiest woman he'd ever seen, that wily Tomasina Valdez. He held still, thinking nothing much at all that might be approved by Regis or Bone. But they weren't there, now, were they? And they chose to leave him in charge of the ranch, which admittedly wasn't all that much yet. A makeshift corral with two horses in it—his and the cranky old pack horse. And the crude shade shelter they'd built to live in until they could get a house built. So, no, all in all it wasn't much to be in charge of.

Yet here she was and here he was, boss of the place. Yes sir, it could be an okay afternoon after all.

"Ma'am," he said, trying to remember what it was people did after they said that. Tip the hat? Then what? Bow at the waist?

She walked toward him. He couldn't help but notice she was even prettier today than she had been in that blue dress, and that had been something else. Today she was wearing trousers, of all things, but not any he'd ever seen on a man. These looked to be painted on, so tight were they.

And her shirt was a button-down affair, open at least to her belly, and about half of the buttons on the way down were missing. And he could see a whole lot of light brown skin between them. The ones that were there looked to be putting up a mighty effort to keep in whatever it was behind there doing all the pushing.

He wanted to tell those buttons to lay off the fight. Wouldn't bother him a bit.

She walked up to within two feet of him, then rested her fingers on her belt. A black tooled gun belt, Shep now saw. And her left side held a leather holster, tooled with a silver concho and fringe. Her trousers were tucked into tall black leather boots, dusted from the trail. Her hat was a black low-crown affair with a ring of smaller silver conchos for a hat band.

Even though the visor was tugged low, those eyes, a cold, deep green and staring into him, held him fast. He tried to keep his eyes gazing up at hers, but he found he couldn't look away. It was odd, but he didn't much care.

"So, Shep, was it? What are you doing here?"

Would she know he was alone at the ranch? Had to, otherwise why show up when she had? He didn't say anything. His tongue failed him.

"I have come to talk with the boss of this place." She tried to hide a sneer as she said it. But Shep saw it, and a vague notion of wariness—something his brother had told him, something about this woman being less than trustworthy—crept into his mind.

But then she must have seen that on his face, because she stepped closer. "Do you mind if I refresh myself down at the river? On hot days such as this, I like to bathe. The water is so cool, and I like how it feels on my body. Do you do this, too? Yes?" She nodded her head, and now her face was less than a foot from his.

He watched her lips move, form words, and send them to him. He heard them, vaguely, as one hears a bird in the morning and knows a new day has begun. And though he is uncertain of the song the bird sings, it matters not. Only that there is a pretty birdsong. And this pretty bird was asking him a question. *Just nod*, he told himself.

"Yes? Good! Then you will join me. Come, come." She took him by the wrist and led him to the river. As they walked, she with long strides, unhurried, he trying to catch up, her long fingers twined around his. She swung their hands as if they hadn't a care in the world.

And really, thought Shep, had they? It was a pretty day, after all. And she was going to bathe in the river. And she'd asked him to join her.

"I only bathe in the river when it is hot, and I only bathe naked because that is the only real way to cool down on such a day."

As they walked, Shep's thoughts flashed to Bone. He promised Bone he'd have the corral posts up by the time Regis arrived. But he wouldn't be there for hours yet. He had plenty of time. The afternoon was young.

Shep watched the side of her face, the line of her jaw, the downy hair curling beneath her ear. Sweat stuck curls of black hair to her neck, and her shirt was tight to her back in spots. *I am a junior partner, after all*, he thought. *Why work like a dog all the time when you can enjoy yourself now and again.*

The path to the river was one he knew well, having carved it out himself by walking to and from camp for morning ablutions and to haul water three times each day. Bone never once hauled water. But to be fair, he did share the cooking duties.

They came to the river, and she looked left, then right, and let go of his hand. "I'll go behind these bushes and take off my clothes, okay, Shep? You do the same here." She leaned in to him, her lips close to his ear. "Then we shall bathe . . . together, eh?"

She pushed out a soft, hot breath, and he felt cool all over his body. He nodded and swallowed and watched as she, smiling, walked behind the thorny bushes. They were thick with leaves, he saw now, and cursed them in his mind for being so clever at shrouding her from him. He'd sorely like to see a woman shed her togs.

He saw that he was once more alone and, for a moment, had the odd thought that perhaps he'd had a strange daydream, that the heat was softening his brain somehow. Then a woman's voice, her voice, said, "Oh, Shep? Could you come here? I am having trouble with these buttons. I can't get them undone."

Shep gulped, not for the first time in recent minutes, and stepped close to the bushes. Yes, he saw as he looked down at the softer riverbank soil, there were her bootprints. He wasn't going off in the bean, as Bone might say.

"Okay," he managed to whisper. "I'm here."

And a voice, not a woman's but a harsh, hard voice, said, "Yes, I see that." The words were followed by a quick series of harsh metal clicks. Shep looked into the dark snout of a revolver. And beyond it, the eyes of a man.

He was a dark-skinned, swarthy man, with deep creases in a sweat-sheened face, begrimed, and with greasy moustache drooping over a wide-pulled smile showing cracked, stained teeth. The eyes were brown and wet-looking, with red veins rimming them.

But what held Shep's attention was the very tall blue-banded sombrero, a hat as distinctive as a hat could be. He wondered briefly how someone might come upon such a topper, who might make such a vivid thing, and who might wear it? Here was the answer.

This was a man he'd seen before. Poking beneath the hat's brim were sweaty, wet-black curls and, here and there, bandages browned with old bloodstains. Where he'd been skinned on the head by shots from Regis. Twice.

The thought brought Shep out of his dazed fantasy. The woman, Tomasina Valdez, stood—fully clothed, he regretted seeing—behind the man. Her arms were crossed, and she was smiling. No, she was sneering. At him. Behind Shep, he sensed others. He turned his head to the left and caught sight of one, maybe two more men.

"Uh uh, no no, senor," said Blue Hat. "That is all the movement you do, eh? Or you die slow, bleeding like crazy all over the dirt. And I don't think anybody will find you for a long time, except maybe the coyotes. Only they won't be so nice. They won't ask you if you need help."

"And they certainly won't ask you if you would like to bathe in the river." This from the woman. Her offering raised howls of harsh laughter from the men surrounding him.

Shep looked at her, and she no longer had the soft, pretty eyes of minutes before. Now they were hard eyes glinting like shards of jade. She shoved Blue Hat's shoulder and stepped closer to Shep, then spit in his face.

He wiped it away with the back of his hand and bit down hard, his cheek muscles bunching. Any harder and his teeth would turn to powder. He'd been such a fool. Of course she'd had no intention of flirting with him for real. Why would she? She was a woman, an outlaw, and he was a . . . a kid. *A stupid kid*, he thought. What would Regis and Bone think?

"Okay." She nodded to the men and turned back toward the trail. "Tie his hands and bring him. We get back to the camp, you can have some fun with him. But remember, don't break anything too bad. I need him for ransom. I mean it. Anybody hurts him too bad"—she whipped out her revolver as fast as anyone Shep had ever seen—"and you fight with this one, eh?"

Chapter 13

The blows Shep expected began as soon as Tomasina Valdez turned her back on the men. They delivered their brute punches and slaps and kicks with near-silent savagery, emitting little more than grunts and low growls of satisfaction as Shep wheezed and doubled over, only to feel the sting of an uppercut to his jaw.

The last jaw blow jammed his teeth together hard. Then Blue Hat stared him in the eye and at the same time kicked up quick, landing a boot toe square into Shep's grapes. Any breath the boy had left in his lungs trickled up, pushed out of his pursed lips by a thin, squeaking wheeze.

He pitched forward and barely stopped himself with outstretched hands before his face smeared into a gnarled clot of prickly pear cactus.

The woman must have been far enough away by then, because the men kept up their low-volume braying and smiling.

"On your knees, gringo." Blue Hat's revolver once more appeared in his hand. "Now."

Shep gulped and waited for other blows to descend on his already aching pate, but none came. He looked up into the chaw-stained teeth of Blue Hat. "You listen to me, gringo. You give the lady what she wants, or I will kill you. And I will do it slow. I take tricks I learned from *mi abuela, si*? She was a half Apache. She always told me, to do it right, you got to do it slow. Make you scream for days, man!"

Someone lifted Shep to his feet and held his shoulders while other rough hands grabbed his arms and bound his wrists together with leather thongs, wrapping them so tight that within seconds his fingers began to throb.

They shoved and dragged him back up the trail to the weak little shanty he and Bone had built. It was a gappy affair and rattled with each blow Tomasina dealt it.

It took Shep a moment to realize she was tacking up a paper to the side of the structure, pounding one nail in each corner with the butt of her revolver. She turned to him. "You are curious, eh? Come, come." She beckoned toward him, smiling. "Walk closer. I'll read it to you."

One of the men shoved him hard from behind. He stumbled forward and stood tall, glaring at the woman. She glared back, then a smile spread on her face and she laughed a big, deep, hearty chuckle, her head bent backward.

"Oh, this is going to be so much fun! Okay, okay, here's what I have written in this note to your brother, Regis, or that other one, the man who stared at me all the time." She laughed again. "Well, that was you, too, *si*? Little child."

She shook her head and made a noise with her lips as if she were scolding him. "To Regis Royle: I and I alone have convinced your brother to accompany me to a place that will remain unknown to you for now. He will be delivered back to you once you have agreed to my demand. There is only the one, and it is this: You will sign over to me the deed to the Santa Calina range. It is mine by right, mine by birth, and it was stolen from me by you, a foul gringo!"

Shep watched the woman's cheeks color as she read the note, her voice rising in pitch. Spittle flecked from her mouth, and by the time she uttered the word *gringo*, she was shouting.

She closed her eyes, and her flexed nostrils pulsed with her quick breaths. She opened her eyes and finished reading. "If you do not meet my demand, your brother, Shepley Royle, will die. And not quickly. I have promised my man Hector that he will be allowed to torture the child to death. It will be a long, slow, steady way to die. Do not seek to involve any pig gringo lawmen, or I will kill the boy. Do not seek to find me, or I will kill the boy. Do not do anything other than what I have told you, or I will kill the boy. You have five days to do as I demand."

She turned her gaze on him. Those hard black eyes glinted with the obvious excitement the situation provided her. "How do you like that, little boy?"

"I'm not a little boy! And I won't go with you!" Shep drove a boot up fast and landed a solid kick that caught the witch in the elbow. It would have connected with her leg, but she side-stepped quick as a cat, though not quick enough. She yelped and grabbed her arm, her teeth gritted. "Knock him out and tie him over a horse. We ride for the canyon."

A raspy chuckle was the last thing Shep heard. The last thing he felt was hot pain, like boiling water leaching over his skull. The last thing he saw as his legs gave way and he dropped to the ground was the once-pretty face of Tomasina Valdez glaring down at him. Her teeth gritted, and that once-perfect mouth twisted in a sneer of rage. She spit on him again, but he never felt it.

Chapter 14

The journey from Brownsville to the ranch was one that Regis was surprised to find he didn't mind at all. It gave him ample time to clear his mind of the concerns of the shipping and docks and of the constant cries for attention from their deckhands, the tenders, the stevedores, all of them. It was good, too, to get away from customers, who never seemed satisfied no matter how fast or how undamaged their goods arrived.

He didn't admit this to Cormac, but he could see a day when he spent all his time working the Santa Calina range and none of it, professionally at least, tending matters at the docks or plying the waters on yet another trek up or down the coast, or inland up the Rio Grande.

Regis breathed deep and closed his eyes for a moment to listen to the warblers and meadowlarks sing. It seemed the birdsong increased in intensity and variety the farther he trekked.

There was birdsong and the steady squawk and clack of the wheels on the supply wagon and the *thunk thunk thunk* of the taut ropes holding the tarpaulin covering the load as the ropes smacked the wagon's sides.

The rhythmic sound was almost pleasant enough to make a man want to whistle, something he hadn't done in forever. In fact, he'd not heard many men whistle while they worked in a long time. The only one he could dredge up in memory was Lockjaw Hames, the massive black stevedore. He was always chuckling, as if to some constant stream of jokes only he heard.

"Wish I was more like that," said Regis to the brace of horses churning forward before him. Then his own voice answered him in thought: *That's what the ranch will do for you. If you let it.* He nodded and smiled, much like Lockjaw, at his little joke. If anybody saw me now . . .

Hours later he drew in sight of the camp, the camp that sat close to the spot where his home would sit one day. A big fine home. Home enough for a family? He shook the thought from his mind. Not yet, Regis. Not yet.

He saw the flutter of something bright, perhaps white, on the side of the sleep shanty Bone and Shep had built. At least that's what he assumed it was, sitting in the right spot and all. But of the two men there was no sign. The only thing that moved was something on the side of the crude shelter. Not even a sign of their three horses in the corral. Where were they all?

Out on the range somewhere, of course. But he was hours late, so he expected at least one of them to be here. Heck, he thought, they'd likely be excited to see him, bearing fresh provisions and all.

He'd carried everything he could pack onto the wagon, from seasonings for food to food itself, fresh work clothes and hand tools to ammunition, coils of rope, horse feed, a couple bottles of whiskey, and a crate of live chickens strapped to the back.

He'd even lugged a stack of books that Cormac insisted he take, demanding he tell Shep that Cormac would quiz him on the contents in two months' time.

"There's no reason on God's earth why that boy shouldn't be spending his free time with his nose in his books. And mind you, take plenty of candles! I'll not listen to the excuse that it was too dark to read."

Regis had nodded and tamped down a smile, as he'd undergone much the same rigorous tutelage years before with Cormac when he was Shep's age.

For his part, he purchased for the boy a used but fine revolver with walnut grips and brown leather holster and belt. There was no tooling or frippery adorning any of it, but the whole was solid and serviceable.

And now here he was, alone in the camp. He wheeled the wagon to a halt alongside what appeared to be a less-than-half-built corral about where he'd expected a full-built corral to sit.

"Hmm," he grunted as he jumped down from the wagon seat and stretched his legs. And then a soft rustling found his ear and reminded him of the thing that had caught his eye minutes before on the way into camp. Or rather the ranch yard proper. He had to start thinking of the place as a ranch and not a campsite any longer.

He strode to the sleeping shanty, a crude affair made of twisted, crooked mesquite lengths with a gappiness that offered scant protection from wind and sun and did nothing to aid the notion of modesty.

He spied a paper tacked to the east-facing wall. It had torn loose from what looked to be three of the four short nails securing it. Another light gust would have peeled the sheet away completely, and then what would Bone's or Shep's note have told him?

Regis snatched it down, and as he read it, his smile slipped slowly from his face. Was this a joke? It was a poor one, if so. But as he got to the end and read the name *Tomasina Valdez* scrawled in haughty if finely wrought hand—hand that was not Shep's or Bone's—he scowled and his jaw muscles tightened. He stood in place and read it through once more, then once again.

He knew it to be no prank or work of fiction. And yet it was so utterly absurd a notion, so ridiculous a demand, no one in his—or her—rightful mind could possibly make it. And so it was as he'd suspected on meeting the woman at Don Mallarmoza's estate that day not long before. Senorita Valdez was deranged.

That was not something he could alter, but that her madness had caused her to abduct his one and only relation, a young man he was only now hoping to come to know once more as brothers should know each other . . .

The rage he felt was instant. It bubbled up in him like already-boiling water thrust on roaring flames. His big hand crushed the note into a crumpled ball, and he spun in place, eyeing the vista all around.

Were they watching him? Perhaps. What were they seeing? A big man, helpless and angry. Yes, that's what they would want, what that devil woman would want. He pulled in deep draught after deep draught of air and willed himself to calm. Half-cocked anger would get him nowhere.

Wait—what of Bone? Where was the man? Action, that's what needed doing. Investigation. When had this happened? Today? Had the woman known Regis was arriving today? Likely, else why the note, which looked fresh and not yet harmed by the sun? But it had pulled away from most of its moorings.

She'd given a time line. What was it? He opened his palm and plucked up the note, smoothed it out against the bony side of the shanty. It was still legible, despite the mass of wrinkles like cracks in the dry South Texas soil.

"Five days," he said numbly, still looking about the camp. He stepped to his left and peered inside the little sleeping shanty, open on the south-facing side, away from the prevailing winds of the afternoons. There was scant sign of habitation, as the men didn't have much in the way of gear and possessions yet. He was bringing it all to them.

But of Bone's kit, his traps, there was little—nay, nothing.

Regis stalked the yard, eyeing bootprints. Recognizing none. He was no tracker. Perhaps one was smaller than the rest? A woman's? He peered closely at those around the holes dug for the corral posts. Dug by Shep, if he knew Bone as well as he knew he did. Okay, those bootprints were recognizable, as Shep's left boot sole looked to have a crack running across its width.

Regis felt a twinge of guilt. He'd not brought the boy boots, hadn't even thought to ask him if he needed new boots. He would gladly have bought him a better pair!

Hot anger flowed over Regis, and he shouted through near-clenched teeth, "Dammit!" and crumpled the note once more.

Chapter 15

From his position, head banging against the great barrel of a belly, where he'd been flopped across his horse's back—the devils had first laid on a rough-wool blanket that itched and rubbed him like the devil, cold comfort there—Shep saw they were approaching more rough, knobby ground ahead. He moaned and closed his eyes. The ride to wherever this witch and her men were taking him had so far been a dance of pure agony.

They'd not pummeled him enough to render him unconscious the entire time. Maybe that had been intentional, to keep him semicoherent and in control of just enough of his senses that he'd suffer the full duration of the trip. If so, it was working to perfection.

He heard a horse's hooves click closer, then felt a harsh smack against the side of his head.

"What's the matter, gringo boy? You don't like the ride?" This was followed with the ragged, braying laugh of a throat long accustomed to raw whiskey and harsh tobacco smoke. Shep guessed it was the demon in the hat with the blue band, the man she had called Hector.

The clout set off a fresh volley of cannonfire between his ears that thudded in counterpoint to the horse's plodding steps.

Someone ahead sent up a quick, hastening whistle, and who-ever held his horse's lead line picked up their pace.

Despite the piercing pains in his head and ribs, Shep tried once more to shift his position, even slightly, but his hands and his feet were bound and then cinched together with a line run beneath the horse's belly.

With each step the line looked to be causing his mount irrita-tion, too. As it sawed back and forth across that soft underbelly, he did his best to lessen this. Not only did he not want to cause the horse pain, but mostly whenever he saw the rope rub, the beast jittered and acted up, and that wrenched Shep as if he were being slowly tugged apart, piece by piece.

"We'll be there soon, cute boy," said a woman's voice. Her voice. Closer than Shep realized. He tried to look up, but be-tween his brown hair hanging before his eyes and his stiff-as-a-post neck, he gave up trying to look at her. If he had the strength he'd spit on her, pay her in kind for the two times she cut loose on him.

Instead, he timed a response between thumps of the horse's steps and said, "Go to hell, devil woman."

Her horse stepped close, kept pace with his. He saw her dusty, tooled black leather boot inches from his face and regret-ted opening his mouth. He'd always had a hearty fear of having his nose broken. That he'd made it this far in life, given the fights he'd been in, without it happening always happily sur-prised him.

But she didn't kick him. Yet. Instead, he heard leather ratch-eting and her leg shifted slightly. She was leaning down, and her long black hair hung on both sides of his face, as if he were standing in a waterfall raining down the blackness of night. Then she spoke once more, almost a whisper: "I think I will make you my pet. I will forget the offer I made to your brother and keep you. I like that you, how do you say, speak your mind to me."

She laughed. "I will keep you for my amusement. As long as other parts of you are as bold as your mouth, anyway." Her long hair pulled away from his face as she straightened in the saddle, but still she kept pace beside him.

"I'd rather be dead." *Man*, he thought, *when will I ever learn to keep my mouth shut?*

She laughed again. "That will likely happen, anyway. I have all the pets I need. Right, boys?"

A chorus of haggard but lively cheers bubbled up around him. How many men were there?

"What about the land? You kill me, you won't get it," said Shep, weakly he knew, trying to make sure she kept him alive, at least long enough to give Regis a chance at finding him.

"Oh, it does not matter. This was merely a polite way of getting what I want. But I will have the land no matter what. In fact, I would prefer if all you gringo thieves die in the process. Yes, that would be just right." She snorted her approval of the idea and heeled her horse into a lope forward, leaving Shep behind.

He had to pee in the worst way, and these bumps weren't helping. He'd almost gotten to the point of not caring, of letting loose right there on the horse, when they slowed once more. Words were exchanged between voices ahead of him. He couldn't hear what was said, but as it would likely be in Spanish, it didn't matter. He couldn't speak much of it.

Then they resumed their march, winding close to rocky juts as though they were riding through a narrow passageway into a canyon, except now they were going uphill, and he'd always pictured canyons as existing as the bottom-most bit of terrain.

This new stretch of trail was harsher, and his horse's hooves slid backward a few inches with each step on the scree-riddled slope. The men had taken to whistling and cursing and barking orders at the beasts. He heard the crack of short whips and leather reins slapping horse flesh. All that did was agitate the beasts more and make them rumble deep in their throats, their breathing labored.

Someone close behind Shep cursed, in English, at the poor choice of taking this trail over another. "This is a fool's way, I told you!"

"Shut your mouth, man! You want her to hear?"

"Gaah, sick of this, I tell you. . . ."

"Shhhh!"

That was all he heard, but it was enough to tell Shep that not all her men were infatuated with Tomasina Valdez. The thought was almost useless to him at that moment, but he squirreled it away in his mind, just in case he'd need it later.

Even from his unfortunate position Shep sensed they'd reached the end of their journey. Mostly it was the slowing of the procession of horses, but it was also the sighs, whispered, from the men. As if they were afraid to utter their relief too loudly before the woman.

He looked around as much as he could, but all he saw, since the day's light was waning, were what appeared to be cliff faces of stone rising up all about him. A canyon of some sort. That made sense, since for the last twenty minutes they'd made up for the uphill scramble by descending once more. Into this place.

It was cooler down here, and given that the sun lay behind him and had been blocked out halfway down the narrow, scree-strewn trail, that way had to be west. Only the barest of the sun's light reached them now.

It seemed an eternity before anyone tended him. For a moment he wondered if maybe he'd been forgotten. Wild thoughts came to him, and he knew he was half-crazed from thirst and pain, but he didn't care. Ride the wild thoughts, ride the horse back on out of there. Maybe he could urge it toward the trail. Heck, in any direction at all. With enough time he was certain he could free himself and really get out of that viper pit.

But none of it happened. He managed a few weak, bucking

thrusts, but the horse, too fatigued from the journey, stood still and seemed only to sag under his spasms. Curiously, the urge to pee had largely left him some time before.

"Welcome to your new home, baby gringo boy!" It was the same raspy voice. Hector. Had to be. "Say, what is it you're doing there to that horse?" He chuckled.

Shep sagged once more against the horse's bowed back.

"Looks unnatural, boy, eh? But I know how it can be. A young fellow like you." A chorus of laughter rose up around him. Great, they were all watching him.

"Cut me down."

"Huh?" Hector leaned close to his face. "What? I don't hear so good, especially since that pig of a brother of yours shot up my head!" He said these last words through tight teeth, as if he were reliving the moments.

Maybe he is, thought Shep. Good. With any luck, he and not Regis would be able to deliver more such moments to Blue Hat and all of them. But first he needed to get off this horse. "I said, get me off this horse."

"Oh, so now you are the one giving orders." This from Tomasina Valdez. He saw her boots and didn't bother raising his head. She stood close to him for a few moments, then turned and walked away. He heard her say, "Cut him down. Then tie him to the post."

It occurred to him as someone sawed on his bindings that nobody ever said a thing once she gave an order. Not to her face. Though he couldn't see anyone yet, he knew she had to still be within earshot, for he heard no grumbling. That's when someone shoved his backside and he slid forward, headfirst, off the horse.

He wasn't prepared, but he thought quick enough to tuck his head forward, chin to chest. And then he hit, shoulder first, and heard something pop inside his chest, maybe off by his shoulder. He hoped it wasn't a broken bone.

He'd busted his small finger once on his right hand, and that had hurt like the devil, but other than that, he didn't think he'd ever broken any bones. He wasn't likely to get a doctor's attention from these outlaws.

He also couldn't breathe. The wind was pushed or pulled from him. Felt as if it was beaten out of him. His left eye was puffed, worse than before, from a punch one of them threw at him back at the ranch, and he ached all over.

They dragged him upright, and hot jags of pain shot up his arms to his shoulders. Then they dragged him backward, his heels bouncing on the gravelly ground, leaving a scant trail as they went. Twenty feet later they jerked him upright hard against a thick wooden post and smooth, as if it had been used for this purpose for some time.

Hector began to tie Shep's wrists behind the post when Shep regained enough breath to say, "I have to go."

The man stopped. "Huh?"

"I have to go. To pee."

"Oh, *si, si*. Ah, senorita?"

Tomasina Valdez stood across the clearing, which Shep saw now was about fifty feet across and dark beyond her. "What did I tell you to do?"

"*Si*, senorita."

"Come on . . ." said Shep, trying to make eye contact with the woman through his haze of pain.

She growled some low word that he didn't think was a compliment, and Hector replied, surprising him. "He might stink up the place, senorita."

She rolled her eyes and waved a hand. "All right, all right, take him off back there where you go. You men are disgusting." She shook her head as if it was something preventable and not one of the most natural things in the world he needed to tend to.

Hector led him around a jut of ledge. Past it, there was even less light, but enough to see that the man had a revolver drawn on him. He prodded Shep in the back with the barrel, and they kept walking along a well-trod trail. Finally he said, "Over there, behind that stone, you'll see. Piss and be done with it."

Shep nodded and walked over. He smelled the spot before he saw it, and a cloud of flies rose up as one creature, then descended again on an open pit that looked to have no drainage. It was a foul, open latrine that looked as if the men merely squatted over it. He nearly gagged at the smell but turned his back on the man and attended to his business.

When he was done, they retraced their route to the clearing in the rocky gorge, and Hector tied his hands and feet at the post. Shep jerked his arms and legs, but Hector pulled his pistol once more and wagged it. Shep decided to wait for a better moment to show his dismay to the heathens.

"I need a drink," he said when he sensed Hector was almost done. The man stood back, hands on his hips, and said, "Oh, so now you're a drinking man, eh?"

That raised another round of half-hearted chuckles from the men.

Shep shook his head. "Water, that's all." He didn't think he could stand another five minutes without water.

"Oh, well, that's different." Hector walked off, and Shep almost sighed with relief when the man walked back with a tin dipper of water he'd filled from a covered half barrel just visible at the edge of an overhang. Deeper in behind it, he saw a glow, and Shep assumed it was a cave.

The man stopped a few feet in front of Shep and held up the dipper, then he smiled and held it to his own mouth and sipped it down. Still smiling, he smacked his lips and dragged a grimy cuff across his greasy moustache.

Shep sneered and wanted to spit on the man as they'd done to him. He trembled with barely suppressed anger, but Hector only smiled and walked away.

When the man lifted the lid of the barrel to hang the dipper on the inside lip once more, a voice from inside the cave spoke. "Give him water," said Tomasina.

Shep felt as grateful as he could be, considering his situation. Hector did as she bade, but as he held it up for Shep to drink, he tipped it fast. Shep suspected he might, so he opened his mouth wide and gulped as fast as he could. He managed to get most of it in and wanted to bite the edge of the dipper as the man pulled it away.

He breathed heavily and licked his lips. The water's flavor was not good, as though rotting meat had been hung in the barrel with the water. Despite this, Shep wanted ten more dippers full of the filthy liquid. The drink only whetted his thirst, and he knew he had to beg for more. Suddenly his desire for another drink was overpowering. "More . . . More water, please."

"No, no, I don't think so. We don't have time to serve you, gringo."

This time the woman in the cave didn't step in and save him. He kept his eyes closed and tried to clear his mind of his powerful need for water, of the throbbing pain of his hands and feet, of the pounding in his head, and of the predicament in which he found himself.

Activity in the camp unfolded about like other camps he'd found himself in, especially as he'd traveled westward. He'd not told Regis, but in an effort to save as much of his money as he could, he had managed to catch rides, early in the trip on stagecoaches, then on wagons, one long train ride, and a few river barges.

The rest of the trip he walked. He'd about worn through his boots by the time he made it to somewhere in Indian territory. Another week of that and he knew he had to either wait a month while his sore feet healed or buy a horse and continue on.

He only considered such a venture because he saw a sign at a trading post in some tiny town that read, "Good horse, hate to sell. $10 or best offer."

He'd looked down at his boots, curled and dried out, and thought, *I could buy that horse, buy a pair of boots, a new pair of socks to go in them, and a meal, and still have enough left over for a used saddle and a sack of provisions for the trail. Heck, I'd even have more left over besides. Why have I been so blamed cheap?* And so that's what he did. And rode the rest of the way to Texas in style, taking his time and working out a story to tell Regis.

That story didn't quite work the way he expected, and in truth he hadn't been so certain he wanted to stick around with Regis after he found out how bossy the man was. But he was his brother, and there was something about that part of things that sat pretty well with him after all. And he'd grown to like Bone, too, even though he could be a moody sort of a morning. Well, every morning.

What were they thinking about now? Bone would still be off trying to hire ranch hands and scout cattle, and Regis, well, Regis would have gotten her note by now and he'd . . . what? He'd be stuck alone at the ranch with a wagon full of supplies and no Bone and no Shep.

Would he bring his own horse with him? He'd said something about that before he'd left to return to town, but Shep hadn't been listening too much. He'd been thinking about playing poker. He had a deck of paste cards, and he thought he might get Bone to teach him a thing or two about the game, after work was done, of course. That hadn't happened much, as they'd both been dog-tired at the end of their days.

But what about Regis? He'd be one peeved older brother. Shep opened his eyes. *Oh no*, he thought. From what he remembered from years before when he'd been a boy and Regis was himself much, much younger, and from what he'd seen in the past couple of weeks, his brother had one heck of a temper when a situation started to go in any direction except the one he wanted.

This was one of those situations, for certain. He'd light out after Shep, and to devil with the letter. Shep bet all the money he'd . . . well, all the money he'd lost back to Regis that he was in for a mighty hard time over the next few days. The only thing he had to do was survive it all.

Darkness draped over the camp before Shep knew it, and still no one paid him any heed, for which he was both grateful and annoyed. He needed to sit down, and slumping against the rope bindings pained him something fierce. He worked to stretch them, in hopes he could squat down and give his legs a rest.

Tomasina walked up, a jug of pulque in her left hand. She swigged from it, passed it to Hector. Shep couldn't help noticing she was wearing a thin white dress that hung raggedly at the bottom, in the front not quite covering her knees. She still wore her boots. And her gun belt. But no hat. Shep hated that he still found her so beautiful.

Beauty, sure, but it's an evil sort of beauty, he told himself. He also couldn't help noticing that from where she stood, the warm honeyed flicker of firelight shone through her thin dress and showed so much more of her than he'd seen before. Even in his thudding-headed gaze he admired this. So did the other men. He also suspected it was intentional on her part. She was a devil in disguise, nothing more.

She jerked her chin at a man seated on a carved half-log bench with his boots outstretched toward the fire. "Paco."

"*Si*, senorita?" He looked up from her legs to her face and smiled a toothy grin.

"It was a rough trip back home, eh?"

He shrugged. "*Si*, maybe."

"I think it could have been easier, you know," she said, cradling one arm by the elbow and tapping her lips with a long finger. "Yes, I think that last bit, taking the rocky trail up and over the rim, perhaps we might have gone the other way, no?"

Again, Paco shrugged. But Shep sensed a tightening in the man's shoulders. What was all this about?

Tomasina walked forward, dropped her hands to her sides, and sighed as if she just couldn't make up her mind. "So much to think about," she said. Then she snapped her finger and pointed at him as if she'd had a great idea. "The good news is that you will have much time to think about such things where you are going, Paco."

He leaned backward, his eyes widening. "G-g-g-going, senorita?"

"*Si, si,*" she said, her bottom lip thrust out. She shrugged also, then faster than Shep had seen her do before, her revolver slipped free of the holster, the hammer peeled back, and the gun purged itself of its foul seed—straight into the center of Paco's head. Smack between his wide, staring eyes a third eye appeared black and glistening in the cooling night.

As the slamming crack of the shot echoed and rolled down and back, through the canyon like a single jolt of thunder, Shep's breath stopped in his throat as if bunged tight with a mallet.

The other men all stiffened and held their seats, eyes as wide as any human's could be. It appeared they, too, weren't breathing.

Hector held the pulque jug halfway to his mouth, his hand trembling slightly, the thonged cork dancing, the only indication the man was alive.

Paco, however, was not so lucky. Eyes still wide and mouth formed into a big O, he slowly rocked backward. It seemed to Shep for a brief moment as if the man might be preparing to rise, but no, he kept slipping backward and flopped on his back in the darkness behind the bench. The other man on the log beside him flinched but didn't look at him, or at the man's legs, his boots dangling stiffly off the ground, propped by the bench.

The left foot jerked inward as if Paco were trying to recall a long-forgotten dance, then that, too, ceased. The man's body sagged then, as if he'd let out a long, long sigh. And Shep supposed he had, somehow, in succumbing to the deepest of sleeps anyone would ever experience.

"Please," said Tomasina, slipping her revolver back into its holster. "If anyone else wishes to talk with me about anything, anything at all. Feel free. I am always listening."

She strolled over to Hector, took the pulque jug from him, and swigged; her eyes settled on Shep, still standing trussed to the pole three yards behind the men and two yards from the sheer rock wall.

"Baby gringo," she said, then smiled and strolled to him. "How are you now? Was that too much for your sensitive gringo eyes and ears?"

He realized after a few moments that she was waiting to hear a response. He shook his head and knew he was staring at her face with a wide-eyed, shocked look on his own. But he could not help it.

He'd never seen anyone murdered before. He'd only ever seen three dead bodies in his life, and one of them had been his mama. Oh, he wondered about her then, wondered what she was thinking, looking down on him from what she had called her "seat of glory," a special spot she'd been certain was waiting for her after death.

"No?" Tomasina said in a soft voice. "That's good, because I could easily . . ." And a long, thin-bladed knife with a stag-horn handle appeared in her right hand. She moved it slowly, blade upright in the night air. It gleamed and firelight sparked off its polished surface. ". . . open up your eyes and ears for you."

Her gaze moved from admiring the serpentine movements of the blade to lock on his eyes. Her soft, placid expression slipped away, and there again was the coldness he'd seen before.

"*Si*, that I could do." She shrugged. "Ah well, perhaps another time." She turned away, then said over her shoulder, "You will let me know, won't you?"

He nodded but saw she wasn't looking at him. "Yes, yes, I will," he said, hating that his voice sounded like that of a mewling child. Hating it, but knowing at that moment that's exactly what he was.

Chapter 16

Regis took stock of his situation. He was alone at this place, a so-called ranch barely more than a patch of scuffed dirt, with a wagonload of supplies; a two-horse team; King, his own riding mount, towed behind; no Bone; no Shepley; and a note that told him both more and less than he wanted to hear. In other words, he had a hatful of headache. And no time at all to deal with it and no idea where to begin.

He was flustered, he recognized that, though it was a foreign sensation to him. And knew he had only himself to rely on to remedy the situation. Didn't mean he didn't wish Cormac, with his level-headed ways, was there to help him sort through this.

The horses perked their ears northwestward while he was unbuckling their harnesses. He noticed and looked in that direction as well. There was something there, little more than a wavery upright shape in the distance, like a pencil mark on wood. But it was advancing. The horses sensed it, and that was good enough for him. He'd learned they were trustworthy beasts where such things were concerned.

He continued stripping off the harnesses, glancing toward the distant form now and again. The form began to take shape, then became two forms, side by side. He paused once more and watched them. Then he recalled his spyglass and fetched it from a saddlebag, which he'd stowed beneath the wagon's seat. He slid apart the leather and brass telescope and worked the focus ring, moving the glass left, right, then there . . . he had them. Two riders. He saw no more behind them.

They were in no hurry, and he didn't think he recognized them. Still, given the note and that this place was largely lawless, despite the fact he had a deed to the land, he opted for safety.

As he pulled his rifle from its sheath beneath the seat, he mused that deeds won't stop bullets but they sure as hell can start them.

He slid his hand over the polished stock, hoped he didn't have to use it, and checked that it was loaded. Then he cocked it and set it so he could slide it out easily. Then he checked his revolver, also loaded, and left the thong off the hammer. At least he'd be as ready as he was able to be.

He resumed work on the harnesses, then led the team, one at a time, to the makeshift corral he'd helped Bone and Shep rig up the last time he was here, nearly two weeks back. He watered and fed the team. He'd expected the new, permanent corral to be further along, but the lack of building progress was the least of his concerns right now.

His own horse had remained tied behind the wagon, where he'd trailed on the slow journey out here. "How are you, boy?" he said, running a hand down the fine animal's broad neck. He'd purchased him before their last trip out here, and he couldn't be happier. He led the horse over to a spot away from the wagon team and watered and fed him.

Where the last horse he'd rented from the livery had been fidgety and flighty, King was solid, seemingly immovable until Regis needed to pick up the pace, then King's power and grace kicked in.

He was a buckskin gelding, and he was eager to move anytime Regis had shown interest in wanting to. He'd taken more

time than he ought, he knew, in working with the horse, but
he'd regretted none of those solitary rides off into the desert
and away from the bustle of town and the docks.

Too many people and too few brains, that was how he summed
up the place. Still, it was the nexus of his business dealings, and
he needed the money to bankroll his ranching venture.

The riders were at a distance where he could make out they
were white. One was wearing a tall hat, fawn with sweat on the
brim. His face was wide and red with what looked like a ginger
beard. The other was thinner and appeared to be wearing spectacles. He was taller, rode such in the saddle anyway, and his
shirt was white enough to contrast well with the first man's
brown shirt. Both men, it appeared, carried gear with them,
though neither was overly laden.

When they were within shouting distance, they slowed and
the red-faced man held up a hand in greeting. "Ho there! We
welcome?"

Regis eyed them a moment longer, then said, "Depends who
you are!"

There was a pause, and the two men looked at each other.

Regis motioned to them. "Come on ahead. Arms where I can
see them."

They looked at each other once more, then did as he bade
them. Up close they were as he'd seen, though with defined
features. Young men both. The first man, with the ginger
whiskers, had a kindly round face, leaning toward fat, and he
smiled and nodded. The second man, while not smiling, was
not possessed of a desperado's wolfish look.

"You Shepley?" said the tall man. "Shepley Royle?"

Regis eyed them but said nothing for a moment. "Why do
you ask?"

"Well, Bone McGraw sent us, said to tell you, or Shepley,
that is, that he hired us on and that he'd be back in not longer
than two, three days."

The smiley man grinned. "He also said to stop lallygagging and get that corral finished."

When Regis didn't smile, their twin grins faded.

"Look," said the thin man. "If we come to the wrong place, you just let us know and we'll ride on. We're not looking for troubles."

Regis breathed out. "No, you came to the right place. But I'm not Shepley. If Bone sent you, then that's good enough for me. I'm Shep's brother, Regis. Regis Royle. Step down. I reckon you work for me now. And I have need of help."

He saw recognition, at least of his name, on their faces.

They swung down out of their saddles and held the reins while they each offered a handshake.

The ginger-haired man said, "I'm John Tuttle, though my friends call me Tut."

"And I'm Percy Grimlaw. Folks call me Percy."

"Good to meet you, Tut." They shook hands. "And Percy."

As Regis explained the situation to them, he kept an eye on their features, their actions. Nether man looked particularly worried or inclined to skedaddle. That was good. He didn't need weak-kneed help. He needed men.

"Can either of you shoot?"

"I'm a fair hand with a gun, long or pistol," said Tut.

"I'm less than fair, but I'm game," said Percy.

"Good," said Regis. "Now tell me what Bone said, everything he said. I need to piece together what happened here."

Percy nodded. "We were drifting east when we crossed his path late yesterday. I'd not met him, but he knew Tut here."

"That's right," said the chubby man. "Few years back we worked for Mack Deemworth at about the same time."

"We shared a fire and a camp with him last night. Told us about a deer he saved from a mesquite snag."

"What?" said Regis. He was starting to lose his patience. None of this sounded useful at all.

"Oh, I reckon that part's not important," said Percy.

Tut shrugged. "Anyway, Bone asked us if we were looking for work and explained your new ranch here to us. We're pards, been riding together for, oh, two years or so now, and we decided to leave Mack's employ and look elsewhere before the rest of the men thereabouts got the same notion. It's the drought, you see. Hard on the ranches thataways. Orliss Pushaw's and such."

He shrugged again. "Mack, he's folding up and there was too many of us left, anyway. Felt bad about eating his vittles and there not being enough work to justify two meals a day. Anyway, Bone said he could pay us a decent wage, but the work'd be hard at the start. We aren't afraid of hard work, are we, Percy?"

Percy shook his head.

"What else?" said Regis. "What did he say about my brother?"

Tut's eyes widened. "Oh, well, Bone told us to ride on in here and give Shepley, that'd be your brother, a hand with the corral. Said you might be here, too. Though he said he couldn't be sure, something about you delivering supplies and then staying or leaving again, he didn't know. Anyway, by then he said he'd be back from Mack's and Pushaw's with more men. We told him he shouldn't have trouble hiring some. He seemed anxious to get back here. We offered to go with him to Mack's, but he wanted us to get here. Said he felt bad enough about leaving Shepley even for a few hours alone until you were due to arrive with supplies from Brownsville."

"Well, I did arrive, nearly a day late, but Shep wasn't here, as I said. Only this note to go on." Regis wagged the sheet, then folded it and stuffed it in his shirt pocket. "Bone said he'd be back in two, three days?"

The men nodded.

"Well, I can't wait that long. I don't suppose either of you can track?"

Tut nodded. "I spent time in the Shining Mountains, worked for a spell for the Boston Fur Company. But the beavers were all trapped out. I drifted south, started ranching. So yeah, I can track some." He shrugged.

Regis decided he'd overlook the annoying habit, especially if the man could help him trace the trail.

"Percy, I'll leave you here to work on the corral. Unload what needs unloading from that wagon. The rest leave covered under the tarpaulin. If we're not back by the time Bone arrives, you fill him in. Tell him everything and take note of whichever direction me and Tut ride off in. Got that?"

Percy nodded fast, eyebrows raised. "Yes, boss. You bet."

"Okay, pack us a couple of grub sacks and feed for the horses. Tut, your mount fit for more trail work?"

He shrugged. "Been better."

"Mine's fresher," said Percy. "Not lugging Tut around, I reckon."

Instead of taking offense to the remark, Tut merely nodded as if it were sage wisdom.

"Okay then, Percy, swap horses. I want to be ready to ride in ten minutes. Tut, you come with me and help me sort out these bootprints. I think they lead down to the river, but I didn't want to sully them until I knew what I was doing. Your showing up could be good."

The chunky man nodded and bent low, forearms resting on his knees as he studied the tracks all about the barnyard. Finally he stood and scratched his curly red beard. "I count four, maybe five men. One of them might be your brother. He have a split sole on his left boot?"

Regis sighed, angry with himself all over again. "Yeah, yeah, I think so."

"Well, that's useful to us. Them tracks there?" He pointed a thick callused finger at the dirt. "You see they're narrow? That's the woman, likely."

Tut dogged them down the trail to the river, nodding to himself and mumbling, then shaking his head and backing up a step or two. Finally, he made it all the way to the river bank, where the prints were ample in the softer, damp dirt. He circled them, assessing them narrow-eyed from all angles.

Regis stood on the riverbank, visoring his eyes and looking up and down, craning his neck in all directions, not daring to walk too much for fear of mussing the prints. He also hoped against hope he'd not see anything that looked like a drowned body snagged along the banks.

Tut kept at his tracking for a couple of minutes more. Finally, Regis said, "Got anything?"

"Yep, more of the same. But them three, four other men besides your brother? Their tracks only lead up from the water."

"Which tells us what? They got here but by another route?"

"I think so, I think so. . . ."

Finally Tut stood upright and stretched his back. "They all went back up to the camp from here."

"Then let's get up there and make sure we know which way they rode. I'll show you where I think they all went."

"Okay, but boss?"

"Yeah," said Regis, already striding back toward camp.

"You said that woman told you not to follow or, well, you know, she'd hurt your brother."

Regis nodded. "Tut, let me worry about that."

Tut watched the big man walk up the trail ahead of him, regretting having said yes to Bone just the night before. This was a mess he hadn't counted on.

When he got a moment, he was going to give Percy what for. He blamed him for landing them in this kettle of soup. Didn't matter if he knew Bone and Percy didn't. He felt like blaming Percy, and that was that. He bit that thought back. He was feel-

ing grousy and knew Percy wasn't to blame any more than the
kid was for getting lugged off by brigands.

It didn't take but two minutes for Tut to confirm that Regis
was correct. They'd ridden southeastward, at least at the start.
Tut guessed they were headed to Mexico. He'd been down that
way once, but that had been up west along the Texas border,
nearer some mountains. Pretty country as he recalled, but that
had been the extent of his experience south of the border.

As they were getting ready to mount up, Percy shook Tut's
hand. "Don't get shot up, pard." Then he looked at Regis, who
was not paying much attention, already saddled and obviously
itching to get on the trail. "Both of you, that is."

"You bet," said Regis. To Tut he said, "You ready?"

Tut mounted up on Percy's roan. "I'll bring him back safe,
don't you worry."

Percy nodded and watched the two men ride away, each
laden with canteens and canvas sacks filled with food and horse
feed from items he'd hastily tugged free from the pile of goods
and gear piled on the wagon. There was enough on the wagon,
thought Percy, to outfit a . . . well. A ranch. Or a small army.

If this was the wondrous operation that Bone had told them
about, he wasn't so sure he could trust Tut's old friend Bone
McGraw, or this new one, Regis Royle. He might be a wealthy
ship owner, as Bone had said, and he might own this here ranch,
but that doesn't mean he's not a surly so-and-so. Still, his brother'd just been stolen. Can't rightly expect a man to behave all
giddy about that.

Percy sighed as he unpacked what he felt he should from the
wagon, outfitted the sleeping shanty with fresh gear, and set to
work adding onto it. By nightfall, he hoped to have doubled the
size of it, for sleeping and for storage. He'd use some of the corral poles, then make more from those trees down along the
river.

It looked like he'd have at least a couple of days on his own, which suited him fine. Unless Boss Royle and Tut came back early. They'd either get shot up, get the boy alive, or get him killed, thanks to his big brother's hastiness and hotheadedness. Or they'd be successful and ride hell-bent back home. Chased by bandits. What a fix we got ourselves in.

"Home, sure," said Percy, looking around him as he set to work on the lean-to addition.

Chapter 17

Shepley Royle groaned and jerked his aching head. Where was he? Oh yeah, the cave—a dry, dust-stinking place populated with beasts that crawl and slide and see in the dark. He'd been dragged in there late in the morning of his first full day held by Tomasina Valdez.

At the memory of the witch, he looked to his left to the entrance of the cave. He saw a faint flicker of dancing light, firelight, on the rough tumble of rock that formed the cave's sides and roof. It must be nighttime, for it would be lighter there, even with the flames' glow.

He sensed no one else about. Still, he said, "Hello?" No response.

But he seemed to recall there had been someone else, someone different in the night. He shook his head and stopped it, too much pain behind his eyes. Still, at least he was in the dark, away from the sunlight. He reasoned she had him dragged in here in case his brother showed up to rescue him. Or maybe she was going to leave him to be feasted on by rats or snakes or whatever else lived in here.

Shep closed his eyes again and felt a faint tickle of coolness, of breeze, on the right side of his head, his sore, aching head. A breeze? He sniffed as he opened his eyes once more and looked to his right. As he shifted, he heard the slide of metal on rock.

Yes, that's right, he remembered now. He was manacled, his ankles and wrists were bound. But for the moment he didn't care, for he felt the mysterious coolness once more. He squinted, thought perhaps he could see some bit of light in that direction as well. It could as easily be a trick of shadow, some deception in the dark. But the breeze, that was no trick. He definitely sensed fresh air.

Maybe there was a way out in that direction. He tried to get his legs beneath him, at least one, to give him leverage to stand. He leaned against the rock and shoved upward, but he was stopped short by the rattle of chains once more.

He felt along the taut links to a cold steel ring pounded into a crevice in the rock. What sort of woman was this? To keep him chained like a beast? In rage he tugged on the chain, his breath clenched behind tight-set teeth, but it would not budge. His breath came out in a burst and he sagged to the floor, exhausted from the effort.

In an effort to take his mind from his burning thirst, Shep's thoughts turned once more to the dream he'd been having, something about a woman wearing a cloak or a veil of some sort. What was she? A vision of his mother come to help him? Did that mean his mind was slipping from him, that he was about to die here in the dark? Alone? After all that travel to find Regis, only to die in a rocky cave somewhere in Texas or Mexico—he didn't really know where he was.

Did it matter? And all for what? Land? Greed? Money? What did the woman want with the land, anyway? As far as Shep could tell, most of it was a wasteland with more death than life in it.

And why did Regis want it, really want it? Money? Power? Why was he so bent on building up what he kept calling the biggest, most powerful ranch anyone had ever witnessed? *Why?* thought Shep. Didn't he care if people died in the building of it?

With that thought settling over his mind like a dusty bed sheet, Shepley Royle drifted from wakefulness back into a fitful doze brought on by exhaustion, lack of water, and too many spiteful beatings.

From the darkest reaches of the cave, a soft scuffing sound drew closer.

Chapter 18

Tut had never been one to complain. He was of hearty English stock, or so he'd been told by his Auntie Jemma back in Ohio, but he'd never much cared one way or another. He was just glad to be alive. So far he'd managed to avoid serious scrapes and dustups, unlike many of his fellow ranch hands, who were forever dragging back to the ranch after a spree in town with bruised faces and empty coin purses.

They never wanted much in the way of breakfast the next morning, so Tut was only too happy to help Cookie clean up the platters in exchange for a few extra bites of ham or beefsteak or a couple of biscuits to tide him over until the noon meal came around.

He liked to eat and didn't care much if it showed. His Auntie Jemma always told him it was just "baby fat" and he'd outgrow it one day. Again, fine with him if he did, fine with him if he didn't.

All this and more bubbled through Tut's mind as he rode either point or side by side with his newest employer, a strange man caught in a strange situation. Or maybe it was just the situation that had made Regis Royle an odd duck.

Tut reckoned he'd feel much the same if his brother had been snatched and held for ransom. Then again, he didn't really know, now, did he? He'd never had a brother, a sister, or anyone, save for Auntie Jemma. Then she up and died when he was sixteen. By then Tut was all but grown anyway, so he sold off what little they had, bought a horse, and rode west from Ohio, where he'd spent his life to that point.

He was generally affable, couldn't help being so, and didn't mind tucking into a task that others found distasteful. He also didn't mind hopping down off his mount when something needed doing about a ranch. Most of his pards on the ranch crews would do about anything to avoid climbing out of the saddle. There was one fellow he'd never even seen climb down to water a tree!

He'd been at this cowboying business for nigh on to six years, and he liked it just fine. But this situation with Bone and the Royles, something about it felt odd. He couldn't put his thumb on it yet, but it felt like danger was closer than he wanted it to be. Trouble was, how do you tell that to your boss, who obviously has a whole lot more on his mind than your concerns?

Twice he'd opened his mouth to commence a conversation with Regis Royle, ease into the topic, but both times he closed it again. He gave it a third go, and Royle looked at him.

"What is it, Tut? You've been cogitating on something for some time now. Must be important to you."

That caught him by surprise. "Well, yes, boss, matter of fact, it is. It's this woman who wrote that note, you see."

"Mmm, thought it might be something like that."

Tut nodded. "It's . . . well, it's no good, is it? I mean, she's laid out her end of the situation, and I wonder if she really is expecting us to respond as we are, or do you think she believes you'll comply with her demand?"

Regis half smiled for the first time since Tut had met him. Made the older man look ten years younger than what Tut guessed was Royle's mid- or maybe late twenties.

"What you mean is, is she expecting me to be honest?"

"Oh, I didn't mean it that way, boss. . . ."

"Don't worry about it. I know what you meant." The boss sighed. "I'll be honest with you, Tut, I have a tendency to go off half-cocked sometimes. This is my brother, and that should be enough. But it's more than that. A man has to live by certain rules, I guess you'd call them. Points he needs to live by if he's to be the man he knows he should be. That make sense to you?"

Tut nodded. "I think so, yep."

"Good. I'm a businessman. Wasn't always that way, but I think I've become pretty good at what I do. Me and my partner, Cormac Delany, we own a fleet of steamers and barges on the coast and up the Rio Grande. Don't owe a thing and we employ a pile of men. And since I don't hear much in the way of complaints from them, I reckon they're pleased with the pay they receive. One of the things I've promised myself I'd never do, and I never have, is give in to people who think they can best me by being deceitful."

"And she falls smack on that point," said Tut.

"You bet she does. But business is one thing and a brother's life is something entirely different. That's why I've made up my mind to go on ahead and find them and get him free, come what may. I figure I know the way by now. So come morning, I'll thank you for your time and you'll be heading back to the ranch to help Percy. I reckon he can use some help setting those corral poles."

Tut's eyebrows rose. "I don't doubt you're right where Percy's concerned. He's a solid cowboy, but he's not what you'd call a workhorse where digging post holes is concerned. But come morning, if it's all the same to you, I'll ride along with you. I can shoot, as I said, and you'll need an extra set of eyes."

They rode in silence a few moments more, the day's gloaming light descending.

"I appreciate that, Tut. But we'll see, come morning. Right now, I figure we should make camp while we still have rock to hunker behind. I could use something hot to drink."

"And maybe something to eat?"

Regis smiled. "You bet."

Chapter 19

It was no shadows and sizzling as Bone rode up to Mack Deemworth's gate. He'd passed through that front gate a number of times in the past, back when he worked for the man as one of the ranch's regular hands. The spread wasn't sizable and the pay was low, but Mack's wife, Martha, was one heck of a cook. A man could get fat and happy, and stay poor but happy, working for Mack and Martha Deemworth. Bone reckoned there were worse things to do and worse places to be. And he'd done a few and been to a few over the years.

But there'd come a time when Bone felt a stirring, an itch that needed scratching, and the only thing he knew that would do it was to move on. He'd gotten to that point several times over the years and it was difficult, as he made friends easily. Though on a couple of occasions, where the rancher wasn't as welcoming as was Mack, Bone was only too glad to see his last payday and get gone.

One had been Rastus Schoenbarger's spread over Poke country way. Man had been little more than a slave master and all but tugged out a whip to lay on his cowboys' backs. He was a transplanted, scrimy Yankee from what he called "pure New England stock."

All that meant to Bone was that Rastus was ignorant of history—the only pure New Englanders were the tribes who'd lived there, as far as Bone was aware, for thousands of years. Mostly, though, Schoenbarger was bone-mean and a cheat. While Bone never had come to blows with an employer, Rastus Schoenbarger had nearly been the first to earn that distinction.

The opposite was Martha and Mack Deemworth. And even though he'd not worked there in several years, he'd enjoyed the pleasure of their company and had stopped a number of times since, usually while riding through on other business.

If he knew his travels might take him their way, he always made certain he had a brick of Mack's favorite applewood tobacco and a skein of yarn or a square of pretty cloth for Martha, by way of thanking them for the fine meal he knew he would not be allowed to refuse.

Mack had seemed to genuinely like him, too, and had even hinted one night over too many sips from the jug that were he to one day sell up, he hoped he could find someone a whole lot like Bone to sell to.

No more had been said of that thing hinted at, and the next day, as Bone saddled up to ride out—he'd been a working Ranger at the time—Mack didn't mention having said it. But it had planted a seed in Bone's mind. Over time that seed had grown into a robust little tree, threatening to choke out other vague ambitions Bone had for himself.

"Curse you, Mack," Bone said with a chuckle as he rode through the gates once more.

This time, he noticed that they sagged on their hinges. Just as Tut and Percy had warned him, Mack had let the place begin a slow drift to ruin once Martha died.

Bone had not known she was gone, but it pained him to learn of it. Not for her but for Mack, who was left behind to suffer the pangs of such a grievous loss. For that reason and a few others, Bone always told himself it was safer to dally with married women and professional ladies. Neither group seemed to want what little he had to offer, save for in the short term.

Twenty minutes later, after following the long, straight lane in, Bone caught sight of the ranch house, stable, and other buildings. He rode up and paused in the midst of it, before the bunkhouse with its dogtrot kitchen that led to the cookshack. To the left sat the stable, where out front dozed the once-tidy corral, now a wide wobbly circle of leaning posts and knocked-loose rails.

It took a whole lot to shock Bone at this point in his life. He'd seen and done things other men daren't even consider, but eyeing the run-down state of affairs of the Deemworth place left a cold knot of sadness nesting in his lean belly.

A dull clunking drew his sight toward the low log, stone, and mud house. It had always been a tidy structure with flowers of some sort when Martha could coax them to grow, which as he recalled had been a goodly portion of the time. How she did it, Bone never knew. She'd been something, a lifemate who would keep a man humble and proud.

The clunking came from the darkness of the house's half-open door. Then a shotgun barrel poked out like the sniffer of an old hound dog testing the air. It was followed by a small old man, hunched and craning his head forward like a mud turtle. He stepped onto the porch, *clunk clunk clunk*, and stopped.

Bone rode forward slowly.

The shotgun raised up. "Hold, I say!"

The voice was wavery, thin.

Bone held up a hand as if waving. "Ho there, Mack! Good to see you. It's—"

"Voice sounds familiar, but I don't know . . . I just don't know." The old man squinted back at him and leaned forward, ranging his head side to side, trying to figure out who or what had just addressed him.

"What's not to know, Mack. It's me, Bone McGraw!"

That did the trick. The old man's face softened and a few of the wrinkles creasing his eyes traded places with those pushed up by his smile, half-hidden behind unkempt moustache and a

settled over the old man. "And in as big a way as this country has ever seen. You wouldn't believe the plans we've been bandying back and forth. I'd say Regis is one of those rare birds who makes a go of whatever he turns his hand to."

"Plans," said Mack, looking past Bone into the distance. "Yeah, me and Martha, we had plenty of them. That was years back, when we come to this place. It ain't a big spread by your reckoning, but it kept us and we were able to feed hands year-round, couple at least, plus when things hotted up in the year with calving and whatnot, we was able to bring on the drifting cowboys such as yourself."

Bone nodded. "Yes sir, and I speak for them all when I say it was a pure pleasure to work for you and Martha."

That seemed to pull the old man from his reverie. He looked at the Ranger. "Why, thank you, Bone. Means a lot to hear the old days are recalled by others as I remember them. If I was to sell you what's left—mind you it ain't worth the spit it takes to talk about it all. . . ."

"Aw, Mack, that ain't true."

The old man held up a hand. "Don't sugarcoat it for me, boy. I've let this place go. Don't know why anyone'd want it. But if they did . . ." Mack ran his tongue tip over his teeth, closed one eye, and cocked his head to the side.

Now there's the Mack I remember, thought Bone.

"If they did, why, I reckon as long as they'd let an old man stay on, sort of oversee the place, and promise not to uproot my Martha's grave, then plant me beside her when my time came, why, I reckon a deal could be struck that the buyer would find most pleasing. If you get my meaning, son."

Bone nodded slowly. He didn't want Mack to think he was too eager, and most of all it made him feel downright spooked to hear his old friend and former boss talking like this. This was not the robust, barrel-chested, burly rancher he knew from years before.

"That would be the case, Mack. You can take my word for it. We'll shake on it now. Percy and Tut mentioned I might be able to hire on some men from over at the Pushaw place. If so, I'll have them drive the stock back to the Royle with us, and those critters'd be out of your hair. Leave you with a wagon and a team, naturally. But I don't mind saying so, you got me worried, Mack. Can't leave you alone out here."

"Oh, I won't be alone, Bone. Naw, naw, I got me a young Negro woman and her son who are coming out from town, due to arrive, oh, let's see, day after tomorrow. Friday, isn't it?"

Bone nodded.

"Yeah, they're going to take up living in the bunkhouse and she's going to do the housekeeping and cooking, tend the chickens and goats, that sort of thing. Woman said the boy's handy, so might be me and him will work on the buildings some." He looked around, his hands in his pockets, and said, "I am afraid I let them go for too long."

The entire time he told Bone about the help he would soon have, he never once looked him in the eye.

But Bone didn't know how to pry any further to get at whatever truth lay hidden beneath the words without hurting the one thing ol' Mack seemed to still have—a crust of manly pride. Even if it was brittle-thin.

Bone stuck out his hand again. "That's good to hear, Mack. Real good." But something didn't sit right with Bone. He'd have to think on it.

"You'll be staying the night, won't you, Bone?"

In truth, he'd not planned on it. He felt an urgency to get his new hires and stock back to the Royle Ranch. But the old man looked at him with wet, rheumy eyes and, other than a crotchety old dog and the chickens and mules, it looked like Mack was indeed alone in the world.

"Of course. I didn't want to invite myself."

"Invite. . . . Why, my word, Bone, when did I give you cause to take such fancified precautions with me? Course you'll stay. We're going to have . . ." He combed his beard with his grubby fingertips, then smiled. "Gonna have chicken and dumplings, that's what we'll have."

Bone knew the old man was fixing to kill one of his stringy old laying hens, and the thought of that didn't sit well with him for a few reasons. He pretended to consider it a moment, then snapped a finger. "I've a thought. What say you let me pop a couple of rabbits? I noticed you have a pile of them running loose, and they're the last thing you need—be bringing in the coyotes."

"Well, if you'd prefer, then sure, that'd work just fine. You are my guest, after all. Martha always said to do what your guests want."

"She should know. Never was a finer cook nor a kinder woman."

The old man's lip quivered again, then he ran his hand under his dripping nose and nodded. "Okay then, you fetch back a brace of rabbits and I'll tend to the cookstove." He walked toward the house, then turned around. "I ain't got a drop on the place, Bone. Else I'd offer you a drink. Old times and all."

"We'll have that drink, Mack. I never go anywhere without a bottle in my bags."

Mack smiled wide and smacked his hands together. "Hoo-ee! Hurry up with them rabbits, boy, I'm feeling peckish."

By the time Bone left his old friend the next morning, he was feeling a whole lot better about the state of things at the Deemworth spread than when he'd ridden in the previous afternoon. Certain that Mack's spirits were buoyed by his unexpected visit, Bone had promised to stop in and say howdy once more on his way back to the Royle Ranch. And with any luck he'd have a few former Pushaw hands with him to help ferry some of the remaining critters southward.

And that's how he'd left it as he rode toward Orliss Pushaw's spread.

Orliss Pushaw nodded. "Yeah. Mack's a good man. Be a shame to see that place get any worse."

"Well, that's the thing," said Bone. "I made a deal with him to buy it. He'll stay on, oversee it, and he won't ever have to leave. Besides, he told me a Negro woman and her boy will be along in a day or so from town to help him out. Said the kid was of an age to help spiff up the place."

Orliss's drawn brow made Bone stop. "What do you know?"

"Just that to my knowledge there's no blacks in town. Far as I know, other than Percy and Tut, Mack's been alone there since Martha passed on."

"What are you saying, Orliss?"

"I'm saying I think the old man is alone as alone can be. Likely made that business up about the woman and the boy so he wouldn't worry you. Heck, I'd say he fed the same line to Percy and Tut so they wouldn't feel guilty about leaving."

Orliss leaned close. "Between you and me, I'd be surprised if he's around much longer. Likely you caught him by surprise."

"What's that mean?"

The rancher shrugged. "Could be nothing. But every time I've seen Mack in the past few months since Martha died—I try to drop in on him when I can—he's looked worse and worse and makes noises about going to see her. Got to be so anyone who was riding through would drift over and check on him. So far, so good." He shrugged again. "He's a proud old dog, though. Won't take much help of any kind."

"Yeah," said Bone, poking his hat back. "Percy and Tut said he just about run them off the place instead of admit he couldn't pay them."

"They're good men for sticking as long as they could. Even better for telling you."

"You don't think he'd . . ."

Orliss nodded. "Matter of fact, I do," he said. "Then again, you know him pretty well yourself."

"I have to go, Orliss." Bone swung up into the saddle. "I'd be obliged if you'd send those men and beasts along to the Royle. I'll get the money to you within a week or so. If that works for you."

"I will. And I'm not worried, Bone. Do what you need to. I'll be seeing you. Good luck with Mack!"

Bone snapped off a solid salute, but he was already barreling toward the trail he'd ridden in on.

Chapter 20

"Bound to be a whole mess of them, huh?" said Tut, licking his lips.

Regis looked over at the pudgy young man. "Still time for you to bow out, Tut. You don't owe me a thing, nor I you. I won't think less of you. I know this is a foolhardy thing I'm about to do, and I'd feel better if you weren't part of it."

"Nothing doing," said Tut. "I say I'm going to do a thing and I do it. I'm here. Let's do what needs doing and get on out of here. This place isn't right. All these rocks—nothing good lives in rocks."

Regis nodded, said nothing. Then he saw movement and a brief flare of orange light as if balanced in the middle of the air, maybe sixty, eighty feet south of them but higher up. He held a long finger over his lips and nodded toward the spot.

The light was gone. It had been a match, and a soft but steady breeze carried the trace of a whiff of pungent tobacco to them. Smelled to him as if someone was huffing on a ripe dog turd.

Regis slid back down and turned over against the rock. It felt good on his back, still offering the stored warmth of the long day's baking sun. He jerked his head, beckoning Tut to move closer. Regis leaned in. "At the ranch, how many besides my brother did you say you thought there were?"

Tut thought back a moment. "Four, I believe, besides the woman. Give or take a couple." He shrugged. "Best I can offer."

"Okay."

That match light meant they knew where one was. Would they have more than one on sentry duty? Likely. He would if he were in charge of a camp such as this. Unless it was so tightly bottled there wasn't much need for more than one. But a shot would alert the lot of them and set the nest to buzzing.

From there, it might not take much to convince Tomasina to kill Shepley. She was as unpredictable and crazy in the head as she was pretty to look at, and that was saying something.

"Look," he whispered to Tut. "We get in there, and you see this woman, she's liable to bewitch you, in a manner of speaking."

Tut moved his head back. "What's that mean?"

"She's pretty as a painting, but she's not right in the head. She'll twist your thinking and you'll be afraid to kill her. Don't be. She needs to be put down, like a dog with hydrophoby. You got me?"

Tut nodded. This was fast turning into something he never expected to be part of. How much of life working for Regis Royle would be like this?

As it turned out, Regis needn't have worried so much about reducing the number of Tomasina's men without sound. As full darkness draped its inky cloak over the bony place, the two men hunkered low. Tut waited for Regis to tell him what they were going to do.

Regis had only a half-formed idea and, not like his usual self, he wasn't filled with certainty about his next move. It galled him. Then they heard bootsteps, one man, then another, crunching on gravel, carrying whispers with them.

They were approaching Tut and Regis's hiding spot, walking not with purpose but not slowly, either. Their steps sounded sloppy, irregular, and one of the men giggled. The other shushed him but giggled too. Regis suspected they were drunk.

Their words were now more than sounds; they were speaking Spanish. He'd not asked Tut if he could speak the language, but it hardly mattered now. He looked at the younger man, barely visible a foot from him, then nodded and pointed his thumb at his own chest. He hoped the kid understood to hang back, that he'd take the lead. Regis didn't need Tut getting hurt. He was game, but he was an oddly innocent kid, and a good-hearted one, too.

The footsteps drew closer, walking the path he and Tut had followed earlier. The two men were nearly upon them, and Regis still didn't have a clear plan. *In for a penny*, he thought, recalling an old maxim his mother used to say when tackling a chore she wasn't particularly excited about.

He could just see them in the gloom, two men walking, nearly staggering, side by side. He let them pass and in one smooth movement got to his feet, leaving his rifle on the rock beside Tut.

Regis spread his broad arms wide and brought them together before him as fast and as hard as he could, as if to hug the men from behind. The only difference was the hug he had in mind for them was anything but friendly.

His forearms caught each man on the sides of their heads, and as they were jostled their shoulders whipped by each other. Their heads smacked hard together like colliding melons. They made no sound as they flopped to the ground.

Once they hit, one of them groaned louder than Regis would have liked, but he reckoned he would do the same if his head smacked on jagged rock.

As they dropped, so did he, bending at the knee, his arms still out before him as if escorting them to the ground. He held the pose, squatting, his hands out as if testing flame, but the two dark lumps before him on the ground didn't move.

"Tut!" whispered Regis.

"Yeah?"

"Help me drag them off."

"Yep."

Regis felt the tops of the bodies, but nobody moved. He rummaged on the flopped men for weapons. Gun belts would weigh them down, but he could stash them, should they be lucky enough to beat a retreat back this way.

Tut came up beside him, also patting the air. "Remind me not to tick you off, boss. That was something."

Regis said nothing but smirked in the dark. In truth, he was surprised it worked as slick as it had. Trouble was, they were only knocked cold. As riled as these devils made him, there was a part of him that wanted to give them a wide, deep throat smile, but it felt too much like murder.

Again, dogged by the foreign feeling of indecision, Regis uttered a low growl deep in his throat and jerked at one man's shirt, freeing the front. He slid out his knife, the blade offering a flash in the emerging moonlight.

"What are you gonna do?" asked Tut in a tight voice.

"Not what I want to." Regis slashed a generous wad of cloth from the man's own foul, sweat-stinking shirt and stuffed it in the drunk's mouth. He felt at the man's throat and found a knotted kerchief. He jerked it upward and cinched it tight about the man's face, holding the cloth gag in place.

"Do the same to him," he said to Tut.

The kid nodded and fumbled with the man's shirt. Regis shoved him out of the way. "Tie the first one, hands behind his back—feet, too—then connect the hands and feet. Use his own shirt, vest, trousers. I don't care. Just go at it fast."

It took a few minutes, but they worked steadily, glancing about, knowing this was likely a primary travel route for the band of desperadoes. *How many more are there?* thought Regis. If what the kid said was true, and the tracks at the ranch bore it out, taking these two out of play put a dent in their number. But if there were lots more of them loitering here at their camp, their effort might be a paltry one.

Regis knew they had many hours before them, hours in

which they had to try to sneak up on as many individuals as they could. These two had been a gift. The rest would not be so easy.

A shout from up the path, from the direction the two men had come, paused them in their work. He'd wanted to get them off the trail, but it sounded as if someone was looking for them. The shout came again, a few steps closer.

"Julio? Marco?"

Now they heard gravel underfoot, the man sounding as if he were getting steamed about not hearing from the two men he sought. Regis pointed at Tut, then pointed across the path, to the west side. He stayed put, partly concealed behind a boulder trailside. He saw Tut do the same, though with less to hide behind.

Their two victims still lay partly on the trail, one of them still half-untied. He glanced up the trail and saw a bobbing orange glow lighting the flat planes of rock before winking out again as the lantern the man carried swung behind rock. He would be on them in seconds. "Marco! Julio!"

From far below, down in the cavernous rocky space they'd barely seen before daylight lost its battle with night, a woman's voice growled, "One more shout and I kill you, bastard!"

The voice was hers, Tomasina Valdez, and it was closer than Regis thought. He bit back the urge to bolt down the rocky slope and gut her right there. All it would do is get himself killed. Tut, too, and likely Shep. He ground his teeth tight and waited to see what the lamp-carrying man was going to do.

Her words had halted the seeking man's progress. Regis half hoped they would have bothered him enough to turn him around, but the man continued toward them, slower and without making a sound, save for the clunk and scrape of his boots on rock.

Regis was set to dish out more of the same rough techniques on this newcomer, but the man's lantern stopped moving toward them. The glow lit the boots of one of the felled men, and the lantern man halted. He bent low, holding the lantern higher than his head, peering forward.

"Julio?" he whispered. "Marco?"

That was all the time they'd be given. Trouble was, Regis was still a good ten feet uptrail from the man. Any second now he was going to trumpet his alarm with a shout. And this time he knew they'd be found out. Unless . . . and that's when he saw a round shape barreling from out of the dark across the trail.

Somehow Tut had angled himself closer to the man, maybe in an effort to find a bigger rock to hide behind. He would have been seen soon, since he was more exposed than Regis, so the kid went with it and lunged. He barely made a sound, then Regis heard a loud "Oof!" and the light swung wild. Metal clanked on rock, and the glass globe rattled but didn't shatter.

Regis was nearly to them. In the swinging light he saw Tut snatching for the lantern while his other hand clubbed the kneeling man in the head with the butt of his revolver. But the man was wily. Though he'd been struck once, from the way he was wobbling, he wasn't yet out.

Then he shouted, "Hey, ha! Oh!" as he dodged Tut's driving blows. They struck the man's shoulders and neck with sledge-like force. The man spent too much effort trying to shout and the rest of his effort trying to maintain his clawhold on the swinging lantern, as if he were trying to use it as a weapon.

Regis grabbed the man's arm and held the bail of the lantern with one hand while trying to pry the man's fingers with the other. His grip was solid, so without much thought, Regis bit the man's wrist. Good and bad resulted from the rash act. Good in that he let go of the lantern, but the bite forced out the rascal's loudest shriek yet. Tut snubbed it off with a vicious blow to the kneeling man's temple.

Regis steadied the lantern as shouts bubbled up from below. Spanish again. There was a pause, and Regis held up the lantern and said, "*Si! Si!*" He looked at Tut and shrugged.

Tut shook his head and rolled the clubbed man off the trail. That was all the time they had, because the ball opened then with a rifle shot lobbed in their rough direction. It pinged off a boulder above them and then hit another. Regis flinched. Last thing he wanted was to be laid low by a ricochet bullet.

Regis shouted, "No, no, no!" in some minor hopes that the shooter might be placated, convinced somehow that he or she was shooting at their chums. Thin chance of that, he thought. But a second shot did not follow.

He grabbed one of the trussed men and dragged him fast off the narrow, boulder-lined trail. Tut followed with the second. Regis snatched up the men's gun belts and jammed one at Tut's belly. "Follow me, stay low."

He snatched up the lantern once more and cat-footed low up the trail toward where the men had come from. No turning back now. Tut had insisted he wanted in on this mess, and Regis had given him ample opportunities to back out, yet he hadn't. So that was that.

The lantern light, he hoped, would make whoever was down below think that the clubbed fellow was on his way back down. Shouts from below, how many voices, he didn't know. More than a couple, maybe five, six? One of them, the shrillest, was the woman. She sounded worked up, likely steamed with her men, for they quieted. Then she shouted, a long sentence, something in Spanish.

Regis paused and glanced at Tut, but from the kid's shrug, he didn't know any more of the lingo than Regis did. He saw a belled-out space to the right side of the trail ahead, a dozen feet or so, before it appeared to begin winding downward and to the left. He nodded and Tut made for it.

Regis left the lantern where he stood, tucked behind a jag of ledge, and joined Tut in the hollowed space. He had enough time to check his guns, saw that Tut was doing the same. Then they heard boots on rock, grinding on gravel, stamping forward.

"Shoot anybody but me," said Regis. Then a quick thought came to him. What if they brought Shepley up here with them? Why would they do that? Still, he couldn't risk it. Tut didn't know the kid.

"Second thought—let's hold off, let them go by, at least until I can see if Shep's with them. Then we'll head down there. Maybe we can take her by surprise, though I doubt it at this point."

"Okay, boss," said Tut, licking his lips.

In the faint glow of the light, Regis saw not raw fear but the solid look of determination of a man thinking in a dicey situation. If he'd been unsure up to that point, he knew then that Tut was a good man to have around.

Three men thundered up. The rough-cut chamber Regis and Tut stood in barely masked them in shadow, but the men were intent on reaching the lantern, not on what they were passing in the dark.

As soon as they rounded the elbow in the trail where Regis had stuck the lantern, he and Tut made for the trail and found themselves winding downward, counterclockwise, on crude, narrow stone steps, uneven and threatening to trip them up. They must have been hewn from the rock by humans; they were too regular for anything nature left behind.

No sounds reached them from up above, on the trail, so the three men must have kept going. They'd soon find the clubbed man and the two others. "We get down there, see if we can keep hidden, then we should split up. My brother's your height, dark hair, needs a haircut, name's Shepley. Tell him you're with me. He's a good hand with a gun. But don't tell him I said so."

"Okay, boss."

From somewhere ahead and slightly below, the woman growled and shouted in Spanish and English. "What are you fools doing?"

No answer, then a flurry of Spanish and shouts from above

were matched with shouts from below. At least one more man and the woman, now barking orders.

Regis guessed they'd found the others. Or at least the first one. Then came more shouts from above. He and Tut paused on the stone steps, backs to the outer wall, guns drawn. They each wore the spare gun belts, bandolier style, across their chests.

Ahead of them, Regis saw wavering light, then a metal lantern clunked against rock. More curses and shouts, urged on by the woman.

They crept downward once more, knowing they had to get to the bottom, wherever that was, before whoever was below started up and before the ones from above started down. Else they'd be caught in a cross fire. *At least the fools would likely shoot themselves in addition to me and Tut*, thought Regis. Not a comforting notion.

Sweat stippled his face despite the night's cooling temperature. He dragged his cuff across his forehead to keep the sweat from stinging in his eyes. He edged past Tut once more, motioning to the kid with his gun hand to keep behind him.

Ahead, the shouts and light grew louder, brighter. Three, four more steps and they'd find out what they were facing. *Here we go*, thought Regis, as he pulled the second revolver and cranked back the hammer.

The first comer nearly bowled square into Regis, so close was he. Royle had no time for thought. He leveled the gun in his left hand square at the mass of the man's broad body. The last thing he saw was a big slop belly barreling into him. He jerked back on the trigger, and the blast was muffled by the big man falling into him.

Regis sidestepped, and Tut had just enough space to jump up over the falling man as the big body flopped to the ground. The man gagged and squirmed as if he were smothering a whore somewhere beneath his massive girth.

A second man jerked short, eyes wide, a lantern in one hand and a gun in the other. He stared from Regis to Tut, caught like a netted fish for the briefest of moments. It was all Tut needed. He drilled the man, blowing a bullet into the man's throat. Regis saw the shocked man's Adam's apple burst apart, the short distance doing nothing for the man's looks.

Before them lay a vast bowl in the rock, as if carved by a giant's scooping hand. It looked to be as big as two corrals. Toward the far side, a fine, warming blaze pulsed, filling the night with just enough light to show him a retreating form. It darted into shadow beyond the firelight. And it looked like a woman.

Regis growled and bolted forward.

Chapter 21

A day after Bone left Orliss Pushaw, the dark, low shapes of Mack's buildings were barely visible in the southern distance, squat black shapes shimmering in the wavering horizon. Bone knew that somehow what he'd find once he made it to them would be another of life's harsh tragedies. And he was right.

He found Mack Deemworth dead. He was scrubbed pink, shaved, and dressed in his Sunday best bib and tucker, all laid out on the bed he'd shared with Martha for more years than Bone knew. Bone had shaken the old man's shoulder, wanting his paper-thin eyelids to flutter open but knowing the truth of it.

Funny thing was, Bone didn't find a thing to show how Mack had died. No brown stains indicating a bullet had ended things, no knife wounds, no foamy mouth showing he'd poisoned himself. He found nothing but a peaceful old man laid out in a suit too big for him now, lost in it like a child playing dress up with his father's clothes.

The room was not untidy like the rest of the house, the home of a man who'd lost a reason to rise each day. This room was spotless. As if Mack had not used it since Martha died. Likely couldn't bear to.

On a bedside table sat a letter folded in three and propped

against a Holy Bible of cracked brown leather. The letter bore
the name "Jarvis McGraw" in black ink in a shaky hand.

Bone seemed to hold his breath the entire time he was in the
room, dreading each moment even as it arrived. He thumbed
open the letter and read:

> *Dear Bone.*
>
> *Funny name you got there. I knew you'd be riding back this
> way. I apologize for lying to you as I did about there being help
> coming. Forgive an old man the fib. I have no one, no living rela-
> tives I'm aware of, and if they're out there somewhere, seems I
> would have known about them before now had they been worth
> knowing. In the drawer beneath the Bible, you will find the deed to
> this ranch. That and this letter should suffice to anyone who ques-
> tions you. I'm not saying we were ever close as man and son, but
> Martha always said you were a good man—I agree—and that's
> good enough for me. Besides, I know you have the same gusto me
> and Martha had for making something of this place all those years
> ago. Maybe you and your friends can make a go of it. I sure as hell
> couldn't.*
>
> *Please bury me out back, beside my Martha. You'll see the spot.
> I've already chiseled my own name on the stone and I started the
> hole, but I'm so stove up I can't make a go of it. I'm sorry to leave
> you with that task, Bone, but I'd surely appreciate it. One last
> thing, if you could maybe see fit to say a word or two over us. I
> marked a passage in the Good Book. The rest of this place, our
> things, in and out, it's yours. Thanks for being a true friend and a
> good man. Don't change. Good luck to you, son.*
>
> *—Macklin Henry Deemworth*

It took the lanky Ranger-turned-cattleman until an hour before sundown to finish the hole. The gravesite was obvious—a
well-tended plot scarcely bigger than the bed of a buckboard
defined on the flat landscape with a wooden picket fence that
had once been painted white. The stone Martha and Mack

would share was pink-tinged sandstone, a sizable slab that must have taken Mack forever to haul from somewhere and plant upright. But in a day of hard shocks, the most surprising lay opposite the big stone. Two smaller, older stones set flat in the ground. Each bore a chiseled heart and the word *Baby*.

Bone, and most other folks, he bet, had no idea the kindly old couple had lost two children. To what, who knew? And it hardly mattered now.

The digging was hard going but he muscled through it, and nearing sunset he was ready to bury his friend. It was another hour and a half, aided by a lantern from the kitchen in the little ranch house, before the grave was filled and mounded and packed and covered with stones, as Martha's was. He read the passages over them, added his own heartfelt thoughts, and stood in silence for long minutes. As he bent to lift the lantern from the ground, a mourning dove cooed, joined by a second. Their hollow, lonesome sound somehow felt just right.

Bone bunked that night on the porch, determined to make decisions only after the morning sun warmed him.

It would be another four days until he neared the new ranch he was building up with Regis, until Bone let the first crack of possibility light the darkness clouding his mind. He was now a ranch owner, though not in the way he wanted to come by a place of his own. It was not as a big spread as Regis's, and not in very good repair, but it beat the sagging lean-to he and Shep had cobbled together.

It was all so new, he wasn't certain what to think, but he couldn't wait to share his news with the Royle boys. If he knew Regis, he'd have Shep hopping, setting posts, and clearing brush in his spare time. And getting hard stares from the kid for his troubles.

What he found at the cattle camp was anything but what he expected.

Chapter 22

By the time Regis reached the fire at the far end of the rocky basin, the vague white-shirted shape running ahead of him had disappeared into the blackness beyond.

Regis barreled forward, knowing full well he was chasing the vile she-devil, Tomasina Valdez, and knowing he was playing the fool, risking all the longer he was exposed by the dancing firelight. There could be a dozen more outlaws drawing a sight on him right now.

Thus far the men had been foolish and poorly equipped, stumbling around drunk and shouting and rushing headlong at him and Tut. Heck, if they were there, let them fire if they wanted. He had no choice. He had to catch that woman and he had to find Shep.

As Regis rounded the fire and neared the spot where he'd last seen her fade into the night, he slowed. What was this gaping darkness within darkness before him? He stayed to one side, felt stone and then no stone beneath his hand as he groped forward. A cave? He shuffled forward another step.

Without warning, from somewhere ahead in the inky gloom, a gunshot boomed and blasted, lighting the dark space before him for the merest blink of time with a yellow-blue burst of light. The bullet pinged and whipped and buzzed, sounding as though it had ricocheted off a thousand rocks all at once.

Then he heard a flurry of Spanish words in a high-pitched rage, shouted as if through a thick snowstorm, then bootsteps fading away. Then there was silence. She was getting away. What had she shot? Then the cold knife of truth slashed him. Shep. Of course she would keep him hidden in the cave!

The sudden thought sent him into the darkness of the cavity, slamming his head, shoulders, arms, and legs into uneven, low cornices and jutting ledges, driving him to his knees at one point. He was up, shouting, "Shep! Shep!" heedless of the danger he had put himself in.

He didn't care, had to find the boy, his brother, his own little brother. The baby of the family, and he'd been here in this hell all because of Regis. It was always because of him, he knew now, all of it. The hardship his mother and brother had been forced to live in when he'd left all those years before.

No matter the money he'd sent back home, it had never been enough, he knew. For it was not the one thing his mother and brother had wanted, which was to see him, to have him near them once more. And that was the one thing he could never give them.

He was his own man, for ill or good. And now that bird had come home to roost. He'd gotten his brother killed.

Regis shouted Shep's name over and over, and then he tripped on something soft. Something that might have groaned. He still had his revolver in his hand, because he heard the metal slam stone as he hit.

Regis shoved up to his knees. "Shep? Shep?"

He stuffed the gun in his holster and plowed forward on his knees on the rocky cave floor, scrabbling like a dog, groping in the dark. He clawed back toward the thing he'd fallen over. He felt it, a leg, then another. A person. It groaned.

"Shep?"

"Yeah." The voice was weak, a whisper.

"Shep, boy, you shot?"

"N-n-no, don't think so. She tried to. Never saw her miss yet. . . ."

Regis's hands felt all the way up Shep's body. He was seated on the ground, leaned against the rough, rocky wall. He got to the kid's face and felt a puffed, battered thing beneath his trembling fingertips. Shep groaned.

Regis said, "I'm sorry, so sorry," over and over as he patted lightly all over the boy's head and neck, his chest and gut, down his legs. He felt nothing wet, no blood, no gunshot wounds.

"S'okay, Regis. I'm okay."

It was a relief to hear, but Regis didn't believe it. He had to get the kid out of there.

Regis traced along the kid's arms and felt manacles matching those on his boots. The chains joining both sets led to a chain that trailed in a small pile beside the kid on the ground.

Regis pulled on it and found that it angled up to the wall above Shep's head. He tugged. It was attached. His fingers told him it was a steel pin sunk in the wall. But the link attaching the chain to the pin felt as if it might have a crack or a gap. If he could pull it apart . . .

Back at the mouth of the cave, Regis heard shuffling footsteps drawing closer. He tensed and pulled his pistol. "Keep still, Shep. Somebody's coming."

Relief cracked apart the moment he heard Tut's voice say, "Boss? Regis? You in there? You okay?"

Regis let out his held breath. "Tut! I'm here, we're good. You okay?"

"Yeah," said the young cowboy with obvious relief in his voice. "You bet."

"Bring a torch, burning stick, anything. Can't see."

"Okay!"

A few moments later, Regis saw light dancing along the irregular surface of the cave walls and ceiling. Good ol' Tut. "Over here," he said as the light came slowly closer. "Anyone else out there?"

"Nah, I heard the ones up above shouting to each other. My Spanish isn't so good, but I think they were hightailing for anywhere but here."

"Good."

Tut drew close and bent low.

From Tut's sharp, in-drawn breath, Regis knew the young man had seen Shep's face. "Yeah, he's been beaten on pretty badly. I need your help with these chains. I almost have that link pulled from the wall pin."

Tut held the torch in one hand and bent low, grabbed the chain with the other. "No good. Hang on." He set down the torch on the rocky cave floor and grabbed onto the chain above Regis's big hands.

"Okay . . . now!" said Regis, and the two men put their all into it. One hard go was all it took. The link separated and, with a *ping*, popped free of the steel pin. Regis and Tut both pitched backward, scrabbling awkwardly for a moment until they righted themselves.

Tut rolled on the barely burning hunk of firewood that offered their only light. It pinched out. "Dang it!"

"Don't worry about it, Tut. You stay here with Shep. I'll be right back. Don't move him yet. He's in and out of it, but I don't know how bad he's been hurt."

"Okay, boss. Where you going?"

"To find a snake and kill it." With that, Regis bent low and continued deeper into the cave. Within a minute he was wishing he had tried to coax that burnt firewood back into flame. He couldn't see a thing. Still, he advanced, gun drawn, into the narrowing dark.

He'd traveled for many minutes and had gone how far, he had no idea, when he felt a breeze from ahead. He kept walking, faster now, and sooner than he expected came to a widening in the walls, for which his head and shoulders were grateful. The breeze here was more prominent, and then he saw purple sky and starlight.

Regis slowed his pace, taking care to make as little sound as possible with each step. He scuffed once and gritted his teeth, pausing and listening. He heard nothing. That witch would be ahead, he knew it. But where?

He ventured farther, farther, then, with the feeling of the cooler night air fully on his face, he smelled something familiar. Horses. That dry, musty smell of dung and horse sweat. Ahead, perhaps a dozen feet, a horse whickered. He kept moving forward, one arm out with fingers grasping the night air, the other holding the revolver at the ready.

The smell of horse was more pungent, and he fancied he stepped in dung. Then his fingers felt a picket line, and he jerked it toward him. A horse to his right made a low sound, then another beyond. So this is where they kept their mounts. Was she here?

Regis held still, eyeing the dark. Unless she was half cat, which he didn't doubt, she couldn't see in the dark any better than he could. And he knew that movement, when stalking or when being stalked, was the simplest way to reveal yourself to predator or prey. He stood locked like that for long, long minutes. He heard a horse urinate, heard a far-off scratching sound, a critter in the night. But that was all.

He was being foolish. He had what he came for, his brother. He should be back there with him and Tut, holed up and waiting for dawn. At least in there he could keep a rock wall to their backs and defend themselves should the rogues return for another set-to.

Regis turned and made his way back, deeper into the cave. He groped his way along the dry stone walls, whacking his head twice and suppressing barks of pain with stifled groans.

He still wasn't convinced that witch wasn't lurking nearby. Mostly he guessed she was gone. Where? He knew not, but there was lingering doubt. She was wily and unpredictable. No, *crazy* was the right word for her. He didn't doubt for a second he'd neither heard nor seen the last of Tomasina Valdez.

"Tut?" he said as he advanced closer to where he thought they might be.

"Yeah, boss. Just ahead of you. We're good."

"Okay." He made it to them, knelt once more, and laid a palm across Shep's forehead. "Feels wet."

"I fetched water from a drinking barrel back at the mouth of the cave," said Tut. "Been cooling him down, trying to get him to drink. He's still out."

Regis sighed. "I patted him down, didn't feel any wounds. I hope he's just knocked out. We'll wait here until daylight. Safer than stumbling around out there with who knows how many of them there are."

A minute passed, then Tut said, "You think our horses are okay?"

Regis nodded in the near dark. "Yeah, we hid them pretty well." In truth, he didn't feel that confident about their horses. But daylight would show all.

"If you're tired, boss, I can tend Shep. You could spell me in a while."

Regis cracked a slow smile. "Thanks, Tut. I'm too keyed up. You go ahead. I'll wake you if I need you."

"Well, okay then, if you're sure."

"Yep."

"Just a minute or two is all I need."

Regis swore the kid barely got the last word out before he heard a light snoring sound. He smiled again and held Shep's hand. Daylight would show all, he told himself.

As it turned out, daylight revealed very much indeed. Shep was a mess, and while he'd been beaten badly, he didn't appear to have any knife or bullet wounds. He could stand, and did so with their help once they dosed him with water.

They made their way to the mouth of the cave. Tut stood watch, scanning the rocky rim above them while Regis stoked the fire and rummaged through what he assumed were the meager possessions of Tomasina Valdez.

He found nothing but skimpy, worn clothes; one broken revolver; a pair of rope sandals; a hat; and, at the bottom of a broken wooden crate and wrapped in brown paper, her blue dress. Regis tossed everything that would burn onto the fire.

Tut found one thing of use. Hanging on a bent nail driven into rock above the water barrel was a steel key. "You think?" he said, handing it to Regis.

Regis shrugged, cursed himself for picking up the habit. "Let's try."

The satisfying click of Shep's manacles popping open brought a much-needed smile to their faces. Even Shep, who'd been awake for several minutes, half smiled. He was looking less dazed, though mighty tired, and asking for more water.

Tut explored and found a rough gap in the side of the rock that led along a path to a foul latrine pit. The path angled beyond that and curved northward. He followed it and found a string of six dejected-looking horses tied to a picket line.

He returned to the fire and told Regis.

"Fine work, Tut. They're likely the ones I stumbled into in the dark last night. Good. We'll follow that path, take those horses, and go find ours—and then we'll ride for home."

An hour later, they had done exactly that and located their horses, uneasy but none the worse for having stood tied and alone all night.

Regis helped Shep mount up onto King, the largest of the horses. Tut rode Percy's roan and led the string of found beasts, Shep's mount and their old pack horse among them. Regis had sorely wanted to track Tomasina Valdez, but he knew she'd likely ridden off into the night, as did the rest of her men. Would they see any of them again? He hoped so. He wanted a shot at that vile creature in woman's skin.

Soon they were plodding along the trail homeward toward the Royle Ranch, with Tut scanning their backtrail and to the sides and Regis tending Shep and looking ahead.

Tut cleared his throat. "Boss?"

"Yeah?"

"I never killed a man before."

So that was why Tut was so quiet. Regis nodded. "I guessed so. I'm not too experienced in it, either. But I'll tell you what, Tut, I was mighty glad and lucky to have you there. You did what needed doing, and I'm grateful."

"Well, I was riding for the brand. Bone told me a long time ago that when you take a man's money, you do his bidding. Unless it ruffles your feathers so bad you can't stomach it. Then you ride on."

"Good man, ol' Bone. That's why he's the foreman."

In truth, up until the night before, Regis had been all set to have it out with Bone, fight him and fire him, banish him from the Royle Ranch and all of Texas, too, if need be, for letting this happen.

But overnight, Regis had done a whole lot of thinking, and he realized Bone hadn't done anything wrong—nothing he himself wouldn't have done. He'd assumed Regis was going to be along soon and so he'd left Shep alone for what he thought would be a few quiet hours. Then he'd gone north to do Regis's bidding in trying to hire ranch hands. Just what his job called for.

And besides, most kids Shep's age in the wilds of Texas were wiser beyond their years than Shepley Royle. Regis hated to admit it, but there it was. The kid was just that, still a kid.

Regis sighed. Bone had not asked for Regis to saddle him with Shep's care. That, Regis admitted, had been unkind to his friend. And yet Bone had barely muttered about it. He'd simply nodded and taken on the task of overseeing the kid while Regis was back in town. No, Bone was not to blame. And he'd tell him that when he saw him. Hopefully later that day.

He shifted in the saddle and reached over to the horse walking close beside him. He gently touched the half-sleeping Shep's arm. The boy woke and nodded.

The kid had taken hard knocks, and though Regis wished they could travel faster getting back to the rough cow camp, it would only succeed in injuring the boy further.

They'd get there, he reasoned. It might take a while longer, but they'd get there in the end.

Chapter 23

Something, maybe an ill omen, carried on the south wind bristled northward as if to beat him back from where he rode. Bone spurred his mount, jamming bootheels into Buck's belly, riding harder back to the ranch. The effort hastened his arrival by hours and cost him the strength of his horse and left him nearly as tired as the hard-worked mount.

Soon he saw Percy's distinctive beanpole shape tottering about the place, with no other figures in sight. Bone's fears began to take shape. "Percy, where's Regis? And Shep?"

The tall, thin cowhand replaced his hat on his head. "Well, good to see you, too, Bone."

"I'll say hello later," said Bone, looking about the place. "Where's everyone at?"

"Well, I'm here," said Percy, hefting the steel bar and turning his back on Bone and resuming setting yet another post for the corral.

"All right, okay," said Bone. "Hello, Percy. Good to see you, Percy. How you been keeping yourself, Percy? There, that better?"

"Yep," said the younger man, turning once more. "And how did you know something went wrong?"

"What? What's happened?"

"Me and Tut got here a couple days since and your friend

Regis was already here. He was fit to be tied. Showed us a note by some woman named, oh, let's see, what was her name?"

"Tomasina Valdez?"

"Yep, that's it. Turns out she absconded with Regis's brother."

"She stole Shep?"

"Yeah, and is holding him until Regis agrees to sign over his deed to the ranch, saying it's hers. She said if Regis tried to track her that she'd kill the kid."

"Let me guess—Regis took off after her?"

"Yeah, he did. All lathered up he was. Took Tut with him, too."

"Good. Tut's a level head."

"And I'm not?"

"I didn't say that," said Bone, stripping the saddle off his horse. "I just don't know you as well as I know Tut. Now lend me a hand. I need a fresh horse, food, water, and I need to trail them. Which way did they go?"

"Thataway," said Percy, nodding southward. He told Bone what he could while he helped the man. Not a half hour after he rode in from the north, Bone lit out southward, the scant information Percy was able to relay the only clues he had regarding what he might be facing.

Their trail wasn't difficult to follow, in part because he had been tracking men and wayward cattle for years and in part because the landscape, with stretches of it soft underfoot, lent itself to a readable sightline.

"Just like Regis," he said, biting back the urge to box the man's ears when he caught up with him. He'd pull back bloody stumps for his efforts, as Regis was a testy sort. But in this instance, he'd earned Bone's ire. This was foolhardy. Two men to surround and defeat a viper's nest? "Dumb of you, Regis. Just plain dumb."

He'd ridden about four hours, following the trail the two men left, when he spied something moving in the distance, the heat blurring the dark, thin shapes. "Who now?"

The horse, a solid beast Percy told him was Tut's mount, perked its ears forward.

"Yeah, I see it, too," said Bone, patting the horse's neck. He slid out his rifle and checked it, then rode forward, hoping beyond hope it was his pard, Regis, with an undamaged Shep and with Tut bringing up the rear.

In the four hours he'd been riding, Bone had cooled down some and began to feel foolish himself, then downright worried. The kid had been nabbed when Regis had assumed he'd been watching over him. Bone knew he was to blame.

"If only I'd been there," he said over and over.

As he rode southward, with the figures in the distance drawing closer, he squinted harder. The figures slowed and then stopped moving. *So they've seen me, too.*

Something told Bone he'd best plow ahead, come what may. And by the time another twenty minutes had passed, he knew who it was. And he raced that horse of Tut's hard, right up to them.

Everybody dismounted and, after much in the way of timid, sheepish, heartfelt apologies all around, they made camp, feasting on the generous sacks of supplies Percy had loaded them with.

It was decided that another four hours in the saddle wasn't something Shep was up to that day, so they bedded down on the spot. In the morning, they rode to the Royle Ranch headquarters, such as it was, arriving there late in the morning, when they had another feast and indulged in a day of rest.

Chapter 24

"I didn't expect to see you back so soon." Cormac eyed his tall, young partner. Regis Royle leaned in the doorway, shaking his head and looking a million years old.

"Regis, what's happened? You look like you've been dragged through a knothole." Cormac set his pipe down in his brimming brass ashtray and walked around his desk in their offices at Beecher Street.

Regis smiled. "Good to see you, too, partner."

"Well?"

"You remember one Senorita Tomasina Valdez?"

Cormac sighed. "Oh no, what's that hellcat done this time?"

"What hasn't she done?" said Regis, folding his long legs and plopping down in a black stuffed leather wing chair.

"You look like a man who could use a drink." Cormac didn't wait for a response as he poured a generous dollop of whiskey for his partner, then one for himself. He handed it over and sat back down, waiting for Regis to settle and sip before he said, "Well?" once more.

Regis nodded and launched into the story of the events of four days ago. Long before he'd finished, Cormac had jumped up from his seat behind the desk and paced the room like a caged wolf. "How's Shepley? Where is he now?"

"Relax, Cormac. He's fine. Well, he will be, I think." Regis leaned forward, elbows on his knees. "That devil and her men beat the living tar out of him. Bruised him up one side and down the other. Doc says he doesn't think the kid has anything broken inside, save for ribs, which will mend. And his appetite's back. He's starting to eat like a mustang."

"Good! Where do you have him? Your digs? Not much, if you'll pardon my saying so. I have room at my house—two spare rooms, in fact. He can have the run of the place."

"Kind of you to offer, but I set him up at the Red Rose rooming house for now. It's not far to here, in case he needs me during the day."

The older man resumed his pacing. "I'll pay him a cheer-up visit after work. But look, we need to deal with this woman once and for all. This sort of thing is unacceptable. I know we're right on the Mexico border, and I know that a number of our clients are Mexican, good men all, but Valdez is part of the riffraff that plagues the border. If we're ever going to make this entire region safe for other good folks—and ranchers, too—not necessarily one and the same. . . ." He winked and snatched up his pipe. He worked a match over the already smoldering tobacco nested within. "Then we have to clear out the trash, preferably starting with Tomasina Valdez."

Regis nodded. "I can't disagree. I also can't help thinking what they must think."

"What do you mean?" Cormac stabbed the air between them with his pipe stem. "You aren't going soft on me, now, are you, *boyo*?"

"No, no, nothing like that." Regis stood, sighing. "What I mean is this land was all the land of the Mexicans. Now, in a short run of time, you have folks such as us ride on in all along the border and lay claim to it."

"That's the way of the world, Regis. I thought you knew

that. The history of humans is one of domination. It's been going on for as long as people have been seeking better lives beyond wherever it is that doesn't make them happy anymore."

"Yeah, I know, Cormac. And I understand. I'm just tired, is all. You don't mind, I'll call it good and be back here bright and early in the morning."

"Take as much time as you need. We'll soon be in between loads and trips, as you know. It'll be a lull time. We planned for it, but the only trouble is we have a number of men with itchy feet. You combine that with empty coin pouches and we might lose them to that blasted Madowski and Sons before we ship out again. I'd hate to lose good men. But the warehouses are all stocked and sorted, and the other vessels are all shipshape."

Regis scratched his chin. "Cormac, how'd you like to keep them busy and doing something to better our lot at the same time?"

"You thinking what I'm thinking?" said Cormac, grinning.

Regis bit back the urge to point out that once again Cormac had taken someone else's idea and laid mild claim over it. It was one of the few annoying traits his older partner had that irked him. He wondered idly which of his traits grated on Cormac. He'd make sure to exercise them regularly, if he ever figured out what they were.

"Yeah, I reckon so. I know Bone could use the help out there. The place is shaping up slow, and the men he managed to find so far are all true cowhands, good with the cattle, but only about half of them don't mind stepping down from the saddle and sullying their hands on a pry bar or a bucksaw."

Cormac looked out the window. "Our men aren't afraid of hard work, and what's more, we can send them with tools and lumber. You recall last month's shipment of planking from up the coast? They sent more than we needed, and I've been saving the rest for some unknown deal. What say we send it out to the Royle Ranch . . . with the men?"

"Now that's an idea I can get behind. I won't be able to leave for a bit. Too much to catch up on."

"That's all right. Why not send them out on their own? They're not helpless. You know that Norbert Shanks and Lockjaw used to be landmen. They'll be the guards."

Regis nodded. "I'm sure they're capable of taking care of themselves. Just the same, I'd feel better if we could send another gunman or two along. With this Valdez business and the rest of the yahoos roving the border country, you never know what might happen."

"How about the off-duty deputies? Marshal Corbin could fill you in on who's trustworthy and who's useless."

"Good thinking. I'll pay him a visit after I see Shep." He headed for the door. "Oh, and Cormac?"

"Yes, Regis."

"Thanks. For everything."

"I could say the same to you, my boy." Cormac popped his pipe in his mouth and settled himself back behind the desk. "Could—but I won't . . . yet! Let's see how this ranching idea works out." He looked up and winked, then immediately began grumbling as he resumed tallying figures in the massive ledger flopped open before him.

Regis smiled and shook his head as he left their office and threaded his way through the light afternoon crowd along Beecher Street to check on his little stoved-up brother.

"What do you mean he isn't here?" Regis peeked into the small but tidy sitting room to the right of the bottom of the stairs. "Are you certain?"

"Mr. Royle," said the flushed, buxom woman drying her work-reddened hands on a flour-sack apron. "I am not in the habit of losing my boarders. Neither am I in the habit of watching their every move. Now, when you locate him, tell him I serve supper promptly at six. If he's late, he'll go hungry. Though in his case I'll make an exception. Just this week, mind you, while he's . . . under the weather."

But Regis heard only half of what she said as he shoved through the front door, sputtering and growling like a testy bruin who's been denied his winter's hibernation.

Back inside, Mrs. Shalinski shook her head and stomped her way down the long hall to the rear of the house. In her steamy kitchen, potatoes in a blue agate pot bubbled out white froth and sputtered and hissed on the hot black stovetop.

"Why I ever got into this boarding house game is beyond me. 'You'll make your fortune in a month!' said Esther. 'You'll love every minute of it!' said Olive. 'You'll want to open more than one!' said Beatrice. Oh, if I could wind back the clock, I'd tell those biddies a thing or three. . . ."

But it was the same each day whenever a boarder brought her a new story of woe and misery. She figured she was owed more now than she'd ever made when she opened the place five years before. "Oh, never mind," she muttered. "Them's that need will get, them's that don't, won't."

Three minutes away, Regis Royle was stepping fast and hard, trembling the puncheons of every establishment he passed, asking folks if they'd seen his brother, and then he had to describe the kid to everybody, to boot. A hundred and one worries fluttered in his mind like summer moths around a lantern.

He shouldn't have let that foul creature, Tomasina Valdez, escape. Should have trailed her right through that cave to wherever it was she lit out for. Gunning her and her verminous men down would have been too good for them. As it was, they left a stinking heap of bodies behind in that foul hole in the rocks.

Tut had grimly dubbed the place "Bone Canyon," and that's exactly what Regis would think of it as for all his days. After ten, nearly fifteen minutes, he'd run out of ideas and figured he'd have to do the inevitable and make for the marshal's office.

Heck, he was going there anyway to ask about getting armed escorts for his men heading out to the ranch, though finding Shep was far more important.

A cold, twisting fist knotted his guts when he let himself dwell on the possibilities. Another block of buildings later and he was in a right lather. He was certain his brother had been absconded with once more by what was left of that band of rogues. This time he knew they'd lay the kid low, and wouldn't have to work too hard at it, either.

Shep was in no shape to travel and was nothing to look at. The kid's face resembled purple and yellow and blue knobs of dough stuffed together, with a wild mat of hair atop. That image reminded Regis that he'd promised to have the barber pay a visit to Shep's room. One more block of buildings and he'd be at the lawman's office.

He was nearing Rudy's Saloon, a decent little hole for a beer after the day's work was wrapped. Regis had been in there a time or three over the years. As he passed, he thought, okay, one more round of questions for one more bartender might not hurt. He shoved through the batwings and was about to say hello to Ivan, the beanpole of a barkeep, all bald head and Adam's apple and bony fingers, when he heard a familiar voice say, "I tell you, boys, it was all I could do to keep from slicing them banditos open, one at a time. Had to restrain myself, I did."

"Looks to me like while you was restraining yourself, those boys took a couple of rounds out of your hide, youngster!"

A chorus of braying laughs bubbled up from around the table of three men—and a very bruised-up, hunched over, half-inebriated boy. A boy, Regis saw, that looked a whole lot like his whelp of a little brother, one Shepley Royle. He stepped over and stood behind the boy's chair. The three men around the table looked up. He knew two of them well enough to know their first names.

"Tom, Skipper, how you been keeping?"

"Oh, okay, Regis. You know, got me a bad elbow," Tom said, holding one arm with the other and pulling a face as if he'd been sucking on a lemon. Regis ignored him and laid his big hands atop his brother's shoulders. And squeezed. "And how are you today, Shepley Royle?"

The kid did not look up, nor did he turn around. But he did groan.

"What are you thinking, Shep?" Regis walked beside his silent, limping, slightly tottering brother. "No, wait, I have that wrong—you aren't thinking. That's the trouble right there. Because if you were, you'd know you're still healing. You've been through a devil of a time and you're still a kid! And what do I find? You drinking, telling lies in a saloon with men who spend their working hours in saloons. This does not bode well for your future, boy. Not well at all."

This last he said through gritted teeth, which finally caused Shep to look over at him.

"Sooner we get you healed and back to the ranch and away from this town and its temptations, the better." Regis muttered this, barely audible.

Shep stopped and put his hands on his waist, leaning slightly because his left leg, which had received more kicks than other parts of his body, was still bruised and sore. "What ranch would that be, Regis?"

His voice was none too quiet, and Regis looked at some of the faces passing them on the sides of the street. He felt himself turning red, then some color far beyond red as Shep's voice rose louder.

"Oh, you mean that dusty snake pit you bought out in the middle of nothing but sun and dirt? Where the horses are too wild to do anything with and the cattle are crazy and weigh no more than rabbits? Where there aren't any buildings? Where a

man named after something a dog buries is in charge? Where
your own brother, your only flesh and blood in the world, was
nearly killed because you weren't there? That ranch? Good
plan, Regis. Because it worked out so well the first time!"

Shep tried to storm off down the boardwalk, but he couldn't
move that fast. He also looked to Regis as if he were a little
dizzy from the sun baking his head. Likely from the booze.

"Hush up now, Shep!" Regis bent low with his face close to
the kid's. "You're attracting attention."

"Oh, pardon me! The wise and wonderful Regis Royle
is getting embarrassed? Is having me around inconvenient
for you?"

Regis worked the muscles in his jaw, alternating between
wanting to punch the kid in the head and put an arm around
him and tell him to calm down. Neither feeling won out.

"Soon as I'm able, I'm leaving, so you won't have to worry
about me anymore. I'll take my chances back in Connecticut
with the Quakers. At least there they respect me. Brother Dom
was a good man, unlike some folks I've met along the way."

Regis crossed his arms. "That ship has sailed away, little
brother. You're a partner now—well, a junior partner anyway—
in Royle Ranch. So you best get used to it."

The kid shoved Regis in the chest and winced, his still-sore
body obviously paining him. "I don't want to be your junior
anything! I never asked for it! You're not my father or my
mother, you hear me? You aren't anything!"

Regis was aware that more folks had gathered about them,
and he wanted to take a few swings at each of them, too.

He bent close so their noses almost touched. "I may not be
much to you, kid, but I am your older brother." His words came
out low, tight, and even. "And that makes me your legal
guardian, and while I am, you will do as I say."

He saw the rage build up, like a frothing pot of stew on a
high-flame fire. The kid's anger-stretched features finally burst,

and he shouted a rush of hot sounds, more animalistic than sensical, all the while flailing with weak fists at his older brother's face.

The first pop caught Regis by surprise, even though he'd seen the kid's rage rise. He touched his jaw where the fist landed, and with his right hand he snagged Shep's haymaking left as it swung in for another clip.

The kid swung his right while tugging, trying to free his left from Regis's clamplike paw.

"Knock it off, Shep!"

"I aim to!" But Regis held both of the kid's arms in his hands. So Shep pulled back his left boot to land a hard kick to his big brother's shin, but he gasped and sweat stippled his forehead as he bent forward, held up only by Regis's grip.

"Shep, you okay?"

He didn't respond for a moment, then nodded. "Yeah, I'm fine. Just where they . . . you know."

"I'm so sorry about it all, Shep," whispered Regis, letting his brother's arms down. He laid a hand on Shep's shoulder. "I never meant that to happen. You were right about the ranch. It's all a crazy dream, something best left to others, I reckon. Especially if it means losing you to the likes of that Valdez witch."

"No." Shep shook his head. "Look, don't pay attention to what I said. I'm fine. Take more than her to lay me low, you know that. I'm a Royle, after all. Besides, I'm going to need a whole lot of money as I mature." He smiled and looked at Regis. "So I'm counting on this ranch of yours—"

"Ours," said Regis.

"Okay, of ours, to be a success. Heck, if it's half as good as you predict it will be, we can't miss, right?"

Regis regarded Shep for a moment. "Come on," he said, turning his brother gently back toward where they'd begun.

"This isn't the way to the boarding house."

"I know. It's the way to Stump's bar. Anybody who can lob a

few punches like that, despite being in such a pitiful state to begin with, deserves a beer to cool him down some. Besides, we have some real talking to get up to."

And they did, with Regis agreeing to be less of a mother hen and Shep willing to work on acting grown up, taking responsibility for himself.

"Mama would like this," said Shep, his thumbs twiddling the base of the half-full beer glass.

"The beer?" said Regis, pulling a false look of shock.

"No, you goober. That me and you are working together."

Regis nodded. "I think you're right. I surely do."

Chapter 25

A week had passed since Regis and Tut had rescued Shep, and they weren't expected back to the ranch anytime soon, though Regis swore he'd send men. Bone and the boys had been busy. By then it sported a tidily built corral and an expanded shelter that verged on cabin quality, all thanks to the industrious Percy and the six Pushaw ranch hands that Bone had hired on his travels northward.

It had been a challenge to convince them that the budding ranch would require them to be off their horse's backs more than in the saddle. Bone had dangled the prospect of lots of eventual cowboying before them like steak before a hungry dog. They bit. They grumbled a whole lot, but they kept chewing.

"Still don't see why we can't go wrangle up some of those mustangs. They're everywhere down here, like flies on dung, for Pete's sake."

"Because," said Bone, emerging from the latrine—one of the first proper structures they cobbled together with planking and a branch-lattice roof—as he tugged up his braces. "I said so."

The complainer was a tiresome fellow named McCurdy who'd come along as part of a package deal with other men Bone knew and liked.

McCurdy wasn't fond of the foreman, either, as Bone had an

annoying habit of popping up when you didn't expect anyone to be popping. It was unnerving and often set the tense little Irishman back on his heels.

He'd sort of thought that because he and Bone shared a lineage that stretched back to the auld sod, he might be able to shirk more than he'd been able to. And on this hot May morning, he'd finally had enough.

"Now then, this ain't exactly what none of us signed on for, you know, Bone," he said.

Bone had been pouring himself another cup of coffee and figuring on the best way to commence the day's chores. They had to get a bunkhouse proper built, and the men, just the day before, had been spooked to their boots by a close-riding pack of what sounded to him like Apache.

Or it could also have been some of the border trash that still tried to pick off his men from a distance. So far only one had been wounded. He managed to squeeze out the lead pill from his forearm before he made it back to the ranch. He'd intended to keep on with rounding up the wild-eyed scrub cattle that roamed the ranch, feral and vicious with their horns if cornered in the brush. But the finicky wound hadn't stopped bleeding, and he figured he ought to seek some of Percy's ministrations.

"This is awful food, Bone."

The boss man's eyes widened. By gaw, but he was getting it from all sides this morning!

The lanky Ranger gritted his teeth. He would dress down the offender in front of the other men to show he didn't put up with any bucking of his authority. As he turned, he found the man who'd said it was Percy.

Percy had come to earn a valued position about the place, not only for his quick mind. He'd often study on a problem in quiet for a spell, then offer a suggestion that usually was better than some other way the men were about to choose.

He was also their first stop for medical woes. He had a well of knowledge that had proven its worth to them in the course of the month, from gunshot wounds to all manner of scrapes with brush and spooked ponies, not to mention setting a popped shoulder and remedying two snakebites. All in all Percy had proven himself a decent man to have around camp.

But he could also be a surly thing. No, surly wasn't quite the word for it. More like he wasn't raised among people who spent time with other people. He had an odd, caustic way about him at times that made Bone scratch his head. It took the men a whole lot of time to warm to Percy. Thankfully there was Tut. Together those two pards talked like normal folks.

Bone didn't really care as long as Percy could sit his horse and help with the day's rounding up of feral beasts, then pitch in with the shoveling and sawing and pounding. He'd been dividing up the tasks with rounding up and building and digging sharing equal measures.

But this was too much. "You think you can cook up something better, Percy, then be my guest." Bone tossed his tin plate onto the already leaning stack of plates. "In the meantime, clean up those dishes and then join us in that back corner section. We'll be along the north bank of the Santa Calina, building on that way-station corral until midday."

That'd show him.

"I can, you know."

"Can what?"

"Cook." Percy had gone back to piercing the thumb of his right leather glove with an awl. The men were forever mending their gear, but Percy was the only one who did so well enough that his efforts looked store bought.

"You can cook?"

Percy nodded. "Used to be a chef in Boston, by the wharves. And in the army before that."

"Why didn't you say so? We've all been struggling with this cooking and here we have a man in our midst who could do it?"

Percy shrugged. "Nobody ever asked."

"Well, consider this as me asking. Or telling. You cook tonight, and if it's up to snuff, why don't you take on the duties you've mostly covered, anyway. Tending camp and doctoring and whatnot."

Percy looked up, then pushed his spectacles higher on the bridge of his nose. "What about the cattle?"

"I'm expecting more men any day. I reckon we can stumble along until then."

"And the building?"

"Don't push your luck, Percy."

Despite that last comment, from the look on Percy's face, Bone knew he'd cracked a nut. The man wasn't much use in a saddle anyway, and more than once Bone had thought he'd have to end up doctoring their own doctor.

A few minutes later, Bone swung his horse close by the fire and spoke as he rode by. "If you have any other talents we don't yet know about, I wish you'd let me know."

Percy stood and stretched, stuffing his mended leather glove into his satchel. "I am a fair hand with numbers, tallying and such. And I once attempted to write a series of sonnets. That, however, is still a work in progress."

"Oh." Bone nodded. "All right, then. Well, if you can cook as good as I suspect, you'll be the outfit's Cookie, and you won't have to dally with the cattle. Unless we're desperate for help, that is."

Percy rubbed a hand across his chin and scrunched his eyes in concentration.

Bone really didn't mean for it to become a conversation. He had work to do and no time to do it.

"Considering the situation, I accept."

"Good." Bone clicked his tongue and rode on out of there as fast as he could, before Percy launched into one of his odd, chattery rambles.

When he got to the river, the men who'd been at it since day-light were churning up a storm of dust about five minutes out, to the southeast, but riding hard toward the corral. It looked like they had a goodly number of head this time.

The beeves bawled and fought like drunk gamblers over a fancy woman's attentions. Much more of this and they'd all end up punctured by horns. Thus far he'd avoided turning their efforts to seeking the mustangs, but it wasn't to be much longer before Regis would want to do something with them, too. They took an awful lot of man labor to wrangle, contain, and break, and they didn't have any spare hands to go around and still get the blasted buildings built and reservoir dug.

"Boss!" It was Hank, riding in hard. "Visitors!" He thundered up and jerked on the reins. The big gelding nearly sent the kid over the saddle horn and up onto the horse's neck.

"What do you mean?" said Bone, standing in the stirrups and looking past the approaching gather.

"Apaches, maybe. Not certain. But it's the second time we seen 'em this morning. They ain't passing through, no sir. Cause the first time they was coming from the other direction."

Bone sat back down in his saddle. "Maybe we can buy them off with a few head."

"You mean we ain't gonna fight?"

Bone looked at the kid, who Bone was all but certain had lied about his age. Still, the kid was keen, was a hell of a horseman, and could throw a rope like nobody Bone had ever seen. And he wasn't full of himself, not too highfalutin to hop down and lend a hand to one of his fellows. Some of the other hands would drape a leg over the pommel and build themselves a smoke while they waited for their pards to finish the ground work.

But now Bone saw disappointment on the kid's face. "Look, Hank, we don't have the men to go off shooting up every band of raiders who want us dead. Better off avoiding a fight when-ever we can. At least for now. Regis'll be back in a couple of days, and he's promised to fetch us a pile of men, guns, horses, the works. Then we'll really give them hell. But for now, don't provoke them. Okay?"

The kid didn't look happy with the decision, but he nodded. "Okay, boss."

"Good. Now help me spread the word."

The closer they rode, the closer the band of raiders across the river rode, from the opposite direction. *They want a piece of us, all right*, thought Bone. And it looks like they'll stop well short of the river and play shadow to us while we work.

Could also be a trap, a group sent to keep our attention focused on them while another group rides in from a different direction and guts us from the rear. He'd seen it before.

He and Hank spread the word among his seven men, and they kept their heads on swivels, their thongs off their hammers, and their gun hands loose.

It frustrated Bone because nearly every day brought with it something of the sort. On top of too few men for the work they had to do, there were increasing numbers of rogues looking to cut them down, or at least take the measure of them. What they needed were men who were willing to work and put up with hardship, ample food but poor cooking—though maybe Percy would remedy that—and little sign of it letting up.

There was promise, great promise—even the men could see that—in the range that Regis had staked claim to. It was vast, and though much of it was useless to anything but raising snakes, the wide valley bordering the Santa Calina for miles on either side was a fairly green place with plenty of feed for a whole lot more cattle than they currently had.

He hoped Regis would show up with the men he promised. Or better yet, surprise him and bring even more. There was no way they could keep up the pace Bone had set for them all, herding cattle and hunting and constructing buildings and corrals. All the while they had to keep an eye on the horizon for killers and thieves and natives who were just plain unpleasant and who would like nothing more than to drive Bone and his men off the land.

He also hoped Shep was healed. The kid had looked like he'd been set on by a dozen angry men. And from what he knew of Shepley Royle, and of Regis, Bone found it difficult to imagine that Shep would take any beating without running that wide mouth of his.

The kid was a decent sort, and Bone recognized a lot of the traits in Regis that made him a good friend, but the kid was just that—a kid. And not afraid to carry on if he felt like he was being worked too hard or if he just plain didn't want to work. Still, Bone shook his head. Kid or no, nobody deserved to be trounced like that.

He sorely wished they'd managed to catch that Valdez woman. What a verminous creature she was. Thankfully, Regis and Tut had managed to cut down a few of her men.

"Boss!"

Bone looked up from his work. It was Hank again, this time riding back to Bone, all out. If he had to travel any farther, that horse'd be in a lather. "Whoa there, boy—what's the hubbub now?"

But before the kid could catch his breath, Bone heard a crack, then another. Rifle shots. They were far enough off, past his men, that the smoke was already drifting skyward, breaking apart against a blue backdrop.

"They're back! Told you they was coming back!" Hank shouted it as he looked toward the group of men.

"Hell," muttered Bone as he kicked hard at his mount. He kept his eye on the band of men, a dozen or two—it was difficult to tell—scattered across the river. Their mounts were the usual assortment; some appeared to sport saddles, some blankets of muddy colors and indistinct striping.

They were thundering close to the river on their side, the

south side. Those in the lead were already near enough. They slid from the backs of their mounts and sought protection in the parched landscape behind whatever they could. A low jut of red wind-sculpted stone accommodated most of them. The stragglers followed, jumped down and kicked up sprays of dust as they came to rest on their knees behind scrags of mesquite and stone.

Bone heard why the bandits were acting so frantic. His men were shooting back at them, returning fire with precision and without a lot of fear. He was proud of their showing. Not a one of them had backed away and fled, which would have been the easiest course of action. Instead they sought their own cover, such as it was.

He was nearly to his men, with Hank thundering hard behind, when he heard a whistling, zipping sound nearby, like an unseen bee. Another, closer, followed with a thudding sound. His horse flinched, and so did Bone.

He looked down to his right, the southward side facing the river and the bandits across the way, and saw a pucker in the brown worn leather of his saddle, inches ahead of his right knee. He hoped Buck hadn't been shot. The bullet was from close enough that it could be a nasty wound.

He cut north, a dozen fast horse strides, and slid from the animal's back, still holding the reins. Buck walked okay—not a sure sign that it hadn't been wounded, but he'd investigate later. He slid his rifle from its boot and smacked the horse on the rump. He'd chase him after he'd killed a few outlaws. What did they want this time?

"Stupid question," he said out loud as he cat-footed back to the nearest of the few men hunkered behind a sparse thicket. It was meager cover, but unless they were willing to get closer to the river, there wasn't much in the way of protection this far back from the banks.

The beeves they'd been herding had scattered or run in circles in the half-built corral, still uncertain if they could bolt free, even though the men who'd been keeping them contained were now scattered, too.

"How many?" Bone asked Jesús, a middle-age, work-hardened vaquero who didn't speak much but put in two days of work for every one of most of the younger men.

"Six there," Jesús jerked his thinly whiskered chin toward their left, the southeast. "Another four, maybe more straight across." He nodded before them. "And there, I have seen three." This time his head dipped toward the southwest bank.

"Apache?"

"*Sí*. And who knows what else. They're a mixed bunch, some Apache, a few gringos, banditos, none of them any good. We should shoot to kill. But that's my opinion."

"Yeah, I guess trying to avoid them hasn't worked out so well. I was hoping to keep our distance until Regis showed up with more men before we took them on."

As if to mock him, the attackers kicked off a volley, raining shots at Bone and his boys. They kept it up for a good ten, fifteen seconds before dribbling to a pause.

Bone shouted, "Let 'em have it, boys! No quarter!"

He heard yips and howls from his ragged band of madmen, and despite the situation, he had to smile and add his own growl of satisfaction to the mix. Their shouts weren't heard for long, as their shots drowned out everything else. Bone took careful aim with his rifle where he'd seen a soot-smeared face jerk out from behind a stump every few seconds.

The man's cheeks wore ragged white stripes, and his hair was a grease-stiffened mass that he couldn't quite hide behind his scant cover. Bone muttered, "One more peek, asshole," and as soon as he said it, the leering man darted his head out and Bone squeezed his rifle's tender trigger.

He felt as though he were traveling astride the tiny lead missile as it coursed true, straight into the center of the man's forehead, coring the fiend's head and turning the smug face into a grease-smeared mess.

Much as he had felt he was riding the bullet to its mark, Bone now saw the man's head ripple, then pulse outward. The fool's greasy hair jerked apart, and shards of bone, snot-clods of blood, and globs of mudlike matter bloomed out the back of the head in a foul cloud. Bone felt as though the man's eyes stared straight at him as he stared back, a tight feeling in his gut, the same thing he felt each time he'd had to kill a man.

He'd thought many times about killing, be it man or beast. He'd concluded that the feeling of guilt at having taken the most important thing that creature would ever have should give the killer pause. That most deliberate and final of all acts should make him say, yes, this I have done and though I'm sorry, I had a reason, be it hunger or self-defense.

It never stopped Bone from doing the deed when he deemed it vital. Nor did it deter him from occasionally allowing a slight grim grin to pull at his mouth whenever he'd laid low someone he knew would only go on to hurt others. Like the greasy-haired vermin he'd just killed.

"Good shot, boss," said Hank. Bone barely heard him because his men were trading shots with the invaders hot and heavy. So far as Bone could tell, none of his men were down, but he'd seen two dead or at least downed among those clinging to the opposite bank.

"Boss!" It was Hank again, but this time the kid was stretched prone to Bone's right, about ten yards away. The kid had been sending shot after shot, and though Bone knew the kid could shoot, he was surprised to see a long red-black slice along the kid's trousers, on the back of the kid's leg behind his woolly chaps. He'd been grazed, but it didn't look life-threatening.

Bone thought the kid was asking for help, but no, he was motioning with his left hand upstream toward the river. Bone followed the sight line and saw a dark shape moving across the flow from the opposite bank and toward theirs.

At least one of them was trying to cross. If one could do it, others would follow. The kid was able to see the man but was not able to get off a shot. Bone nudged Jesús with an elbow. He jerked his head upstream. "The river."

Both men leveled on the black shape two seconds before it disappeared behind the low-hanging bankside growth.

Their bullets danced along the water, seeking their target, spraying plumes of water as they marched. In seconds they heard a high-pitched scream as their shots found their mark. A figure of a man whipped upright, not quite to their bank. The arms, those of a white, jerked to the heavens, a revolver whipping high, arcing then dropping into the water.

Then the man flipped backward and flopped with a splash. He bobbed in the pulsing wash, then flipped over and drifted downstream a dozen feet before snagging on an old dead tree jutting into the flow.

"Another devil sent back to hell," said Jesús.

Bone nodded, then scanned the far bank for a new victim.

Chapter 26

The group of nine men, eight from the docks and one part-time deputy, rattled, rolled, and rode their way northwest-ward from Brownsville toward the new Royle Ranch. Norbert Shanks, one of the men in the lead and one of two ahorseback, tugged free from an inner vest pocket a folded piece of paper and as he rode would scrutinize it.

Once or twice he looked up from it to the surrounding land-scape, and once, to the worry of the men behind him who rode in the jarring, jouncing wagon, he turned the paper halfway around and seemed to scrutinize it more deeply.

"You notice how Norbert will work his chaw faster every time he tugs out that map Mr. Royle gave him?" The man who spoke, Alberts, was a watch-capped man of the sea and river and did not think much of this inland venture. He took each opportunity to mock something about it and call into question anything that appeared unsafe or out of the ordinary.

As none of the other men were familiar with that word, and since Alberts could be a prickly sort, they chose to accept that what he talked about was of little concern. This meant Alberts was ignored much of the time. To be polite, Lockjaw Hames, who rode beside Alberts in the work wagon's seat, said, "Huh."

"No, I mean it. I think we're plumb lost. I've been navigat-ing on sailing vessels long enough to know when a man's confused. I have a good mind to jump down and snatch that map out of his hands. I could read the thing, I'll wager." He crossed his arms and stared up at a wheeling hawk pinned high up in a clear blue sky, as if by not looking at the back of the man with the map he could set them back on course.

"I ain't lost!" growled Shanks from his horse. He didn't look back at Alberts, but the raspy edge to his comment conveyed his perturbation with the surly old salt.

Turns out Shanks was not lost, he was merely an overly cautious sort and had never been trusted with a map before. That Regis Royle chose him to oversee it meant to Norbert Shanks that the boss man was impressed with him. He'd secretly hoped for an opportunity just like this for some time now. Helped him forget regretting his decision of years before to run away to the sea.

He was born on a farm in upstate New York carved dab between a lake and a knobby rise that on a good day and from the right angle might be construed as a mountain. He'd always missed the old homestead, and now his cousin, Merle, was running the place.

But Norbert now fancied he wanted to be a man of the land once more, a farmer, if you will. Trouble was, he hadn't managed to save more than a small sack's worth of coins, and that wouldn't earn him entry into a piece of property big enough to spit across.

But now that Regis Royle was trusting him with a proper landman's task, why, he felt certain he might be able to set to whatever task Regis needed doing of him. He'd prove he was once more a man of the soil, a fellow who belonged not on boats but inland.

Why, could be Royle might offer him a position right there on the ranch. Away from the temptations of towns and docks, he might finally be able to save himself coin enough to buy his own place. Maybe back East.

He missed full seasons and snow most of all. Through the

prism of memory, he recalled good times in winter; even hauling wood and frosted fingers weren't a deterrent, at least in memory.

Why, these Texas ranchers didn't know a thing about privation and hardship! They were too busy whining about snakes and heat.

"Shanks?" said the deputy sheriff.

"Yeah?" Norbert said, a little testily, annoyed at having been plucked from his thoughts about winters back East.

"What's that map say about how far we're to go?"

"Oh, map don't show that. But Mr. Royle said we'd know it when we saw it. Said there would be a corral and a small abode built of mesquite, and we'd like as not see his friend, Bone, who would be expecting the arrival of our help."

"Could that be it? If so, I'm sure glad I'm not staying around. I'll take my chances alone on the trail back to town." He was grinning when he said it, but Shanks didn't like his tone.

Norbert visored his eyes. His short-brim flat cap didn't do much in the way of keeping the sun out of a man's face. Another thing he'd have to change once he was a worker out here.

"I think you may be right. There's a corral. But I don't see an abode." He turned to face the young deputy. "I'm pretty certain he said there was an abode."

They held up when the deputy raised a hand. The wagon was riding close enough to pull alongside, then squeak to a halt. "What's the trouble?" said Alberts from the wagon's front seat.

Two of the men in the back hopped down; they'd all been walking as much as possible anyway, as the wagon, even with sacks of feed to sit on, was brimming with goods and was not accommodating to the backside.

Norbert tugged out the map once more, and Alberts walked up beside his horse. "Hand that map down here. Let me take a look."

Shanks didn't look at the man or pay attention to his outstretched hand. He did, however, flex his jaw muscles. One more comment from that cranky old man and he'd kick him square in the chin. He'd enjoy doing it, too.

But he needn't have worried. As a new distraction came into view. "A rider!" said one of the men, pointing past the cobbled corral. All heads swiveled up, and sure enough, there was the telltale dust cloud, low to the earth and drifting southward.

The deputy checked his rifle and said, "Any men with weapons, come on up. The rest of you stay back by the wagon."

"Well, who is that?" said surly Alberts.

"I don't know. But that's no reason to stand here with our trousers down around our ankles, now, is it?" The deputy checked his revolver, then his rifle again. "Who else is armed?"

Turned out two more of the men were. One with an old hand cannon more relic than reliable, and one pulled a revolver of more recent vintage from the depths of his floppy old canvas seabag.

"Okay then, we'll wait him out."

As the man rode closer they saw he was a white, tall in the saddle, with big moustache and a tall fawn hat, sweat staining the lower half of the crown. Likewise, his white shirt, though soaked through with sweat, bounced as he rode toward them astride a tall grulla.

He slowed as he neared them. They saw he also carried a rifle cradled, mountain-man style, across his middle, set to swing at a moment's notice. "Ho there—who sent you?"

Alberts began to answer, puffing up and saying, "What's it to you?"

But the deputy nudged his horse forward. "Mr. McGraw, that you? It's Mark Havert."

"Mark! Good to see you, boy. What are you doing out here?" Bone eyed the bunch and halted his horse. "Transporting prisoners or something?" He smiled when he said it, but not a one of the men standing by the wagon seemed to take it well.

"Regis Royle said we might find you out here wandering around and rubbing your head. His words, not mine," said the young deputy, holding up a palm in mock defense.

"Yeah, that's about the size of it. I was expecting men from Regis soon."

"We're from Mr. Royle," said Shanks, tugging out his map once more. "He said you could use help, and we're in between runs on the Rio Grande."

"Oh, he did, did he?" Bone backed his horse away from the deputy, then rode over to Shanks. "Sailors." He sighed. "That a note from Regis?"

The man looked at the folded map. "Oh, no, not exactly. It's more of a map, to keep us on track to get to the Royle Ranch."

"Well, you don't need that anymore, gents." Bone extended an arm and pointed, turning in his saddle. "You been on it all day, and longer."

The men looked all about them and didn't say much. Norbert held the map pinched in his fingers. "Mr. Royle said there was a corral and an abode."

"An abode?"

Norbert nodded. "That's what he said."

"Well." Bone nudged his hat backward, his sweat-matted hair stuck to his head. "Only abode we have so far is the lean-to. But Percy added on to it. We mostly use it as storage for gear and provisions."

"Where do you all sleep?"

Bone's drawn brows answered Albert's question. "Why, we bed down about the cookfire. Snakes don't bother us much, and the nights can get nippy. Did Regis send any word to me? Any notion as to when he'd be out here again himself? And how's Shep doing, anyway?"

Mark Havert nodded. "Yep, almost forgot. He said to tell you that he had too much to catch up on this week, but he'd be out by end of week next. And seeing as how Regis and his little brother caused a ruckus right in the middle of main street two days back, I'd say the boy's healing up."

"What sort of ruckus?"

"They were shouting and whatnot. And that, as you know, ends only one of two ways with brothers, smiles or fighting."

"You don't say," said Bone.

"Yeah, the kid tried to get the better of Regis with a few punches, but he's still weak as a kitten and Regis is . . . well." The deputy shrugged. "You knows Regis."

Bone smiled broadly then. "Yep, reckon I do." He faced the others. "So, you men are sailors by trade? Any of you handy with a shovel? A bucksaw? How about mudding a wall?"

By the time Bone had asked all the other questions he had in mind, and received increasing silence from the newcomers, he was groaning inwardly. Then Norbert Shanks cleared his throat. "I was raised on a farm back East, sir. I know my way around tools."

Shanks gestured to the men about him. "And loading and unloading cargo and rigging ships and loading boilers is hard work. We're none of us afraid of a full day's work. We've been trekking too long out here, and we all would like to lay into a task to work out the kinks. Am I right, men?"

Their nods and mutters of "Aye, aye" were all Bone needed to hear.

"Good. Because me and the rest are about worked to death, and we sure could use your help. We're close to commencing work on an . . . abode, you know. I reckon now we can light into it soon."

He turned his horse and beckoned the deputy and Lockjaw to follow. The rest of them climbed back into the wagon, and soon it was rolling a few yards behind the three mounted men toward the ramshackle corral ahead.

"I have a couple of Mexican fellows I found who know more

than I do about mixing adobe, so there's that. First thing we need to build is a stockade."

"What for?" said Mark Havert. "Thought you needed a bunkhouse and a barn."

"We need all those things, but the attacks have been coming quicker than we're able to keep up with."

"What attacks?"

"Apaches, banditos, you name it. This place has been lawless and border free for long enough that the outlaws have nested right in here such that you'd think they had the deed to the place and not Regis. We've been doing our best to keep them away so we can gather beeves and mustangs. But soon we're going to have to take the fight to them. That's all there is to it."

He leaned closer to the deputy and glanced back behind them. "Been waiting for Regis to send troops enough to do just that. Between you and me, I think I'm going to be waiting awhile longer."

He straightened and raised his voice once more. "Next best thing is to build that stockade. Something to keep us safe while we're waiting on troops and working on the other buildings, abode included." He winked and shook his head. "That Regis. I'll wager he knew the word would make its way to me."

"Well, we have another week's worth of supplies in the wagon. Then I expect Regis will bring more."

"Good," said Bone as they neared the corral. "Percy over there by the smokey mess he calls a fire is, believe it or not, one hell of a camp cook. Surprised us all with his abilities with a ladle and a fry pan. Might keep him another week before I shoot him."

The men from the docks stiffened. Through the smoke a voice shouted, "Don't pay him any mind. He calls himself the boss, but Bone is little more than a hindrance to the work of the day around here."

"That's it, Percy. I'm about through with your lip." Bone slid his revolver from its holster and the men from the docks, still wide-eyed, each backed up a step.

Bone regarded them. "If I didn't know better, I'd say you men don't have much of a sense of humor. That'll change. Now come on over and have some coffee. Percy here'll work up some grub, then we'll get at it. We try to use as much daylight as we can around here. Elsewise we'll be caught with our trousers flapping about our ankles when the banditos arrive."

Chapter 27

Four days after the sailors arrived, Regis rode in with Shep in tow. As was their custom, Bone and Regis caught up over cups of coffee.

The riverboat captain looked at his friend over the rim of his steaming cup. "You like this? I mean all this." He gestured at the surrounding landscape.

"Oh, I like some of it," said Bone. "None of it's the worst thing I ever have done. But let me ask you a question: What man likes everything he gets up to in life?"

"True, but I guess what I mean is, Why are we doing this?"

"I should think that was plain as the hair on your lip. Man's got to do something in life, might as well spend your time making your later years comfortable. And if you happen to like what it is you get up to, so much the better."

Regis smiled and shook his head. "I can't figure you, Bone. We've known each other a long while now, and you are the . . ."

"I think the word you're looking for is *confoundingest*."

"That's it! Perfect for you. Now, take these longhorns you've been wrangling. We won't ever make a ranch pay with such critters. They're lean and small, and there aren't enough of them to establish a spread the size I have in mind."

"Little late for you to get cold feet, ain't it, Regis?"

The big man sipped his coffee. "Not cold feet exactly, but we could make so much more money if we had real, honest-to-god beeves."

"I won't argue that, but where you going to get those? The market right now for hides and tallow's not so bad. Everybody needs leather and candles, after all."

Regis stood and began pacing before the fire. "See now? That's what I'm talking all about. There's more to this business than candles and leather, Bone. Has to be if we're going to have a ranch our grandchildren can be proud of."

"Hold up there, Royle. I don't normally think that far ahead."

"One part of you does, anyway," said Bone, half-joking.

"Yeah, that's why I'm out here. I'm taking a break from the hard work of . . ."

"*Womanizing* is the word you're looking for, I believe," said Regis.

Bone let that one roll off. "What do you suggest we do?"

"Funny you should ask." Regis rubbed his big hands together as if he were about to kindle a fire between them. "What if we could herd genuine fat and happy cattle to far markets, where the people live, and I mean lots of people?"

"You mean cities," said Bone, all set to roll his eyes. "Richer men than us have tried that, Royle. Some make it, but for the most part they end up poorer and with a herd of dead or dying cattle no bigger than coyotes and twice as ravenous."

"I heard tell of folks driving their cattle from Texas to New Orleans and Chicago. And there was that fella drove his herd all the way to New York City. Can you believe that? I'm telling you, Bone. There's cash money to be made with cattle, real money, not this local foolishness for pocket change for tallow and hides. They're worth at best about three dollars a head in these parts, but you drive them to a sizable market, say a railhead, at least a town with some substance, and the market price right now for the same beast is thirty dollars. Think about that."

"I am, and don't think I haven't." Bone shifted and smoothed his moustaches. "Okay, then, let's play that game. Say we could get them to a market. Even at half that, we're still turning profit. And we maintain our numbers. Once we get a leg up and over these raiders, the herd will double in size in about three years."

Both men let the thought linger a moment, then Bone said, "It might could work."

"Yep," said Regis. "What are the other expenses? I know there are a lot, but I want to hear you tell me, Bone. You're the cattleman, after all."

"Correction to that, Regis. I'm a Texas Ranger first, and a man with ranching experience second."

"Fine with me."

"All right. Thinking down the lane a bit, we pay a cowboy twenty-five dollars a month and found, and he and maybe one other fella tend five hundred, hell, a thousand established grazers. You've paid for them for the month with two head of cattle. That leaves nine hundred ninety-eight head at thirty dollars each. I'm not a fast numbers toter, but that's a fair profit."

"Yeah, it is. And the golden key, as far as I can tell, is railroads. We need one to make it to south Texas. Heck, even north Texas. And when it does, I want to be ready with a herd bigger than anybody else in this place."

"When's the railroad coming, though?"

"That's the trouble, not for a while yet. But when it does . . ."

"We need to be ready."

"Yep."

"And then we'll be rich."

"Yep."

"And that's why you went to all the trouble to track down the original Spanish land grant, eh?"

Regis nodded. "Biggest part of it. Sure it's a gamble, but everything in life is, right? I don't want to be caught using this land, having spent years building up a vast herd, only to be told when the railroads come in that I've been here illegally and I'll have to leave—and take my cattle with me. No sir, where would we go?"

He shook his head. "Look at all these other ranchers who are doing that. Like your friend, Pushaw, was it? They're in for a hard time of it in years to come. No sir, we may lose money in the early days, but no business venture worth its salt for the long trek ever made much money at the outset."

Regis rubbed his long fingers through his hair and kept pacing, excitement sparking in his eyes. "We've only owned the land for a couple of months, but look at what we've done already. You've been rounding up the longhorns. . . ."

"Wish we had as many of them as we do those pesky wild mustangs. They're eating the range down to nothing."

Regis nodded. "Okay, then, we'll round them up and sell some of them off. There's a solid market for them, too. Plus, we'll need more horses, even those crazy wild things. Point is, Bone, we're building up a ranch base proper, not just a cow camp anymore."

"If it's going to be as big as you say, we're going to need proper bunkhouses and stables and a cookshack, to begin with. And that means more men. A lot more." Bone leaned forward. "And not just a handful of sailors, either." He held up a hand to deter Regis's protestations. "I'm not saying they're not good workers, 'cause they are, but we need more permanent men who are skilled at cowboying."

Regis nodded. "It'll happen. Trust me." He sat down again.

"Oh, I'd like to live here before long. I'm tired of town living, and even life on the boats has lost its flavor for me."

Bone whistled. "Sounds like this place has worked itself under your skin. Yep, I'd say you have it bad. And there ain't no cure, pard."

"Not sure I want one. But first things first. I have a man coming out with a crew next week to survey the boundaries so we know exactly where our land begins and ends. That way there won't be any trouble when other ranchers try to claim our land and the cattle on it."

"You unsure of what we have?" said Bone.

"Nope, but I want to be dead right, because when the time comes and we get challenged, and it'll happen—especially out here in this Wild Horse Desert where it's every man for himself and has been since the Lord was a bairn—we want our boundaries to be surveyed, recorded, and deeded. Solid as bedrock."

"Can't argue that. But a surveyor, huh? He'll need help carrying chain and such."

Regis nodded. "Mighty humbling work. Long days. I'll put my time in. There are sections of this ranch I've not seen yet."

"Heck, Regis, it'll take you years before you see all of it."

"I know. But I had in mind another person who ought to see it."

"Shep?"

"Yeah." Regis looked around, lest the kid be listening. He was apt to be lurking most anywhere.

Bone didn't have the concerns Regis did and spoke openly about the boy, as he did about anyone else, for that matter. "Be good for him. Humble him a little and get him out from underfoot. You think he's up for it? Long days, hard work."

"I know what you're saying, and I can't disagree. He needs it. I'll mention to the surveyor to go easy on him for a spell, use his judgment. He's still healing. But yeah, I think he's ready. More to the point, I think I am. He's a trial at times, that kid."

Bone snorted. "I can't imagine you were much of a saint."

"When I was his age I was crewing on a riverboat for Cormac."

Bone nodded. "I was his age, I was a full-bore ranch hand on a spread up in Missouri Territory. The man thought he was going to go into ranching, anyway. Turns out all we did was run from the Indians. Lucky I got out of there with all my hair."

"Uh-huh, imagine all those ladies you'd have cheated out of running their fingers through it."

"It's a trial being me, it surely is," said Bone, stretching like a lion waking from a nap.

"Before the surveyor gets here, I've been meaning to talk with you about water. We have a good thing with the Santa Calina, but it's too far from the grassy knob we've staked out as this spot to build up the ranch proper. It's good here because of the streams. They feed the river."

Regis pointed to the northwest, visoring his eyes from the sun. "You see that stream over there? I've been keeping an eye on it, and I think she's spring fed. We could carve that out. You see where the land makes a bowl on three sides?"

Bone nodded. "Having a dam would make life easier, especially when the weather turns prickly. It's ain't always this green, you know."

"You say that like I'm about to argue the point with you."

"Oh, I'm not surly, just ready to play with cattle, spend the day in the saddle again. This business of building, it's not my favorite way to spend my time."

"Not too much longer, my friend," said Regis, smiling.

Bone sighed and grinned. "I'll take that in writing, if you please."

Later, talking with his brother at supper, Regis tried his best to answer a question the youth asked about why he liked the ranch so much.

"Being a captain of ships is all I've ever known, really, and it's a good life and a profitable one, too. But there's something about this place, dry as it is, that's different."

He looked at Shep to see if that explained it. Shep did not look convinced.

"Look, boats sink, rot, break apart, you name it, and a vessel's likely to do it. But land, now what can you do to it? It's always going to be there for you. And this land has value. Sure it's dusty, but not all of it. Some of it's downright lush. There's hay to be made here, enough to feed the cattle in the lean months. And what's more, there's clear sweetwater springs. Not lots of them, but it takes only one to make a ranch grow. It takes land and water, and we have both. Work with me on this, Shep, and we can have something Mama would have been proud to see."

"Mama's why you're building the Royle Ranch up so much?"

Regis thought a few moments, then nodded. "I never really thought of it that way before, but yeah, maybe so. Part of it, at least. I feel like I owe her, and since it's too late on that score, I can do right by you. And should I marry one day, I want something to pass on to my own offspring."

Shep shook his head and turned away, but Regis could see he was blushing. "You find that funny, do you?"

"Naw," said Shep. "Just odd how things turn out. I thought you were something else way back before you left home. Then I grew up not knowing you, save for letters. Then I find you again and you're a grown man with thoughts of marrying and children."

"Whoa now, I never said I was getting married. I said one day."

"Same thing, ain't it?"

"Isn't it, and no, it's not the same thing. But you mark my words, you'll feel this way one day too."

"Ha! No sir, not Shepley Royle. I aim to be like Bone."

"Somebody say my name?" said the Ranger through a mouthful of beans, plunking down beside them.

"Yeah, me," said Shep. "I was telling Regis how I aim to be like you, not ever getting married, not settling down, dallying with all manner of women."

Instead of the usual mirthful look on the Ranger's face, Shep saw the man's features slacken. He swallowed the mouthful of food and looked back to his plate. "Yeah, well, it's not all you think it is, boy. Lot to be said for settling down and enjoying the company of a good woman. You'd do well to look elsewhere for inspiration. Heck"—he motioned toward Regis—"you could do worse than take after your own kin. Except for them moustaches. Hoo, that's pretty near a crime the way you carry that weasel around on your lip, Regis."

"At least I have enough manly sand to grow hair. You look like a fuzzy little girl half the time."

That was all it took. Bone set his plate down, dragged his hand over his mouth, then walked sideways in a wide circle, beckoning to Regis with his fingertips. "Come on now, let me show you how a fuzzy little girl fights. Unless you're too busy combing your manly weasel, that is."

Shep grinned and looked at his brother. There was that glint in his eyes, and even under the big moustache he saw Regis smiling. Just enough. He set down his own plate and proceeded to unbutton his cuffs and roll his sleeves up past the elbows. The two men circled each other, not saying much, but each smiling. Just enough.

The silence and emerging spectacle of what was about to happen quieted the other men, and they nudged one another and formed a half ring and watched.

Percy walked in the middle of them, drying his hands on his long, grimy apron. "You two take this silliness away from my cook camp. I am busy and I don't have time for child's play. I don't care if you're the bosses or not. Now git!" He stalked back to the fire and stirred with vigor whatever he had bubbling.

Neither Regis nor Bone made a sound or nod to acknowledge Percy's admonishments, but both men stepped sideways, clearing the unofficial cooking and eating area in deference to the odd man's scolding.

Chapter 28

The time had been spent building roads and improving what they could. Rounding up the feral longhorns was slow and dangerous work, only slightly more so than all the slow back-breaking construction. One group worked on the stockade fence at the same time as another built the first true ranch building, a daub-and-timber hut the men only half-jokingly called the "mud pile."

"Looks like we'll be living in a dung heap."

If Tut hadn't said it with a grin, Bone might have taken offense. But the men deserved to mock their own efforts. At least it was a place to store their gear, sleep out of the elements, and anything they did to the place was an improvement. They knew it couldn't get much worse.

Both Bone and Regis ached for the day when sufficient structures had been built and they could begin the real work of ranching, when they could set out to buy cattle to fill their vast—and growing—acreage. It would have to wait.

The men were dog-tired, bone-tired, and Regis knew it. He'd seen enough overworked, underpaid men in his time. He'd been one and still was much of the time.

For as many hours as he put into maintaining the shipping fleet and now the ranch, there was no bank in the world that could pay him for those hours. But as hard as he worked, Cormac had always worked twice as hard. The man lived, breathed, ate, drank, and slept shipping.

Regis had often wondered—and once, years ago, had even asked—why Cormac hadn't ever married. Rarely had his boss and best friend lost his temper with him, but he did that time. He'd poked a finger in the air at him and said, "You'd do well to mind your own business instead of that of others, thank you kindly."

Regis had felt his cheeks and ears burn red and that was it, the beginning and end of the only talk they'd had on the subject.

But now, with ranch hands and vaqueros mixing with sailors and dock laborers from town, he'd not given much thought to how the men would get along. He had to say that the men from the docks tended to work harder than the cowboys, with the exceptions of younger hands eager to impress and show off that they'd grown up working hard.

Now that they all grunted and sweated and labored side by side all day without letup, Regis began to see signs of discontent. He couldn't blame them. For his part he was preoccupied with wrangling the surveyor, who sent word that he would be several days later beginning the job than he anticipated. Regis was also keeping close tabs on his brother, who, despite their long talk in town, still showed signs of chafing under his direction.

Now that they were all back at the ranch, instead of flourishing under the tutelage of so many men and removed from the temptations that abounded in town, Shep seemed to shrink in on himself somehow. He spooked at the slightest sudden noise and rarely wanted to leave Regis's side. And from the purple-and-black smudges beneath the kid's eyes, it looked as if Shep were the only man in camp not getting a full night's sleep.

Except for Percy, who was proving to be an excellent cook

and all-around solid hand. But Percy was a worrier of the first order who tended the fire and rose to begin his morning culinary maneuvers at an ungodly hour. He was fairly quiet about it, though.

He was also becoming cantankerous in an amusing way. More so than he was when he'd first landed among them. Tut, who knew Percy the longest of them all, merely shrugged and said the young man had always been an odd duck.

One morning while the men were making quick work of a platter of Percy's buckwheat flapjacks and pot on pot of hot, thick coffee, Regis sidled over to the cook, who was busy putting beans to soak. "Percy, I'd like to talk with you a minute."

"What about?"

Hold your tongue, Regis told himself. You can't afford to lose a man, so let the skinny drink of water have his lippy way. He'd been complaining long and loud about needing an extra set of hands. Here, maybe, was a solution for both men. Didn't hurt that Regis would finally be shed, at least for a few hours a day, of his "Shep Shadow," as he called him when talking with Bone.

"I heard you were complaining that you didn't have enough time in the day to do everything you need to. That about right?"

"You bet it is. I could work around the clock trying to feed you rascals and all I get is a bunch of complaining belchers who come in like a herd of buffalo, stomp on through, upend my equipment, then stomp on out again!"

"Okay, calm down. I only came over to tell you I have a helper for you."

The man didn't pause in his measuring and scooping and shuffling of dry goods from one spot to another on his vast worktable. Despite this, Regis thought he saw the man smile.

"I don't have time to train anybody! You think what I do is easy? Why, I—"

Regis set a big hand on the man's shoulder and squeezed,

turning Percy to face him. "Hold up, Percy. Save that grumbling crap for the men. They find it amusing. I don't. And don't forget I'm the boss of this outfit." He bent his head closer to Percy's and in a low voice said, "I want you to do this as a favor to me, understand?"

Percy's eyes widened. "Okay, boss."

"Good. It's my brother, Shep. He's not been right since he was taken by that she-devil. His body's mostly healed, but he's jumpy and can't settle on a thing. It's in his mind, you see. I need to go with that surveying crew once they get here, and I'm afraid he'd not find the work to his liking. I thought at first I'd take him along, but he's too skittish."

He waited for Percy to say something smart, but the skinny cook just nodded, so Regis continued: "I'd appreciate it if you'd take him under your wing. He's a good worker when he sets his mind to a task. I won't have to leave for a couple of days yet, as it turns out, so why don't we give it a go, see how you two get on together?"

"You bet, boss." Percy nodded, looking once more like the somewhat humble younger man he'd met when he and Tut rode up that day some weeks back.

"Okay then. I appreciate it, Percy. I'll talk with him and send him your way shortly."

Chapter 29

It was late on a Tuesday, a day sooner than Regis expected, when a small work wagon towed by a muscled mule rolled up. It emitted slight clunks and clanks as it wheeled along the roadway they'd established. As it approached, Regis paused in stripping the saddle off his horse. He laid it over the nearest corral rail and walked to meet the wagon as it rolled to a stop.

He waved a hand to the man in the seat. "Mr. Bulmer, I assume?"

The man nodded, touched his cap, and said, "G. Rothschild Bulmer, land surveyor, at your service, sir."

"Given your letter, I wasn't expecting you until later in the week."

The man was a slight, bespectacled fellow in a rumpled collarless shirt, braces, and tweed jodhpurs above tall lace-up brown leather boots. He smiled and said, "I was able to complete that job earlier than expected. That is to say, on time. And so I am here."

"Good to have you. Drive your rig over to the stabling area yonder." The man nodded, lightly snapped the lines to his mule's back, and they rumbled forward.

Regis walked alongside. "I see you are traveling alone. Unless you have a helper tucked in one of those boxes in the back of your wagon, that is."

Bulmer smiled. "Nothing like that, I'm afraid. My assistant has gone and joined an expedition to the Arctic, of all places. I made the mistake of granting him a night off back in Corpus Christi, and he attended a traveling explorer's magic lantern presentation. He was overwhelmed, to say the least, spoke of nothing else, and visited the man again the next day, wherein the man informed him of a new trek he was putting together and offered my junior the opportunity to become the expedition's lead surveyor and cartographer."

Bulmer stepped down from the wagon and winced as his back stretched and popped. "I daresay he's qualified, skillwise, but he's . . . how might one say it kindly? Less worldly and mature than a twenty-two-year-old should be. Have you ever known anyone like that, Mr. Royle?"

Just then Shepley caught sight of Regis and made for him.

"As a matter of fact, Mr. Bulmer, I do know just such a fellow." Shep walked up and Regis said, "Mr. Bulmer, I'd like to introduce you to my younger brother, Shepley Royle. Shep, Mr. Bulmer."

The two shook hands.

"In fact," said Regis, "we were just talking about you." He traded a quick glance with Mr. Bulmer, who nodded knowingly but betrayed nothing.

"Mr. Bulmer is the surveyor I've been talking about. I'll be riding out with him come morning to get a fix on where our land lies and where it doesn't."

"Great. That sounds like fun."

Regis rasped his hand across his chin. "When I said I'll be going, I meant *I'll* be going. You'll be staying here, to keep helping Percy. He's overworked enough as it is. Wouldn't be fair to pull you away from him just when you're becoming useful."

The cloud that descended on Shep's face and that narrowed his eyes presaged hot words that even the newcomer, Bulmer, could foresee. The surveyor coughed and said, "I should relieve poor Gretchen of her load."

"Gretchen?"

"Yes, my mule. I named her after my sister. Equally willful and stubborn, but endearing nonetheless."

"Very good, then. Gretchen is most welcome. You'll find feed in that plank bin there and ample water. We've a good spring not far to the north."

"Excellent."

"When you're through with that, Mr. Bulmer, I hope you'll join us for our evening meal. It's not fancy fare, but it's tasty. Our cook's a rare find in these parts. Isn't that right, Shep?"

He got no answer save for the continued glare.

Bulmer smiled and nodded and commenced unfastening the traces.

"You're going to leave me here?" Shep squared off, his temper showing on his reddened face and in the opening and clenching of his fists.

Regis walked away from him, in part to get him out of earshot of the newcomer. As he expected, Shep strode right on his heels, continuing to growl his complaints.

When they'd walked thirty feet or so away from the camp, Regis spun, thrusting a long finger in his brother's face. "You listen to me, little man."

Shep's ire was still in evidence, but he'd been set back on his heels and his eyes widened.

"Another word, one more word, and you will be sorry you ever opened your mouth at all today. You understand me? We've been down this road before, you and me, and by God, if I'm not half-tired of it."

"Then take me with you."

"Why? It'll be hard work and long days out in the field. We won't be back here for some time, I don't know how long. You want that? I'm doing you a favor, you little whelp. Ever think about that?"

"I don't want any favors. I want to . . ." Shep said through clenched teeth. His face shook, and he turned away and stalked toward the river. He made it about twenty feet from Regis when he stopped suddenly. Though the day's light was waning, Regis could see the young man's shoulders shaking slightly. Was he cold?

No, fool, thought Regis. I am such a fool. The kid's afraid, full of fear right to the bone. Afraid to go too far from me. Afraid to walk to the river, afraid to rove from the camp at all. What did those animals do to his little brother? He'd not talked much about his ordeal, though Regis had tried to pull it out of him.

Regis pulled in a big breath, let it out, then walked to the kid. He stood just behind him. "Shep, I'm sorry." He waited, but his brother said nothing.

"Shep?"

The kid folded his arms over his chest and in a low, thick voice said, "What?"

"I didn't realize how bad it was . . . how tough you've had it. What they did to you . . ."

"Yeah, well, you've been busy, right?" He turned and faced Regis, his puffy eyes wet and rimmed red. "You have a big ranch to run and a riverboat business, and you make sure everybody knows it, too. I'm sorry I ever came here. I should have stayed back East. As Bone would say, I'm a burr under your saddle."

"Shep, that's not true."

"Well, I have nothing of my own, so you're stuck with me. At least until I can earn enough money to go somewhere else. You said eighteen, right?"

"What?"

"You said I have to be eighteen before you'd let me make my own decisions, right? Well, I have less than a year to go. So until then, I'll do what you say. I'll get over whatever problems I have, don't worry. I'll help Percy, even if he is a grump."

Regis seemed to sag before him. He hung his head and rubbed his big-knuckled hands together. "That's not what I want, Shep."

"Regis, it's not about what you want. It's about me this time."

"I know. I know. That's why . . . I think you should come with me and Mr. Bulmer. I was wrong, I see that now. If you're up for it, we're down a man, so we'll for sure need the help."

Shep said nothing but looked Regis in the eyes.

"I mean it. I said it before, I thought I was doing you a favor, leaving you here. But if you're up for it, we can use you. He was supposed to have an assistant with him, but the man left on some feather-brained adventure."

"What sort of adventure?"

"What? I . . . uh, he said some expedition to some fool place."

"That sounds good to me."

"Really? Why?"

"Bound to be nicer than slowly roasting to death out here in the Desert of the Dead."

Regis recoiled as if he'd been slapped. "Where'd you heard that?"

"It's what one of the vaqueros said everybody south of here calls this place. I can see why."

Regis sighed. "So what do you think? Going to help me and Mr. Bulmer plot out this land? Seems to me you should be part of this, anyway, seeing as how you're one of the partners."

Shep ran a finger under his nose and snorted. "Yeah, I guess so. If you really need me."

Regis clapped a hand on Shep's shoulder. "You bet we do. Now let's go talk with Bulmer. Ask him about expeditions and such."

Chapter 30

Sunrise the next say found Shep yawning and hopping on one foot, tugging on a boot while Regis and Bulmer finished loading the wagon with provisions.

"I expect to have the southwest and perhaps some of the west boundaries defined in a week, give or take, as we indicated on the map last night. Then we can either make for here again to renew our provisions or stay out and have someone bring supplies to us."

"What's your preference?" said Regis.

"I'd prefer to stay out, but that makes everything more logistically challenging."

"I'm glad you see that, Bulmer. If I had the men to spare, we'd have even more hands with us, but I just don't. And I need all the rest down here, working for Bone digging the reservoir and building the stockade fence."

"Stockade?" Bulmer's eyebrows rose.

Regis nodded. "Mmm-hmm. We need to protect what little we have built up here. It's been one thing after another. More than we expected, in fact."

Bulmer looked up from repositioning a brass-cornered box in the wagon bed. "What's that mean?"

"It means we're being attacked more often than I thought

we'd be. Turns out a whole lot of people who used to use this land aren't taking our presence as it's intended."

"And how's that?"

"We intend to stay. They can't keep butchering our stock and lobbing potshots at us and expect us to run, which is what we've had to do, though it grinds my teeth to admit it. Bone and his men drove another bunch off a couple of weeks back. Since then we've seen a few here and there. What sort of rancher am I if I can't protect my men?"

Bulmer buckled a shoulder strap on the mule's harness. "It would seem to me, Mr. Royle, that if the brigands are as thick as you say on this land, you'll need more than a stockade. You'll need a veritable blockhouse."

Regis's smile slipped, and he nodded slowly. "You know, Mr. Bulmer, that is not a bad idea. Not a bad idea at all. Let me talk with Bone before we leave."

The surveyor's eyebrows rose. "I wasn't serious," he muttered as he watched the big man striding away.

The surveyor's tripod pressed down on Shep's shoulders. "Can't we take a breather, Regis?"

He said it and regretted it almost immediately. They'd decided to begin at a point along the Santa Calina where the ranch holdings crossed the river. That had been days before, and since then they'd crossed back over. None of it made much sense, but Bulmer seemed to know what he was up to.

Shep was trying his best to see what Regis found so fascinating with the land. Sure, they were in the midst of a pretty and green massive sea of long grasses silvering and rippling in a breeze. But the sun was still a blistering thing.

Bulmer was proving to be a quiet but steady professional. Working his compass and transit, he roved ahead, a massive sidearm swinging from his belt.

"I assure you both I know how to use this," he said even before they'd left the camp.

Now he was the one giving orders, putting Regis in a new and unnatural position as the one on the receiving end of directives. It amused Shep, but he found it of interest that Regis found it acceptable, so he figured he ought to make more of an effort, too. And he had, for a time.

He lugged the surveying chains and tripod and nodded and did whatever Bulmer told him to. He'd even managed to forget the fact that Regis and Bulmer drifted pretty far from him at times.

He did not forget that Tomasina Valdez was still running free out there somewhere with her crazy man, Hector, in the blue-banded sombrero. The one who'd be there staring at him, sneering whenever he woke, tied too tight and slumped against the post. The man would be there, shaking his head as if he'd asked Shep a question and he'd gotten it wrong. He would always be there. Of that, Shep was certain.

The three men came together for midday meal. With the surveyor's help, Shep rigged up a tarpaulin and poles off the side of the wagon for shade. While Shep tended Gretchen the mule and Regis's horse, King, Bulmer walked around the back of the wagon to where Regis was tugging free the vittle box.

Percy had insisted on calling it that. He said it sounded more authentic than *food*. Bone had shaken his head and walked away. "Authentic? What's he think we're doing out here? Play acting?"

Regis recalled the exchange while he flipped open the leather-hinged lid to see what the cookie had packed for them. They had plenty of cooking of their own to get up to at the ends of their days, but for midday meal, he was more than happy to gnaw through a couple of leftover biscuits and maybe a few dried apple slices.

"You know," said Bulmer, "they say you should never be able to see one before it's too late."

"What's that?" said Regis, not finding any apples.

"Indians. Apache, perhaps."

Now Regis looked at the slight man. "What makes you say that?"

Bulmer didn't turn but said, "The rise to my left. Don't give us away. I just saw six, perhaps eight, all ahorseback. Still there?"

Regis kept his head bent as if still looking in the box but glanced askew over the smaller man's cocked hat. He saw nothing but grass. "Are you certain? Lots of mustangs hereabouts."

"Mr. Royle," said Bulmer, smiling, "I've seen and been seen by just about everything you can think of in my line of work, including Apaches. I know what I saw."

Regis checked his urge to make for his horse and the rifle resting uselessly in its scabbard. But Bulmer was right. Take the time in each movement, act as if nothing were happening, don't tip off the enemy. They might just be watching them, after all.

Then he saw Shep holding a nose bag up before Gretchen but looking west of the rise. Had he seen something? And then the kid turned his face toward Regis and caught his eye. Regis saw that same shrunken, frightened boy he'd seen in the cave when he rescued him from Tomasina Valdez's clawhold.

He needed the boy to get strong, to stay strong. "Hold there, Shep. Keep acting as though you've seen nothing." He smiled and said it as though he'd just told the boy to pass the coffeepot.

Bulmer nodded and nudged Regis's elbow. "Two rifles under that long tarp just behind the seat. And ammunition. You're taller than I. You stay close to the wagon so you can retrieve them should the need arise. I'll continue with our midday meal preparations."

"Okay. But I need Shep to be safe. He's had a rough time. I only hinted at it, Bulmer. But he can't go through such again."

"I'm afraid he may not have a choice." Bulmer nodded and jerked his chin upward, looking past the big man's right shoulder. "They've flanked us."

Regis angled his head and caught movement of something dark pulling just out of sight behind grasses, several hundred feet away. He cursed himself for not paying more attention. He'd been caught up in the surveying process, and in seeing, really seeing, his land for the first time. It had been fine, like rubbing balm on an ache he hadn't known he'd had but had been there his entire life.

From that day he'd first ridden through the Santa Calina range, and every day since spent at the ranch, and even more so on this day, he'd been awakening to the realization that this is where he belonged. In all the world, in all the journeys he'd been on, this was the one place that made him feel, really feel, like he was home. And to be able to share it with Shep was even more special.

And now it could all be stripped away by an arrow or a bullet to the back. *Well*, he thought, *not if I have any say in the matter*. He moved forward along the left side of the wagon, sliding his right hand inside as if he were musing on what to do next. He hoped that all outward appearances showed a casual man about camp. But his left hand hung at his side, fingertips brushing the holstered revolver.

As far as he knew, the Apaches were farther away on this side of the wagon. To their rear, toward the east, from the direction they'd traveled, he saw nothing, and as the land dipped slightly downward from their position, he saw a vast distance in that direction. Past the front of the wagon, waving grasses revealed more of nothing. He could not assume they were only on two sides of them, but it was a good start.

He made his way to Gretchen. So far Shep had taken his advice and had not revealed much sign he was frightened or that he knew they weren't alone out here.

"Might be nothing, Shep. But I'd like you to make your way over to King and bring him closer. I'm glad you didn't strip off his saddle yet."

It had become a joke between them because Shep always left Regis's horse chores until last in a lazy, half-hearted effort to get Regis to do them himself.

"Lead him over here and make like you're going to unsaddle him, but don't. We may need to use him. Keep on the right side, close to the rifle. That'll be yours if you need a long gun. And don't forget you have your revolver."

"What about you? And Mr. Bulmer?"

"Two rifles in the wagon, plus our pistols. We're covered. If shooting starts, you stick close to the wagon and try to keep it between you and whoever's coming. I think they're to both sides of us, but not to the rear. So that's your safe side."

He saw Shep's face whiten, as if the blood were being squeezed from him. Regis fought down the corpse-like vision and smiled. "Likely nothing will happen. They're probably curious, that's all. They see we're harmless, they'll ride off."

But that's not what happened. Before Shep could lead King back to the wagon, a high-pitched birdlike sound rose up from the grass to their left followed by the same from their right. Then, as Regis suspected it would, a bullet sizzled in and struck the wagon's right side.

Regis looked up to see Shep standing still, eyes wide, staring across the wagon toward the land beyond. It was as if he were carved from stone.

"Shep!" Regis shouted the name again, harder, and the kid looked at him. "Get over here—grab the rifle!"

That shook the kid from his daze, and he untied King's reins and the pair bolted to the wagon.

He handed the reins to Regis, who used one hand to hastily tie them to a rail. He had the rifles in the wagon uncovered and was thrusting one, butt-end first, toward Bulmer's reaching arms. "Hope they're loaded!" shouted Regis.

Bulmer nodded. "They are."

"Good, then get firing!"

With Bulmer on the wagon's north side and Regis at the front and Shep behind him along the south side of the wagon, they commenced.

Regis measured his shots, firing only when and where he saw something move. He'd had enough experience by now to know that if something seemed out of place out here, it was. But knowing that and getting the mind to respond quicker was something he'd not yet trained himself for. Still, he gave it his best.

But he noticed, too, that Shep kept firing.

He looked at him, but the kid had gone from white to gray-faced and shook as if palsied. He wasn't aiming at much of anything, just firing. And too close to King, who thrashed and churned from side to side.

"We're in a bad spot here, Mr. Royle."

"I know it, Mr. Bulmer, but we're stuck with it."

"Will you two stop talking like you don't know each other," shouted a voice Regis was surprised by.

If Shep had talked to him in that tone before Tomasina Valdez nabbed him, he might have given over to the urge to box the kid's ears. But now he found the surly sound welcome. Maybe the kid was going to be all right. He hoped that tone transferred to a sharpening of thought in the coming fight.

"Shep!" Regis growled at the kid, who wisely didn't look at him but kept his eyes roving the grasses before him. "When I say 'Now!' I want you to get out from behind that horse and break for the left, get to the rear of the wagon. I'll cover you. And keep low!"

No response, not surprising. Regis glanced briefly to his right.

Bulmer was still whipping off random shots, though he looked to be taking aim. So far he was still upright. Regis shattered the lull from the left side, plowing a bullet toward the spot he'd last seen a peering face.

"Now!" he shouted, and Shep didn't move. "Now, Shep! Move! Get back there!"

The kid glanced at him, his eyes wide and his skin a gray-white as if it were the face of a dead man. *Great, the kid's still a mess. Time for a new plan*, Regis told himself.

He covered himself this time, crouching low and pounding out bullets as he cat-footed the dozen feet to Shep's side. Regis grabbed him by the shoulder and shoved him down. "Come with me—now!" That roused Shep from his daze.

"Get to the rear of the wagon and keep low. I'll cover you— now go!" Regis shoved him from the back and nearly drove him face-first to the grassy ground. Shep got up, but a shot sounded and Shep's right leg whipped inward, knocking him to the ground once more.

"Shep!"

"I'm okay!" snarled the kid as he used the rifle to shove himself upright. He bent low at the waist and crouch-hopped to the back of the wagon.

Regis banged two more wild shots southward and bumped into the kid as he rounded the rear of the wagon. He barked, "You shot?"

"Don't think so," said Shep, looking oddly focused and red-faced again.

"Get in the wagon and keep your head down, you hear me?"

Shep nodded and hoisted a leg up over the gate. As Regis boosted him he tried to see if the kid's right leg was bleeding but saw nothing. He shoved roughly at the boy's boots and felt only part of a boot in his big palm.

Shep's right boot's heel was now a ragged hunk of stacked

leather. The attacker had shot the boy's heel, nothing more. He shoved hard and sent the kid sprawling forward, his butt sticking up in the air as he tried to get his knees beneath him.

"Get down, Shep!"

Regis hoped that since the attackers hadn't shot the horse and the mule, they might need them. Maybe they'd be less inclined to kill a man's mounts, as horses were regarded as valuable trade goods. Unlike a human. At least one that bit back.

There was always the worry that someone might want to make off with Shep, being the smallest and youngest. They might want him as a slave, though that happened mostly to women and children. He'd heard of it happening too many times to discount it as a bad rumor.

He hated to leave the animals standing there wincing as shots whipped past them, but he had no other plan. Other than to get Bulmer into the wagon as well. Then he was going to . . . do something. The situation wasn't one he'd expected to find himself in, and he didn't see any simple solution.

Then things began happening even faster. Bulmer dropped from sight, a spray of blood ribboning upward the only indication that a man had been standing in that spot a second before. Regis dropped down himself and knee-walked under the wagon, smacking his head hard on the underside planking. It knocked off his hat, but he didn't stop to fetch it.

The shooting from the left had stopped, at least for the moment. Regis sucked air through his teeth and fought to clear his head of the dizziness from whacking his bean, as Bone would call it.

"Bulmer!" shouted Regis. The man was but a few feet from him, on his knees. His rifle lay in the dirt, his left arm hanging to his side, red blood dripping steadily from three fingertips. He was trying to bend low and pull his arm in at the same time but seemed confused by how to do so.

"Bulmer, get down!" Regis reached out a big hand and

tugged the surveyor's shoulder toward him. The man spun with it, his usually trim look now frayed and haggard. "Got to get you into the wagon bed, Bulmer!"

As he dragged the groaning man backward, a bullet whistled so close to his nose that Regis gasped, jerking his head back like a turtle retreating into a shell. He let go of the man, who sank to the dirt, his groans louder than ever, and poked his rifle through the wheel's spokes. He squeezed the trigger and was rewarded with the best sound a lucky shooter could ask for—a strangled scream. It was followed with a sight he'd not forget for the rest of his days.

A dark-skinned man in rough-weave clothes emerged from behind a wide tuft of grass. He held his hands to his head and lurched in Regis's direction. Though much of his face was hidden by his hands, his screams were loud, growing in volume and intensity as the man staggered forward.

Most shocking of the scene was the flow of thick, bright blood leaching through his fingers. There was so much that it covered his entire head, arms, and shirt as if he'd been dipped in a vat of gore.

The man howled and staggered and wobbled. Then he stopped walking and stiffened as a shot from behind him blew through his back and burst out his chest. It looked as though he'd been punched from behind. The force of it shoved his arms outward as if he were begging a crowd for sympathy. He pitched to his knees and slowly flopped forward.

"Well, I'll be. . . ." Regis almost whistled, the effect was so impressive. "I . . ." A bullet whistled in from his left and snapped his reverie—and almost pierced his skull. It lodged in a span of cross-trussing. A shot from within the wagon's bed reminded him he'd best get Bulmer to safety, as the man was darn certain not able to do it himself.

He'd check on the extent of his wounds later, if there was a later. For now he'd do his best to get him to safety. "Shep!

Help me with Bulmer, but keep your head low, below the side boards!"

The wagon wasn't but five feet wide at best, and maybe eight, nine feet long, but its sides were high. Bulmer rode with a flat canvas tarpaulin stretched across the load ("to keep the dust off," he'd told Regis and Shep when the boy had pestered him with a hundred and one questions within the first half hour on the trail). The sides were high enough that a man could nearly sit up and have only his head exposed from within to those without.

Regis reckoned it would do to keep the surveyor and his brother somewhat safe. Because, as he thrust the groaning, ash-faced man into the wagon from the tailgate, then the man's rifle in after him, a plan had come to him.

It was a thin plan, to be sure, but better than the one he didn't have a minute before. It would require that he get to the front of the wagon and reharness Gretchen.

"Shep, gonna need you to cover me again. I'm going to hitch up the mule. You grab the lines and drag them back into the wagon. I'll cover you while you make a hard tug to the right—slight dip there where you can gain momentum—not much, but it might help. Then snap the lines hard and roll like hell toward that arroyo we passed about a quarter mile back. I'll cover you."

"What about you?"

"Going to be right behind you on King. Don't worry about covering me. I'll fire in every direction at once. You got me? It's our only chance."

"Yeah, okay, but Regis, Mr. Bulmer doesn't look so good."

"I know, but—"

"Do what your brother says. I'll make it—just my shoulder."

"Bulmer! Good man," said Regis, and resisted the urge to clap him on the shoulder, even the good one. Might not be the best thing he could do to the fellow.

Regis bent low and hustled forward once more, nearly got a stout kick from King to his breadbasket, but a few soothing words seemed to help the skittery beast. Maybe it was just Regis's imagination. The horse still danced away, tugging at the looped reins and exposing Regis to the shooters to the south of them.

He ran a trembling hand along Gretchen, who was in a whole lot better mental condition than King, and jammed together the fewest number of buckles and straps he needed to and still have the mule connected to the wagon. Enough so that it wouldn't tear loose halfway to the arroyo.

"Shep! Time to move! When I say 'Go!' you go, by God!"

"Okay!"

Regis thumbed back the hammer on his rifle, squeezed the trigger, and the hammer fell. Nothing happened but a dull metal click. "Gaah!" he growled, and tossed the rifle into the wagon, then dragged out his revolver, sending a shot southward. The attackers had to know what they were up to, but no shots came at them. Yet.

"Go, Shep! Go! Hee-yaaa!" He smacked the mule on the flank once, twice, and the beast showed more life than she had the entire short time Regis had made her acquaintance.

Shep had dragged the lines back into the wagon, and Regis saw the top of the kid's head bouncing and peering up now and again. He resisted the urge to shout at him to keep his head down and instead lunged for the reins still barely holding King to the wagon's rail.

He heard Shep's shouts and shrill whistles, and while he was grateful that the kid wasn't buckling under the pressure of the moment, he wished like hell he'd thought to untie his horse before the situation exploded.

King danced, bucked, neighed, thrashed, then crow-hopped in an effort to get away from the rolling wagon and the stumbling, shouting man beside him. "Hey!" barked Regis as another gunshot pounded. Even in his jumping rage Regis tightened, half expecting a bullet to core his brain any second.

Any kind thoughts he'd had about his horse vanished like smoke on a stiff breeze.

Somehow the wagon turned, and King didn't go with it. Didn't mean the horse lost any of his momentum, however. Regis flailed outward with his right hand and felt his fingers smack hard against the saddle horn. He snagged it and didn't let go.

The horse had turned, and now, freed from being tied to the wagon, King bolted eastward, the general direction Regis wanted to make for, anyway. Trouble was, Regis wasn't yet in the saddle. He barely had a purchase on the saddle horn. But he had long legs and gave chase, then kept apace with the running buckskin.

He also managed to bark and growl a number of choice words that, had the attackers heard them and provided they knew English, would likely have caused them to turn and run. But judging from the sound of trailing gunfire dogging him, they were deaf and free of his mother tongue.

Regis wasn't certain what heavenly entity he should thank for keeping him on the opposite side of King from the southern mob of attackers. Then as he hopped forward, trying to gain an extra few inches on the horse so that he might leap into the saddle, he remembered that there were attackers—likely an equally large number of them, save the one who'd been shot—on the northern side. Which is the direction he was exposed to.

The sun-baked air about him sizzled with whistling, buzzing sounds as shots rained in at him from both directions. He hoped they weren't yet closing in on him from behind, though he knew they would be soon. And ahead?

Ahead, Regis saw the surveyor's once-tidy work wagon slamming and bouncing along the rutted, unforgiving earth. The tarpaulin they'd attached as a sun shade on the wagon's right side flailed like a luffing sail on a ship, then snagged in the spinning wheel and ripped away, balling in the dirt.

The left side of the wagon caromed into, then over, a mesquite that must have been tougher than it looked, because the wagon tipped up away from it before slamming back down. The mesquite looked as surly as they always do.

As it hit, the wagon jostled and jerked side to side, and Regis saw the bodies of the two men inside jouncing up, then disappearing once more behind the tailgate. *Stay hidden*, he thought. *And get to that gulley.*

A sudden conviction came to him as he loped beside the horse, revolver in his left hand and his right still gripping the pommel, that the odds were not in his favor that he'd make it to safety before getting shot by these determined bandits.

But an equally fierce urge shoved the first out of his mind, telling him that all costs, even at the ultimate cost, he must make certain Shep and Bulmer get to safety. As he ran, Regis swung his left arm up and squeezed off a shot to the north, then aimed across his chest, over the galloping horse's back, but held his shot.

He knew he wouldn't hit anything—how many lucky shots was a man entitled to in his life, anyway? But he thought it might keep their heads ducked. Every second bought by a blazing bullet was another second, another long stride toward safety.

He could see the arroyo now, and knew Shep could, too, for the slamming wagon was cutting southward. He was relieved that the kid had seen the gulley on their way past it but a few hours before. It looked as if Shep had also noted the lay of the land, the best way to enter the scant cover the gulley would afford them. Scant but better than nothing.

As if time had once more slowed, Regis felt sound sharpen, close in. His breathing became loud, louder than he'd ever heard it, as if he were hearing it from within himself. The pounding of his bootsteps and the hurried slamming of the horse's hooves began to pinch out. The rasping of his breaths was replaced with his own heartbeat, thudding in steady, measured time.

He felt the sun's heat bleaching everything beneath it, the brightness like the flare of a struck match before his eyes. Still he ran, seeing only twin points of burning light before him. Then he heard a scream, loud, deep-chested, raw, animalistic.

It was a horse's scream, and he was certain the beast beside him had been shot, and yet he kept running. Pounding the earth to get there, to see that Shep was safe, somehow. He had to be, just had to be. He'd promised their mother he'd keep the boy safe. Promised her in his deepest thoughts. Had to be safe. . . .

"Regis! Regis!"

Someone was shouting his name over and over, so close it seemed almost real, like the voice of someone he knew. Then he felt a hard blow to his face, and his eyes widened. Standing over him, looking down at him, was a face he recognized.

"Shep?"

"Regis! You okay?"

"Yeah, I think. . . . What happened?"

"You made it! We all did, to the arroyo. You were right on our tail—heck, you were almost dragging that horse behind you. You're the only man I ever saw so impatient he drags his horse to get somewhere."

"But how . . ."

"I had to jump you, you fool!" said Shep from beside him. "Never saw anybody run so fast in all my life." But the kid was no longer looking at him. He was crouched, holding a rifle, inching up to peer over the top edge of the gulley.

Regis shook his head, laid a hand across his chest, felt his heart still hammering away as if a team of blacksmiths were in there, competing. But his breathing was slowing, and their predicament came back to him in full force. "How's Bulmer?"

"He's okay." Shep jerked his chin to the right, and Regis saw the surveyor leaned against the sandy sloping side of the gully. Beyond Shep stood the wagon, the lines hastily wrapped around a jutting arm of rock. His horse was nowhere in sight.

"Where's King?"

Shep shrugged. "I grabbed you and yanked, and the horse got even more spooked. He kept going."

"How long was I . . . dazed?"

"Not long. I jumped out of the wagon, had enough time to drag Mr. Bulmer with me, then you came ripping up."

Regis rolled onto his side and nudged up beside Shep, both scanning the vista before them. "Too quiet. I know they're still there."

"Wait, look—someone's moving. From the south."

Regis looked and saw a low shape move out a few feet from the jumble of rocks they'd been hiding behind. The shape moved once more.

"Too far to shoot," said Shep.

"You sound disappointed."

"You want them to live?"

"No," said Regis. "But neither do I go around wishing for someone to shoot at."

Shep shrugged but didn't say anything. He kept his eyes on the terrain.

"And stop doing that," said Regis.

"Doing what? Scouting?"

"No, that thing with your shoulders."

"Huh?"

"Never mind."

"You two would argue the hair back onto a bald man, I swear it."

They both glanced over at Bulmer, who was grimacing, trying to rip a strip of fabric from the bottom of his shirtfront.

"Glad to see you're among us still, Mr. Bulmer," said Regis.

"Oh, you won't be shed of me that quickly. I've not yet tendered my bill."

"You've not yet done anything worthy of payment." Regis smiled when he said it, then he turned to his brother. "Shep, help him. I'll keep an eye. And bring over what weapons you can find—and ammunition. And keep your head down. Oh, and give me that rifle, will you?"

The kid looked at him as if he'd just belched in his face. "Anything else I can do for you?"

Regis glanced at him and sighed. "Not right now, but I'll think on it." He held out a big hand.

"Okay, okay." Shep jammed the rifle at him.

And that was all the time they had for small talk, because the figure Shep had seen darted out to where they'd parked the wagon for lunch. He was looking for something, anything, it seemed. And he knew he was beyond range of their bullets. Or was he?

Regis raised the rifle and leveled on the man. It was difficult to tell, given the distance and his limited experience in such matters, but from the looks of the man he'd shot and from the looks of this one, they sure resembled what he suspected an Apache to be. Not that it mattered. Attackers were attackers.

They were men set on killing him and his brother and their new friend, Mr. Bulmer. That meant they were his enemy. And to be an enemy of Regis Royle meant he would do to you what you were doing to him.

He raised the rifle, tried to feel the wind on his face, and felt nothing but stillness. And heat. An odd, fleeting thought nipped in and out of his mind: Could the sun's heat affect a bullet's trajectory over a long distance?

He raised the rifle again and then thought, no, no, this would waste a bullet and they would soon need all of them they could get.

"How are you, Bulmer?" he said, still watching the man in the distance.

"Better than I thought. Shoulder, but I believe it went through."

"That's good to hear," said Regis, knowing if they didn't get the wound cleaned and bandaged he would soon pop a fever, get sicker than a man ought to be, and that could quickly lead to bad things. The worst.

He knew of the probably sequence of events Bulmer had in store because he'd seen it in the Mexican War and a handful of times aboard ships, when gambling among the crew or passengers got out of hand and weapons came into play. In most of those cases they were able to get the wounded to a doctor who could use his tinctures and powders to clean and bandage the wound.

"Any water in the wagon, Shep?"

"Yeah, most of our supplies are still in there. A little banged up, but they made it."

"That ride was something," said Regis. "You were laying in to ol' Gretchen."

"That mule can fly, you bet." Shep whistled low and popped his head up again, looking around before reaching into the back of the wagon.

"Hey, why don't we keep rolling east, back toward the ranch. Well, to the cattle camp. We're already on the ranch."

"I thought of that, but we'd be sitting ducks. Good as she is, Gretchen can't keep up that pace for long, and there weren't any other places that I remember where we could hole up and defend ourselves. Pretty soon we'd be in the same pickle we were in back there. Only worse."

"Worse how?" said Shep. "Ain't like we're in tall cotton here."

"That's true," Bulmer cut in. "But your brother's right, Shep. Now a couple of us are wounded."

Shep looked from Bulmer to his brother. "I thought you were the only one who took a bullet," he said back to Bulmer.

"Not so." The surveyor gritted his teeth as he shifted to a more upright position. "You see that shot-up boot of yours?

That's the sort of wound that slows a man down. And out here, that's downright dangerous."

Shep didn't say anything as he slid out a couple of wooden equipment crates from the back of the wagon. He stacked them on the ground as steps to make retrieving the rest of their gear simpler.

"Easy on those crates, Shep," said Bulmer. "Once we make it through this, I'm going to need all my equipment in functioning order. Some of it's delicate."

"I'm sorry, Mr. Bulmer." Shep moved the others more gingerly, then crouch-walked over to Regis with the two rifles and four boxes of bullets.

"You see my horse anywhere?" said Regis, looking around, eastward toward where he assumed the horse bolted.

"Naw." Shep opened one of the boxes. "He was lathered and looking to be anywhere but here."

"I ever catch up to him," said Regis, "I'm going to tell him how smart he is. Here, I'll do this. Go help Mr. Bulmer. But splash water, then whiskey, in that wound. I think he has a flask. I had a small bottle of it, but it's in my saddlebag. And that's with the horse."

They waited there for a couple of hours, with no more movement from back where they'd run, to either side. That meant the attackers were cutting wide far to the north and south, maybe planning on pinning them down.

Despite the logic of staying put, a whisker of doubt nibbled at Regis, and he wondered if they should have tried to make a run for it. Maybe the Apaches weren't numerous or didn't have decent mounts. "Maybe maybe maybe," he muttered.

"You talking to yourself, old man?" said Shep, followed with a little laugh. Again Regis found himself glad to hear the kid was able to laugh at the situation. To laugh at all. He appeared to have been shaken out of his fearfulness. At least for a time. He was worried it might be otherwise. Still might be, he reminded himself. The day is young.

"Shep, why don't you spell me. I need to stretch my legs."

"Okay." The kid slid down beside him and held out a hand. Regis handed him the rifle. "Give it the full look, both sides and the front. I'll keep an eye out back."

"Yep."

Regis made his way over to Bulmer. "How you feeling?"

"Not great, but Shep helped me clean it out, and I even managed to save some of the whiskey in my flask. Care for a pull?"

Regis wanted one worse than just about anything. The thought of a bracing swallow of gargle, as Bone would call it, sounded fine, but he shook his head. "No, you're going to need it. You keep it."

"I expect they're waiting until dark to move in on us."

"So you think they're still out there, eh?"

Bulmer nodded. "Doesn't mean we can't make a fire while it's still light out."

"Are you cold?" said Regis. If so, that didn't bode well for the man's situation.

"No, I'm thinking about coffee. I always brew up a pot in the afternoon when I'm on the trail. Helps the rest of the day's work go smoother."

"Oh, I like the sound of that." The temptation of whiskey in his mind was replaced with a sharp, sudden urge for a good, bold cup of coffee. "While I'm at it, might as well toast the last of those biscuits."

He gathered scraps of wood, dried branches, and made a mental stock list of their supplies. They had plenty of water for two days, maybe three if they rationed, and more than enough food to keep them, if not fat and happy, at least alive for a week.

All we need, thought Regis, is to get through tonight, and then come the morrow he'd have a new plan. Had to. Else they were going to slowly dwindle. He sort of hoped the attackers would make a move in the night. He was not one for sitting back and waiting for life to happen to him.

"Regis, I don't see anything moving anywhere. Not even a snake, rabbit, no bugs, nothing."

"I saw a vulture circling over us a while ago." Bulmer smiled. "Maybe he thinks I'm beginning to look like something toothsome."

"Oh, don't say that, Mr. Bulmer!"

Shep's reaction shocked Regis, and he was about to say he was certain the surveyor was only kidding when something paused him. He tilted his head back and sniffed. "There, I did smell it."

"What?" said Bulmer, leaning forward with a wince.

"Smoke, I think."

"Hmm, I'd guess our Apache friends had the same idea. Maybe they're making coffee."

"Or they're trying to burn us out," said Shep.

Regis didn't say a thing, but he looked hard all about them. He saw nothing, no smoke rising. Just a long, low line of land, brittle brown below, dotted here and there with rocks and mesquite and patches of grass, but mostly barren. And above and beyond, nothing but clear blue sky.

Maybe they, too, were fixing a meal for themselves.

They waited and waited, cooked their own food while daylight was with them, brewed a pot of coffee, tended to Gretchen, hoping she wouldn't be shot, as her head was likely visible poking up out of the gully. And they waited. And while they waited, Regis doubted himself, worrying that they should have at least tried to escape while the opportunity was with them.

Regis looked over at Bulmer. The surveyor was still sleeping and didn't look to be red-faced and fighting a fever. He looked back over the rim of the gully to the west. "That was my plan, you know."

"What?" Shep looked at his brother. "What are you talking about?"

"I was going to send you on King to get help."

Shep was silent for a moment, then he said, "You think I didn't try hard enough to stop your horse, don't you?"

"No, I didn't say that."

"Well, I don't know if I did or I didn't. I was too busy trying to stop you from running yourself to death. You were crazy, you know. Still are."

Regis smiled. "So are you." He shoved Shep on the shoulder. "Still glad you came out here looking for me?"

Shep's raised eyebrows told him all he wanted to know. "Ask me once this is over with."

"Before dark, we need to figure out a few things."

"Like what?"

"Like we need to get Bulmer"—Regis looked around their little hidey-hole—"over there in that corner. Are you still able to work that rifle, Mr. Bulmer?"

The surveyor shook his head. "No, I don't think so. But I can manage my revolver."

Shep and Regis helped the man, with much grunting and groaning on the small surveyor's part, over to a slab of stone that marked the rough corner. Once there, he sat upright but still leaning, as comfortable as they could make him. From this vantage point he had a wide view of all directions, save for the northeast, directly behind and above him.

"Shep, in that long, narrow crate. Yes, that one, still unopened. It's my second tripod. It should make a solid truncheon. I also have a long dagger. The blade is keen, though I usually use it for rough work, slashing brambles and limbs that are an impediment to my work. If you'd bring it to me, I'll use that should the brutes close in."

"Good thinking," said Regis. He sighed as he looked around. "Sorry about all this, boys. I knew setting up a ranch out here was going to be a gamble, but this is downright hairy."

"Don't lose heart, Mr. Royle." Bulmer shifted his left hip

and raised his leg, pointing the toe of his boot to stretch out sore muscles. "I've surveyed much land in my time. Been at this for, let's see. . . . Oh my, it'll be twenty years next spring! And I've seen some plots of land that are real dogs. But this one, Royle, this one has promise."

"I'm pleased to hear you say that. What would you say if I told you"—Regis glanced at Bulmer, then Shep, then back to the surveyor—"that I might be purchasing more land?"

"More land?" said Shep. "How much does a person need?"

"As much as he can afford, I reckon."

"How much more land are you talking about, Mr. Royle?"

Regis smiled and glanced at them each again. "Nearly twenty-four thousand acres."

The stunned looks on their faces kept the grin on Regis's face. He nodded. "Yep. And at a few pennies an acre, I can't pass it up. Nobody wants it, hard to believe."

"Not for me, it isn't. Look at this place," Shep swiveled his head from north to south and back. "I can't imagine why nobody else hasn't snapped it up before now."

Bulmer laughed. "You'd be surprised, Shepley. There's value here. There are springs, more than you might think, and there's grassland, and herds of wild mustangs and cattle and game. Even if you only held on to it to sell it off piecemeal over time, you'd still make a tidy fortune, I suspect. Or your heirs would."

Regis nodded. "Except I don't intend to sell it off."

"I rather suspected not."

"But Regis, you just heard Mr. Bulmer—you could make a fortune!"

"Never sell land, Shep. Whatever you do, never sell it." Regis let his hard stare linger on the boy a moment longer, then he plopped down beside Bulmer. The men chatted in low tones, with Regis explaining the impending purchase. He scratched in the dirt with a forefinger, pointing here and there, and Bulmer nodded and commented now and again. For the time being, their predicament, and with it all thought of Apaches, was gone.

Shep rolled his eyes and flopped back down along the west edge of the arroyo. "Well, I think you're both crazy."

Neither man indicated they heard him.

Shep looked across the land, his brother's land, once more and noticed the day was slowly darkening. Already the horizon toward the west was shading to a purple-gray dimness that seemed to harbor scuttling figures he knew weren't really there. Or were they?

Chapter 31

The attack came in the night, as Regis had expected.

One moment, Shep's head snapped and bobbed, his chin nudging off his shirtfront, fighting the hard battle with sleep, and the next instant he felt something hit him. "Huh?"

"Shh!"

It was Regis.

"Wake up—they're here!"

Shep dragged a hand down his face and sucked in breath. Skyward the night was not black but speckled with stars, brilliant glittering dots way up there in the blue-blackness of full night.

That was all he had time for, because quick yet soft thudding footsteps sounded to his right, then stopped as two seconds later something hard like a log slammed across his shoulder, a blow thrown by someone who can't quite see who he's fighting. Shep shouted, remembered Regis had told him to keep his mouth shut no matter what, lest he give himself away.

Then he remembered he had a hip knife, an eight-inch blade hanging off his right side. He rolled again, felt something—a hard hand—clip the side of his head, and kept snatching for the bone handle of the knife.

He thought he heard other sounds of struggle. Regis had

been off to his right. The mule still hitched, jerked, and stomped in place.

Then his attacker closed in on him once more, as if he'd been unable to see Shep and had been swatting the ground and the air before him. His sloppy blows landing on Shep, who squirmed away, still trying to free up the knife.

But what about his revolver? He flailed for it and felt its walnut grips, but as with the knife, there was no time to peel it free of its leather holster.

The attacker growled and grunted, sounds a desperate, cornered animal might make.

Then the attacker laid himself, as if he'd tripped, right over Shep. The man's torso was bare and thickly muscled, sweaty and greasy all at once. The frenzied man shifted as if trying to reach for something—his own weapon?

His armpit slammed Shep's face, and he tasted slime and hair and sweat. He tried to bite the flesh jamming into his mouth, but it pressed against his teeth too hard.

An awful stink from the man's armpit clouded Shep's face. The man would have a knife or gun, and Shep knew if he didn't get out from under the attacker or draw his own weapon, he was going to die, and in a very few seconds.

The thong on his gun's hammer was still looped tight, but his hip knife slipped free of its sheath, and he closed his fingers over the handle. A fine fit, he'd thought when he'd selected it from the store in Brownsville with Regis.

He liked the heft and the thickness in his fingers, the balance of it. The man selling it had been insistent that the balance of the blade feel right in either of his hands. He never said why the balance was important, but Shep didn't really care.

It was a pretty knife, and he'd wanted it. Liked the way he felt when he walked around with it and his six-gun. "Heeled," as Bone said.

Now that pretty knife had a job to do, and Shep had no way to draw the knife back for a blow upward, no way of knowing what part of the attacker he was stabbing at. Quick visions of a man staggering into the night with Shep's knife handle jutting from his eye gritted the youth's teeth.

He jammed upward with the blade, and it met no resistance. He tried the other, and he felt the man ease back slightly. One of the man's arms released its pressing hold against Shep's gut, but it moved up, away from Shep, then . . . oh no! Shep knew he was going to be stabbed.

Shep used the slight easing of the pressure against him by the arm and jammed the knife hard upward toward what he hoped was the man's body. At the same time he jerked his hips hard in the opposite direction and bucked, hoping to shove the smelly bastard off him before the Apache, or whatever he was, delivered something more lethal than a reeking armpit.

He didn't quite make it out from beneath the man. Then several things happened at once. The man, though still wriggling, trying to gain purchase on Shep's torso so he could land a knife blow of his own, spasmed and jerked atop Shep. His wriggling slowed. A high-pitched growl, as if from a lion, sounded close to Shep's right ear. Wordless sounds of rage and anger mingled and shoved at his face in a gout of hot, foul breath.

At the same time, Shep's arm kept jamming and ramming above him, but the man sagged all his weight against it. Shep felt the hilt of his blade's handle shoving harder and harder into his side, grating against ribs, ribs that had barely healed from his ordeal with the Valdez gang.

And now he felt two of them pop again, and sharp, hot pains welled inside him. But that was nothing compared with the pain the man atop him was feeling. The warm rush of something hot and wet gushed down Shep's arm, and the man thrashed once more, his growl tapering to a pitiful mewling.

For a moment, Shep did nothing but hold still. The man atop

him was also still, sagged over him. Dead weight. And that's when it came to Shep—he'd just killed a man, stabbed him deep, into the very blackness of death itself.

All about him Shep heard signs of struggle. Gunshots had been echoing, some close by and some not so close, but not as many as he expected for a fight between people who earlier had not worried about throwing lead, filling the still, hot air with cracking shots and smoke.

Then he heard a man bark, "No!" and he knew it was Regis. *And here I am lying on the ground with a dead man atop me, bleeding and crushing my ribs, and I can't breathe, let alone move and help my brother.*

But that last thought, *my brother*, burned like a smithy's fire-stoked tongs deep in Shep's gut, and he jerked his leg higher, got the knee up enough to plant his heel beneath him—what was left of it, anyway—and shoved with all his effort. That leg bore most of the work, and his hand was still wrapped tight on the gore-slick handle of the knife.

He shoved harder, harder; the knife dug deeper into the body above him, and then the wound opened and his hand shoved inside the man. Something hot and slick flopped out and slid down his arm.

Shep screamed through tight-set teeth and, with a final grunting shove, the dead man slopped backward, wrenching the knife from Shep's stiff fingers.

"Shep? Shep!"

The kid tried to shout that he was okay, but it was difficult to gag and gasp and cough all at once. Then a gun cracked from the far back corner of the arroyo and spat a burst of yellow flame, and he knew Regis wouldn't hear him, anyway.

Footsteps pounded all about him. Shep saw something light-colored approaching fast. A man in a flapping white shirt and trousers bent low, ran right by him, within an arm length of his face. At the last second, Shep saw it was definitely not Regis or Mr. Bulmer. He slid free his revolver, but the man disappeared into the gloomy dark.

He pulled in another breath and stumbled after him.

From his spot close by the wide, low mouth of the arroyo, a likely spot for the attackers to approach, Regis heard a rustling and low sounds as if someone whisper-hissed, "Shhhh." Then he saw them, several shapes, hunched low and stalking, stopping, starting again, slow and searching. They were light-colored shapes, skulking forth, specters out of the fog of darkness.

He counted at least eight and wondered if the two groups who'd attacked them earlier had come together to descend on them as one. They must feel confident of themselves and their superior numbers. *They must think we have something more valuable than we do,* he thought. Maybe they suspect the surveying equipment is worth money. Maybe they're just hateful.

The group of eight or so split, the shapes moving apart as if blown by an unfelt breeze. Three made straight for Regis at his end of the gulley.

They wouldn't see him because he'd tucked himself low. He would be on their left as they entered and, with any luck, he'd be able to swing the stout steel-and-maple leg of the tripod hard enough to crack them all on their heads and lay them low. At least long enough for him to jump on them, knife pulled, and revolver, too, if need be. He didn't want to tip off the others as to his location in the dark.

Stealth. Move slowly and surely, strike one, two, three, then get out, back to the shadows and let them writhe and bleed out while he waited for another. Then another. These evil creatures deserved nothing from him but his enmity.

Over the course of the day's long hours spent sweating, squinting, holed up like cornered animals, whatever thin feelings Regis may have harbored hours ago toward them as fellow humans were gone, replaced with seething annoyance at being tormented.

And this hadn't been the only instance. Bone kept him apprised of the various attacks, running or full-on assaults, to his men and to their cow camp. It had to stop, and the only way Regis knew to do that was by becoming the aggressor, the attacker. And that began tonight. And from here on out.

Closer and closer they stepped. Regis gripped the smashing weapon tighter, ready to split their heads like overripe melons.

The first stepped almost into range and stopped, some animal sense telling him to hold. Regis held his pose, the tripod leg rigid in the air behind his right shoulder as if he were setting up for a mighty swing at beating a rug on the line.

The man pulled his head back—a movement, judging by the man's torso, that told Regis he was skittish. All the work and time and money that went into this land, all the torment Shep had gone through for it, all that and more bubbled up in him at that moment. The Apache leaned forward again, and something made him look to his left, at Regis. It was the second-to-last thing the man did.

The last thing he did was to utter a short, clipped bark of surprise. It was short because Regis swung the solid pole hard and fast, straight into the man's head. He felt it meet flesh and bone and keep right on traveling.

The force of the blow whipped the man backward. His knees arched up and shared the same air his last sound was busy polluting, even as his head burst apart and whatever had been the man's blood and brain and bone sprayed away from him.

It covered another man because he'd been right by his fellow raider. Regis didn't wait for the second man to regain control of himself and step over the body of his fallen cohort. Regis Royle kept going, swinging back the wood-and-steel tool, pleased that it had a much longer reach than he did.

Regis stepped in close, and the man he was about to club

pulled the trigger on his gun. Regis felt his shirt tug backward but felt no pain, no wetness, and so he kept moving forward. Before the man could pull the trigger a second time, the big rancher's blow met its mark, well beyond the range of his fists.

The blow caught the man low, glancing off his jaw, before collapsing his throat. The brute gasped and wheezed through blood bubbles that boiled up out of his mouth and through his newly split neck, then up his mouth and out his nose. He tottered on one heel, then collapsed. Regis heard a third man shoving off hard and running into the night. There was no sign of the others.

Behind him, Regis heard grunts and random yips and howls far off into the night, from all sides. Men behaving like coyotes, surrounding them. And they were closing in. And it sounded as though there were far more of them than Regis had guessed.

He could make out the shapes of others, ranging beyond the scant light the moon and stars gave. The illusion the shouts and yips offered came to him as he was looking in the one direction he shouldn't have been, for he heard the pounding of feet and shouts from his own small group, and then the night was once more alive with savageness.

Something slammed into the backs of his legs and he nearly toppled, sidestepping in time to avoid flopping to the ground. He dropped the tripod leg he'd used to fell two of their number and clawed free his revolver, thumbing back the hammer as he raised it.

A ghostly shape, low, hunched as if it were ashamed of itself, hurtled at him in the dark. He knew by gut feeling more than anything else that it was neither Shep nor Bulmer. And he squeezed the trigger. His gun thundered in his hand, and the night lit bright for that sliver of time.

It was enough to see the attacker—a swarthy, wide-shouldered little brute with black hair and a shining face—jerk backward. His feet whipped out from beneath him, and Regis knew the brute was dead before he smacked to the earth. He didn't care; he was already spinning in the dark, pistol out. He heard a muffled grunting sound from where Shep had been when he'd last seen him.

"Shep!" he shouted once, twice, before his voice gave away his location. This time, two men attacked—one from behind, the other scrambling down the embankment to his left.

Yips and garbled shouts still seemed to sound all about him. He needed to get to Shep's side, to help him defeat whoever was attacking. But first, these two needed his attention.

Regis sidestepped just in time as a gun boomed. It was a rifle, close in, and it cracked the night once more, its sound tripping over the crack of twin shots from the far end of the gulley, where Bulmer sat.

Before dark he'd told Regis he might move about only if needed once the show began, but not much, as he felt ill in his gut and head all at once whenever he tried to stand. But seated, he was fine, so seated he would stay while the fight raged. That was useful to Regis, who counted on that to help guide him as he ran toward Shep's spot in the gulley, ducking low and holding the revolver out before him in a rigid hand at the end of a long unshaking arm.

"Shep?"

If his brother was unhurt, he should respond. Simple. But he heard no response. He was either busy defending his life or . . . no, he couldn't think like that. Already Regis smelled the thick, greasy stink of hot blood. Spilled for what? Greed? On whose side?

Men who sought violence for the sake of the momentary thrill were not men but base creatures. Few beasts under the name of nature will kill for sport, but among those few, man stood supreme.

Some of the things Regis had seen in his life made him disgusted to be part of a foul breed such as man. And yet most of the time he was reminded of the goodness of his fellow humans. Of their caring, gentle ways toward one another, of their happiness and inventiveness and ingenuity. Those were the people he sought to fill his life with. Good, solid, happy people all pulling in the traces together to accomplish a task, to achieve a goal.

Not—he ducked low as he spied the glint of a knife or a belt axe whistling toward his head—not a brute bloodbath. But sometimes, as abhorrent as killing sprees were, they could not be avoided.

Then Regis heard the slapping of feet, moccasins on gravel, perhaps, grinding and scratching and scurrying away. And as suddenly as it had begun, the attack seemed over.

"Shep?"

"Regis!"

"You okay?"

"Yeah . . . Mr. Bulmer?"

"I'm good—save for a dead brute lying across my legs!"

"I'll light a lantern," said Shep.

"No, don't. Not yet." Regis made his way to the boy and knelt, feeling in the dark with a searching left hand. It patted a shoulder. "Shep?"

"It's me." He thumped his brother on the arm.

"You sure you're not hurt?"

"I'm okay. Can't say the same for one or two others."

"Yeah, me too. Let's go help Bulmer and sit tight and think for a bit. They might be regrouping, and we need to be ready."

As they dragged a dead man off their friend, Shep said, "Should we make a run for it?"

"No," said Mr. Bulmer, "and I think Regis will back me up on this. It's dark enough that we'd need to light our way to see where we're going, and that would only serve to show the rest of them where we are."

"My guess," said Regis, sighing as he sat back next to Bulmer, "is that we sent them packing for whatever hole in the ground they crawled out of."

"What if they do come back? And with help?"

"It's a risk, but we don't have much of a choice right now."

"How's the arm, Mr. Bulmer?"

A sharp intake of breath was the response, as Bulmer flexed his wounded wing. "It's been better. But it beats being dead."

"You're right on that score," said Regis. He patted his vest pocket. "Jerky, anyone?"

"Mmm, yes, please," said Bulmer. "Not as satisfying as a draw on a well-packed pipe, but it'll do nicely, considering our present circumstances."

The three men sat in quiet then, chewing the jerky and waiting for sunrise. It was slow in coming, but as it crept up on them, Regis was the only one awake.

He looked at his younger brother and saw a chin-to-chest young man, spattered head to waist with drying blood. His right arm looked as though it had been dragged in a river of it. But he slept steadily, soundlessly, his chest rising and falling in the slow rhythm of deep sleep.

The same went for Bulmer's breathing. His shoulder wound had bled during the melee, but it looked to have stoppered itself some time in the night. It was a peaceful scene, and Regis let his vision linger on the two sleeping friends. But he knew once he turned his head, as more of the dawn's creeping light leached into the gulley, that he would see death and the raw evidence of battle. And he was not robbed of that sight. He let his eyes rove and take in the scene.

A dozen feet from them lay a dead man, where he and Shep had dragged him off Bulmer's legs. He lay facedown. In the center of his back, high up, was a ragged black, blood-matted hole where Bulmer's shot had plowed through and gone on its own way in the night to parts unknown.

The man had thick black hair and what looked to Regis as

some sort of ribbon or grass woven into it. He wore leather leggings, much worn at the creases and missing the backside, so that it looked as if the morning light would burn him to a blister, not that the dead man would know.

One foot wore a leather moccasin, the other was bare, and the man's foot sole was lighter in color than his leg's skin tone. But it was hard, covered in callus, and it looked as though two of the man's toes were missing. What stories did each of these men have? Or rather, what had been their stories? Who would mourn them?

And that led him to look on the rest of the gulley.

Far to his left stood Gretchen, the mule, one leg tugged up as though she'd been hurt. He wasn't certain. She might also be standing hipshot. Her ear twitched, and she lowered her head a few inches. He'd check her when full light came.

Down the gulley another fifteen feet, a hunched form emerged from the darkness and Regis started for a moment, certain the man was wounded but sitting, ready somehow to spring at them.

But no, the man was nothing now but a dead thing, propped in a hunched form by one knee jammed awkwardly beneath his belly, a thick rope of blood tethering him to the gore-stained earth. Already bluebottles buzzed sluggishly, settled, rose up again before settling once more to feast on the blood. This was the man Shep had tangled with.

He couldn't recall hearing shots from the kid, so he must have used his knife. That would explain the bloody arm and filth-matted look of Shep. He glanced once more at his brother, who still slept, and looked back to the dead man.

He looked beyond and saw two more bodies, flopped close to where he himself had dropped them. He felt no sympathy toward them. He supposed this was because they had been trying to kill him. But wait, hadn't he shot a man, closer this way?

In the brief flare of the gun's flash he had seen the bullet knock the man backward, had seen his feet fly up before he slammed to the ground. So where was he? Regis wanted to stand and stretch—and find out where the man had gotten to. He thought he might see a blood trail leading back up to the low rim of the gully, but beyond that was lost to him from this position.

"Good morning, brother," said Shep in a whisper. It wasn't quiet enough, though, as Bulmer twitched, and an involuntary grimace of pain pulled his mouth wide.

He let out a breath and looked about him, then smiled and nodded. "Good morning, gents."

For a long minute the three men looked before them. Then Bulmer said, "Could you check Gretchen for me, Shep? That leg doesn't look right. The poor thing has more patience than sense, but I'm afraid she may have been nicked by a bullet, or worse, in the night."

Regis and Shep both stood slowly, keeping low and peering up over the rim of the arroyo. They saw nothing move but kept low just in case as they made their way to the mule.

Regis ran his hand up and down the mule's back before sliding it down her leg. She flinched and drew the leg up until the hoof no longer rested on the dirt. Higher up on her left rear flank, close by her tailhead, he felt a pucker, then another on the side closer to him. She'd been hit by a bullet, but it had exited.

"Just like you, Mr. Bulmer," said Shep, reporting back to the surveyor. "She's been hit, but it passed through."

The man sat up straighter. "There's more alcohol in the wagon. It's a raw blend I use to help clean my instruments. It's in a cork-stoppered bottle in a leather drawstring sack stood upright in that dark brown toolbox with the brass corners. You know the one, Shep? Behind the seat?"

Shep nodded. "I'll tend to her."

Regis came back. "It's not going to kill her," he told Bulmer. "But it's not going to let her tow us. In fact, I'm not certain she'll be able to walk too far. But we need to get out of here this morning."

Bulmer nodded. "I know. You and Shep should leave me here with Gretchen. I can handle myself, and you'll be able to travel faster without me slowing you down."

"No, no, we can't leave you. Those men might come back and you'd not be able to hold them off."

Shep overheard them. "Send me back. I can do it. You two stay here. Together you can hold them off, I bet. I'd go fast. As fast as I can."

Regis shook his head but said nothing. Shep had a point. He hated to admit it, but it was a consideration. Not a solution he liked, but likely the best. "Let's see if Gretchen can walk. If she can, we'll get as far as we're able, then we'll consider sending you on ahead."

"I know what you're thinking, Regis," said Bulmer, taking the offered canteen from Shep. "But it's no good. She'll not be able to walk too far, nor I. And then we'll be stuck out in the open, no convenient arroyo to hunker down in."

"I'll make coffee," said Shep, smiling. "Everything's clearer after a cup of coffee."

"Can't disagree there, Shep." Regis nodded. "I'll help you."

"Hey . . ." said Shep, looking eastward, then pointing. "What's that?"

"What now?" said Regis, his first thought of Apaches.

It looked to be men, possibly on horseback. But whatever or whoever it was, it was still too far away.

"Wish I had my spyglass," said Regis, visoring his eyes. He saw a glint from the front of the group, then it seemed a few seconds passed before the group resumed moving toward them. They watched, joined by Bulmer, who leaned on Shep's shoulder and said, "Hmm . . ."

Within another minute they could tell it was a handful of riders kicking up a dust cloud, showing they were galloping at a decent clip. Toward them.

"Shep, get the guns ready. Let's stand behind this wagon. If they wish us ill, they'll split, cut around us to the north and south. But we can take a few out at least."

Shep began to turn, then spun back around and visored his eyes once more. "Hey . . . I think that's Bone."

Regis leaned forward as if it would help him gain a better view. "My word, I think you're right!"

Shep waved his hat and shouted. "Hey, Bone! Hey!"

Within moments they could tell it was indeed their friend, the Texas Ranger, and thundering up behind him rode four more men, Jesús and Tut among them. Two of the men led spare mounts, one of which was King, Regis's spooked horse.

"Well, I'll be. . . ." Regis smiled a genuine grin for the first time in days. How in the heck did they know?

Bone was the first to come thundering in. He jerked the reins, and his big grulla fairly slid to a halt, chomping and stomping. "Boys! Boys—you okay?" He was down and out of the saddle before the words tumbled from his mouth. From beneath his hat peeked a bandage. His left leg was wrapped tight with more of the same, and he stiff-legged his way to the edge of the arroyo and jumped down. He stumbled over to them and grabbed Shep and Regis, each by a sleeve. "You whole and alive?"

"Yeah, yeah, we're good. Well, except for Mr. Bulmer and Gretchen. They each took lead."

Regis could barely get the words out, given the brute squeezing of a hug Bone was giving him. The Ranger nodded to acknowledge he'd heard, then switched his rugged hugging to Shep, pounding the kid on the back, even though Shep winced and groaned.

"Shep, boy! So glad you're okay! We rode hell-for-leather to get here, wherever here is. Didn't think we'd find you! And if we did, wasn't sure what sort of shape you'd be in."

As he spoke he approached Mr. Bulmer, who held up his

good arm and said, "If it's all the same to you, I'll refrain from the hugging, Mr. Bone."

"Aw, don't worry. I only wanted to check your wound. I've tended plenty in my day. Got some medicinals in my bag, too."

He stood back, looked around. "Apaches?"

"How'd you know?" said Regis.

"Dead men talk plenty." He nodded at the nearest corpse. "From the looks of it, you give 'em something to chew on. If I know Apaches, and I do, they'll be long gone by now. But they'll be back." He toed the facedown man. "Attack you in the night?"

"Yep."

"Huh. I expect, from the looks of this one, that they're hungry. Lean times we're in. It's the drought, making folks do crazy things."

Regis nodded toward Bone's leg. "What happened to you?"

Bone waved him off. "T'weren't nothing. Tell you all about it later."

By then the other men had slid down and gathered around, Tut among them. He hung back, red-faced, but Regis went over and shook his hand. "I appreciate you coming. Means a lot."

Since their initial adventure together saving Shep from Tomasina Valdez, Tut and Regis had forged a bond that each man understood and accepted as far more important than employer and employee. Regis regarded the young man as one of the best of the best, and Tut had given him no cause to doubt that estimation. For his part, Tut felt the same toward Regis.

Regis nodded to all the men. "We should build a fire and have something to eat, now that we don't have to figure out how we're going to get back to camp!"

One of the men gathered wood and laid out the fixings. Another man tended to Gretchen, and Bone sent another for his saddlebags. "Don't worry, Mr. Bulmer," he said, helping the man up onto the wagon's tailgate. "We'll have you playing violin in no time."

"But I don't play violin."

"You will when I'm through with you! That's how good I am at doctorin'. Just ask any of my one-arm friends!" He winked and rummaged through the bag.

While he tended the man, Regis hammered him with questions.

"Yeah, yeah, yeah," said Bone. "Your horse, King, dragged in to our outpost camp late yesterday, and I knew something bad was in the air. No way you'd have let that beast off on his own like that, not with your goods and such onboard. So we followed our sniffers, and here we are. Good thing we decided to mosey back out to the outpost camp we're building, elsewise you gents would still be mired out here, pondering your next move. Course that means we're not rounding up cattle or working on mud huts and such, but I think this counts as a day off, don't you, boys?"

"What do you mean, 'mosey back to the outpost camp'?" said Regis. "You mean you were there, then you weren't, and then you went back?"

Jesús turned red and looked southward, as if he spied something there of great interest. The men chuckled and shook their heads, but nobody said much of anything by way of response. Even Bone reddened a bit and made a meal of working on Bulmer's arm.

Regis let it go and promised himself he'd call off the work for a day of rest once they all made it back to the main camp. "So, other than chasing after us, has life been quiet at the ranch?"

Again, his query was met with silence.

Finally Regis could take it no longer. "Bone? What happened while we've been gone? It has something to do with your bum leg, doesn't it?"

"Well, sir. Now you mention it . . ." The Ranger massaged

his jaw and looked everywhere but at Regis. "We did have what you might call an occurrence."

"An occurrence."

"Yep." Bone nodded. "Mmm-hmm, that's what I'd call it. Yes, sir."

"Out with it already!" said Shep, spooning up pancake batter into his mouth.

Bone leaned back against the wagon and sighed. "Okay, but you better have some coffee—and a dollop or two of that whiskey in my bag won't hurt none, either. Make the story go down smoother, if you know what I mean." He winked and waited until the coffee was served and the bottle passed around before he commenced.

"It all started with the women."

"No, no, it did not," said Jesús, a normally quiet vaquero. *He's showing particular interest in the proceedings*, thought Regis.

"Oh yeah, okay, let me back on up the trail a bit. Let's see," said Bone, sipping his coffee. He snapped a finger and nodded. "Yep, it started with that rascal and his tincture wagon."

Chapter 32

"Tincture wagon?"

"That's what that thing is?" said Tut, visoring the sun with his hand over his eyes.

Jesús paused in rolling a smoke. "How can you tell that from this distance?"

"Can't."

"Then how come you to know it's a tincture wagon?" said McCurdy.

Tut shrugged. "Just know is all."

"I think that means you are crazy from the heat."

"Yep. Don't mean I'm wrong, though."

Nobody said any more until the weird slowly rolling thing drew close enough so they could see the driver's face. The three cowboys had all retrieved their long guns from their piled gear. Their mounts were picketed such that each could seek shade beneath a sparse scatter of mesquites while the men worked.

The trio was setting up a small outpost some hours southwest of the camp proper as a place to deal with the balky range cattle that were proving a trial in every way.

Bone wanted it taken care of in two days' time, then wanted them back at the base camp for the final push to get the bunkhouse and reservoir in shape. The stockade was already built up enough for use.

The men suspected Bone was pushing hard so as to impress Regis once he ventured back to the ranch with his brother and the surveyor. Trouble was, the entire affair was turning out to be more of a trial than any of them had expected.

Their days were filled to brimming with snakes and heat and bugs and more heat and snakes and a whole lot of work, very little of which had been actual cowboying.

Still, the food had gotten a whole lot better once they let Percy have full rein of the situation. Man was one hell of a cook, it was roundly agreed. And there was plenty of it, even if most of the meat was that stringy beef they were rounding up for tallow and hide. The worst of it, they were hoping, might soon be behind them.

Regis Royle had promised them to a man that if they stuck with him and Bone on this venture, they'd get thirty dollars and found a month, higher than the going rate of twenty to twenty-five dollars, plus the chance to cowboy to their heart's content, no more building of mud huts or corrals. Royle said there'd be a whole other permanent crew just for that sort of thing.

There was even talk of cattle drives northward to market towns. Tut claimed he overheard Royle and Bone talking one night after grub about bringing in fatter beeves from back East to breed in and mix with the longhorn brush rats they were used to.

Said that's where the money was at, said the fancy folk back East and up far north wanted tender meat and lots of it. Didn't make sense to most of the boys, as driving cattle that far would likely walk the fat right off of them, but if Royle was paying and the boys got to stay in the saddle and wrangle cattle, who were they to mope and act bitter?

The closer the wagon rattled, the more of it came into view.

Two outriders trailed behind. The wagon was a sizable affair lugged by two large-boned mules. And it did, indeed, turn out to be a former tincture wagon.

The lettering had been covered by a poor green paint job. The outline of the word *nostrums* was in clear evidence arching along the wagon's near side, along with fancy curlicues and fili-gree that told of a once-grand lettering job with a proud past. But no longer, if the man in the seat was any indication.

He sat hunched as if he were trying to cover his own sunken chest and ample belly with his shoulders. A tatty black wool jacket that could have benefitted from mending years before now hung in frayed edges about the man's wrists and collar. Atop that stared a thick, pocked face, and pronounced jowls bulged beneath the spidery hairs of an unkempt black-and-gray beard.

The juice of a long habit of chewing tobacco had stained the man's mouth, as evidenced by the twin brown runnels beneath the corners. Thick black-and-gray rings of sweaty hair were matted down onto the man's grease-shiny forehead by a dusty bowler with a rodent-chewed brim.

"Well now," he said, as they squawked to a stop. He set the brake with a boot and leaned back. "Well now," he repeated.

The outriders also stopped but did not ride forward.

"Looks like we have ourselves a little cow camp operation." His harsh voice dribbled from his mouth like gravel, and he leaned back and squirted chaw juice at the ground below. The two bone-rack mules swayed, flicked ears, and looked beyond weary of life's travails, and the day hadn't reached but eleven in the morning.

"Who's this 'we' business, mister?" said Tut. "You got your-self a mouse in your pocket?" He smiled to show he was just funning the man, but the driver didn't smile back.

"Trying to be friendly, son." His gaze rose up, and he squinted

past the Royle Ranch cowboys, all three of whom, standing before him, cradled rifles and kept their eyes up on the man in the
wagon seat and on the two outriders who still flanked the rear of
the wagon, stone-faced and unmoving astride their horses.

"And yonder comes another."

One of the three cowboys looked back. Jesús and Tut kept
their eyes on the man. McCurdy said, "It's Bone." Relief washed
a little of the worry off their faces.

The stranger sensed something of the approaching person's
importance to them and sat still, waiting for him to arrive. A
long minute passed. Little moved save for sluggish flies, one
mule's ear, and sweat sliding down foreheads.

Bone rode up and sat his horse abreast of his three men. "Boys,"
he said, not looking at them. "How do," he said to the newcomer in the wagon. "Can I help you?"

"Didn't expect to see anybody out here. Other folks are rare
in these parts. This is the Desert of the Dead, after all. Called
that for good reason, you know."

Bone nodded. "Can I help you?"

"You already said that," said the man. "Names Figgs. Julius
Figgs. That's with two G's."

"I don't expect I'll be writing it anytime soon, but thank you
for the tip." Bone did not take his eyes from the man.

"How many of you all are there out here?"

Bone assessed the man a moment before answering. "As
many of us as needs to be."

The man smiled. "You setting up a camp? What's your
story, son?"

"You might say that. You're on Royle Ranch range now,
mister."

"Royle Ranch? Ha! Ain't never heard of it, and I been traveling this route for years."

"What is it you do?"

"I trade goods with the Mexicans. Gringo goods they can't get easy down there." Only high-dollar items, though." He leaned out and nodded toward the rear of the wagon, as if his men could have heard the conversation. "Ain't that right, boys?"

The two outriders never flinched. They sat their horses, their rifles butted on their thighs, barrels upraised to the heavens, ready to swing down and level on anything before them.

The man's explanation didn't impress Bone. "You're trespassing."

"Trespassing? Ha!" Figgs snorted and slapped his thigh. Dust rose from his grimy trousers.

A muffled sound came from inside the wagon. Bone's eyes flicked there, then back to the fat man.

"So you're saying we're on private property? Owned land? Ain't nobody can own this land, mister. It's, well, it's just its own self. That'd be like trying to own a cloud or a rock or something."

"Nothing you're saying is making sense, Mr. Figgs." Bone smiled at the man in the wagon. "But as it happens, I have ridden out here to surprise my men. See, today is what I have decided to be a day of rest in these parts."

"Wish he had decided that this mornin'," said McCurdy under his breath.

Bone's big bird-wing eyebrows rose up like hawks taking flight. He continued, "I've been working my men like demons, and we've prepared a big feed back up the trail a ways."

Bone leaned close to Tut, standing to his right, and in a low voice said, "You and the boys head toward your horses, but keep your rifles ready. There will likely be shooting, and soon."

"But the outpost. We ain't finished with—"

"Don't worry about that right now. Time enough for that. Man's a criminal, I'm sure of it. If I'm right, bound to be stolen goods and worse in that wagon. Seen his type before, maybe even him."

"Criminal?"

"Say it louder, damn you!" Bone growled. "Now do as I say. And tell the others."

"Okay, boss." He nodded to the other two, and they moved toward their horses and gear, clutching their rifles.

Bone continued smiling over at the man in the wagon. "Since you're weary travelers and all, I'd be honored if you and your men would be our guests."

For the first time, the man's lazy squinted grin slipped. "Mighty kind of you, but naw, naw, I got to push on. Got people depending on me." He smoothed the lines between his hairy, grimy fingers and snapped them hard on the mules' backs. They jerked from their dozing and the wagon squeaked, rolled backward a foot, then started forward as they dug in and pulled.

Bone angled his horse in front of the mules. His revolver appeared in his right hand as if he'd conjured it, leveled at the man in the wagon. "Oh, I insist."

Bone's men did as he bid them, though they wore confused looks. But Jesús and McCurdy knew to trust Tut and, of course, any orders doled out from Bone. Nobody ever thought to cross Bone.

He was a legend of sorts among the men, a genuine Texas Ranger and all. Even though some of the Rangers weren't overly regarded, Bone had distinguished himself in a number of scrapes in the past. Anyone who'd ever ridden with him knew him to be a fair and solid character who expected a lot but didn't offer any less of himself.

So they split and saddled their mounts, all under the watchful eye of Figgs and his two outriders, who looked squintier eyed and grimmer with each moment that passed.

"Jimbo! Rollo!"

The two outriders hadn't seen what Bone had done, as they had been too busy throwing hard looks at the three lanky, dirty cowboys. So when their boss shouted their names, they looked forward a moment. That's when Jesús, Tut, and McCurdy leveled on them.

"Drop those rifles!" shouted Tut. "Now! And keep your arms high. Higher, damn you!"

From the front of the wagon Bone saw the one man on the near side drop his rifle—Rollo or Jimbo, whomever he was. Bone grinned, in part because Tut was sure enjoying lobbing orders at the two outriders and in part because he felt like smiling at the smug bastard in the wagon seat.

"Now, fella," said Figgs, "what say you simmer down and let me and my party pass through. We'll give you a tribute if that's what you're angling for. Isn't that what the injuns beg off people for using their land? See, I can be generous and you didn't even have to beg. I'm so close to the border anyway, and you know that's where I'm headed."

"Mister, I was all but considering a full pardon for you and yours and then you had to go and insult me." Bone shook his head and pulled a frown as if he'd just experienced a big ol' disappointment.

"Insult you? Me? How did I do that?"

"You tried to buy me off. And as a Texas Ranger, when someone tries to do that, why, I immediately take offense and begin to suspect something's a bit whiffy, if you catch my meaning."

"Hey, hey!" It was Jesús.

From the corner of his eye Bone saw his man's rifle was poised, arm muscles bunched tight. He caught the nervousness in the vaquero's voice and saw the tension among his three men. *They're cowboys, Bone,* he told himself. Don't get them killed because of this foul outlaw. That said, of the trio, Jesús was the most seasoned in a scrape, followed by the solid Tut. Even McCurdy would do in a pinch.

The nearest outrider was turning in the saddle and swinging his rifle down fast.

Jesús should have shot him by now. Bone swung the dragoon

he'd worn on many a hard-knuckle campaign and sent a bullet into the center of the outrider's heart.

The mules stomped and jerked the wagon.

The black-clad form whipped backward, and his horse bolted. The man, laid out faceup against the bucking horse's rump, would damn sure suffer a broken back, even as the bullet had done him in.

As if given permission, Tut and the boys opened up and, since none of them dropped, Bone assumed they'd shot the other man, too. He looked back to the man in the wagon. No longer than a few seconds could have passed, yet the man was gone. Trick door in the seat? Nah, too narrow. Then he saw it— a crack in the wall behind where the man sat. A door, of course. He'd just not noticed it before.

"Come on out, you greasy oaf!" thundered Bone as he swung his horse hard to the far side of the wagon. To his men he shouted, "Tut, get those horses and bodies, truss them up, and saddle your own mounts!"

He suspected the man had a peephole in there, likely drawing down on him at this very second. Bone kept moving, rounded the back of the wagon, and saw two of his men steadying the horse of the second man.

When they shot him he'd flipped off the far side of his mount, but the first, the one he'd shot, had gone on a jolting ride south a few hundred yards. Jesús hopped aboard the other dead man's horse and was making for it.

What did the slovenly man hope to gain by holing up in there? And what did he have in there, anyway? That slight sound he'd heard before had prickled Bone's suspicions.

He rapped hard with the butt of his pistol on the back door of the wagon. It wasn't locked from the outside, so entry must be through the front. Maybe the only entryway.

He heard muffled sounds, like shouts or screams from beneath water or mounds of quilting.

"Tut! Get up here!" Bone shoved his revolver into its holster and shouted as he kicked free of his stirrups and stood atop his steady mount, Buck. "Hold, boy, hold, whoa. . . ."

He leapt for a steel rail that ran around the top edge of the roof and felt the structure sway beneath him. Although the wagon was sizable, it was an old, tender thing. The man would likely shoot at him through the wall or roof any second. He had to act quick.

Bone reached his hands over to the center of the rear wall and swung out as far as he could, ramming his heels into the big rear door. It bucked and sagged inward, emitting a cracking sound. He vaguely heard more of the muffled sounds from inside. He swung again and, as he rammed his boots into the door once more, a shotgun boomed.

The middle of the door blew wide and dissolved in a powder of dust and shreds of old wood. The hole it left was big enough for Bone to stick his head and shoulders through, but he wouldn't do it on a drunken bet.

From inside he heard coughing from the greasy man, and smoke clouded out the hole as if it were a chimney.

"You had enough, you dumb bastard?"

"Okay." More coughs, then, "Okay! I can't see and I can't hear much! I'm coming out!"

Bone jumped down and drew his gun. "Back door! And hands high—no tricks or you'll die like Rollo and Jimbo!"

"Okay. . . ." The word tailed off in another coughing jag. Presently, Bone and Tut, who stood side by side, guns drawn behind the wagon, eyeing the still-smoking hole in the door, heard chains rattling and metal grinding, then a cursing and a kicking sound. Then the door nudged open two, three inches.

"All the way!" shouted Bone.

"Yeah, yeah, it's stuck." More coughs.

"You best get it unstuck. Now!" Tut shouted it, then looked

to Bone for approval. Bone nodded, suppressing a smile. Boy was enjoying this power position a little too much, he reckoned.

They heard more thuds as the man kicked at the door, then it popped open. Hinged on the left side, it swung wide, creaking on grease-starved hinges. The interior of the long, dark wagon was still smoky, but clearing. Mostly it was dark.

Figgs stood in the middle of the door, his slop gut hanging down over his trousers, the bottom of it visible, bare and hairy. His held-up hands framed his sag chest.

"Hands higher—and hop down to the ground. Now!"

Figgs did, and ended up collapsing to his knees and then rolling onto his side.

"Stand up, you fat bastard!"

He grunted to his feet, and Bone didn't bother suppressing a sneer as he jammed a boot into the man's back and knocked him face-first into the dirt. "Hands out like I'm about to crucify you."

"Hey, Bone. . . ."

"What?"

"Something's movin' in there. See the wagon?" Tut jerked his chin toward the dark hole of the smoky wagon's innards.

Then they heard a muffled sound, like a whimper. "Tie him up," said Bone, and he held his revolver up once more. He edged to the wagon door, peering in around the shredded wood side.

Though the smoke had mostly cleared, it still stunk of powder and something else . . . human stink, the unwashed stink of people. It was rank. As if someone had soiled themselves.

"Who's in there?" he said. "Answer me!"

He wasn't even certain it was a person. Might be a critter. A berserk dog, scared and ready to tear out his throat.

He heard wet sounds, then grunting, throaty sounds, still muffled but clearer than they were before.

"Hello?"

Then a thudding, as if someone were pounding on something.

"Someone in there? Trapped?"

More thuds and muffled sounds, a voice, maybe.

Bone turned back to the driver. "You have somebody in there?"

Figgs said nothing. Bone strode over to him and kicked him in the side of the belly. "Answer me!"

The man nodded, his face turned to the right. "Yeah."

"Who? How many?"

"Just . . . just whores."

Bone's eyes widened. "You bastard," he hissed, and turned back to the wagon, shouting, "Jesús, you watch him, tie him tight. I ain't through with him! McCurdy, you stay with the horses. Tut, you get in here and help me!"

Bone swung himself up into the wagon, nearly tripping over a short set of three leaning steps, and tossed them down. "I'm coming, ladies! Hang on, hang on. Where are you?"

Wagon's sizable, but not all that big, thought Bone. *Have to be in here somewhere. How many?* He wanted to gag, the stink was so bad.

The aisle in the middle was narrow, and lining it on either side were solid wood boxes with crude slats. He felt along the sides of the nearest and heard thumping within, and more of that muffled sound. But now it was desperate sounding, a crying, sobbing, screaming coming from similar such boxes all around him. Floor to ceiling and along the front, save a narrow spot where the sneaky door was located.

The first crate he came to was locked on the outside with a steel padlock. "Get the key off him! They're all locked in!"

Tut peered in. "Boss?"

"Get the key, then get in here! Go up front, open that damn door, then help me! Women trapped in here!"

Bone heard Tut berating the man, demanding the key, then a

low growled response followed by a hard hit and a groan. *Good*, he thought. Beating's too good for the pig.

He grasped the lock and hasp of the first box, tried to see in through the thin slats but couldn't. "I'll get you out of there right quick. All of you. We're working on it."

He realized his voice shook. Rarely had he been this angry. No, not angry, disgusted, enraged, seething, ready when he was done with freeing these poor creatures to jump out of this dank, piss-smelling wagon and beat the innards out of that greasy slaver.

Bone gritted his teeth and turned his anger on the lock, since the key didn't look to be showing up anytime soon.

He growled and jerked on the lock, and there was give under the lid, enough to wedge his fingers under. He jerked and strained and grunted and finally managed to snap off a corner of the box, enough to reach in with an arm. He felt something wet, but it moved. It was a head, someone's head. He patted it and heard a whimpering.

"All right now, it's all right. I promise you, it's going to work out, ma'am. We'll get you out of there right quick."

The head leaned into his hand, and Bone felt his heart tear in half. It took all his strength not to jump down out of the wagon and beat Figgs to death and beyond. Instead he shouted, "Key, Tut! Where's the damn key?"

"Right here, boss." Tut was outside the door and tossed up a steel ring with a single skeleton key dangling from it. Bone caught it in his right hand and swung fast, jammed it into the lock, and clawed the half-rusted thing apart.

Tut was beside him then, staring wide-eyed at the box before them. "Tut, wake up and help me."

He thrust the key into the youth's hands. "Open the other locks, now!"

That did the trick. The young cowboy groped in the dark and fitted the key in all the locks he could find. Meanwhile,

Bone reached in and gingerly lifted up a woman light as a feath-
ered hat, it seemed to him, and carried her to the back of the
wagon. Her ankles were bound with rough hemp rope; though
loosened through time, it still encircled her ankles. It had worn
through the woman's socks until it had rasped the skin raw and
bloody.

Her wrists were the same, and a rag gag had been stuffed in
her mouth with another strip of filthy cloth wrapped around her
head, forcing her mouth apart and tied at the back.

She was drenched with sweat and whatever else had come
out of her body. Her dress had once been a green plaid pattern,
he noticed. And her hair looked to have been a dark reddish-
blonde, like the sun's rays at sunset.

Her eyes had each been blackened at various times, and her
left cheek was bruised and swollen. Blood matted that side of
her head beneath the hair, and her nose looked to have been
broken, then healed crooked. Her top lip was split in two spots,
and there was a trail of dried blood from beneath her nose.

Bone hopped down and set her on the edge of the doorway.
Her eyes fluttered and squinted in the sudden light. He tried to
go easy as he removed the gag, but he had to use the tip of his
knife to pry apart the knot. She stiffened when he pulled it out.
"It's okay, ma'am. I need to get this thing off you. I promise I
won't hurt you."

He realized as he worked how foolish a thing it was to say.
How could she possibly be hurt any worse? Curse that fiend
trussed on the ground before him.

"Can you walk?"

She never took her eyes from his, as if by keeping an eye on
him she could foretell what he was about to do. But she nodded
and set her sock-covered feet down gingerly on the hard
ground. The socks were anything but, having mostly worn away
some time before. The soles were more hole than wool.

He held out a hand, and she looked from it to his face, back to his big-knuckled hand. "I'll help you over to that rock yonder."

She nodded once, he thought, though he couldn't be certain, and he led the woman to the rock. She did not sit, and he thought perhaps she'd had enough of sitting. She walked tenderly, as if she were more than a hundred years old.

He noticed the hand he held had two fingers that had been broken some time before and had not set quite right. They would pain her in her dotage, he thought, recalling his own mama's bent fingers, gnarled from a lifetime of hard work.

She stood there, her hair matted and dirty, but in the sunlight he saw it was a deep red-gold. Even the grime couldn't hide her prettiness, in a solid-plain way.

Bone cleared his throat. "Ma'am? Any of you speak English?"

She looked him in the eye, then held her head up, chin out, and stared past him at the blue sky. "Of course. Do you take us for animals?" Her voice was quiet, little more than a hoarse whisper, but strong.

Bone felt his face heat up. "No, ma'am. Never that. I'm just trying to figure out what's what, that's all."

She offered a slight nod but did not look at him.

"I'll be right back, ma'am. Stay right here, will you?"

He didn't wait for a response, but returned to the wagon. By the time he entered, there were three more boxes open, and Tut was struggling with another. Bone began carrying the other women outside, one by one. With Jesús's help, and Tut inside the wagon freeing whoever else might be in there, they were able to get their charges into the blue, bright, clean air.

"McCurdy, get these women some water and food, all you can spare."

But the normally contrary McCurdy was already on his way back from their gear pile with their three canteens and a pair of Percy's food sacks draped over his shoulders.

That made five women in all. Bone walked back to the first woman he'd helped out. "Ma'am? Is this all of you?" It was a dumb question, he knew, as the wagon was now emptied, but something compelled him to ask nonetheless.

She looked at her companions as if she'd never seen them. Then she shook her head and looked toward the wagon. "A girl. Last place we stopped. Two, three days ago. Where's the girl?"

"You don't see her here, ma'am? What'd she look like?"

She shook her head, a helpless look in her eyes. "I only heard her."

Bone felt the rage flood back into his fevered mind. He turned on the prone slaver and snatched up the back of his head by a handful of hair, lifting his fat torso off the ground as he squatted to face the pig.

Spittle from his growled words flecked the man's thick, shaking face.

"There was a girl," hissed Bone. "Where's the girl, Figgs?" He jerked the man's head hard, higher. The fat man gagged and snotted himself. "I don't know what you're talking about."

Bone jerked the head even higher, then slammed the man's face into the dirt. He fancied he heard something snap. Must have been his nose, thought Bone, because he heard a strangled yip and saw a quick pool of blood leach from beneath the wobbling head.

Bone strode fast to the wagon, wiping his hands on his trousers, shaking off a wad of greasy, bloody hair that had come loose from Figgs's head.

"Tut, did you empty the wagon?"

"I did, yeah, boss," said the young man, helping McCurdy to fill cups for the women.

Bone looked back toward the women. All of them were staring at him with a look that told him he'd better investigate.

He climbed back into the wagon and struck a match, bending low and eyeing every space. The stink was powerful, and he held his nose with his other hand. There were rags in the boxes, little else. Most of the spaces were big enough for the women to sit with their legs drawn up but would not allow them to stretch out fully.

None of the boxes were uniform in size, and though strong enough to contain the weakened women, he saw they were poorly constructed and looked to be built by someone who knew little about using tools.

Bone's anger at Figgs grew beyond anything he'd thought possible. It increased as he made his way forward, checking each crate on each side, six empty. Perhaps the first woman was confused and had heard one of the other women.

He checked and found nothing but the same in each—soiled rags and worn wood and filth. The front of the space was a low, wide step, perhaps with storage beneath, that led to the door to the driver's seat.

Bone kicked at the face of it with his toe. It sounded hollow. He felt along the top, worn from someone stepping to get in and out. He lifted, but it was solid, nailed down. He tugged harder.

Something gave. He wrenched it upward, groaning as he did, and wood and nails squawked as the board lifted free.

A sweet, sickly smell greeted him, wafted up and clouded his face. He pinched his nostrils again and struck another match, then pinched his nostrils again as he bent to look in the box.

He saw a lantern and a rat's nest of junk—lengths of used rope, small hand tools, bits of chain, small grease-stained sacks. He pulled out the lantern and shook it. Fuel inside. He felt the thing and found the wheel, coaxing up the wick. He lit it with the last flare of the match, and he almost wished he hadn't.

Now visible, the inside of the wagon was even fouler than he'd expected, with the lantern's slanting gold light creating shafts of shadow and darkened corners. Bone bent to peer into the space again and saw a dirty canvas tarpaulin. He brought the lantern low over the length of it and seized at what he saw midway up.

It was a hand, that of a woman. No, more that of a girl, curled yet relaxed, drawn up like the claw of a dead bird. His breath snagged in his throat, and he reached for the tarpaulin and tugged it down. There lay a girl, as if in sleep, but he knew otherwise. He'd seen enough death in his days.

She couldn't have been more than thirteen years old and was turned away from him, her face's right side visible. She was very pretty, even under the bruises and matted dark hair. Dried blood clung to the side of her face.

Even though he knew the answer, he whispered, "Girl? Girl?" and touched his fingertips to her cheek. It was cold, though yielding.

What had she done to deserve this? He reluctantly tugged down the rest of the tarpaulin and was relieved that she was at least clothed. Her dress was in better condition than those of the other women, though that was not saying much. Hers was of flowered calico, light blue in color, and torn and soiled with blood and darker stains.

Her legs were bent at the knee, and her topmost hand, the one he'd seen first, jostled. He saw it held a scrap of something, mostly white and thin, and on it were stains. He held his breath and tweezered it out with two large fingers.

It was a scrap of cloth, muslin perhaps. The stains on it were letters, crudely spelling out the word *help*. The first finger's tip was stained dark red, the tip and beneath the nail. She'd used her own blood to spell out the word.

"Please, girl. . . ." He tried one last time, then touched her knee beneath the tarp. Her body was not yet stiff. She'd died recently, perhaps that very morning.

Bone did not want to do what he knew he had to do, but he could not ask any of the boys to do it, and certainly not the poor women.

He held his breath and once more covered the girl's face with the tarp. Then he slid his right arm beneath her knees. He inched his left hand slowly beneath her shoulders—thin, bird shoulders. *Just a child*, he kept telling himself. *A child, dammit.*

He lifted her up out of the crude crate and carefully made his way, in shuffling sidesteps, through the narrow space to the rear of the wagon. He emerged into the sunshine and squinted, getting his bearings. A tear slid down his big nose, then disappeared into his moustache.

"Tut," he said, clearing his throat from the hoarseness there. "Tut, help me now. We need to wrap her. Lay her out proper and wrap her."

But the first woman he'd brought out walked over, still unsteady on her holey-socked feet, and pushed Tut aside. The other women, too, filed over, in their slow, unsteady way, and the first woman nodded toward the ground over where they'd been standing.

Bone nodded and walked the girl over and laid her there. One arm and her bare feet stuck out from beneath the tarpaulin.

"We'll tend her," whispered the woman.

Bone stood and, nodding, backed away. "Jesús, bring them whatever they need, maybe some rope to bind the tarp."

The vaquero nodded and fetched rope.

A sound to his right caused Bone to look over. It was the fat, greasy man. He'd rolled over and grunted himself to a sitting position.

Figgs caught Bone's eyes and smiled wide for the first time, showing them all his black, stump-rotten teeth. "Tell you what. I'll let you all have at them. All of them. For the night. Free of charge! My gift to you. Told you I'd make a tribute to you, seeing as how you're a land owner and all. That's the way the world works, right?"

"Not here, it doesn't. See . . ." Bone walked over to him and stared down at the sag of a man. As he spoke, his voice shook with rage he was not certain he could contain any longer. "Here we take offense to someone, anyone, abusing ladies. You understand that?"

Figgs snorted. "Ladies? I don't see no ladies. Just whores. Dirty whores who begged me to take them along on my travels. And believe me, I am taking them to a place they want to go. No matter what they tell you."

Bone ground his teeth together tight enough for them to powder. "That's it, man." With no warning Bone bent low, bringing with him a big-knuckled right hand that whistled down as a fist and plowed into Figgs's sloppy, sweaty, bearded face. The man's head snapped backward, and Bone hoped he had broken the bastard's foul neck. But the beast moved and moaned and tried to back away from the large man standing over him. It didn't work.

"Where are you crawling off to, vermin?" Bone took two steps and stood over the mewling man once more. He bent low and balled the man's shirt and coat front in his fingers and hauled Figgs upward. Then he dealt him a savage backhand with his right, swinging hard from left to right, his knuckles mashing into the blubbery, soft face. He gave him three hard licks before Tut grabbed his wrist.

"Bone, stop!"

"What are you doing?"

"Stop it, Bone!" said the young cowboy, trying to grab Bone's fist.

"I aim to kill him!"

"It isn't right, Bone!" This time the rugged young cowhand snagged Bone's wrist.

The big man shook him off. "Ain't right? Ain't right?" He looked over toward the women and the girl, and all, save one, looked at him. "That ain't right, Tut! What he's done to those women and that poor girl, that ain't right! And you're stopping me?"

"Bone, I don't disagree with you, but you're a Ranger. You can't just kill the man without him attacking you. It ain't right. Might be he could tell us other names, something. . . ."

The two men stared each other down, Bone's big face shaking and purple with rage, his nostrils flexing like those of a tormented bull. Tut held his ground and stared back, uncertain if the big man was going to lay into him as well to get at the verminous Figgs behind him on the ground, moaning and spitting blood.

Finally, Bone growled low and spun away from him, stalking off westward, his fists flexing. All he wanted to do was kill the pathetic bastard, take him apart one limb at a time, then fling the parts to the coyotes to feast on in the cool desert night.

He'd walked a hundred yards before he began to calm down. He breathed out slowly and stood still, his back to the camp. He was doing no one any good acting this way. Tut had been right, of course. But he also hadn't been in there, found the girl dead, found her note.

Bone touched his left breast pocket, pulled out the scrap, and held it up on his palm. "Help," he said in a small voice and breathed out slowly. "I'm so sorry, girl, that I couldn't have helped you sooner."

He turned, tucking the scrap back into his pocket. There were five other women who needed help, and he had to be the one to ride point. The three cowhands were solid sorts, but no more than that themselves and awkward around women, he'd wager.

He didn't want the women to feel any odder than they already did. Most of them were poorly clad and likely ashamed of how they'd been found, even if they were also likely thrilled to have been found.

He walked back to the camp and saw the women closing the tarp over the girl. They'd laid her out full length and had tried to wash her, judging from the damp rag in the first woman's hand. She looked up at him, then away again. He didn't know how old she was—twenty-five or thirty or one hundred and thirty. She'd done more living and dying inside than any person ought to.

"I'm guessing we'll have to camp here tonight," he said. "It's a stretch to the ranch, and we have a few things to figure out. But I have an idea we can try first."

His men looked eager to help. "Jesús and McCurdy, take your post maul and shovel and that steel bar and knock the ceiling and walls off this wagon. We'll make a buckboard to carry these ladies back to the ranch."

To Tut he said, in a low voice, "We got enough food and water to last the night?"

Tut nodded. "Yeah, we're good. Especially if me and the boys go easy on it. We packed expecting to be out here for a few days, anyway."

"Good. Hopefully we can light out in the morning. Might have to wrap that girl again. You know. . . ."

The reason didn't have to be explained to Tut. "I'll make a fire. Rig up something so they can have privacy of some sort."

"Good. Use the corral posts and the wall pieces of the wagon."

The afternoon waned and evening descended. The women kept to themselves, though they took the food and drink offered them.

His men set to work dismantling the wagon, knocking it down to the planking of the floor. They made a pile of items hidden here and there within the wagon, and Figgs shouted once, "Easy on my possessions, you dirty dogs!"

"Shut it. Now." Bone pointed a big finger at the battered, greasy brute who'd been dragged away from the rest of them and propped against a rock large enough to lean against and little more.

The man leered at him, showing off his blood-stained, stumpy teeth and his swollen nose.

The fire was becoming a welcome thing as the temperature dropped with the daylight's slow disappearance. Bone had tried to build makeshift benches from the lumber pilfered from the wagon, but the women didn't use them.

He could understand that, but he wondered how they'd be the next day when they had to ride in the transformed wagon. Even open-topped he imagined they'd be balky about it. After all, he wagered that the worst things that ever happened to them took place in or close by that wagon. But he had no choice. There were too many of them to haul on the horses and mules, plus the girl's body and Figgs and their gear.

"I'm sorry we're not able to move on tonight, ladies. But given the situation, I don't think a few hours will harm much. Once we can see again, come first light, we can roll home."

At that, a black-haired woman let out a choking sob. *Home*, he thought. It was the first time Bone had given much thought to where they'd come from. They obviously had homes of their own. Were they family women? Taken from their own children and husbands? How was that possible? Did this man just snatch them?

He looked once more to Figgs, propped against the lone rock. He was lolling, his arms behind him and his feet tied at the ankle, but Bone saw the man's open eyes.

Bone walked over and stood looking down at the fiend. "You're lucky they pulled me off'n you. But we aren't through, not by a long shot."

Figgs leaned forward. "Come closer when you threaten me, boy," he growled, a false smile pulling his grimy, blood-stained face wide.

That was all Bone could take. He bent low to grab the man's shirtfront, and Figgs's right arm lashed wide. A hair of time before it slammed into Bone's left leg, Bone thought he saw a glint of steel. Then the fist slammed into his leg and instant agony sizzled through him, up the leg and throughout his body.

He collapsed to one side even as he clawed free his revolver. Figgs bulled harder into him, and the gun spun from Bone's grasp and thudded to the dirt six feet behind them.

As Bone hit the ground, the side of his head whacked into a stone and his hat popped off and rolled away. A sound like the thundering hooves of ten thousand wild horses filled Bone's head, and his vision blackened, flecks of light flashing at the edges of the scene he could no longer see. What had happened? He wondered, trying to speak, to move, to shake his head.

Figgs ground the blade into Bone's leg as Bone kicked feebly at Figgs with his right boot. The fat man slammed into him again, laid out halfway over him, and tried to yank free the short-bladed knife.

He couldn't do it, so lodged had it become either in bone or boot. He scrabbled for the dropped revolver several feet away and grunted his way toward it.

Sounding assured of his vicious victory, Figgs growled a gravelly cackle and lunged, his hand snatching at the gun. But a grimy socked foot stomped beside it and slid it away just before his hand curled over the grips.

The first woman Bone had rescued, the red-gold-haired woman, snatched up the gun even as Tut and the boys bolted to Bone's side. In one smooth, clean motion, as Figgs cursed her, bloody spittle flecking free of his wide mouth, she thumbed back the hammer and shot the filthy little slaver square in the forehead from less than two feet away.

Figgs's eyes widened as if he'd heard surprising news. Then his head seemed to inflate and then collapse in on itself before the entire back of his head exploded outward. He died in fingersnap speed, but the woman who'd pulled the trigger, and the women standing behind her, all wished he had suffered for a very long time.

Jesús said something behind her as Tut and McCurdy bent to Bone. The other women huddled together and eyed this woman in their midst as though they'd never seen her before. She tossed the revolver to the ground and knelt by Bone's head, elbowing Tut away.

She bent and looked close at him, smacking his cheek lightly with a firm hand. "Mister, wake up!"

Bone's eyes flickered. "What . . . what happened?"

"You took a knock to the head. Can you see me?" She held his face in her hands and stared at him from inches away.

"Yeah, yes." He tried to nod but winced.

Tut, kneeling close by, said, "Bone, she saved your hide! Shot that devil Figgs as clean as I've ever seen anybody shoot."

Bone's eyes widened. "Well . . . thank you, ma'am."

She didn't smile as she inspected the side of his head. Then she tore a strip of rag from the bottom of her dress and dabbed his bleeding leg. "Been a long time since anyone called me ma'am."

"Best get used to it," said Bone, then his eyelids flickered and he sagged into unconsciousness.

She sat back on her heels, staring at the man, then without looking said to Tut, "Pull that knife from his leg while he's out so I can tend the wound."

"Yes, ma'am."

She held the leg while Tut jerked the blade twice before it popped free.

He held it up and whistled. The bloody blade was short, maybe two inches, but squat and wide like its owner and filed like a fang on both edges.

"Boil water," she said. "And I'll need clean rags."

"Yes, ma'am." Tut hustled to it while McCurdy retrieved Bone's revolver from where she'd dropped it.

"I'd be obliged if you men would bury that filthy creature."

She nodded toward Figgs. "But don't bury him with his money pouch. He doesn't deserve our money. It's in his coat."

The men did so, digging a wide, shallow hole, then rolled the three dead men into it without ceremony and without words spoken over them. The men covered them over and dragged what rocks they could easily ferry to the grave, placing them atop the low mound.

Later, after Bone had been doctored and whiskey had been poured on his leg wound and some down his throat, the ladies seated themselves on his makeshift benches, across the campfire from the four cowboys. The silence was broken only by the occasional jostling of a horse or the snap of wood on the fire.

A half-dozen yards to the east of them sat the remnants of the wagon, the sides and top stripped off. Floor planking and a couple of pieces jagged up that McCurdy deemed might be too dangerous to rip off the base, lest they make the already wobbly affair even worse.

In a while, as the fire dwindled, the men built the flames up again, piling snapped planks and lengths of mesquite beside it so they all might have warmth through the coming cool night. They offered the women what blankets and spare clothes they could. Some of the women murmured their thanks; others still looked petrified and never let their backs be turned to any of the men.

Before she lay down beside the others, the woman with the red-gold hair checked Bone's head and leg once more.

"May I ask your name?" he said.

She looked at him a moment, then while dabbing the side of his head with a damp rag, she said, "They'd take us out . . . one at a time at night, feed us, water and old bread. And then . . ." Her voice trailed off to less than a whisper as she looked into the darkness.

"I'm so sorry. But it's over now."

She looked at him, anger narrowing her eyes. "You're wrong.

It will never be over." She leaned back and wrung out the rag. "Margaret," she whispered.

"What?"

"My name." She didn't look at him. "It's . . . Margaret."

She walked away and left Bone McGraw wide awake to think about a good many things long into the night.

Chapter 33

Regis was impressed with the progress they'd made at the ranch headquarters. Despite being tired and worried about Bulmer, Bone, and Shep, and now the women he felt were under his care as well, he hopped down to greet the men.

"That looks great," he said, pulling his eyes from the stockade to the earthen berm retaining wall dug by the men for the reservoir in the distance. It looked all but complete.

Bone nodded. "You won't find a more dogged bunch of no-accounts as this lot," he said, grinning as he waved an arm wide. "Now, I believe you had something you wanted to tell the men?"

"You bet," said Regis. "Let's take a day off. I have a lot of catching up to do." He draped an arm around Bone's shoulders. "Starting with the lowdown on the women you saved. How many are still here?"

"Why, all of them are still with us. It's only been a few days since we got back here with them, Regis."

"I know, I know. Not that they're not welcome for as long as they need the ranch, of course. I just mean as far as the men go. You take a group of far-from-town men and add a handful of women into the mix, there's a recipe for trouble."

"The men have minded themselves. Besides, those women

need to hole up and get well, well as they can get. Then we'll see about getting them back to their families." Bone leaned close. "Some of them don't have families. I don't know what they're going to do." Bone's words sort of drifted off, and Regis followed his sightline.

"Who's she?"

"Huh?" Bone looked at him.

"That handsome woman there, with the reddish hair."

"She ain't handsome neither. Well, she is, but she's none of your affair." His color thickened, and he looked away. "Her name's Margaret. Doesn't have anybody to go home to. She's the one who doctored me after that slaver nearly laid me low. Saved my life and all," he said, nodding. "Solid sort . . . for a woman."

"Uh-huh. And the black woman with her?"

"Oh, that's Daisy. She's nice enough. Hard worker. I get the impression she's got troubles of her own dogging her. Might be a runaway."

Regis shrugged. "Seems to me that's her business. As long as she's at the Royle Ranch, she's safe."

Bone nodded. "Good to hear you say that."

"Looks like she's talking up a storm to Lockjaw. Or else he's talking enough for both of them."

"Yeah, that's a funny thing. Those men you brought here from the docks? For the most part, a decent bunch of workers. That Lockjaw Hames, though, he's top of the heap. Man won't stop working. I'd take another dozen of him anytime. At day's end, I have to threaten him or else he'd never lay off. Makes the rest of us look bad. And as soon as that woman came into camp, he's been worse!"

Regis could tell Bone's exasperated tone was mostly in jest. He also knew Lockjaw was one of the hardest-working men he'd ever met. "I wonder if she'll accompany him to Browns-ville when the men head back tomorrow."

"I wouldn't doubt it," said Bone. "Too bad they're leaving so soon, but Bulmer needs to get to a doctor, even though Percy has tended him as good as any medical man can, I reckon. Bulmer hasn't popped a fever, which is something. Tough little bird, he is. I put his mind to rest where his mule's concerned. He was awful worried about her. But Percy tended her, and the wound's clean. I told him we'll keep her here, in the shade, and won't work her. She's earned some rest. We can get her to him when he's ready."

"I imagine Cormac's pulling his hair out about now looking for his workers. They've stayed on a lot longer than they were promised to us as it is. You've got a good bit of chores done around here because of them, though."

"That we do," said Bone.

"So there were six women, huh?"

"Yeah, but as I told you, there's one of their number who didn't make it." Bone nodded toward a far stand of huisache trees. "We had to start a cemetery, Regis. I chose that spot. Hope you don't mind."

"No, no. I trust your judgment."

The big Ranger grew silent a moment, then said, "We put up a simple wood cross. When we get time we'll carve a proper marker for her."

"Don't you know who she was?"

"Nope. Nobody knew. Best we can do is hope someone comes out this way looking for their daughter someday. We can describe her, show them the grave."

Regis sighed. "Well, you did what you could. I don't mind the women staying here as long as they need to. As long as there's no trouble among the men."

"Trouble?"

"Distractions. Already I can see Shep's going to be a pain in the backside, fawning and preening whenever the women are nearby."

Bone laughed. "Yeah, he's got a bit of the rooster in him, that's for certain. Didn't get that from you."

Regis's smile disappeared and his big moustaches drooped at the corners. His eyes darkened. "Nope. Got that slice of foolishness from our daddy. A fairly useless creature, I can tell you."

Bone said nothing. He knew the Royle boys' father was a sore spot with Regis that likely wouldn't ever heal.

Chapter 34

"It's good you're going to stay on while Bulmer and those sailors of yours ride back to Brownsville."

"Why? You like my company that much?"

Bone gave Regis the narrow eye. "Nope, but I know you'd rather be here than there."

"Yep. Something about being out here. If I'm back in town, I'm near useless to Cormac because I'm thinking about all that needs doing out here, all that we want to do, all that we can do. The possibilities for building a genuine empire are here."

"Save the fancy words for Shep. He's a good kid, but he needs steady reminding."

"Yeah. He'll be old enough to make his own choices soon, and then he can decide where it is he thinks he needs to be."

"When you're not around, he's a good kid, you know. Hard worker, too."

"But when I show up, he's . . . what?"

Bone shrugged. "He's a kid, nothing more. Looks up to you but can't help sparring with you. That's the way it is with brothers."

Regis nodded, decided to let it drop. He'd put more than enough thought into his situation with his brother. "Now, about that ranch you inherited from your old friend, Mack."

"What about it?" Bone regarded Regis with a cocked eye.

Regis knew, despite Bone's easygoing demeanor, his friend could be prickly at times on various subjects. The Deemworth spread was one, but he bulled ahead with his thoughts, anyway. "I've been thinking on it, and I have a proposition for you. What would you say if we were to fold its day-to-day operations in with the bigger Royle Ranch proper. You'd still own it all, live there if you wanted, but it'd make life easier if it was part of the operations. And if we go ahead and buy that new parcel west of here, your place will border the Royle Ranch. Pards and neighbors. What do you think?"

Bone continued to rub down his horse. "That'll work nicely with my plans."

"What plans are those?"

"Now that you're here, I aim to head out there tomorrow, first thing."

"Okay, how long will you be there?"

"Oh, a few days. I'll be taking some folks with me, though."

"How many of the men? You know we have to get that last berm firmed up by the reservoir."

"Easy, pard. It's the women I'll be taking along. You can keep the men. The ladies are beginning to heal up and it's odd for the men, like you said. Awkward for the women, too, for that matter. So I thought they'd be better off there. They can have some privacy, and they can keep an eye on things at the ranch, too. Place needs people in it."

"Is it livable?"

"Oh yeah. Well, it was last time I saw it. I hired an old Mexican to tend to it. Good fella, but it's a lot for one old buck, you know?"

Regis nodded. "You're a good man, Bone McGraw. I don't care what all those husbands back in town say about you." He laughed and dodged the sensitive Ranger's darting fist before it connected with his upper arm.

Later, when Bone talked with Daisy, he found that—as he suspected—she had already been asked by Lockjaw if she'd like to try her luck with him.

What did surprise Bone, however, was her refusal to accompany Lockjaw back to town. She said she didn't mind the snaky desert, but she had no desire to live in a town among people who would look at her as if her skin color were a disease.

Bone admired her sand and wondered, though did not give voice to his suspicion, that part of her desire to keep away from town might be that she was a runaway slave. If her refusal to move on to town gave him a moment of surprise, Lockjaw's response was even more of a shock.

The big man nodded, smiled, and said, "Then I will ask Mr. Bone here if he might have need of a sailor turned ranch hand." Lockjaw turned to Bone. "Mr. Bone?"

"Just Bone, Hames. And if I had a half-dozen men as hard-working as you and as big as you, I do believe we'd have had this place whipped into shape a month ago."

"That's a yes, then?" said Daisy in an unusually quiet voice.

"You bet it is. But . . ." Bone held up a finger of warning. "I don't want to get crosswise with my partner, Mr. Royle. You've worked for him for a long time, Lockjaw, and I expect you'll be leaving a mighty big hole to fill down at the docks. You think that'll sit well with him and Cormac?"

"I do believe so," said the big man. "But to be honest with you, as long as you feel I'd be of use to you here, and earning a living wage for a man with prospects of starting a family . . ." He cut his eyes to Daisy, then reddened.

He ran a big finger under his nose. "Well, put it this way, Mr. Bone: I am a free man and, more to the point, I am a man of my own mind. So my doings are my own affair. But I understand your not wanting to peeve your partner, so I'll talk with Mr. Royle right now, if you happen to know where he might be."

"Somebody need to talk with me?" Regis walked around the far side of the half-finished bunkhouse shade porch.

"Yes sir, that'd be me," said Lockjaw, stepping forward.

Regis looked at Bone, Lockjaw, and Daisy in turn as he pulled off his gloves and mopped his forehead with a bandanna he tugged from his rear trouser pocket. "You all look so serious," he said. "Somebody hurt?"

Shep walked up, ambling slightly on his shot-up boot. Percy had done his best to devise a useable heel, but the boots would need the help of a professional cobbler. He stood by Regis, arms crossed, hugging his sore ribs.

"No, nothing like that," said Lockjaw. "You see, I would like to stay here at the ranch instead of returning to Brownsville."

"Uh-huh," said Regis. "Well, the part about you staying on and working here at the ranch is up to Bone, as he's the ranch manager. I know Cormac and I will miss you at the docks and onboard the steamers, but your life's your own, Lockjaw. Anywhere you land, they're lucky to have you. Can I ask what's caused this change?"

"You can. I like it here, always did like doing more than toting and moving freight from one place to another. Not that it was bad work, mind you, but I have more to offer. And being out here has been good. Hard work, but fun."

"Fun?" said Bone. "Now I know the heat has got to you." He smiled.

"Isn't there any other reason, Lockjaw?" said Regis, looking at Daisy, who elbowed past the big man.

"What you want to say but are too polite to say, Mr. Royle, is am I the other reason?" She nodded. "Me and Mr. Hames, we have an understanding. Isn't that right, Mr. Hames?"

"Yes'm."

It was the first time Regis could ever remember big Lockjaw

Hames being at a loss for words. He just stood there behind this solid woman and nodded, half smiling.

Daisy nodded. "That's right. And as for me, I can take in laundry, I sew, I am a fair hand at cooking. I get along nicely with Mr. Percy." She leaned forward and lowered her voice. "And from what I can tell, precious few of you all can say the same."

She straightened and counted off on her fingers. "I am also experienced at midwifing, plus all manner of other work—gathering firewood, chopping and splitting it. I have never been taken ill a day in my life, except for recent events, which not a one of us needs talk about, and I have helped build a good many cabins and barns in my time, toting lumber and timbers, and I am not afraid of killing rattlesnakes. In fact, I like it. They are nasty things." She nodded as though they had all agreed with her, which they did.

"Most of all, though, I am beholden to Mr. Bone and the rest of the men of the Royle Ranch for saving our hides when we thought all was lost." Her eyes glistened, and she looked away briefly.

Regis rubbed his chin and pooched his lips and looked to the sky. "Ma'am, if you weren't already ensnared by that big brute over there, I'd ask you to step out with me. But as he's bigger than I am, I will bow out and say, Welcome to the Royle Ranch—and don't get snakebit!"

"It's the snakes who should be fearful," said Bone.

Lockjaw and Daisy shook the offered hands, then they walked away, the big man leaning slightly so he could rest his arm around the woman's shoulders.

"Now that is something, huh?" Shep sighed. "Any chance another wagonload of ladies will wander through here anytime soon?"

"You know," said Bone, clapping a hand on Shep's shoulder

and turning him to face the reservoir. "I heard tell there's a distinct possibility of that very thing any day now. But you have to be up by the reservoir to spot them, else they might miss us altogether and drive right on by."

"And while you're there," said Regis, "you might as well take that shovel with you. Moving dirt is considered to be a great way to pass the time. Plus, ladies like to see a man who's gainfully employed."

"Oh, I see how things fall with you two old-timers." Again, Bone reached out with a playful clout, but it landed on empty air. "Glad to see your ribs are mending, boy. But it's your head I'd be worried about. Something might come swinging in before you know it." He winked and went back to his own work, whistling.

Regis and Shep stood together watching Bone walk away. "Have you ever heard him whistle before, Regis?"

"I have not, Shep. And I do believe it means that something about our friend, the Texas Ranger, is changing. Now let's get back to work. We're soon to be down on men and we still have more work than we know what to do with. We also have to get to Mexico and buy some cattle before the month is out."

"Month ends next week, Regis."

"I know."

"Can I go along?"

"Of course—how else are you going to learn the trade of ranching?"

"How did you?"

"Didn't," said Regis. "I'm making it up as I go along. With Bone's help, of course."

Early the next morning, Bone, Margaret, and three other women made their way northward toward the Deemworth place.

It took them that full day and all the next, mostly because the wagon they were hauling gear and goods in was solid but not lightweight. And the mule team towing it was a methodical duo.

There wasn't much talk on the ride, and since Bone was the only one ahorseback, he had even less of an opportunity to talk with Margaret, though he surely wanted to. Something about her confused him and excited him all at once. She seemed to know what he was thinking, and yet she would barely speak to him except to answer whatever half-baked notion he'd decided to ask her about.

For the life of him, it was easier to track a gang of killers across the Llano Estacado than it was to conversate with Margaret. And that was another thing—he didn't even know her last name. For that matter, he didn't know much of a thing about her. Except that she was handsome and annoying and he couldn't stop thinking about her.

They rolled in at his little ranch as dark settled down over them. Ramon, the limping old Mexican he'd hired to oversee the place, gimped on out of the bunkhouse, where smoke drifted up out of the chimney.

He toted a sawed-off double-barrel that looked as heavy as the old man himself. But Bone knew the old buck was tough and likely to lay down an opening spray of death seed as he was to welcome in stragglers to a pot of tea at this, or any, hour.

"Ramon! It's me, Bone. Don't shoot me, you crusty devil!"

"Senor Bone, is that you?"

"Yep, already said so. Maybe you could scare up a lantern. I have brought visitors to the ranch."

"*Si, si, si.*" The old man scurried back inside and returned presently carrying a lit lantern by the bail.

"Ramon, I'd like you to meet . . . the ladies."

The old ranch hand held the lantern up high and squinted at

them, then seeing they were indeed what Senor Bone had said, he straightened and pulled in a deep breath, expanding his bird chest with air. With his free hand he palmed his sparse hair and smoothed it to his scalp. "The pleasure is all mine, senoras." He bowed low, and the four women murmured greetings in kind.

"Okay then, Ramon. Maybe you could go on ahead into the house and get a fire going, light a lantern or two. It's been a long couple of days, and we all could use some grub and shut-eye, in that order."

"*Si, si*. It will take but a minute."

"Just enough time for me to tend to Buck and these mules." As he unbuckled the beasts, he looked about him. Even in the near dark, Bone could tell that old Ramon had made a difference in the appearance of the place. He hadn't realized how much he missed it here. And now that he had full say in the running of the ranch, he felt pangs of regret at taking on the foreman job for Regis's ranch.

Sure, he had a share, but this, well, this place was his, lock, stock, and all. Wonder how long it would take to fill the range with his own beeves? He heard the flutter of a woman's laughter from the house and smiled. It was a good thing to hear. How long before he would be able to fill the house with his own kin? A wife and children? What made him think that way?

He shook his head to rid himself of that dangerous thought. No doubt Ramon was entertaining the women with a funny story. Man was a born raconteur.

Without seeming to do so, Bone watched Margaret help the other women fetch items from the wagon. She didn't let grass grow under her moccasins, that was for certain. He felt a sting of kindness then for the ranch hands he'd left behind at Royle Ranch, tending things while he was gone.

They'd all taken the women in as if they were their own mamas and sisters, giving them their camp moccasins, mending and washing spare shirts and trousers for them, loaning soap and whatever else they thought the women might want. Even removed themselves from the nearly finished bunkhouse back to the out-of-doors so the women could have the run of the place for privacy.

It had been good for them all. He saw now that he and the men had been living increasingly like savages, working, eating, sleeping, and back at it again the next day, toiling like fools without cease.

As bad as life had been for the ladies, he reckoned that discovering them and bringing them to the ranch had made a big difference at a good time, for all of them.

"This is your ranch."

Bone looked up to see Margaret standing a few feet away. The other ladies had gone back inside the little house. She'd not asked it as a question. Odd.

"Yes. Yes it is. It was given to me by a good friend, who has since died."

She said nothing but set to work stripping the harness off the other mule.

After a few minutes of silence, she said, "Why do you work for Regis Royle if you own this place?"

Bone tugged off the second harness and hung it on his shoulder while he led the tired mule to the corral. "Well, I didn't have this place at the time. Besides, he's a good friend and he asked for help."

"I had no right to ask."

"Course you did. I don't mind talking with you, Margaret. Ask me anything."

She didn't. So as they walked side by side, leading the mules, Bone said, "You take this place, for instance. I know more about the lay of this land than most anybody alive, I reckon, now that ol' Mack is gone, and his wife, Martha. Good people. Buried up

William W. Johnstone and J.A. Johnstone

yonder behind the house. I'll show you tomorrow in the light, if you like. I worked for them for a spell some years back but got on well enough that I'd stop in on my travels in these parts and lend a hand. Martha was maybe the best cook I have ever had the pleasure of knowing. Her biscuits were as tall as a man's hat, and her gravy was so delicious I about tear up every time I think on it."

"Good thing for you it's dark, then," said Margaret.

"Why do you . . . oh, ma'am, I do believe you cracked a joke on me. That was a good one. Ha!"

"Is it that surprising?"

"Nope, just good to hear." They continued their tasks in silence, but something kinder, gentler had blossomed in their midst without them quite knowing it had happened.

Later, Bone commended Ramon on the fine job he did of repairing things about the place, of keeping the house cleaned and tidy. It looked and felt fresh, not stale and sad, as Bone had feared it might.

They all enjoyed a late-night feast seated around the table. Two of the women helped Ramon turn out a fine rabbit stew. Bone watched the women come out further from the quiet shells they'd dwelt in since he and the boys had found them. Over previous days, Margaret had emerged among the women as a quiet but firm sort, and she had been deferred to as their leader, by both the women and by Bone's ranch hands.

Later, Bone showed the ladies about the house. And though he insisted they were to divvy up the use of the two bedrooms, he gently urged Margaret to use the master bedroom.

She regarded him with narrowed eyes and he backed to the door, hands up, saying, "I'll be bedding down with Ramon in the bunkhouse. So you ladies will have the run of the place. Feel free to treat it as your home and stay as long as you'd like."

The next morning, Bone gave the ladies a quick tour of the grounds and made certain they had ample weapons, food, and clothing. There was a trunk in the bedroom with all manner of garments old and in good repair. He urged them to do what they liked with them, perhaps make themselves all new clothes.

Martha had been a heck of a seamstress, so they were pleased to discover an ample supply of threads and fabrics, all waiting for permission to get on with their lives.

Who knows, he thought. *Maybe one day soon we'll be able to find their families.* He couldn't imagine that many women could be lost without someone seeking their whereabouts. He knew Regis would make inquiries in Brownsville. Then time would tell all.

While Bone prepared to leave, the women busied themselves in the house, tidying and making it a home. An hour after breakfast, he was ready and led his horse over to the hitch rail in front of the setting porch on the house. He peeked his head into the kitchen and said goodbye to the ladies. For the first time, each one of them smiled.

"Margaret, can I have a word?"

She looked at him, waiting for him to speak.

"Um, outside?" He walked out onto the porch and waited for her. He hated that he blushed as he asked, but what could you do? He was forever plagued as a blusher, despite the fact he was also known roundly as a handy sort with the ladies. Notably, he now winced to recall, with a number of women who were actually married.

Thus far he'd been able to avoid any slipups, but he knew that sort of behavior wasn't a recipe for a long, quiet life. A short, exciting one, to be sure, but he was sensing he didn't want that sort of thing any longer. Maybe now and again wouldn't hurt, but events of late had tempered something in him he was only now becoming aware of.

She came out and leaned against the other center post, looking toward the barn.

Bone cleared his throat. "I have to get back to the Royle. This droughty weather's leaving folks in a pitiful situation. Whole towns are drying up and blowing away. That's how come we're headed south to Rio Verde. We're to look at their cattle, and Regis wants to get there before anybody else gets wind of it. I heard from a friend that the entire village is selling its stock just to make it through until next year."

Margaret was visoring her eyes to the sun and looking across the barnyard toward the plain of land that seemed to stretch away forever. "What'll they live on?"

"Oh, they'll be paid cash money."

"And after that?" she said, still looking away.

Bone regarded her a moment. She made a good point, something he'd think on while he rode back to the Royle. In a quiet voice he said, "How come you don't ever look at me?"

She continued staring into the bright distance, then let out a breath and looked over at him. "Because I don't want to see pity in your eyes, Mr. McGraw. I couldn't bear that."

"If you'd bother to look at me you'd not see pity but . . . something else. I don't know rightly what it's called, but it sure ain't pity. You can't pity someone as strong—" He looked away then, blushing in the afternoon heat. "Nor as pretty as you, Margaret."

"Oh, Mr. McGraw. You . . . you don't know me."

"No, ma'am. You're right there. But that doesn't mean I wouldn't like to." He stretched, plopped his hat atop his head, and stepped off the porch and down into the sunlight.

"I'll be back soon as I'm able—a week, ten days. Will you stay, Margaret, at least until I return?"

She smiled, the first time he ever saw her do that, and looked away, then looked back, straight at him. "At least until then . . . Jarvis."

He nodded and smiled—couldn't help it, in fact. "Okay then. For now." He tugged his hat brim, mounted up, and looked back at least twice, maybe five times, until he had ridden too far to see that the woman still stood on the porch, staring, he hoped, after him.

Chapter 35

"You'll pardon me, but you say 'gringo' like it's a disease or a bad flavor on your tongue. Hard to tell under all that grime, but aren't you a so-called gringo yourself, mister?" Percy dried his hands on his apron and didn't take his eyes off the man's pocked, sweaty face.

The cowboy paused in chewing his quid, squished the mouthful of spittle, then sluiced a ropy long brown stream at the cook's feet. It hit the parched earth and spattered on Percy's boots.

"Pretty good aim, huh?" he said, not looking away from the cook. "My shootin's even better."

Percy turned away and busied himself at his worktable, cutting biscuits. "If that is a threat, mister, you'll have to do better. I've been bullied and harassed my entire life by men far superior to you." He glanced over his shoulder and looked the steaming man up and down. "In every way, beginning with stature and ending with intellect."

"Why you son of a—" The stranger lunged at the cook with a haymaker, and the cook held up a cast-iron fry pan at the last moment of the swing. The stranger's scar-knuckled, meaty fist collided at top speed with the unyielding black pan.

For the briefest of moments a smile appeared on Percy's otherwise taciturn face, and his attacker's eyebrows rose as if they were tugged upward by hidden strings. Then the pain set in, and he collapsed to his knees in the dirt by the cook fire, cradling his swollen hand.

Regis stormed over. "What was that all about?" He looked at Percy.

The cook shrugged and continued with his biscuits. "Ask him."

"That . . . that . . ." The coarse brute pointed with his good hand, shaking in counterpoint to his red-cheeked, rage-filled face. "He tried to—"

Regis grabbed the back of the man's collar and lifted him to his feet—no small task, as the man didn't cut a modest figure. "I gave you the chance not to lie, mister. Percy did nothing I wouldn't have done . . . gringo . . . I saw the whole thing."

"What about my job?"

"Oh, you mean the job I never offered to you?"

"What?"

"You assumed when you rode in that because you have a horse and a big mouth that you are qualified to work at the Royle Ranch? No sir. And no again, I say. Even if you didn't have a stoved-in hand, you'd not be in my employ. I have little need of someone who will start a fight for no reason. And now that you're a gimp, well . . ." Regis shrugged. An annoying habit he'd picked up from Tut or Percy or Shep—somebody was to blame. He told himself he'd have to stop it.

"I had reason," said the man, cradling his shattered, swelling hand.

The red-and-purple thing looked to Regis about as painful as a busted limb can be and still be attached to a man's body. He suppressed the desire to shudder and kept his head cocked, eyes half-lidded. "Oh yes, but having a thin skin isn't much of a reason, mister."

"You . . ."

"Choose what you're about to say with care."

"You at least owe me a hot meal. I rode all the way out here and . . ."

"And?"

"And I ain't et in days!"

"And that's my fault?" said Regis.

"Well, no," muttered the man through tight-set teeth. His face had gone white around his mouth from the pain beginning to set in.

"Just the same, you're welcome to a hot meal, and because it's late in the day, you're also welcome to pitch your bedroll by the fire and have a cup of coffee in the morning before you light out."

The man sucked breath in through his teeth. "Big of you." He flicked his eyes to Regis. "I mean that."

"Okay, then. And that fellow you wanted to hit? He's our cookie. And our doctor. I'll ask him to make up a poultice for you."

The man grunted and grimaced as he cradled his big knobby claw of a hand.

Regis stomped back to the bunkhouse porch where he'd been working on the ranch accounts book, annoyed he had to deal with such foolishness. He couldn't wait for Bone to get back from ferrying the women to his ranch.

He wasn't certain how the tough Ranger managed to keep the ranch running so well. He wasn't here but a few days and it was all he could do to keep a lid on things.

A few minutes later, Regis glanced up and watched Percy bandaging the mouthy drifter's bunged-up hand and appreciated that the cookie appeared to be doing a gentle job of it. And the drifter, for his part, was keeping his mouth shut, though his squinting eyes told Regis the man was biting back on some fierce throbbing pain.

Regis decided he'd take the measure of the man again in the morning. If he appeared to have the ability to humble himself, maybe there was a place for him, on a trial run, at the Royle Ranch. Maybe even as Percy's right hand. Or left. That notion brought a smile to Regis's face.

Still, he'd have to talk with Percy. Lippy or no, he couldn't keep annoying every cowhand who rode through looking for work. At this rate they'd never hire on another soul.

Chapter 36

A day after Bone returned from his ranch, Regis set out with Jesús for an overnight trip of his own to a spot the vaquero had mentioned where they might be able to view a herd of ten thousand mustangs. The thought thrilled Regis, and though he offered to bring Shep, the kid declined, saying he would stay behind and fill in for the void left by Jesús's absence.

This impressed Regis, and Shep felt downright good about making the decision, which, in truth, he hadn't wanted to. He'd much rather go see a mess of wild horses than work on the stockade or the bunkhouse, which never seemed to get finished. But something inside told him to hold his tongue.

The appreciation and surprise he'd seen on Regis's face told him he'd made the right choice. *Maybe*, Shep thought, *that means I'm an adult.*

That thought had carried him through much of the day's travails with an extra bit of muscle he didn't know he possessed. And at the end of it, Shep felt downright good. Tired, bone-deep tired, but good.

Later that night, the men in the bunkhouse woke coughing. The stinging stink of smoke fouled in their throats, gagging them, and their nostrils quivered and ran. They stumbled out of the bunkhouse coughing and waving their arms.

"Get down! Get down!" someone shouted to them, but his

shouts were overpowered by shots ripping in from what felt like all directions. One of the men barked a quick, clipped scream that turned into a low growl.

"Ben, that you? You okay?"

"Grazed. Been worse."

A paltry orange flame throbbed and flickered against the far back wall. Hard footsteps sounded on the puncheons, then the flame pinched out and stomping was heard again. "Got it. A lit rag on an arrow, I think."

"Might be more coming! Get the bucket!"

"Empty!"

"I'm soaking beans and the coffee water's all ready," shouted Percy. "Somebody help me get to the cookfire!"

They weren't that far from Percy's outdoor kitchen, but any distance felt like miles on miles when you were being shot at by someone who apparently could see like a cat in the night.

"What do they think they're going to do? Burn us off the range?" Bone stomped out another flame.

A volley of gunfire whistled in fresh, splintering wood, dropping everyone as if they'd been shot themselves. "Dang it! Anybody see where the shots come from?"

"South, mostly." It was Bone. "Another one to the east."

With no warning, Bone ground gravel as he cat-footed away from the bunkhouse, sending shots in both direction as he ran. He moved fast so they wouldn't pin him down easily. As for the rest, it occurred to the men that nobody could see them. Not that the notion made them feel much safer.

"Lucky shot," said Tut. "Must have been watching us and guessed where the bunkhouse was in the dark."

"I'd call that more than luck," said Percy. "Everybody should scatter. Don't give them a lot to shoot at. We don't know how many, or where they are. And get your guns!"

This shouted advice from their cook, even if he was surly more than was good for him, spurred them into action.

One by one they slipped back into the smoky bunkhouse,

bending low and scanning, then bursting in and slapping every-thing in sight trying to find their own bunks. They all returned toting boots and guns and hats, breathing hard and wishing they'd chosen any other way to spend their days—and nights—than grubbing in the desert for low pay and all the hard work they could stomach.

"Dang it, should have slept with my boots on!"

"I'm about sick of getting shot at. We need to ride on out there and blow them all to hell."

"I know it," said Bone, who had been largely silent, instead scurrying low and patting each man he bumped into, making certain nobody was shot up. Yet.

"Everybody have their guns?"

"I do." It was Tut. "Just by luck I had my hand on my rifle when the shooting commenced."

"Where are they?"

"Don't know!"

The shots continued at random, pinging and zipping over-head, keeping the men still and spread out in the dark.

An hour and change later, the shots had ceased and dawn's first light began to brighten all but the edges and corners of the cattle camp. Bone stood out front, his back to the south range, where they guessed most of the shots had come from. "Every-body over here! Now!"

Even in the day's new light, the men could see Bone's color was high. It took a whole lot to rile the boss, but when you did, it took a whole lot longer for him to calm himself. He stormed up and down in front of them, glaring, his nostrils flexing like those of a berserk bull, his face red-purple, and the muscles bunching beneath his stubbled cheeks as he ground his molars.

"Take watch in turns, I said. Spell each other, I said."

"We did," said Tut.

"Oh yeah? Then that means one thing!"

Nobody said anything.

"Okay, let me make this simple," shouted Bone. "Whoever was on watch, just get on your horse and get gone! You have no place working at the Royle Ranch if you fall asleep when you're depended on by the rest of us! Who was it?"

Nobody answered for a few long moments. None of the men looked around, instead finding their own boots of particular interest. Finally one among them stepped forward.

"It was me," said Shep. He pulled in a deep breath and looked at Bone.

Bone, his teeth clenched tight, his face shaking, stared hard at the young man. "Dammit, boy," he said in a low growl. As he turned away he pushed out a hard whoosh of disgust, then spat on the ground.

For the better part of a minute the men stood silent, watching the back of their boss, Bone, the legendary Texas Ranger, a man they'd all come to know and respect mightily, walk away from them.

He wore his gun belt, boots, but no shirt. His braces dangled from his trouser tops. His head was bare. His back was pocked with welts and scars from past battles, fights he did not talk of, not even when pressed. "There's no glory in violence," he'd tell them, then he'd wear a somber mood for a time.

Shep was the first to break the spell. He began walking away toward the barn. He'd gone three steps when Tut said, "Where you headed?"

Shep stopped but didn't turn.

"Hey." Ben walked over and laid a hand on Shep's shoulder, his other arm wearing a fresh bandage. "If anybody has a right to be ticked with you it's me, but I'm not. We've all been there, Shep. They work us like dogs all day and then expect us to spell each other and keep watch. Don't worry about it. I'll talk with Bone."

Shep spun. "No! Thanks, but no. I appreciate it, Ben, but it wouldn't be right. I . . . I don't want to be treated any different

William W. Johnstone and J.A. Johnstone

than anybody else, don't you see?" He looked at all the men. "I screwed up, and it's only right that I go. I've put everybody in danger too often."

"What are you talking about?" said Tut. "Getting kidnapped by that she-devil? That wasn't your fault. And as for Bone, he needs to cool down. He'll be right as rain in a while."

"I've never seen him that riled before," said McCurdy. Tut shot him a hard look, and the man shrugged and turned away.

"He's right, Tut. I have to go. I'm too young for all this, you said so yourself."

Tut began to protest, but Shep shook his head. "No, Tut. You were right. I'm not suited to this. It's Regis's dream, not mine. I'll go hash it out with him. Maybe head back East." He walked toward the barn.

Percy cleared his throat. "Shep, if you're bent on leaving, at least let me pack you a sack of food. I assume you're headed to Brownsville. I'll get it ready. You stop by my kitchen before you ride on out."

Shep nodded and continued on to the barn.

Tut braced Percy. "What did you do that for? We have to keep him from riding off!"

"I know that, you oaf. He's bent on leaving, least we can do is create diversions, slow him down some. Maybe Bone will wise up and get back here before Shep leaves."

"Oh, good thinking."

"Yep," said Percy. "One of us had to."

Shep caught up his horse and tied him to a corral rail and retrieved his saddle. He felt calm, maybe for the first time in the months since all this ranching business began.

He pulled a deep breath and saddled his horse. *Yeah*, he thought. This was Regis's dream. Not mine. He can tell me all he wants that I'm under his care, but it's my life.

If I'm old enough to be kidnapped by his enemies, not mine, then I'm old enough to live my own life. It made clear, perfect sense to Shep, and he led his horse to the bunkhouse to get his few things—blanket, his saddlebag with his notebook, a pencil, his knife and gun belt, and his spare shirt, socks, and undershorts.

The smell of smoke stabbed him like a knife, and he felt a wash of fresh guilt. The men had gone to Percy's kitchen and stood huddled about the cookfire waiting for the coffee to brew.

He'd miss that, the camaraderie he'd begun to feel with the men. Even the ones who at first treated him differently once they found out—not from him—that he was Regis's kid brother.

But a sudden thought buoyed him once more. He'd show them all. He'd go off, find his own dream, make his own fortune! And then he'd return, maybe driving a fringe-top barouche pulled by fine high-stepping horses and with a fine high-society lady by his side.

And he'd have his servant set out a crate of champagne and whiskey and he'd invite them all to gather around while he told them just how very well he'd been keeping since they last saw him that sad day a couple of years before.

A couple of years, that's not too long, thought Shep. Just enough time to do it up right. Somewhere, somehow. Those were details he'd explore on his long ride back to Brownsville. Alone.

That thought lumped in his throat as he stuffed his goods into his saddlebag and buckled it to the saddle, then lashed his blanket roll behind the cantle. He'd not thought about the fact that he'd have to ride all the way to Brownsville alone.

There was a time not long ago when that thought never would have bothered him, not in the least. He'd been unafraid of just about anything then. No, he told himself, that's not true. He'd been ignorant of the consequences, not unafraid. Two different things.

As he led his horse over to the men, he wondered if maybe because he recognized that, did that mean he was growing up? Getting smarter? If so, his smarts were taking their own sweet time getting into his head.

"Won't be but a minute, Shep," said Percy. "Been busy with

the coffee. I'll have your traveling sack ready in a thrice." He snapped his fingers.

Shep would miss Percy, who'd grown on him. He'd come to find out the cook wasn't really surly, just sensitive, and intelligent, too. Maybe one of the smarter men in the entire camp.

Of course, as he'd gotten to know them all, he realized they each had a particular skill or two that the others didn't have. Maybe there wasn't anybody who was dumb, maybe everybody was just different. Something else to think about on the ride.

He tried not to think about how he'd be riding alone through bandito country. That alone would steam Regis and Bone. The thought of that almost made him smile. *Good*, he thought. They'd see what they drove me to, and then if something did happen to him, why, they'd never forgive themselves.

What am I saying? I don't want anything to happen to me!

"What in the name of all that's smart in the world are you doing, boy?"

Shep turned to see Bone striding back from the way he'd come, at a long-legged clip. He was still a good dozen yards off, and while Shep was sure he could jump on his horse and outrun the Ranger, he dampened the childish notion. That was not the way he wanted to leave the camp or his friends.

"Would you act this way if your brother was here?" said Bone.

"Would you?" Shep regretted saying it as soon as it slid from his mouth. Then, seeing the big Texas Ranger's eyes flinch at his words, Shep felt all his hell-bent drive of moments before to leave the place drain from him. He looked back up at Bone. "I'm sorry, Bone. Sorry about the fire, sorry about Ben's arm, sorry I said what I said. Heck, I'm sorry I ever tried to find Regis. I should have stayed back East. I don't belong here."

For a long minute, Bone said nothing. They weren't but two, three paces from the rest of the men, who stood by the coffeepot, trying not to look like they were listening. Bone finally spoke in a tone they all could hear. "Look, Shep. I was just letting off steam. None of us belongs here. Look at this place."

He raised his arms wide, then let them drop. "It's not much more than a desert with patches of grass and snakes. But a man's got to be somewhere. Got to do something in life. Might as well be here as back in Connecticut. At least here you aren't liable to run into many Quakers." He nearly smiled.

"Besides," he said, "here you have a passel of new pards. Friends. Could be a whole lot worse. And it will be if I catch you sleeping on watch again. Okay?" He stuck out a big work-hardened hand.

Shep looked from the offered hand to Bone's face, to his friends at the campfire, then shook the hand. "Okay, Bone. I'll try. I will."

"That's all we can ask of each other, kid." He turned to the group. "That work for you bunch of Nosey Nellies?"

The red-faced cowboys nodded and mumbled.

"Good, now let's all have some of that coffee and count the bullet holes in the new bunkhouse. And figure out how to get rid of those scorch marks before Regis and Jesús return."

He turned to Shep. "Time to get out the bar of lye soap and a stiff-bristle brush, boy."

Chapter 37

Of the incident with the night raid and Shep's snoozing while on watch duty, the men never said a thing to Regis, figuring he'd be none the wiser.

Bone suggested to Shep that silken on the matter would be advisable, as his brother was under a whole lot of pressure to make everything work. The last thing he needed was to hear that his kid brother had tried to burn the place—and the cowboys—to a cinder.

To his relief, Shep agreed, though he did say he felt like he was being deceitful.

"Good to hear you say that, Shep. But I tell you what," said Bone. "There'll be a moment, maybe in the near future, when it'll be a better time. Then you tell him what you want."

Regis, Shep, Bone, and six hands saddled their horses and, laden with sacks of provisions, they rode out early in the day several days after Bone returned from escorting the women to what he still called "the Deemworth spread."

It still warmed him to think back on how he'd left it with Margaret. Hopeful, that's what he felt. Something he'd not felt for some time, years maybe, certainly not about a woman, even those he dallied with in a room above a bar in one of two-dozen cow towns and the occasional whistle-stop.

"How far do you think it is to Rio Verde?" Regis looked to his right at Bone, but the Ranger didn't answer. "Hey, Bone. You still thinking about your lady?"

"Huh?" he said, then sharpened his gaze. "What's that supposed to mean?" He set his jaw as if daring someone to reply.

Regis tamped down a grin, and Bone changed the subject. "The town Felipe told me about is still a good half day's ride from here. I suggest we pitch camp soon so we'll be—"

"Fresh and ready to negotiate," said Shep, wedging himself into the conversation.

"Don't you have somebody to annoy other than me?" said Bone.

Shep beamed and shook his head. "Nope. I reckon you're growing on me. Lucky you."

"Lucky? Not hardly. Now you and Tut and McCurdy go and fetch firewood—look out for snakes—and we'll tuck into some of this food. Then we see who's going to stand watch."

"Watch?" said Shep, looking around.

Regis hadn't seen that instant fear on his brother's face since before the incident with the surveyor. Bulmer was currently back in Brownsville, healing and—Regis assumed—deciding if he wanted to continue with surveying the Royle Ranch once he was mended.

"Easy, boy," said Bone. "It's something any travelers with sense will do once they're this side of the border. Plenty of folks who wouldn't mind seeing fewer gringos down here."

Later, after they ate, Regis talked in low tones with Bone. He felt out of his depth and had a number of questions for his friend. "Bone, your Spanish is better than mine. How about you translate once we get down to business."

"I could, but I'd be afraid I'd miss something important. Liable to cost you money you might not have, especially if you keep on buying all that land."

"Yeah, well, that land makes certain all the plans we have for the Royle Ranch will work out."

"You mean your plans."

"What's that mean? I thought you were in all the way with this venture?"

"I am, but that doesn't mean I might not want to work my own spread, too."

"Thought we talked about that? It'll fold nicely into the Royle, and we can share the duties. Besides, it's small enough that . . ." But Regis saw his friend's cheek muscles bunching like he was about to storm off or throw a punch in his general direction.

"All right, I get you. I understand. But if you plan on pulling up stakes, give me plenty of warning, will you?"

Bone rolled his eyes. "Regis, for a smart ol' businessman, you sure are thick sometimes. All I meant is that I might have more irons in the fire than just living in a bunkhouse on your ranch."

Regis nodded. "Fair enough." He hid his smile behind a cough. "Now what do you think, would Jesús translate for me? You trust him enough to do the job right? I want you there to back up my play, anyway."

"Sure he's trustworthy. Ain't met a straighter shooter."

They saw the little withered, dusty town of Rio Verde, Mexico, the better part of an hour before they rode slowly up the main street. It was a desperate place, sunbaked and stark. Everything about it looked to be bleached by never-ending heat and puckered by too little water for too long a time.

The smell that hung over everything was sweet, dry, and smoky all at once, the smoke rising in lazy wisps into the hot blue sky, in no hurry to get anywhere.

From within dark doorways that stared like unblinking, hollow eyes, gaunt-faced children peered out, their brown faces framed with black hair. They were soon tugged back inside the dark spaces within the adobe homes, some of them little more than cracked-wall hovels.

It was a long, slow walk that felt to the men as if they were being spied on with every step. Some way down the lane they saw an old man sitting on a bench beneath the partial shade of a leaning ramada. He was barefooted and bareheaded. He had a nearly bald brown head and a face gaunt with speckles of wiry white whiskers and drooping moustaches that accentuated the sorrow that seemed to drape over everything about the town. He smoked a pipe, or rather he held a pipe in his teeth, but no smoke rose up. His horned hands rested on the knees of tattered white trousers.

Ahead, a cur dog, black with a skinny, curving tail, trotted toward them from the far end of the street. Still fifty feet away, it stopped and bayed once, then decided it was too much work. He flopped in the scant shade by the cracked wall of the church, which sat squat and mournful, anchoring the far end of the street.

Regis called a halt to the little train of horses and riders. They had traveled the length of the main street and saw only the children, the old man, and one woman. She'd caught sight of them and ran in a shuffle step, lugging a terra cotta jug that looked to be far from full, considering how fast she jackrabbited.

"This place is as dry as a cork," said Regis. "Not much Rio or Verde."

"That's why we're here, ain't it?" said Bone, eyeing the long strip of ragged buildings. "Should be more folks about. Must have seen us coming."

"You'd think they'd be curious," said Shep. "Living way out here, I'd want to see new faces."

"Yeah, but maybe their patron, the local big landowner, rules them with a hard hand. Or maybe banditos keep them skittish."

"Either way," said Regis, "we're here, so we best get to it, see if your friend's information was correct. See if they have any stock they want to sell us. If not, we'll move on. There are other villages hereabouts to visit."

It took Jesús a moment to convince Regis that not only did he need the vaquero to go with him to inquire but that Regis should hold back and let Jesús ride up first. Regis chafed, knowing he was riding second fiddle to his own hired man. But this was the man's home country, after all, not his.

He had to remind himself of that adage Cormac told him and retold him through the years whenever he wanted to push a situation and try to bend it to their advantage sooner than later: "You trap more flies with honey than with vinegar."

Of course, Cormac was also the man who'd said, "If wishes were horses, beggars would ride," which Regis found curious, considering he himself had been wishing and then making his wishes come true for much of his life. Heck, he'd showed up at the docks all those years before as little more than a beggar himself.

"Okay, Jesús, let's scout up somebody who knows something. The day's burning."

Turns out they didn't have far to go. The second door they knocked on brought a not-so-timid woman out to the edge of her ramada. She was stout, almost burly looking, but not from too much food, rather from hard work.

Regis suspected she was far younger than she appeared, but the work had hardened and aged her too soon. Still, her eyes glinted and, even without a smile, Regis guessed she would be one of those people who has a hidden spring of humor bubbling beneath a quiet surface.

Jesús slipped down out of his saddle and led his horse to within ten feet of her. He loosened his stampede strap and tugged off his hat. Regis rarely saw the competent vaquero without his big topper and was surprised once more at how striking and perfectly swept back the man's black hair looked. Regis felt a twinge of envy. He always felt as if he'd just been rolled over in a dusty street by a rogue mule team.

The vaquero began talking, leaning forward as a sign of slight deference to the woman. Regis saw her demeanor soften a pinch around the edges. *Must be because he's handsome*, Regis thought.

Several times Jesús gestured toward Regis as he talked, and the woman's gaze did the same. Regis, too, swept off his hat and held it to his chest, nodding and smiling.

He made out a word here and there: "*patrón*" and "*el jefe*" and "*rancho*," but the rest was beyond him.

He wanted to tell Jesús to make sure he reminded her how dry it had been the previous year, how dry this one had been, and how it was likely the next year would bring more of the same. But just as he was about to interrupt the quiet chat, mostly one-sided, as the woman rarely spoke, their conversation ended.

The woman held up a finger as if to tell Jesús to wait. She turned her back on them and entered her house, then closed the door behind her. Presently, Regis heard a door slam, some shouting in a woman's voice, then a thin whip-snap of a boy sprinted from the rear of the house, speeding across the barren stretch of land behind the buildings.

He disappeared over a rise toward a nearly dry riverbed they'd passed on their way in. But instead of continuing in that northerly direction, the kid cut east hard and disappeared over another low rise.

"What's going on, Jesús?"

The vaquero turned and walked over to Regis. "She has sent her son to the fields to tell the men. They have, as a village, just last night decided what they will do."

"What did they decide?"

"If this dry time continues, they will, as Senor Bone says, pull up their stakes and move on."

"A shame, but I respect that. Still, this is business, and I am the best cash buyer they are likely to meet."

The vaquero said nothing, but Regis thought the man smirked as he looked away. Maybe Shep was right and he was getting to enjoy, as Bone called it, "bein' bossy and speechifyin'" a little too much since he'd bought the ranch.

In the distance a figure appeared, walking along, kicking up dust. It was the boy, returning slower than on his outward trip. They watched him for a few long moments, then another figure appeared on the rise behind. Then another, and another.

Long minutes passed as a group of men drew closer. Finally, twenty-five feet from Regis and his crew, they stopped. One man stepped forward and Jesús did the same, then the two men talked in low tones.

Finally, the vaquero walked over to Regis. "They said they keep the stock far from the village, farther each day, in order to graze them. The beasts are very hungry, and the land, as you can see, is nearly stripped close by the village."

Regis nodded. *How thin were they?* he wondered. "Ask him how many head of cattle they own."

Jesús did and in English said, "Nearly one hundred."

It was a bigger number than he expected, but then again the village was not small. "Tell him I'd like to take a look at them. If I like what I see, I'd like to make an offer to buy them. All of them."

Jesús spoke to the man, who nodded. Regis thought perhaps he spied a look of hopefulness about the eyes.

"First, we'd like to water our horses. Is that possible?"

Jesús asked the man, who hesitated, then nodded. *"Si, si."* He turned and beckoned them to follow him. Regis motioned to his men who had climbed down from their mounts and were clustered in a ragged line along the wall of the church.

One by one they followed, leading their mounts, to what Regis had assumed was the backside of the village. It looked more like a gathering place. There was an assortment of shade-giving ramadas, and beyond, a stone water well with a stout tri-pod spraddled over it. From the middle of the poles, a rope trailed down to coil beside a wooden bucket resting on the lip of the waist-height stone and stucco well.

A low trough, hewn from a big old log who knows how many years before, stood not far from the well. The man began lower-ing the bucket down, down, down, into the well. Regis heard the wood clunking against the sides.

Finally, when the rope had nearly played out, the rope went slack and the man worked it back and forth, around and around, and began to retrieve it, overhanding the rope and letting it coil at his bare feet.

Regis watched the sweat-stained shirt, the powerful muscles on thin arms and bony shoulders pushing through the light fab-ric, the tatty, wide-brim woven hat offering scant shade to the man's dark neck. He was reminded once more that these peo-ple had very little.

He'd thought he and his men had been living hand in hand with privation at the Royle Ranch, but though they weren't ter-ribly far from that range, the Santa Calina provided so much more than these people had that he felt a rare and odd blend of pride and guilt.

As if he could read his thoughts, Shep said in a low voice, "Regis, we can't take their water. These folks barely have mud down at the bottom of that hole, let alone anything drinkable."

Regis nodded. "I see that now, brother. Even before eyeing their beasts, I believe we will be buying some. Be helping us both, mostly them."

Jesús had overheard and said, "They are a proud people, the villagers of Rio Verde, as are all the people of Mexico. They will not want to feel as though you are doing them a favor out of charity."

Regis nodded slowly. "Tell him we apologize, but that we will use our canteens for the horses. Maybe our men could drink from the bucket he raised up."

"Very good, *patrón*."

After his men made a show of sipping from the dipper offered by the villager, they were led out to the grazing area. As they crested the hill he'd spied the boy disappearing beyond earlier, Regis was impressed by the number of beasts, if not with their general condition. Scattered here and there, mostly seated under scant shade trees or leaning on rocks, were more men from the village, a dozen or so.

The cattle were ganted, ribby, and dumb, as most cattle, standing in the dust and bawling at one another instead of seeking the shade of the cottonwoods lining the nearly dry riverbed beyond. He also saw donkeys and sheep and goats, a few dozen, at least, of critters that were not cattle.

Though he'd been told once, he asked the man himself, "How many?"

The man looked from him to the cattle, as if the animals would begin counting themselves, then looked back to Regis. "*Cien*." Then he wagged his hand in that universal gesture indicating more or less.

Regis nodded, understood it meant one hundred or so, as he'd said before, and rode down slowly closer to the cattle. He knew enough not to get too close. Though some of them weren't balky, a good many scampered off, ran a dozen feet, then stood, tired from the effort expended in the day's heat.

He still wasn't too disappointed in what he saw, though he longed for the day when he would own acres of fat, sluggish cattle grazing in knee-high green grasses.

A tall order in southeast Texas, but with the Santa Calina's flow and the handful of springs, it would happen. And with the massive lands the purchase of the adjoining land grant would bring to the Royle Ranch, it wouldn't be long before he could afford to bring in beefier stock from the breeders back East to mingle with his balky longhorns.

"Okay," he said, turning to Jesús. "Tell him I would like to buy every animal I see here. And if he has any others—goats, sheep, mules, horses, chickens, I'm interested. I'll pay the going rate for cattle, and we can figure out a block price for the rest."

Jesús looked at him. "All of them?"

"Yeah, tell him."

"Okay, boss."

Regis wondered for a moment why Jesús would question what he'd said. Did he not think the offer was generous enough? Not that he was worried much about what his vaquero was thinking.

The man related the offer in Spanish, and the news surprised the village man. For a moment his guarded, taciturn look dropped. He said something in a low voice to Jesús, who nodded quickly. "*Si, si.*"

The vaquero turned to Regis. "He thought you were mocking him."

"No, tell him I'm serious. Tell him it'll help his people and it'll help me, so everybody wins."

Regis swung down from his horse and extended his hand for a shake. The man hesitated, then looked across the way to his fellows across the herd. Regis didn't see any nods or hand signals pass between them, but the man still hesitated.

"Okay, is he holding out for a better offer? Remind him he's in a drought," said Regis.

"I don't think that's the trouble, Regis," said Bone. "Am I right, Jesús?"

The vaquero nodded, looking down. "*Si.*"

"What's the matter, then?"

"It's not the way it is done," said Jesús. "A decision as big as this must be discussed among the men of the village. It affects everybody and their families. Manny here doesn't have permission to speak for them all."

Regis felt himself redden, embarrassed, and he hated that. But he'd brought it on himself, through ignorance of the situation. "Okay, what is the way it's done, then?"

"Easy now, pard," said Bone in a low voice, smile still in place. "You're on their dirt now. They didn't ask you to come down here."

Regis sighed. "I know. It's frustrating."

"You know, Regis," said Shep in the same low tone Bone used. "Not long ago, you told me I was impatient. I see it must be a family trait. They're not going anywhere."

He looked at Shep. "Since when did you get so smart?"

Then Regis smiled and said to Jesús, "Tell him to call his friends over here and we can discuss the particulars over a drink of the whiskey I brought." He patted his saddlebags and noticed that the man's eyes brightened. He damn sure knew the word for whiskey.

Turned out that the man wasn't much of a negotiator, he only wanted to make certain his amigos were in agreement with him in accepting the offer.

After a second round of drinks, one of the men asked Jesús why the gringo rancher wanted their goats and sheep and chickens, too.

"Tell him it takes a whole lot of animals to establish a ranch as big as ours. Tell him it's going to be the biggest ranch anybody has ever seen. Tell him . . . oh, hell, tell him we like goats and sheep and chickens!" Regis raised his tin cup and upended it.

The translation brought a round of laughter from the men. Bone leaned over. "I'd say you have made fast friends here, at least of the men in the village. "

"You don't think the women will feel the same?"

"Not hardly. They might not be here making the deal, but that doesn't mean they won't rule the roost later."

Regis and his men stayed near the village overnight, camping close by along the bank of the rocky riverbed, ready to round up the cattle and other beasts in the morning.

"How are you going to get your chickens back to the ranch?" asked Bone that night over a cold supper and a cup of hot coffee.

"I hadn't thought that far ahead. Maybe we could buy a wagon from them. Or maybe I'll ask them if they'll take care of my chickens until another time."

They sat in silence for a spell, then Regis said, "One thing troubles me, though."

"Just one thing?" said Bone, shaking his head. "You're a lucky man. I got a hatful of troubles on any given day."

"What I mean is, if we can keep doing this, buying up stock, and at decent prices, we're going to need more cowboys."

"Or vaqueros."

"Yeah, same thing, right?"

"Not hardly, if you ask them. But I think you just solved your problem."

"How so?"

"You know, Regis," said Bone. "I'm not one to question what you do, being as how I'm a junior partner and all. But don't you think it was a little coldhearted to buy up all those animals from them folks?"

"Coldhearted? Why, I gave them a new lease on life. With all that money, they'll be able to buy new ones, buy food, do most anything."

"Maybe, but what about right now? Where are they going to get replacement animals? And what are they going to eat right now? And if they can find new critters, what shape will they be in? How long will those critters last? Those people will burn through that money in no time, just to stay alive, through no fault of their own. Then they'll be right back in the same situation they're in now. In no time at all, I tell you."

"Hmm, I never thought of that. What do you suggest?"

Bone shrugged. "We have need of help, and if you keep buying up more range, we'll damn sure have need of a new generation of help."

"What are you driving at, Bone?"

"For a businessman," said Bone, "you sure are obtuse."

"That's a two-dollar word if I ever heard one from you, Bone McGraw."

"I ain't just a range bum, you know. I got me an education. Can read and write and cipher. How about giving the same opportunity to all them kids from Rio Verde?"

"Huh." Regis stared at his coffee cup, not really seeing it.

"Yeah, huh is right. Build a school, hell, build them an entire village. Move the lot of them onto the Royle Ranch. They already call you *el jefe*. That's a sign you got their respect. Now, how about earning it? And then keeping it? Take them on, and they'll mean it when they call you that. You always talk about the future like it's a sure thing. Well, it takes a heap of people to run a ranch. If you treat them right, their kids and their kids' kids will be right here, living and working for you and your kids' kids."

Regis liked the sound of that, Bone could tell. The man's big ol' black moustache got twitchy at the ends. "You think they'd go for it?"

Bone shrugged. "Only one way to find out."

Regis strained more coffee through his moustache and sucked the tips. A sure sign he was mulling over something deep. Then he smacked his knee, and dust rose up. "Okay, you talked me into it. First, though, I'll ride back to the village and talk with them. Give me time to think it through. I'm going to need Jesús's help, though. You can get started back to the ranch with the animals, and we'll catch up."

He walked a couple of feet, then turned. "You know, Bone, it's not a bad idea. Not bad at all."

"Shoot, I always suspected my head was good for something more than a place to set my hat."

Chapter 38

"You mean . . ."

Cormac nodded. "I mean that even Don Mallarmoza might not have had the right to buy or then sell the land."

"How can this be?" Regis Royle stared across the desk at his business partner and friend, Cormac Delany.

The Irishman sighed. "It seems the land wasn't Tomasina Valdez's father's land to sell. It was deeded to the firstborn grandchild of her maternal grandfather."

"Okay, let me guess. Tomasina Valdez isn't the firstborn grandchild."

"You hit that spike right on the head."

"So how do we know this?"

Cormac sighed again and flopped back into his chair. "The alleged rightful heir has made inquiries via a lawyer."

"Has this heir said what he wants?"

"She."

"Huh?"

"The heir. It's a she."

"Oh no, not another one."

Cormac nodded and packed his pipe.

"So where does that leave me? Us?"

Cormac shrugged. "I don't know yet, son. But the lawyers are looking into it. It does mean that the purchase of the new parcel will take longer."

"Why?"

"Formalities, really. But given that it's also a Spanish land grant, we should make certain all the T's are crossed and the I's are dotted."

Regis growled low in his throat and paced back and forth in the small office.

"I do believe, yes, yes, now that I look closely, I do believe I see blue steam curling out of your ears. Yes sir. You're not careful, you'll curl that lady charmer of a moustache of yours."

"Stop it," said Regis. "This is serious, Cormac. It's the ranch." He stopped pacing. "Just what did I buy, anyway?"

"As of right now, I'd say you bought a big, expensive headache. But don't forget you aren't the only one in on this. Me and Bone, we have a say in this, too."

"And Shep," nodded Regis. "Don't forget Shep."

Cormac laughed. "Who can forget Shepley Royle? That boy's a mindsticker."

As if summoned, the door whipped open and Shep burst in. He shut it and leaned there, his eyes wide and wild, his face gray and shaking visibly. He looked around the room as if searching for someone but didn't seem to notice Regis or Cormac.

"Shep?" Regis laid a hand on the kid's shoulder and his brother spun, swinging his arms and jumping away from him.

"Easy now, son," said Cormac, rounding the desk. "What's wrong?"

"I saw her!"

"Saw who, Shep?" Regis held the kid by both shoulders.

"The she-devil!"

"Tomasina Valdez?" said Regis, looking toward the closed door as if she might burst through it any moment.

"Yeah, just for a second."

"What did she say?"

"Nothing." He shook as if gripped by a palsy. "She was across the street. She looked at me and smiled. Then she pointed her finger like a gun and pulled the trigger."

Chapter 39

Two days later, following a five-day trip in town, Regis rolled up at the ranch in the wagon pulled behind two brace of mules. Shep rode beside the wagon atop King. The wagon didn't jostle or clunk as it rolled over stones and ruts.

Bone tugged off his gloves and nodded. "Regis. Shep." He nodded again, this time toward the wagon. "Heavy load there."

"Yep." Regis set the brake and stepped down, stretching his back and legs and looking about, trying, Bone knew, not to look overly eager to take in all the work they'd done since Regis left a week before.

No matter how much they did, he knew his friend wouldn't find it enough. It annoyed him, but that's the way Regis was, and nothing could change it. Except maybe a woman. She might temper that edge of the man at some point, but it didn't look to be something Royle was interested in anytime soon. Too much ranch on his mind.

"How's the shipping business?"

"Oh, fine." Regis didn't meet Bone's eyes, so the Ranger knew something was amiss. Likely with Regis bulling for this new big land purchase. He was the single most impatient man Bone had ever met.

"Cormac's got it well in hand," said Regis.

"Well, that's something, anyway." Bone turned to the kid. "How we doing, Shep? Ready for all manner of fun and games? Cause if you are, this ain't the place to be."

He winked, but Regis heard the tart edge to the man's words.

"That reservoir about finished?"

"About," said Bone. "I had more men, we'd be further ahead."

"Working on it."

"I know. That's what you said last week. I tell you, Regis, I can't seem to get a leg up on them."

"Who?"

"Oh, you name it, the Apaches, the Comanches, the banditos, not to mention the snakes and bugs. We're about cooked out here in the sun. It's plenty, I tell you. Plenty."

Regis was about to answer, but Bone kept right on. "Not because we ain't trying, but there are so many of them and not enough of us. We run up to the west border and the couple of men I leave behind to watch things do all they can not to get killed by some other band of yahoos with knives and bows and arrows and rifles and all manner of men. It's enough to drive a man to drink. Except camp's been dry since forever."

Regis scratched his chin and looked past his fuming friend. "Not like you to complain, Bone. That tells me things aren't all that peachy."

"Whatever gave you that notion?" Bone looked at Regis and saw a smile and a bottle of whiskey in his outstretched hand. He started laughing, and pretty soon Regis did. Then the entire ragged gaggle of men who'd trailed over were chuckling, too. Bone uncorked the fresh soldier, swigged deep, dragged his cuff across his mouth, and passed it around. It didn't last long.

"Don't worry, I brought more. So long as you don't forget I have a wagon that needs unloading."

Later, once they'd begun unloading the freighted work wagon, Bone said, "I only see crates and whatnot, but four mules?"

"Wait until you get down to the bottom layer."

Soon, they were there. The Ranger pulled back a double-layer of canvas tarpaulin to reveal something big and bold and brass.

"What in heaven's name is that?" said Tut.

"That, youngster," said Bone, "is a cannon."

"No kidding!"

Regis stepped up and patted the gleaming brute. "Yep, specifically it's a ship's cannon. But as the war's over, for the time being, anyway, I figured we could use it out here to play holy hell with the next gang of savages who dare to knock on our door."

"I imagine a blast or two from this thing and word will get out that we aren't easy pickings anymore."

"That's the idea." Regis turned to the men. "Now, how about it? Who's going to unload this thing?"

"How many men did it take to load it onto the wagon?"

"Six."

Bone smoothed his moustaches and noticed Shep was unusually quiet. More often than not, he would be one of the first in line for horseplay. "Okay, then," he said, smacking his hands together. "I'll need a man or two—to spot me should I falter."

The hoorahs were loud enough that Bone quieted them. "All right, all right. I'll let you little girlies have your chance. Let's drive it close to where we think it'll live, and then we'll unload the thing."

"Oh, one more thing. Bone?"

"Yeah?"

"Should be a wagon of men along later today, more likely tomorrow. More men from the docks, but hard workers. I know them all, and there isn't a lazy seed among them."

"Hoorah!" Bone smacked his dusty hat against a dusty trouser leg. "That's the best news yet, boss."

"Not boss, partner."

"Okay, pard. I know just where to put them to work."

"The reservoir?"

"You bet. The men are getting a might whiffy, and I can't hardly take it anymore."

The looks and red faces and quiet that descended on the group of men made Bone smile.

"Now I know I'm not the sweetest-smelling flower of this bunch, but boys, you all need to spend more time washing down at the crick and less time whining and snoring at night. My sainted old mama always said 'Soap and water are dirt cheap.'"

That didn't change their red faces and hangdog looks, so Bone said, "If I've offended you all, I don't care. The stink off some of you would curdle milk. And the rest of you are downright rank!"

Later, around the campfire, when they had a moment without nosey cowhands nearby, Bone asked a question he'd been wanting to ask since Regis mentioned briefly earlier that the first land deal had gotten complicated, something about another heir with claims to the land. But he'd said no more, indicating it was not the time to go into it.

"Okay, now can you tell me how everything's working with that lawyer? What about this heir's claims?" Bone asked, knowing it was a tender spot with Regis, but he figured he was entitled to hear of it, considering he was a partner in the Royle Ranch enterprise.

To his relief, Regis shrugged, then filled him in. Including Shep's scare in town.

Bone sipped his coffee and whistled low. "That sounds like a headache and a half."

"Yep," said Regis. "But I'm proceeding as if it's all our land. And it will be. Has to be. Cormac thinks it will all work to our favor. Just going to take time. And money. Both of which I'm running low on."

"I thought that was patience."

Regis grinned. "Yeah, that, too."

"So how's Shep doing since seeing that woman?"

Regis scanned the darkening distance through squinted eyes. When he finally spoke, his reply shocked his pard. "That's just it, Bone. I looked all over that town for her and found not a sign, nor anyone who'd seen her." He faced Bone. "I'm not so certain he saw her."

"Naw. Shep isn't the type to make up such things."

"I hope you're right. But to be safe, I figured getting him back out here to the ranch was the best place for him. And wonder of wonders, he didn't argue with me."

Chapter 40

Bone and Regis had been riding side by side, eyes swiveling because of the attacks they knew could come at any time. In addition to that ever-present danger, the new parcel of land Regis was in the midst of buying, even if the process had stalled for a spell, all 24,000 acres of it, came with its own riddles and headaches, with new ones appearing when and where they never expected them.

"I sure was surprised when Shep agreed to hang back at the camp and work with the boys for a few days so you and I could ride on out and explore this new land." Regis shook his head. "Kid's getting so I can't hardly go to the outhouse without him pacing around outside."

"Well, don't forget he went through something most men will never have to. And he ain't a man yet, so it'll take him time to settle down. But he will, you'll see."

Regis was about to respond as they rode up a slight rise. Before them lay a man, dead or asleep, on a slab of sandstone.

"Ho there!" shouted Regis, slowing up and eyeing all around them. The patch was relatively flat and blistering hot. The man on the rock didn't move.

His position was one of comfort and ease, with his legs bent at the knee, the right thrown over the left and his fingers woven together and resting atop his chest. An old flop-brim hat, more sweat stain than felt, sat canted over his face. A curling gray beard leaked out from beneath.

"Maybe he's dead," ventured Bone.

"No, I ain't dead neither."

That caught them both by surprise, especially as the man didn't make a move to rise or even lift off his hat and look at them.

"You okay, mister?" said Bone.

"Course I'm okay, can't a man take a much-needed nap of a morning?" He sighed and lifted the hat off his face and looked over at them. His eyes blinked at the bright sunlight. "What do you want?"

"I want to know who you are," said Regis.

"Well now, isn't that nice. A fancy man like you wanting to know something about me. I'm all aflutter, I tell ya."

They rode closer and halted right beside the man's resting rock. "I'm pleased to hear you're worked up. That's good," said Regis. "Because as the owner of this land, I need to know who's visiting my range, how long they aim to be here, and what they're doing while they are here."

He'd barely gotten the words out before the man commenced to laughing. He laughed so hard he began coughing. Then he swung his legs over the side of the rock and sat up. "That might be the funniest thing I've heard in a long time. Yep, yep, I think it is."

"It wasn't intended to be humorous, mister. Who are you, and what are you doing here?"

The man straightened his back and stretched and yawned. "You really take the cake, you know that?" He stood and eyed the two riders, his hands on his hips.

Regis looked the man up and down and saw an average-height man with a sloppy little paunch. The gut strained a be-grimed and pinked-with-age longhandle shirt over rough-cloth trousers patched more times than Regis could count. One side of his braces hung by his waist, and Regis noticed that although the man didn't seem to be any older than forty, he looked like he'd been rode hard and put up soaking wet.

"Tilden Wormsley's the name. And as it happens," said the man, "I own this here land. About all you can see." He waved his left arm lazily, then let it flop to his side as if the effort of holding it up was too much to bear.

"Well now, how do you figure that, mister? You have a deed? Something that says this land is yours?"

"No, no, not exactly. But out here a man doesn't need any such thing. Why, this land is here for the taking. That's what my Ethel told me, and in near nineteen years of bein' wedded, she ain't steered me off course yet."

"And where is this Ethel?"

"Why? You aiming on robbing us? I should tell you I am a dangerous man! Got all manner of weapons about the place. Don't take kindly to strangers."

"The feeling's mutual. But what place are you referring to?"

"My ranch, man! Ain't you been listening?"

"Where is this ranch of yours?"

"Ain't you listening?" he said again. "You're standing on it. It's pretty much everything you see all around you."

Bone spoke under his breath to Regis. "We're getting nowhere."

"I meant," said Regis through clenched teeth, "where's your house? Your barn?"

"Oh, them. Why, they're yonder. You can't seem 'em from here, but there's a gulley about a quarter mile west of here. We built down there to keep the wind from stripping off our hair."

"Surprised nothing else stripped off your hair."

"Say what?"

"Apaches, border bandits. Haven't you had trouble with them?"

"Naw. They come around now and again, but they're harmless."

"Take me to your place, Mr. Wormsley. We have some business to discuss, and I'm afraid I have some bad news for you."

"What bad news? Ain't one of my boys, is it? I can't bear it. Oh, my life's been one wrong turn after another. Finally settled down out here to get away from the hard times, and it's been nothing but tough going. And now one of my boys has had it! Oh, woe, I tell you. Woe to me and mine. . . ."

He waved his arms and blubbered so much that Regis couldn't get a word in. But as he blubbered he walked down what looked like a well-worn path that led toward the gulley he'd pointed at.

Bone smiled and shook his head and Regis frowned and shook his head, and both men slowly followed the mumbling, blubbering man.

The hovel they approached could well have been a trick of light were it not for the scatter of goats and chickens and grubby children, most naked or nearly there. They ranged in size from toddling to teenage, and all wore the hollow-eyed look of undernourishment and poor maintenance.

"You have older boys elsewhere?" said Regis.

"Why, you should know. You're the one what's bringing me news of them!"

"No, no, I never said that. Where's your wife, Mr. Wormsley? Where's Ethel at?"

Tilden Wormsley narrowed his eyes. "How come you call my beloved by her given name? You a dog in my house, mister? If so, you step down and I'll settle your hash right here and now."

The man straightened his shoulders and raised two bony-knuckled fists and danced in place. "Step down, I say, and I'll show you what it's like to wish you wasn't never born!"

"Mr. Wormsley, please, I . . ."

A woman, the visual equal of the paunchy, stringy little

rooster-man, stepped out of the dark eye of the dugout of a home. She wore an oft-patched dress, so faded the original calico pattern was a ghost of a memory on the fabric. Over the dress, a feedsack apron was tied high, tucked under her sagged bosom.

Her long gray-black hair was trussed in a bun pulled back so tight it gave her eyes a permanent look of surprise. She, as with the rest of her brood, was barefoot. But so begrimed were all their feet, Bone had to look twice to see if maybe they weren't all wearing thin moccasins.

In one clamplike hand, Ethel held a still-writhing rattlesnake easily as long as her body. The other cradled an ancient-looking shotgun. "What's all the noise out here? Trying to put the young'uns down for a spell and all I hear is foolish palaver!"

"You tell me, Mother! That rascal yonder claims to know you, and I want to know why!"

Ethel craned her stringy neck forward and peered at the two horse-riding strangers. "No idea who they be."

"Ma'am." Regis touched his hat brim.

"Watch him, Mother. He's oily. Claims to bring us bad news. I fancy it was a trick to get me to lead them here."

"And you fell for it, didn't you, Tilden? I married a fool. My mama always said I could have done better had I married a stone, and I am beginning to think she wasn't wrong. Now, what's this bad news?" She held up the snake and shook it for emphasis. It writhed and tried to coil about her arm, but she didn't seem to notice. "I got me a shotgun and I ain't afraid to use it."

"No, ma'am, I don't doubt that," said Bone, clearly enjoying himself.

Regis shot him a hard look. "Ma'am, as I tried to tell your husband here, I own this land."

"How much?"

"Pardon me?"

"How much land you own?"

"On this parcel, roughly twenty-four thousand acres, give or take."

She nodded. "And how much land you reckon we are using and have used for nigh on to four years now?"

"Well, I . . ."

"That's what I thought." She advanced a few paces on them, toting her snake and shotgun. "And you come riding in here all fancy and tall and handsome and you figure to tell me I got to pull up stakes and skedaddle? Why?"

"Ma'am, as I said, I own it."

"And I said—"

It was Regis's turn to cut her off. "Look, I intend to run cattle all over this range, and I didn't come here to run you off but to see what's what. And now that I have, I will say I'm not impressed. You have a number of offspring that look as though they could use more sustenance and a husband who clearly hasn't popped a sweat a day in his life. And you live in a hovel. Now, if you will kindly stop trying to interrupt me, I aim to work with you to come up with an equitable solution to your problem and mine."

"Don't look to me like you have much in the way of problems, mister."

"I do at the moment, and it is you." Under his breath, Regis muttered to Bone, "A little help here."

Bone cleared his throat. "My pard here mentioned we're going to run cattle on this range. And we can't have naked children running here and there spooking them."

Regis nodded and continued. "But we do have need of somebody to keep an eye on this end of the range. Until we can set up a proper cattle camp, that is."

"What you proposin', mister?" The woman gave him the squinty eye.

"Ain't nobody doing any proposin' to my wife but me!"

shouted the still squared-off rooster of a man. Regis noticed the stringy fellow had edged somewhat behind his frightening wife.

"Shut it, Tilden," she said, but her eyes never left Regis's. "Let the handsome man say his piece. No, no, better yet, you let me do some talkin'."

She spat on the ground, then commenced to shaking the rattler once more, in time with her words. "You build us a proper house and some place to keep our critters, and we'll run your cattle station for you. Take care of this whole end of your range, too."

She nodded. "Yep. Me and my boys and girls, we're hard workers. Him"—she gestured to her husband—"he's so useless and lazy he'd eat in bed and kick out the crumbs, only we ain't got a bed to ourselves. Just as well." She shook her head in hangdog fashion. "He's about wore me out."

Tilden scuffed up behind her and poked her in the arm. "Always seem to find you though, don't I?" He grinned like a schoolboy who'd gotten away with the entire cookie jar.

Amazingly, Ethel giggled, a horsey little snort that still bore a tinge of schoolgirl to it.

Regis cleared his throat. "Yes, well, you mentioned you had sons? Are any of them of age to work as ranch hands? Cowboys?"

"Yep." She nodded. "Four oldest could. They're off hunting, but they'll be along presently. And the same for our three girls of age, too."

She held up a hand, the one with the snake who looked tired of being strangled and had ceased writhing. "I know what you're thinking, but them girls ain't like girls. They're more like boys than the boys sometimes. Anybody dally with them, they'll wake up missing their oysters!" She chortled and nodded, her face beaming with maternal pride.

"Mother taught them everything she knows!"

"Hush up, Tilden. Go tend the young'uns. Little Amos is fussing."

Tilden walked, slump-shouldered, into the dark cavelike space of their home.

"Okay then, Mrs. Wormsley." Regis touched his hat brim. "Good talking with you. We'll be back at some point to hash out this matter further."

As they turned to ride away, Bone said, "Send your sons along so we can put them to work. We have plenty of it for them." He turned his horse and touched his hat brim. "Good day, ma'am."

All the young—Regis had counted seven outside—still stood wide-mouthed and gawking at them as they rode away.

"Never occurred to me there might be squatters on my land," he said after they'd ridden in silence for a full minute.

"Yeah, well, I believe they call themselves settlers, Regis. And while I don't know how many more there are of them— hopefully not many, since this is a foul place with more snakes than signs of hope—some of them have been here a good long while. Some of them might not be so obliging, however."

They rode in silence for a few moments, then Bone said, "She's a feisty critter, no mistake. I like how she got you to whistle a different tune."

"What do you mean?"

Bone chuckled. "Don't play dumb with me, Royle. It don't suit you. You rode in there ready to run them off, and now you're fixing to give them all jobs and build them a house! Yes, sir, she's good."

Regis scowled. "That's not what happened at all."

"Oh? Must be my ears hear different things than yours. Seems to me you have some thinking to do."

The sigh that leaked out of Regis Royle's mouth was not the last he'd be uttering. "Let's get moving. See how many more surprises we can turn up before the sun sets."

"And how many more promises you'll make to your squatters!" Bone was laughing too hard to hear the barrage of choice words Regis fired his way.

But both men were smiling as they rode ever deeper into the Royle Range.

Regis, Shepley, Bone, and the Boys of Royle Ranch will be back.

Visit us online at
KensingtonBooks.com
to read more from your favorite authors,
see books by series, view reading
group guides, and more!

BETWEEN THE CHAPTERS

Visit us online for sneak peeks, exclusive
giveaways, special discounts, author content,
and engaging discussions with your fellow readers.

Betweenthechapters.net

Sign up for our newsletters and be the first
to get exciting news and announcements about
your favorite authors!
Kensingtonbooks.com/newsletter